The Lunch Witch

Deb Lucke

PAPERCUTZ™
New York

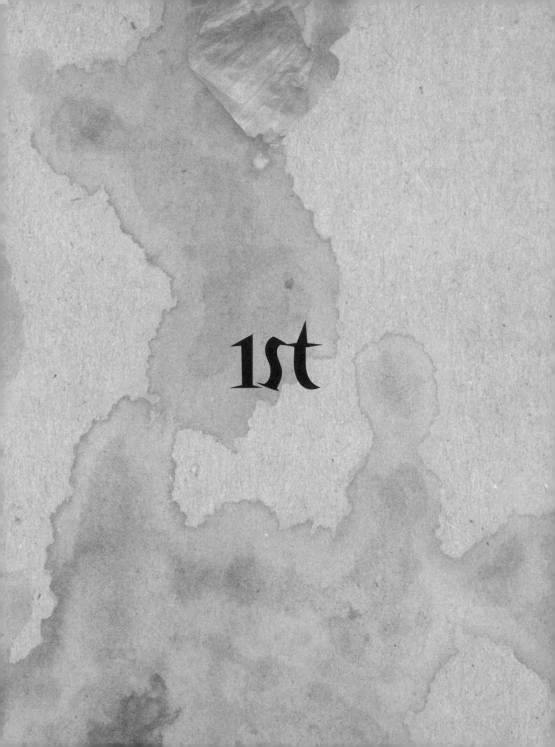

1st

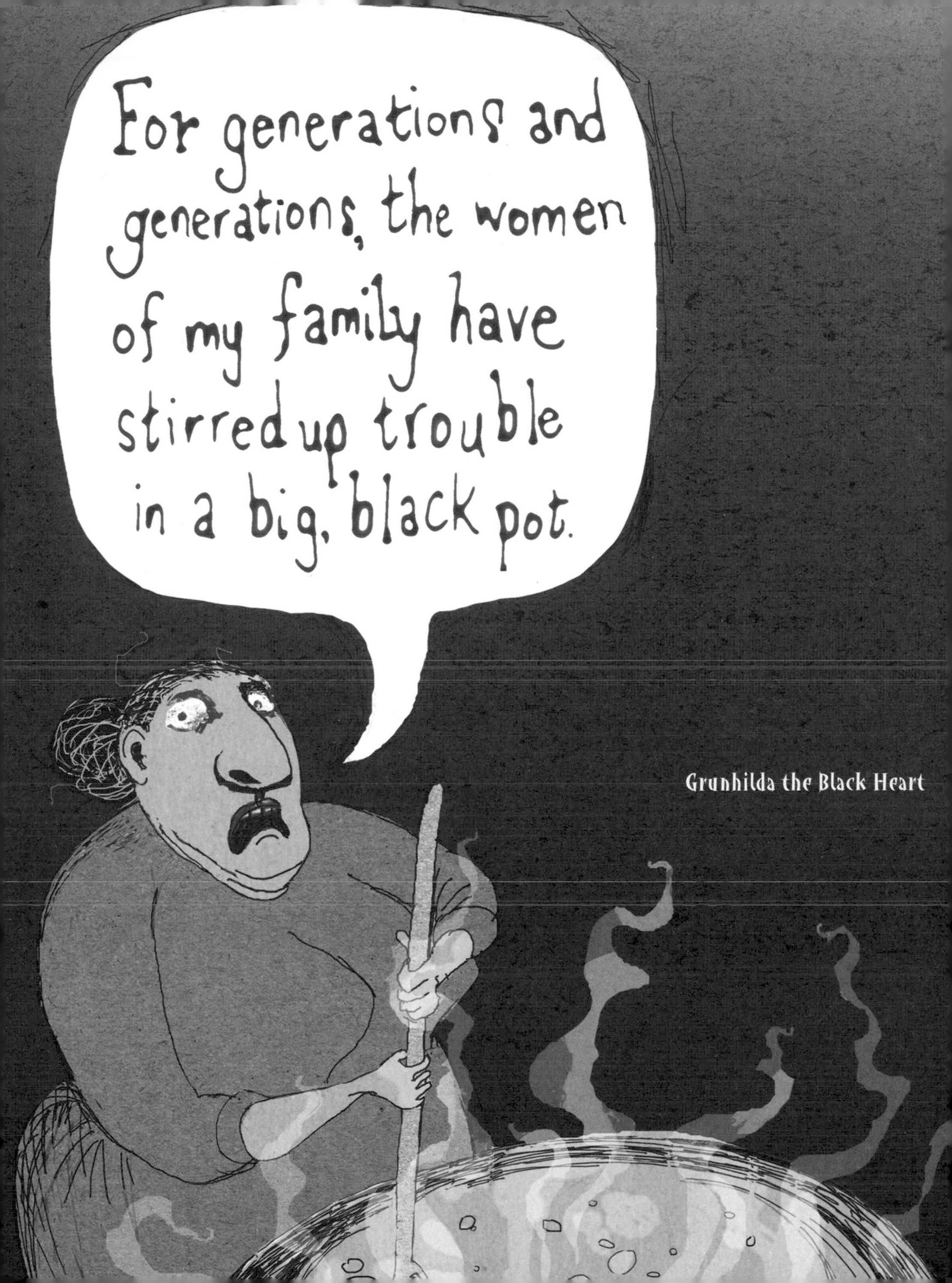
For generations and generations, the women of my family have stirred up trouble in a big, black pot.

Grunhilda the Black Heart

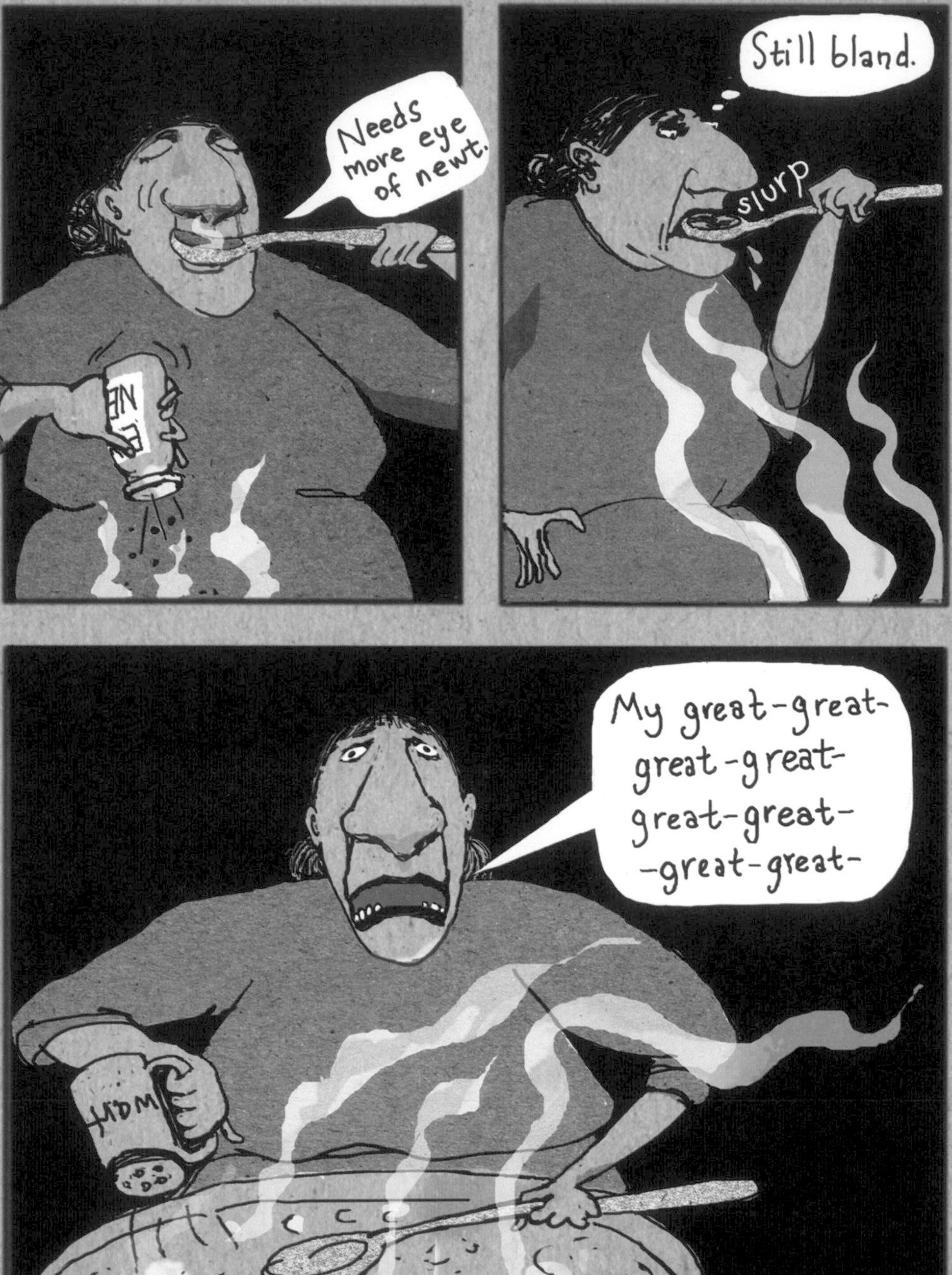
Needs more eye of newt.
Still bland.
slurp
My great-great-great-great-great-great-great-great-

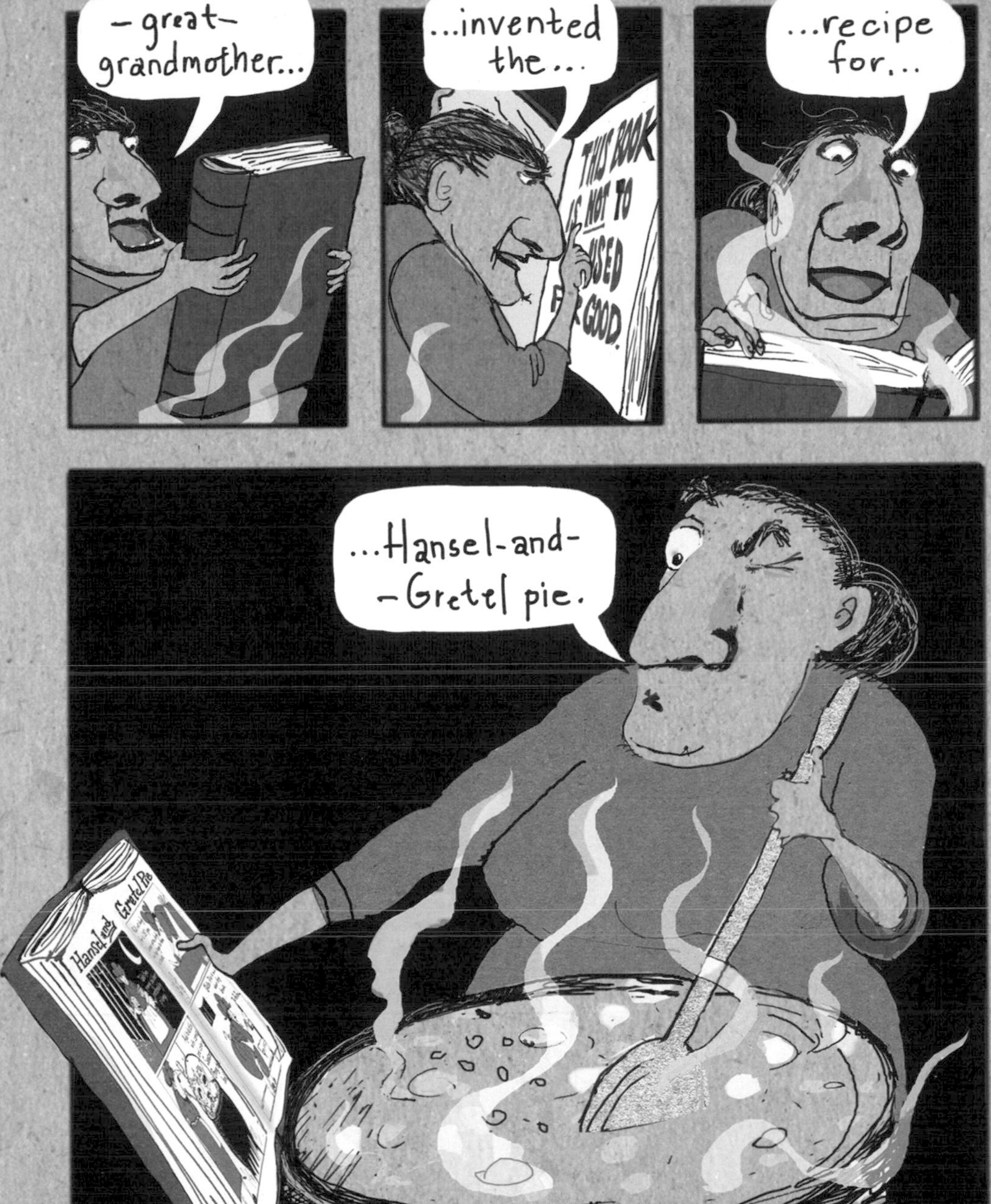
-great-grandmother...
...invented the...
THIS BOOK
IS NOT TO
...recipe for...
...Hansel-and--Gretel pie.
Hansel and Gretel Pie

Hansel-and-

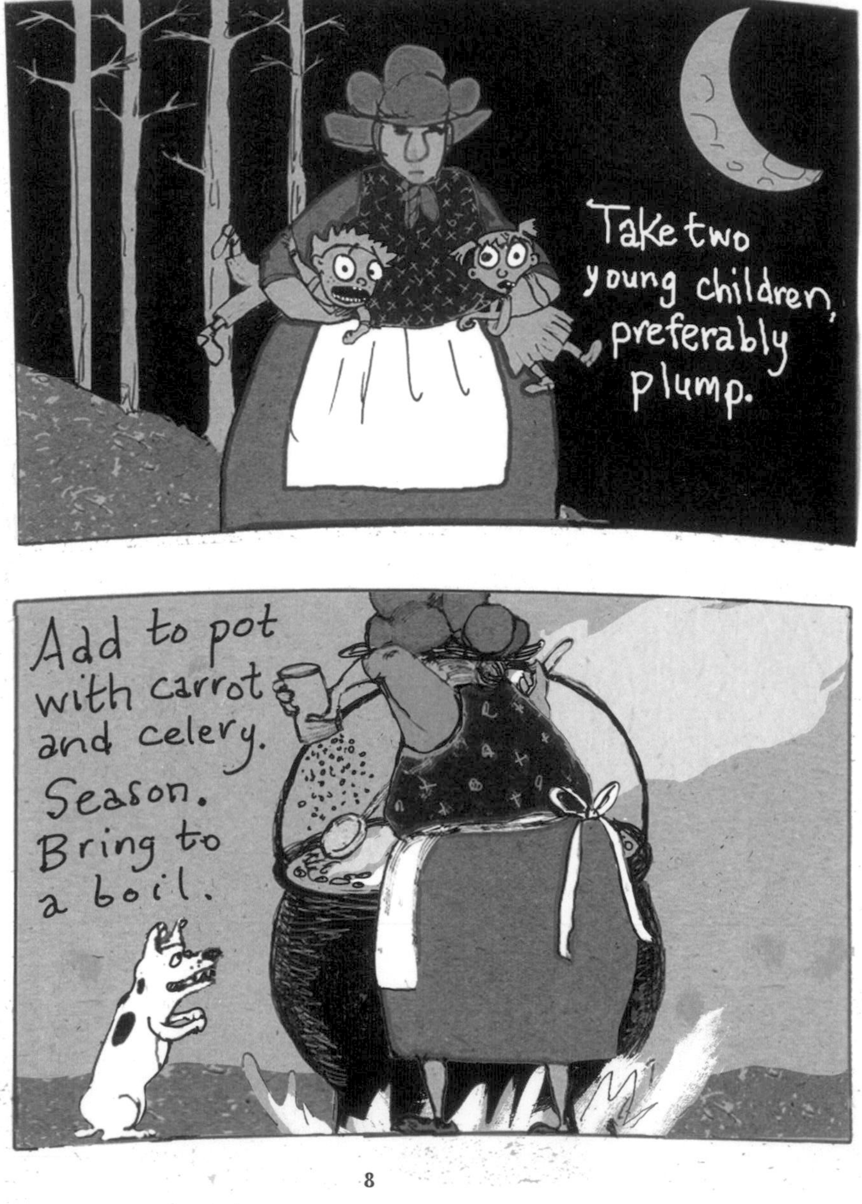
Take two young children, preferably plump.
Add to pot with carrot and celery. Season. Bring to a boil.

-Gretel Pie

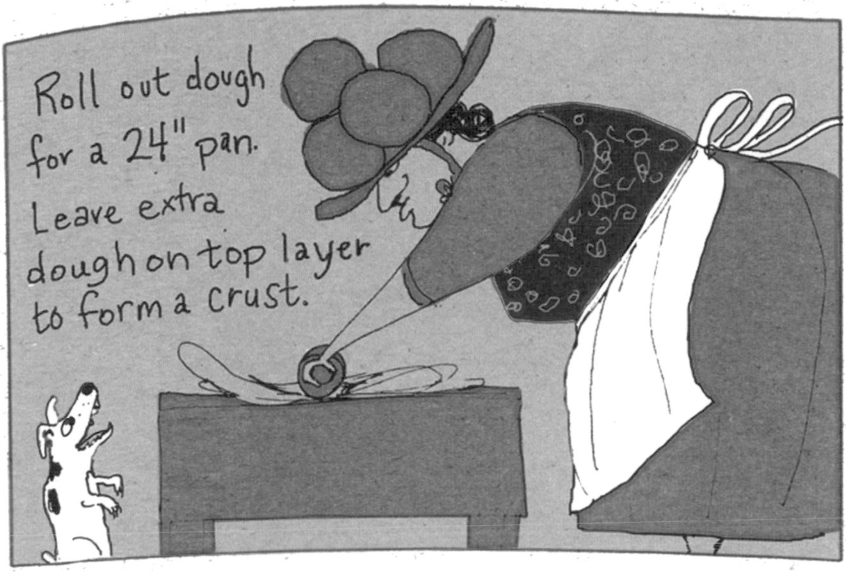
Roll out dough for a 24" pan. Leave extra dough on top layer to form a crust.

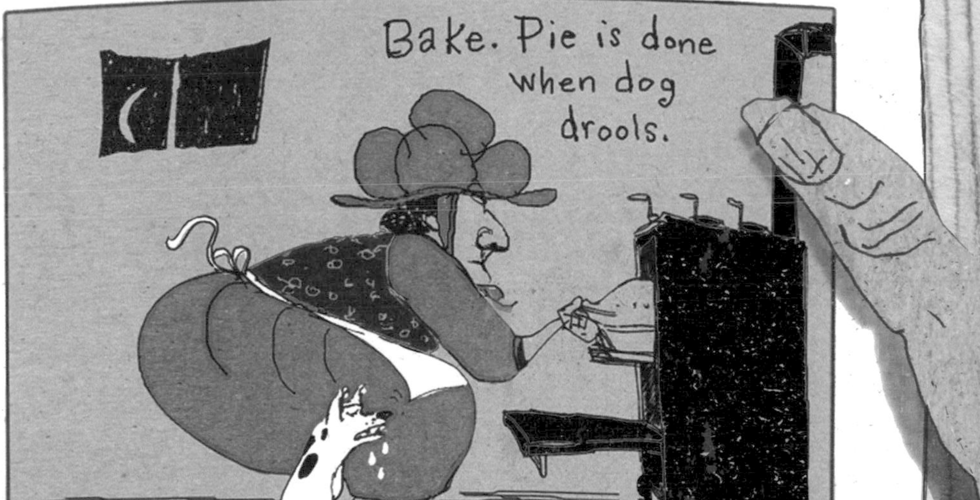
Bake. Pie is done when dog drools.

Tituba's Most

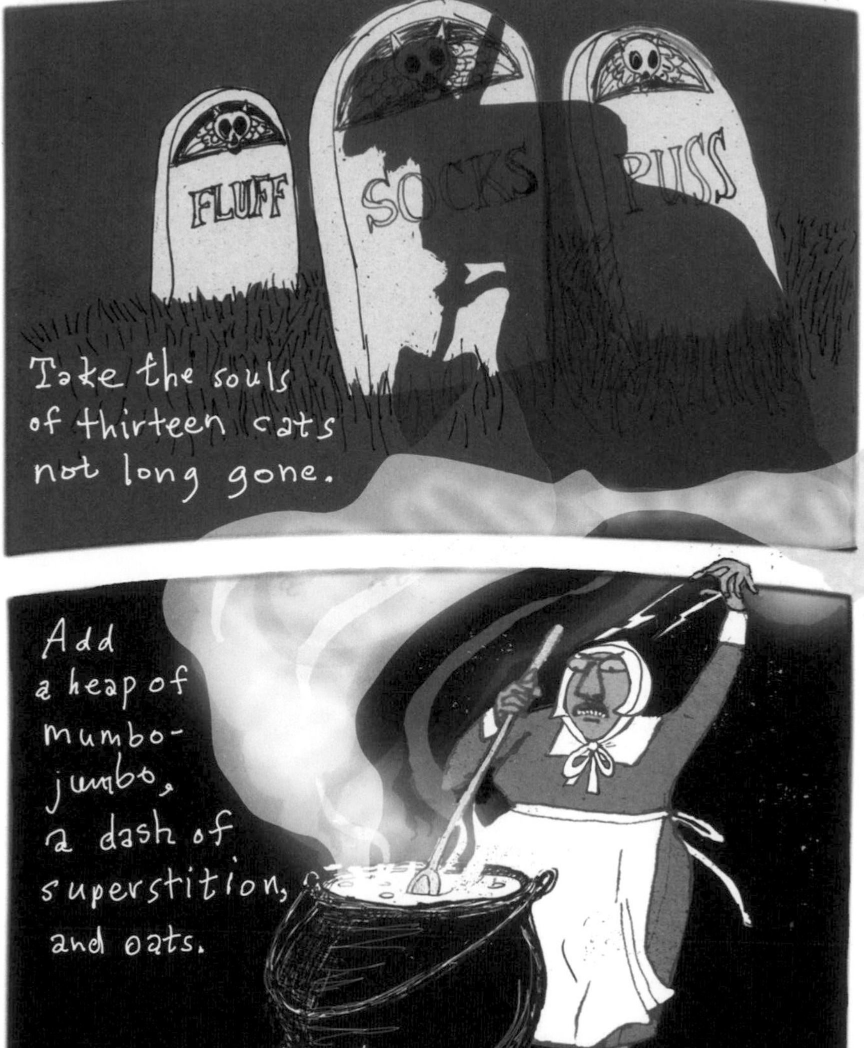
FLUFF
SOCKS
PUSS
Take the souls of thirteen cats not long gone.
Add a heap of mumbo-jumbo, a dash of superstition, and oats.

Foul Porridge

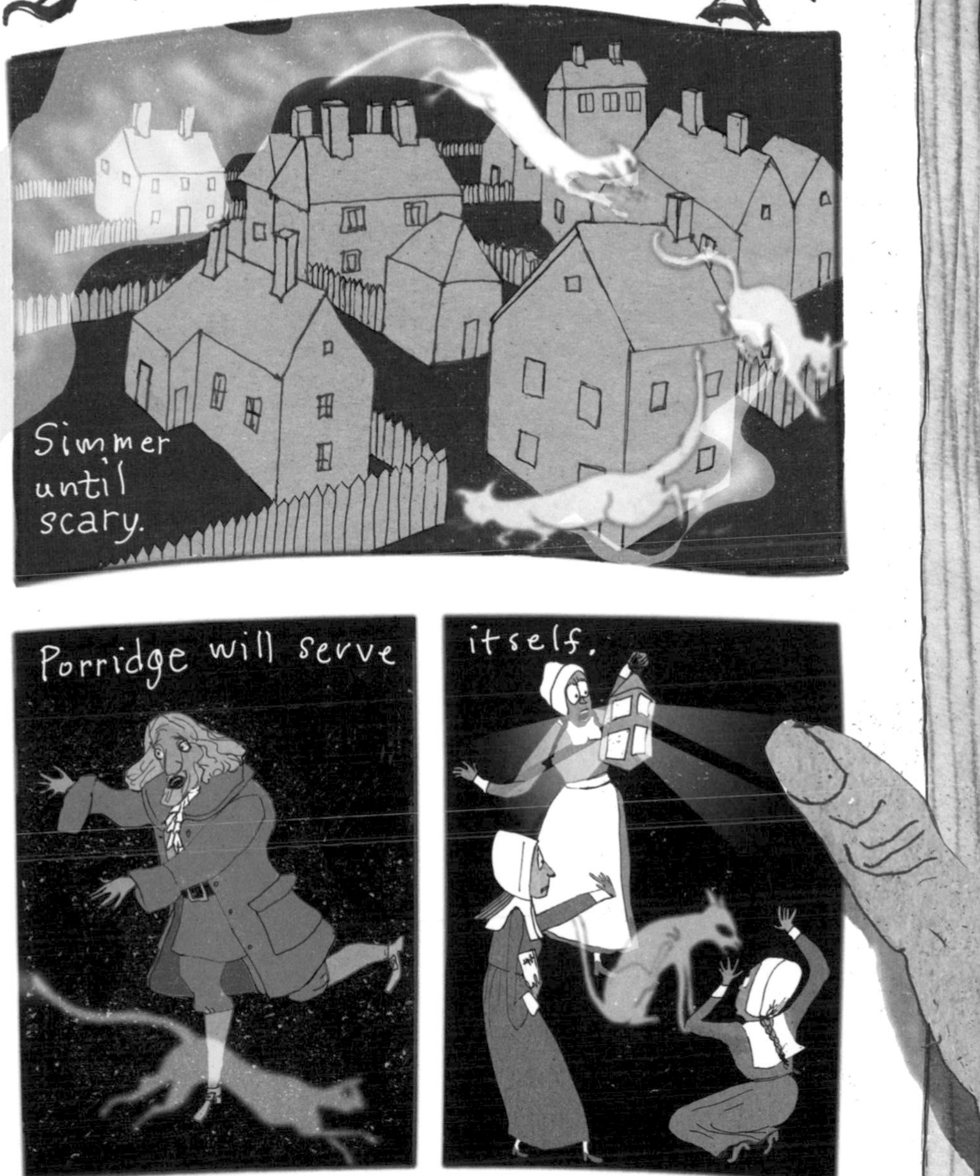
Simmer until scary.
Porridge will serve
itself.

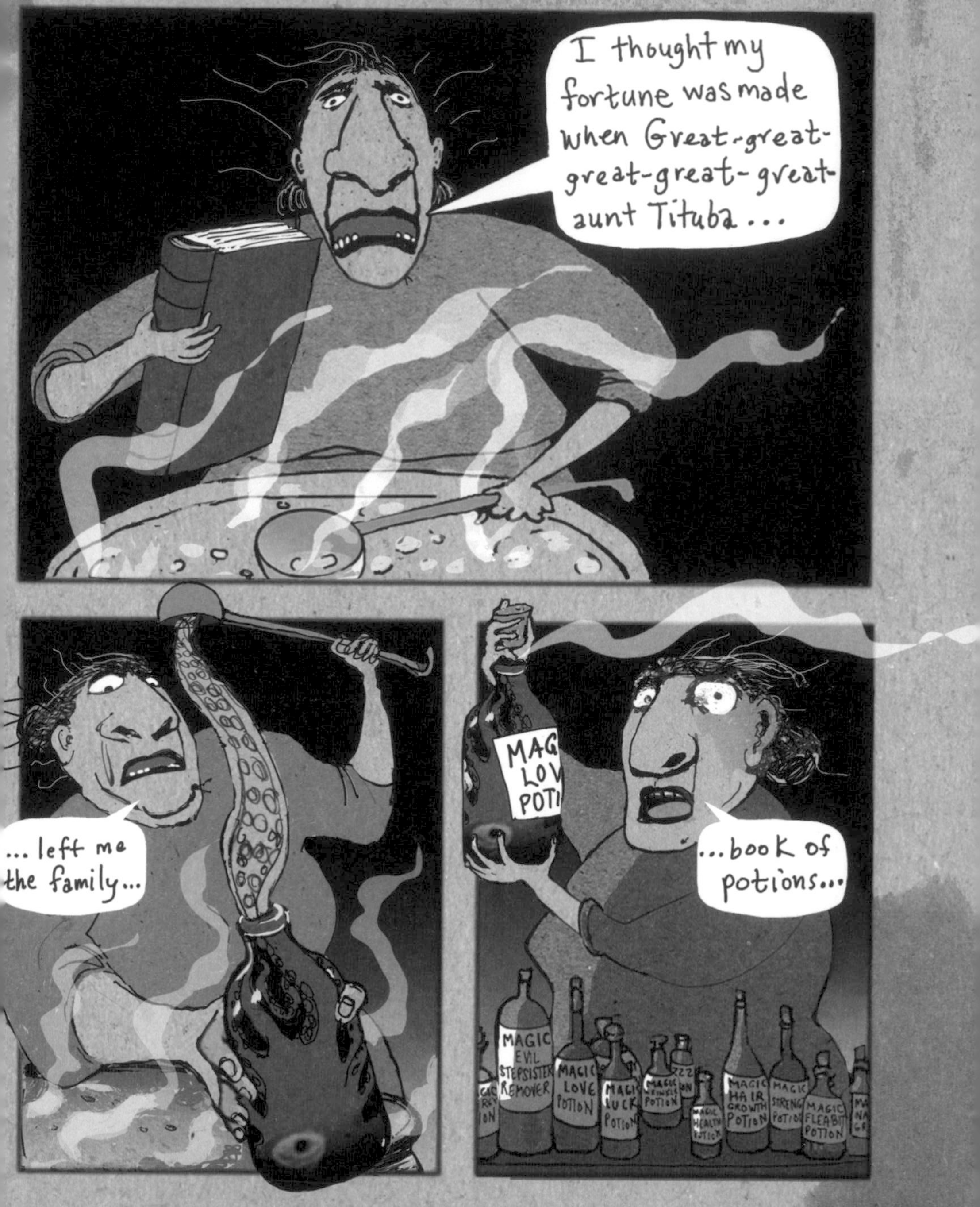
I thought my fortune was made when Great-great-great-great-great-aunt Tituba...
... left me the family...
...book of potions...
MAG LOV POTI
MAGIC EVIL STEPSISTER REMOVER
MAGIC LOVE POTION
MAGIC LUCK POTION
MAGIC HAIR GROWTH POTION
MAGIC HEALTH POTION

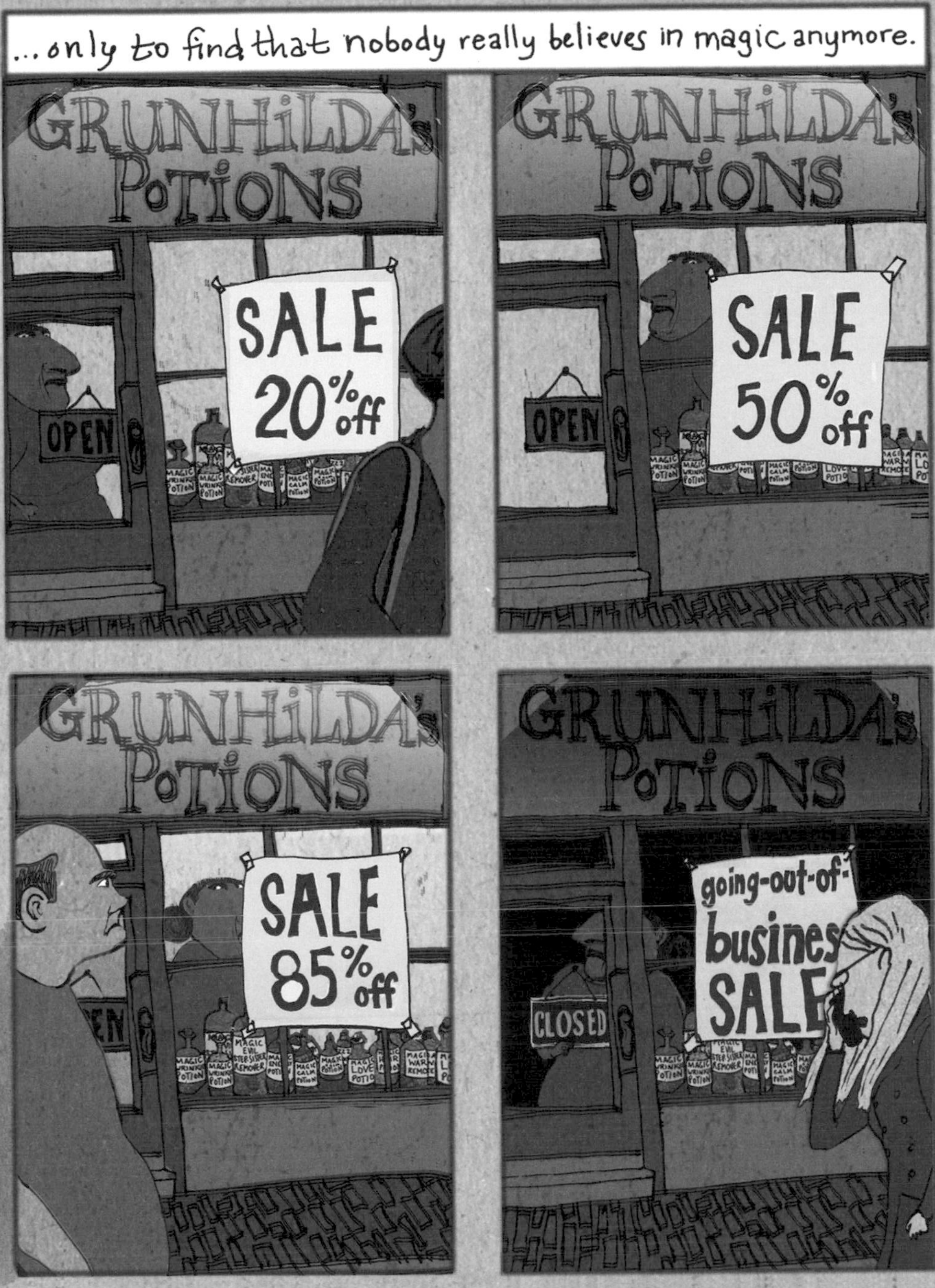
...only to find that nobody really believes in magic anymore.
GRUNHiLDA's POTiONS
OPEN
SALE 20% off
GRUNHiLDA's POTiONS
OPEN
SALE 50% off
GRUNHiLDA's POTiONS
SALE 85% off
GRUNHiLDA's POTiONS
CLOSED
going-out-of-busines SALE

2nd

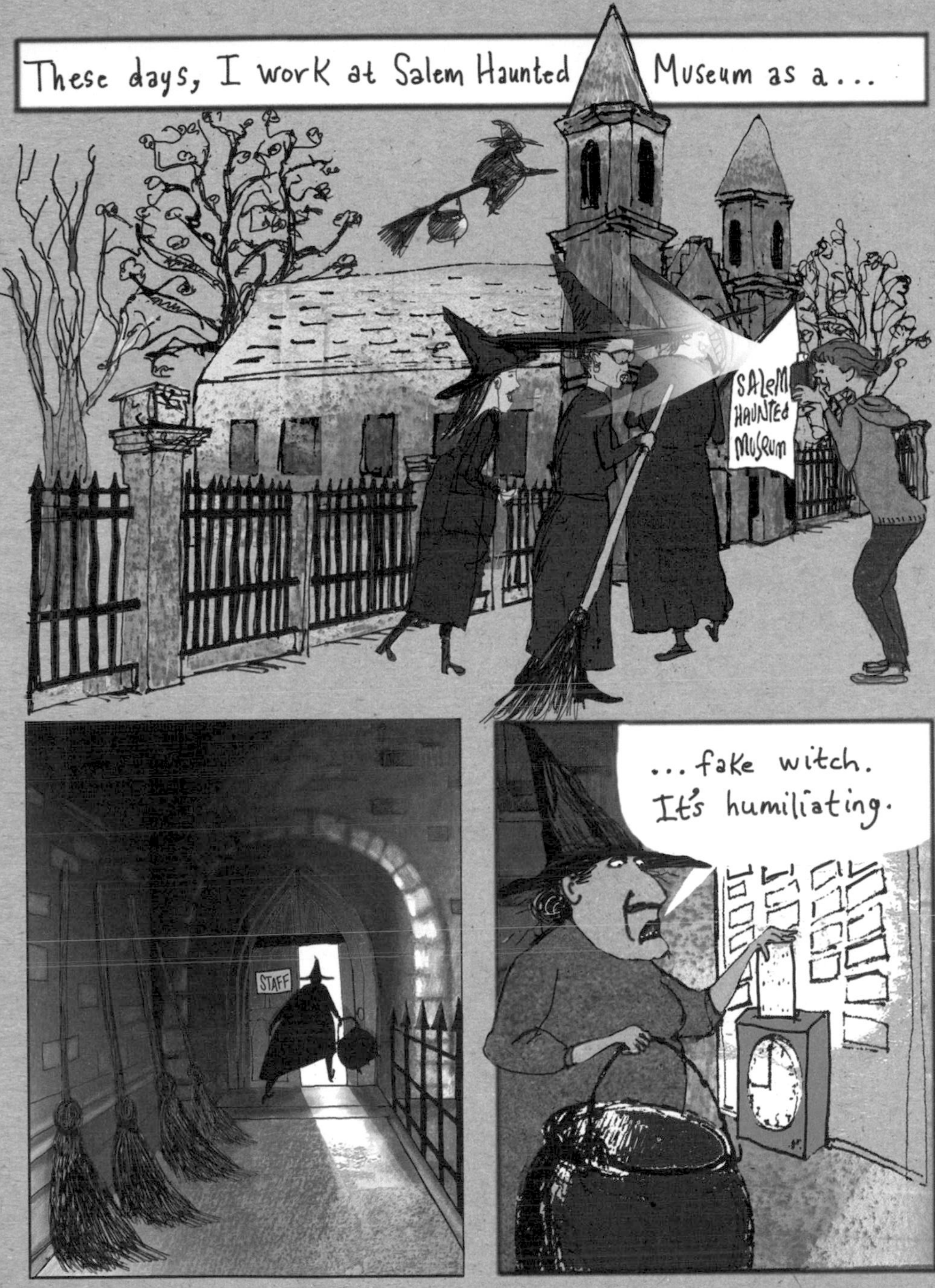
These days, I work at Salem Haunted Museum as a...
SALEM HAUNTED MUSEUM
STAFF
...fake witch. It's humiliating.

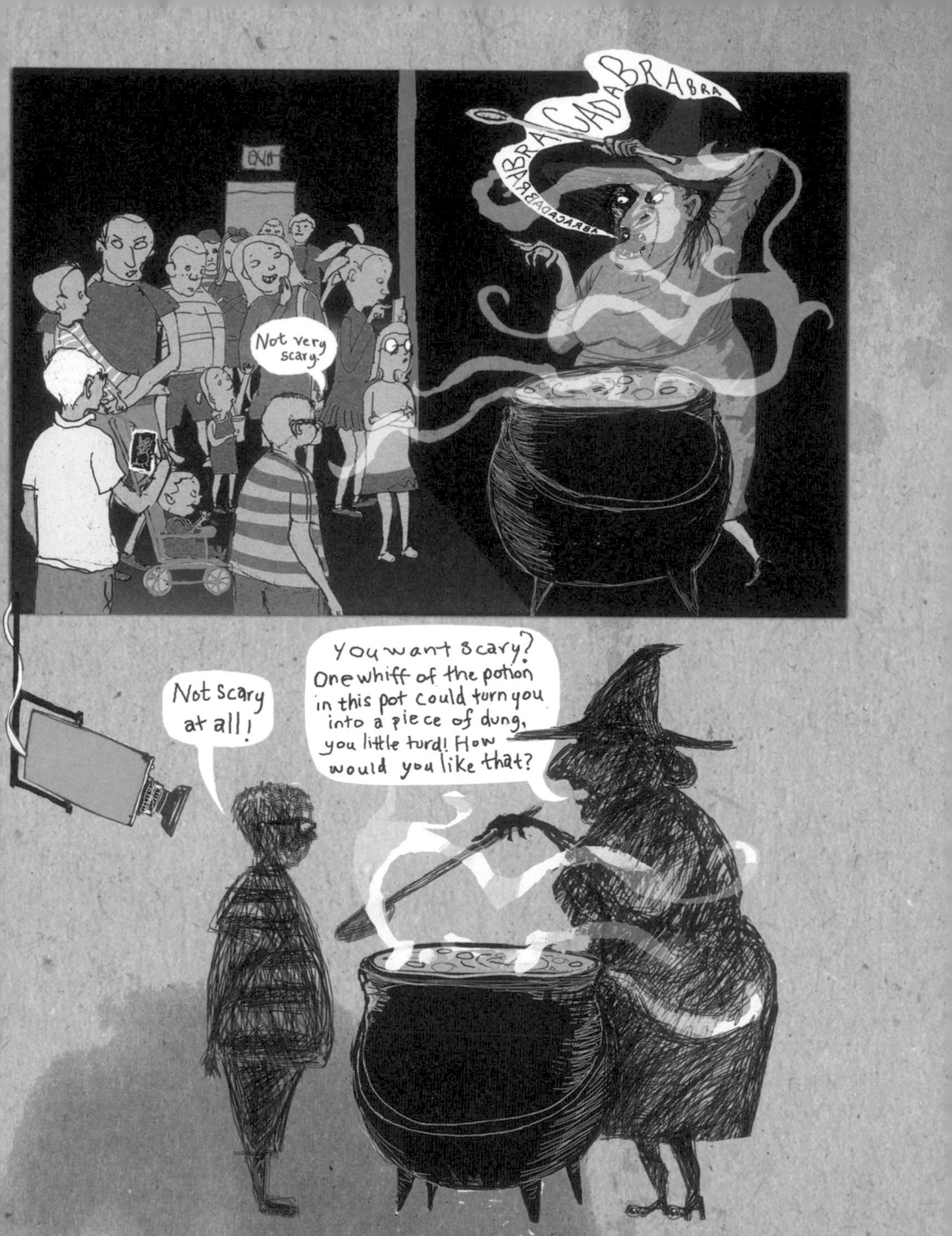
EXIT
ABRACADABRA
ABRACADABRABRA
Not very scary.
Not scary at all!
You want scary? One whiff of the potion in this pot could turn you into a piece of dung, you little turd! How would you like that?

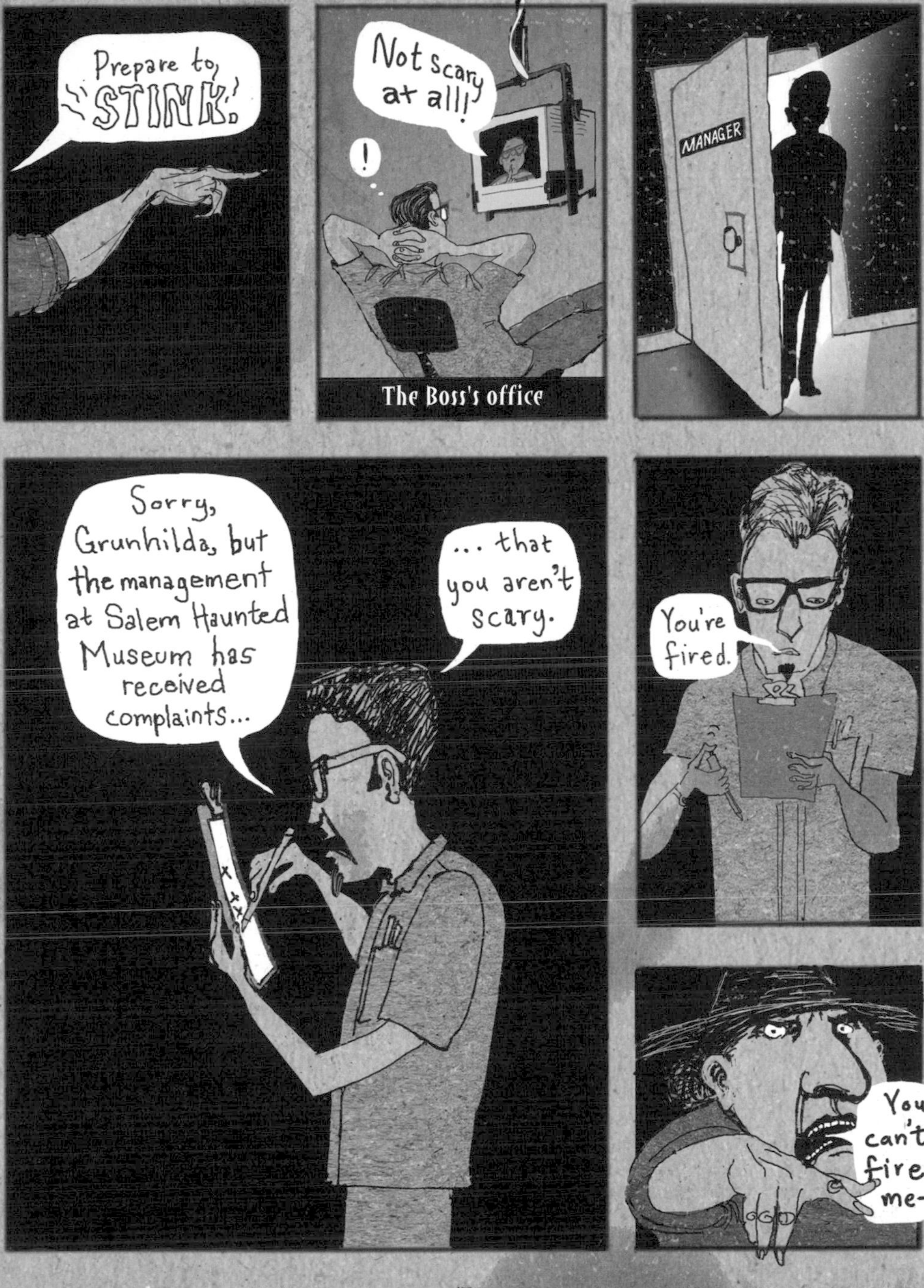
Prepare to, STINK.
Not scary at all!
!
The Boss's office
MANAGER
Sorry, Grunhilda, but the management at Salem Haunted Museum has received complaints...
... that you aren't scary.
You're fired.
You can't fire me—

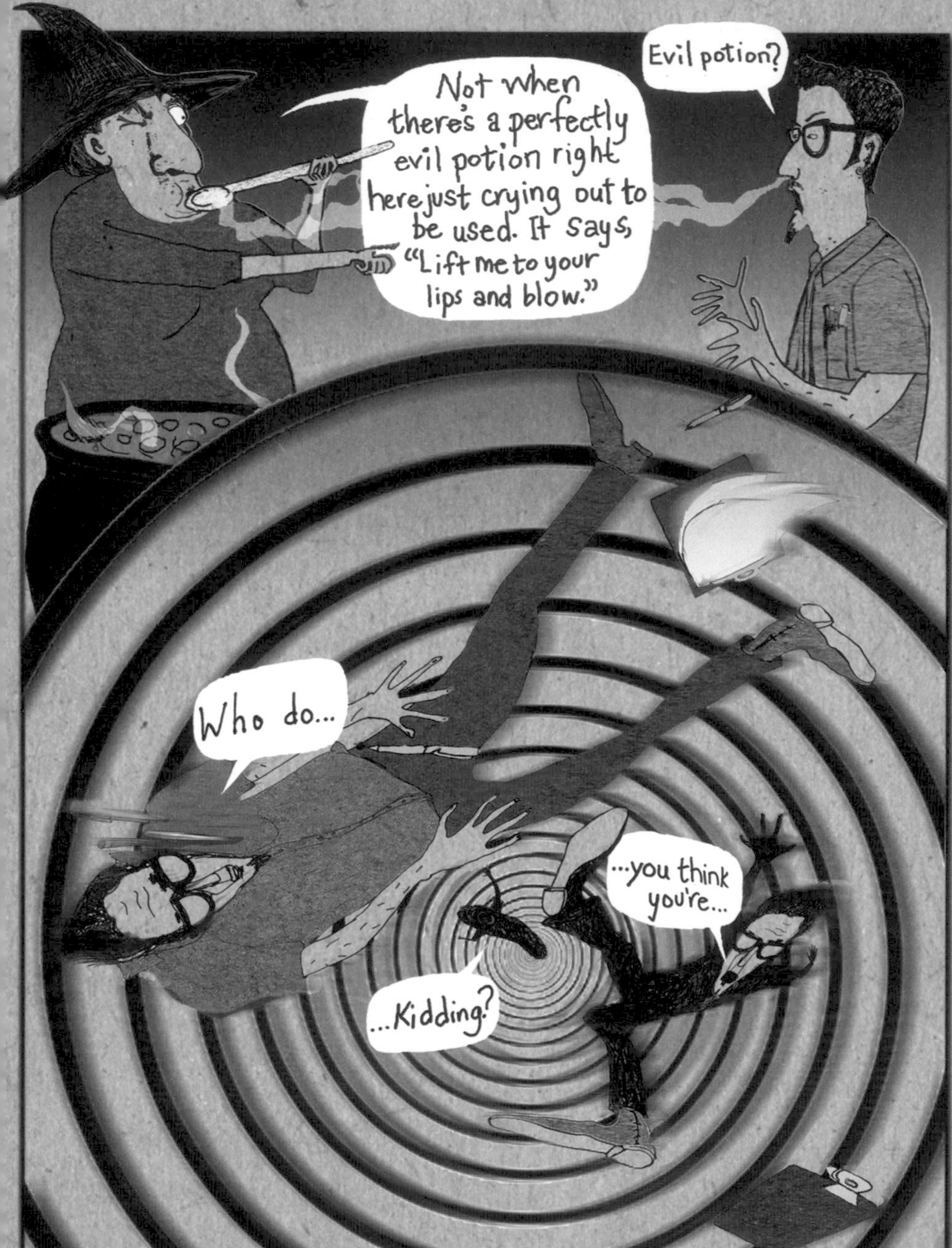
Evil potion?
Not when there's a perfectly evil potion right here just crying out to be used. It says, "Lift me to your lips and blow."
Who do...
...you think you're...
...Kidding?

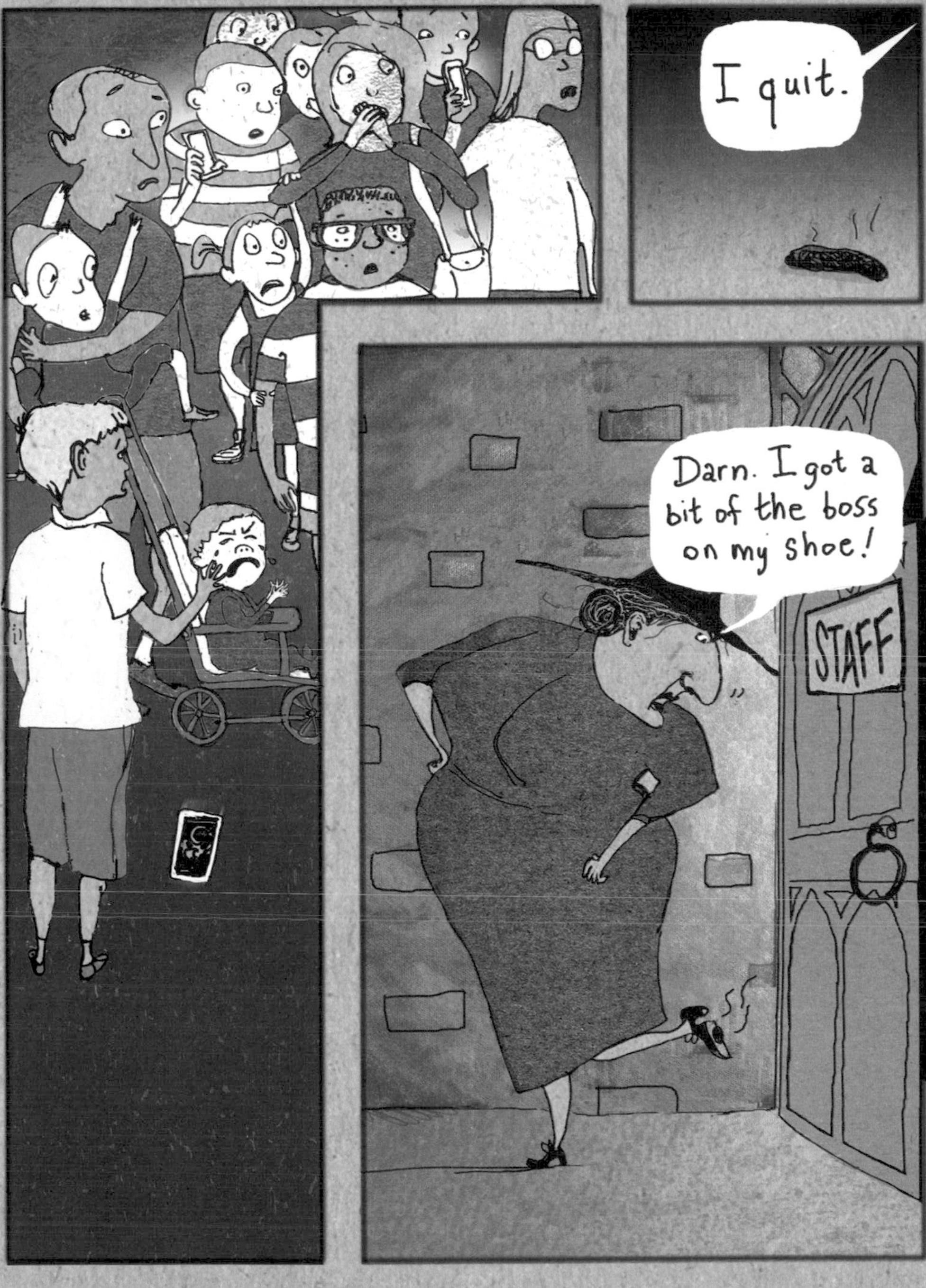
I quit.
Darn. I got a bit of the boss on my shoe!
STAFF

3rd

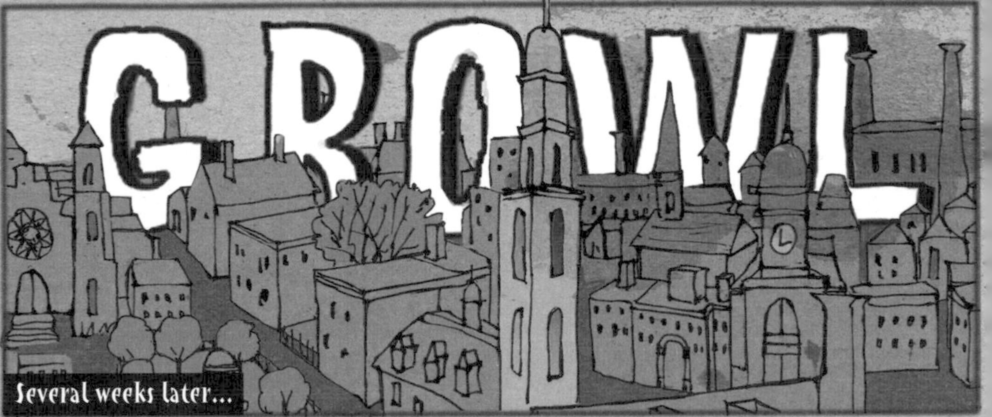
GROWL
Several weeks later...

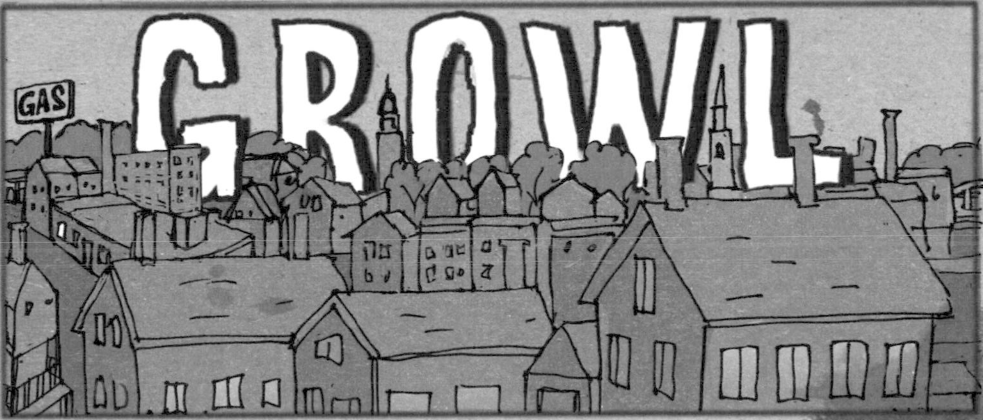
GROWL
GAS

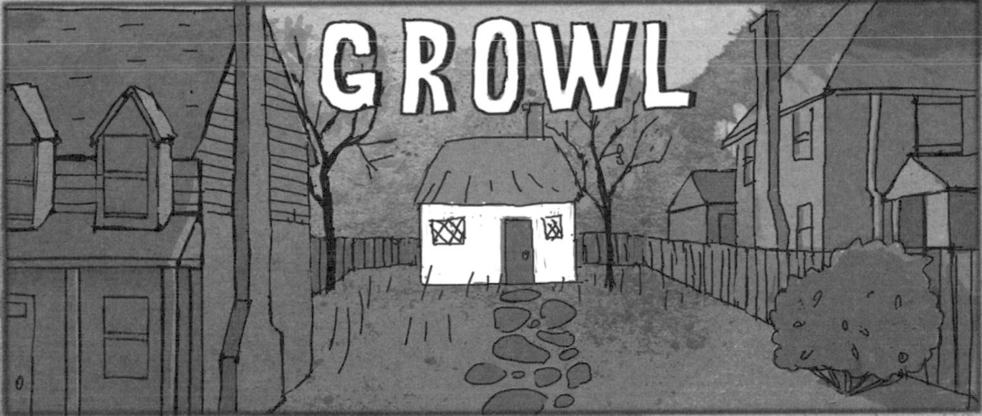
GROWL

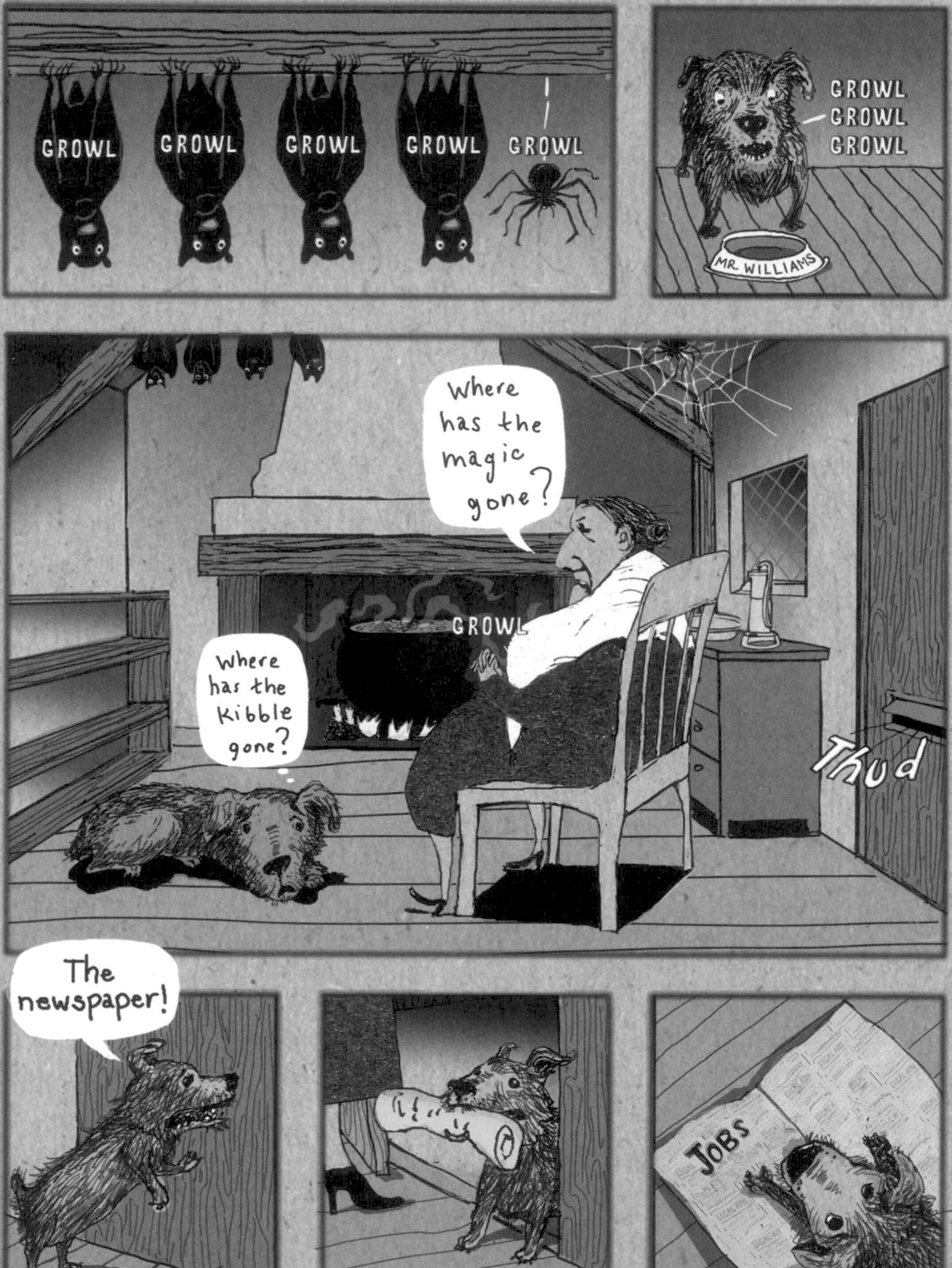
GROWL
GROWL
GROWL
GROWL
GROWL
GROWL
GROWL
GROWL
MR. WILLIAMS
Where has the magic gone?
GROWL
Where has the kibble gone?
Thud
The newspaper!
JOBS

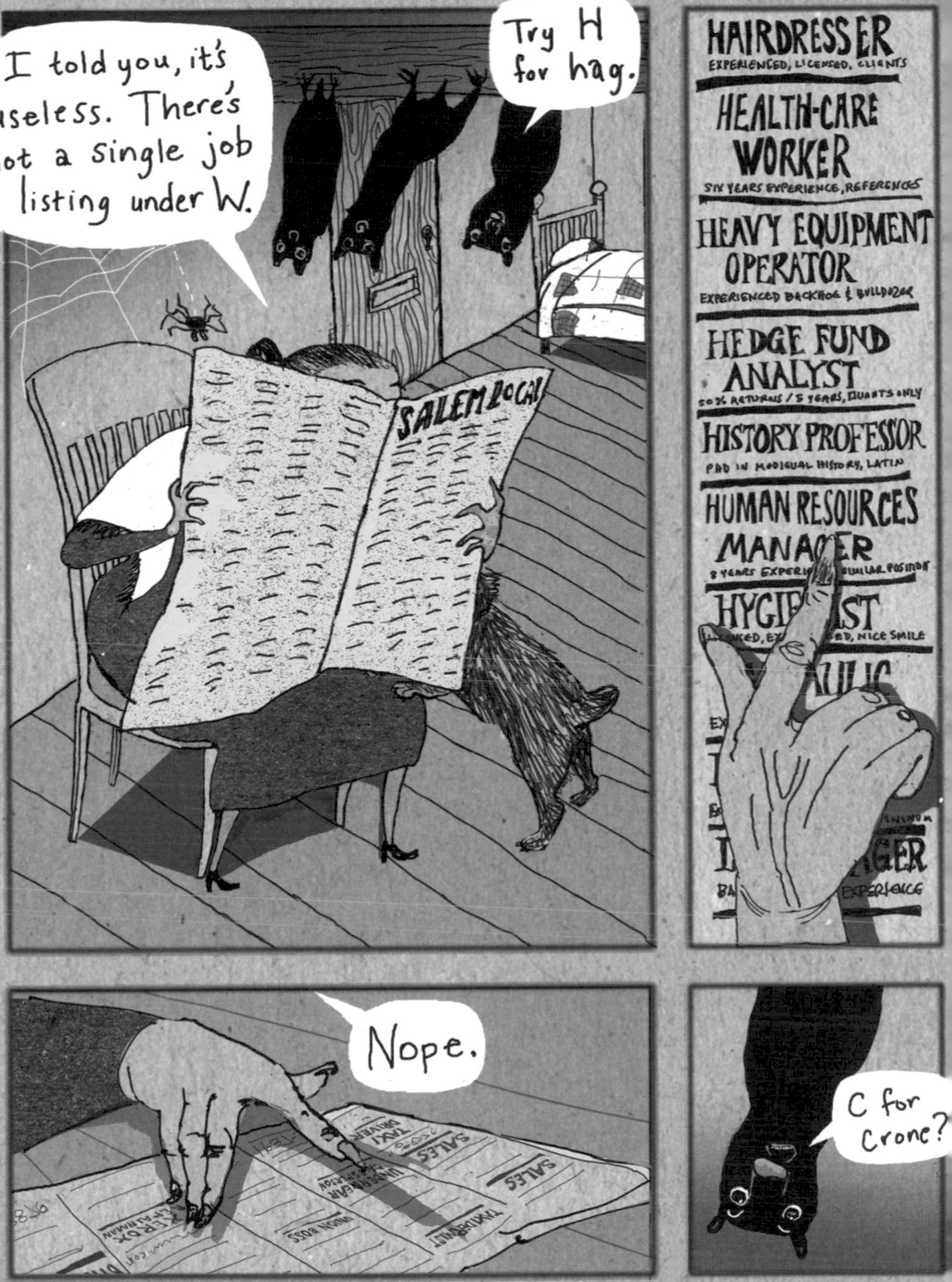
I told you, it's useless. There's not a single job listing under W.
Try H for hag.
SALEM LOCAL
HAIRDRESSER
EXPERIENCED, LICENSED, CLIENTS
HEALTH-CARE WORKER
SIX YEARS EXPERIENCE, REFERENCES
HEAVY EQUIPMENT OPERATOR
EXPERIENCED BACKHOE & BULLDOZER
HEDGE FUND ANALYST
50% RETURNS / 5 YEARS, QUANTS ONLY
HISTORY PROFESSOR
PHD IN MEDIEVAL HISTORY, LATIN
HUMAN RESOURCES
Nope.
SALES
TAXI DRIVER
UNION BOSS
C for Crone?

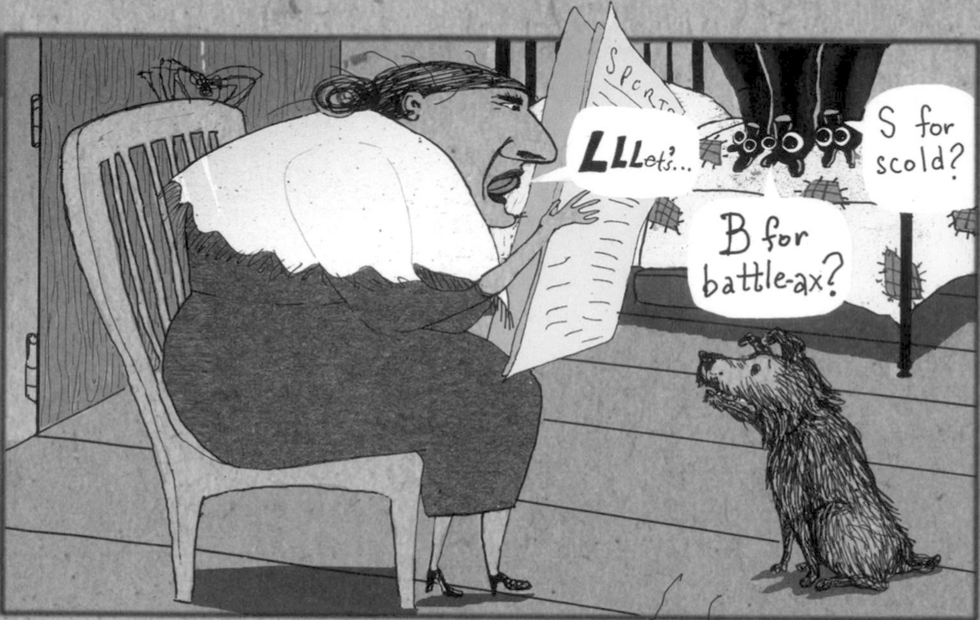
LLLets?...
S for scold?
B for battle-ax?
SPORTS

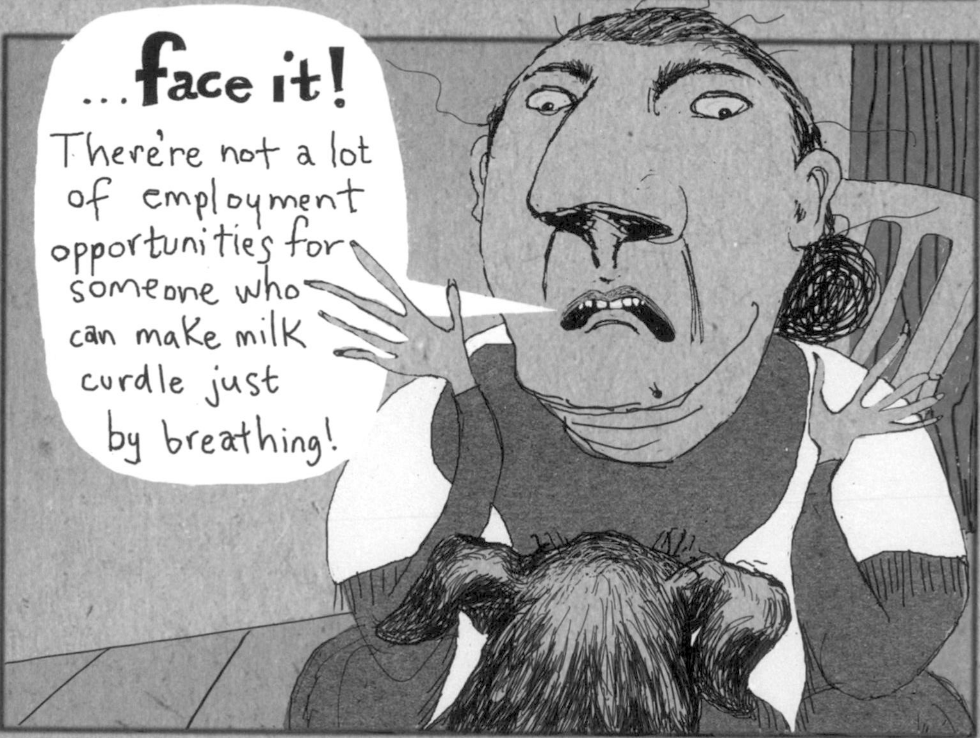
...face it!
There're not a lot of employment opportunities for someone who can make milk curdle just by breathing!

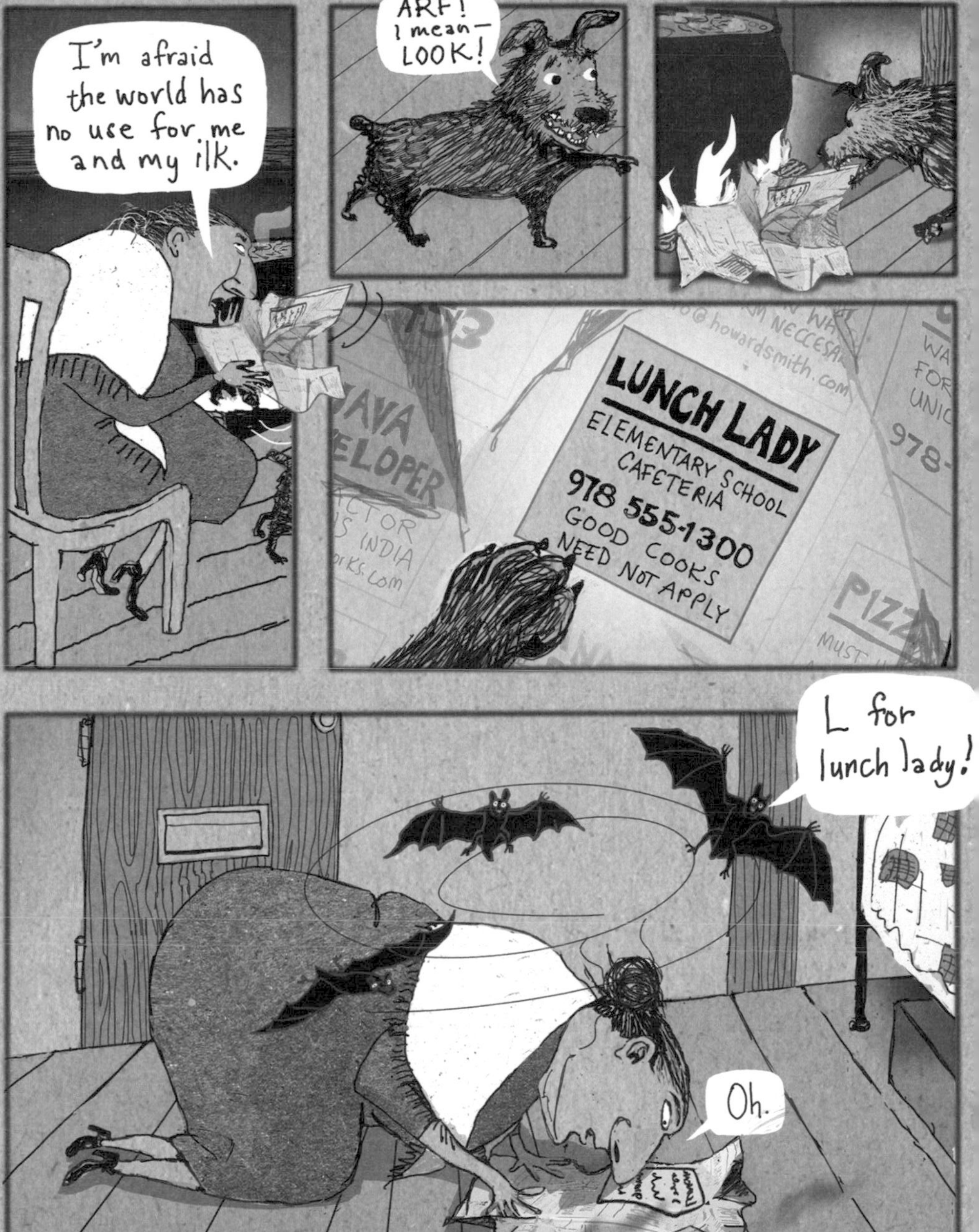
I'm afraid the world has no use for me and my ilk.
ARF! I mean— LOOK!
LUNCH LADY
ELEMENTARY SCHOOL CAFETERIA
978 555-1300
GOOD COOKS NEED NOT APPLY
L for lunch lady!
Oh.

4th

Pull!
ZIP
Wish me luck.

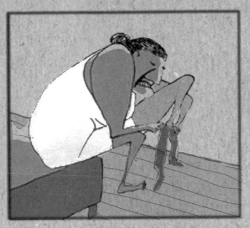

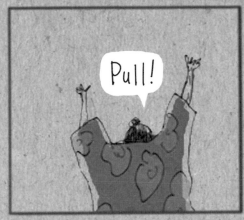

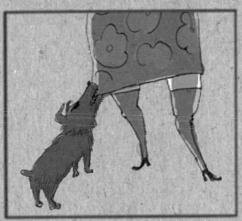

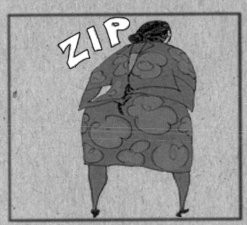

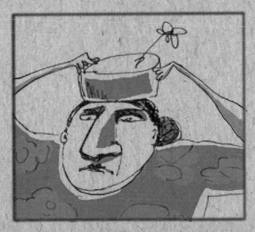

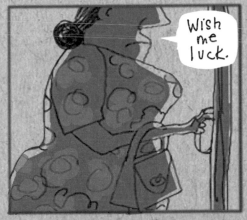

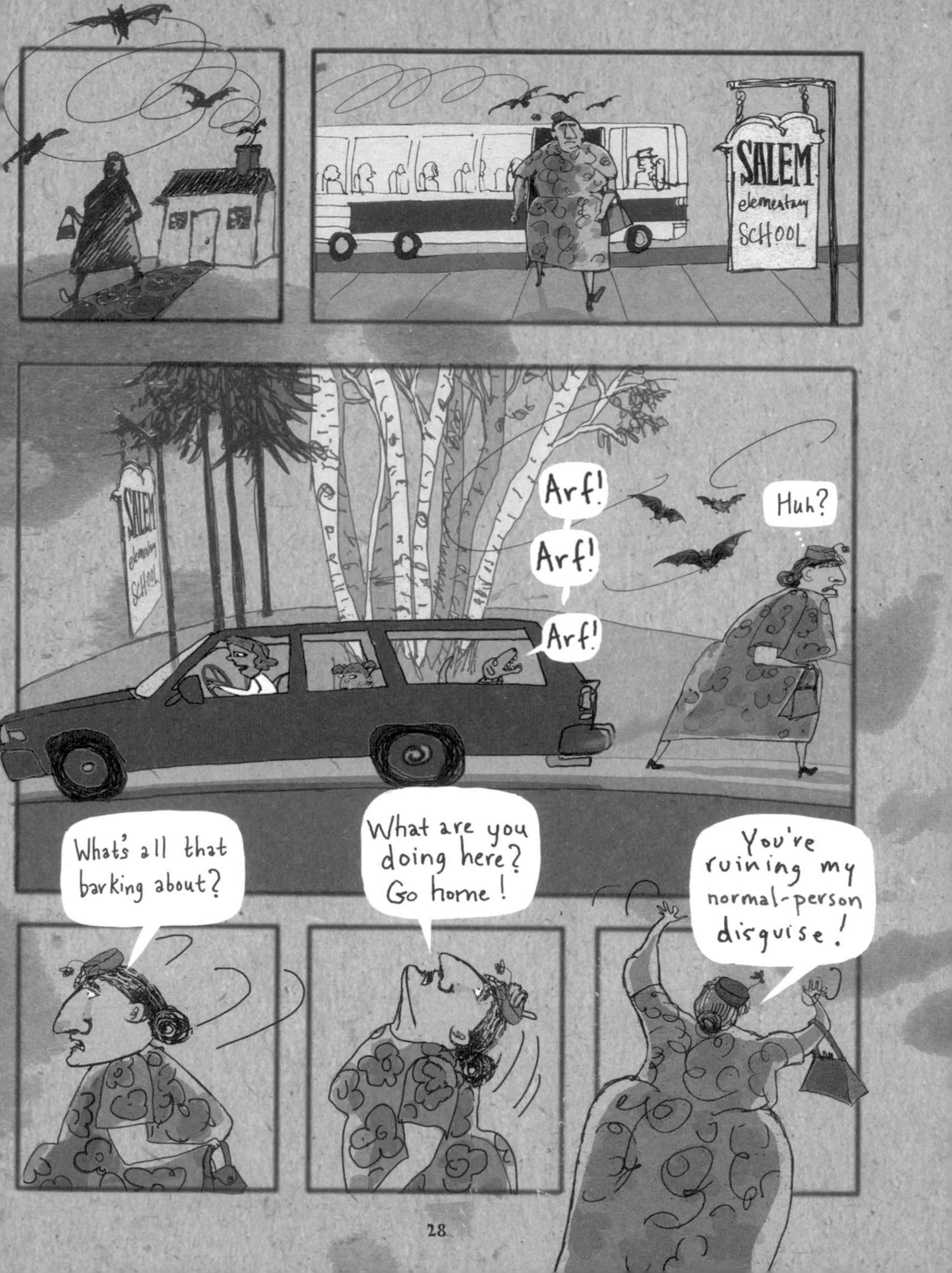
SALEM
elementary
SCHOOL
SALEM
elementary
SCHOOL
Arf!
Arf!
Arf!
Huh?
What's all that barking about?
What are you doing here? Go home!
You're ruining my normal-person disguise!

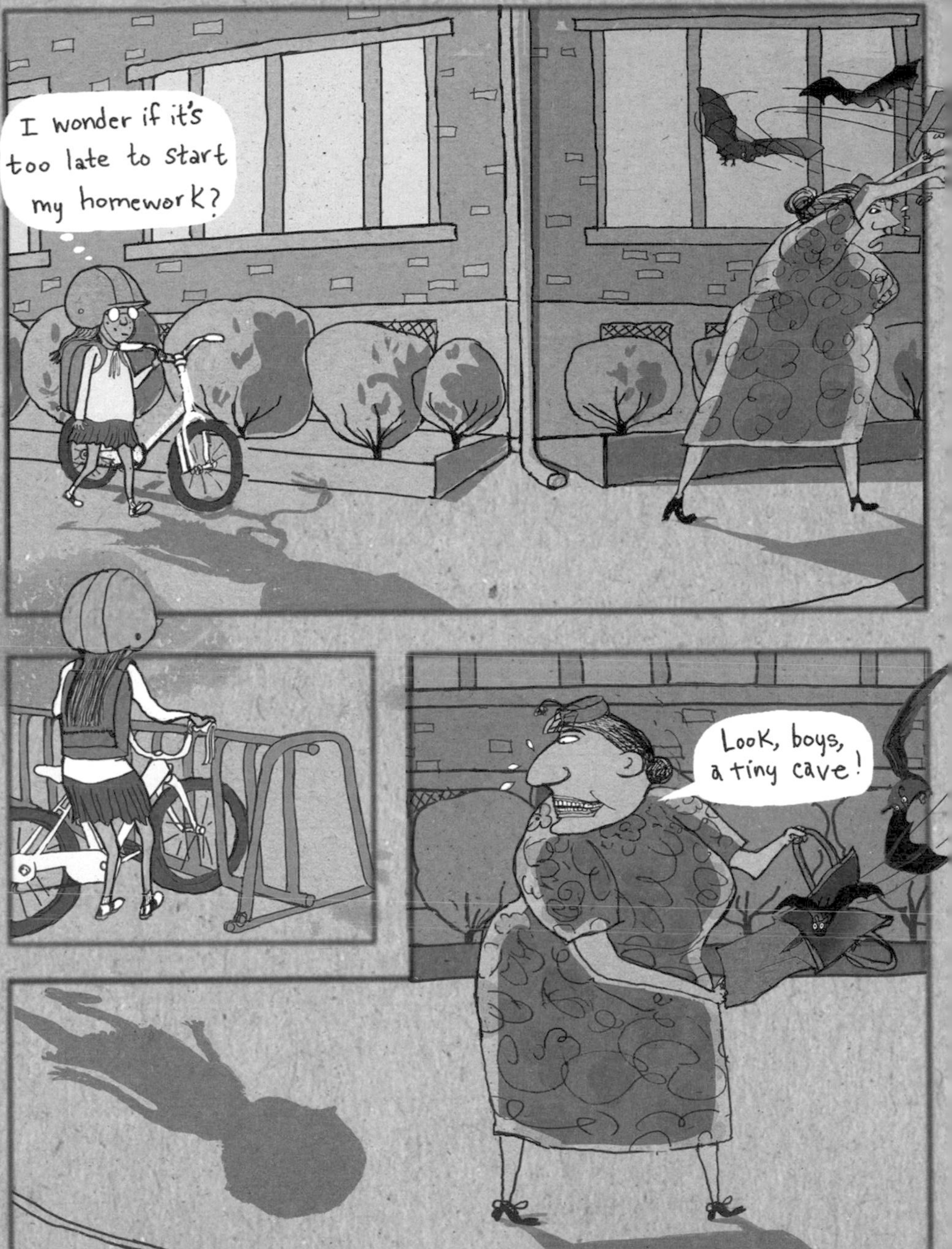
I wonder if it's too late to start my homework?
Look, boys, a tiny cave!

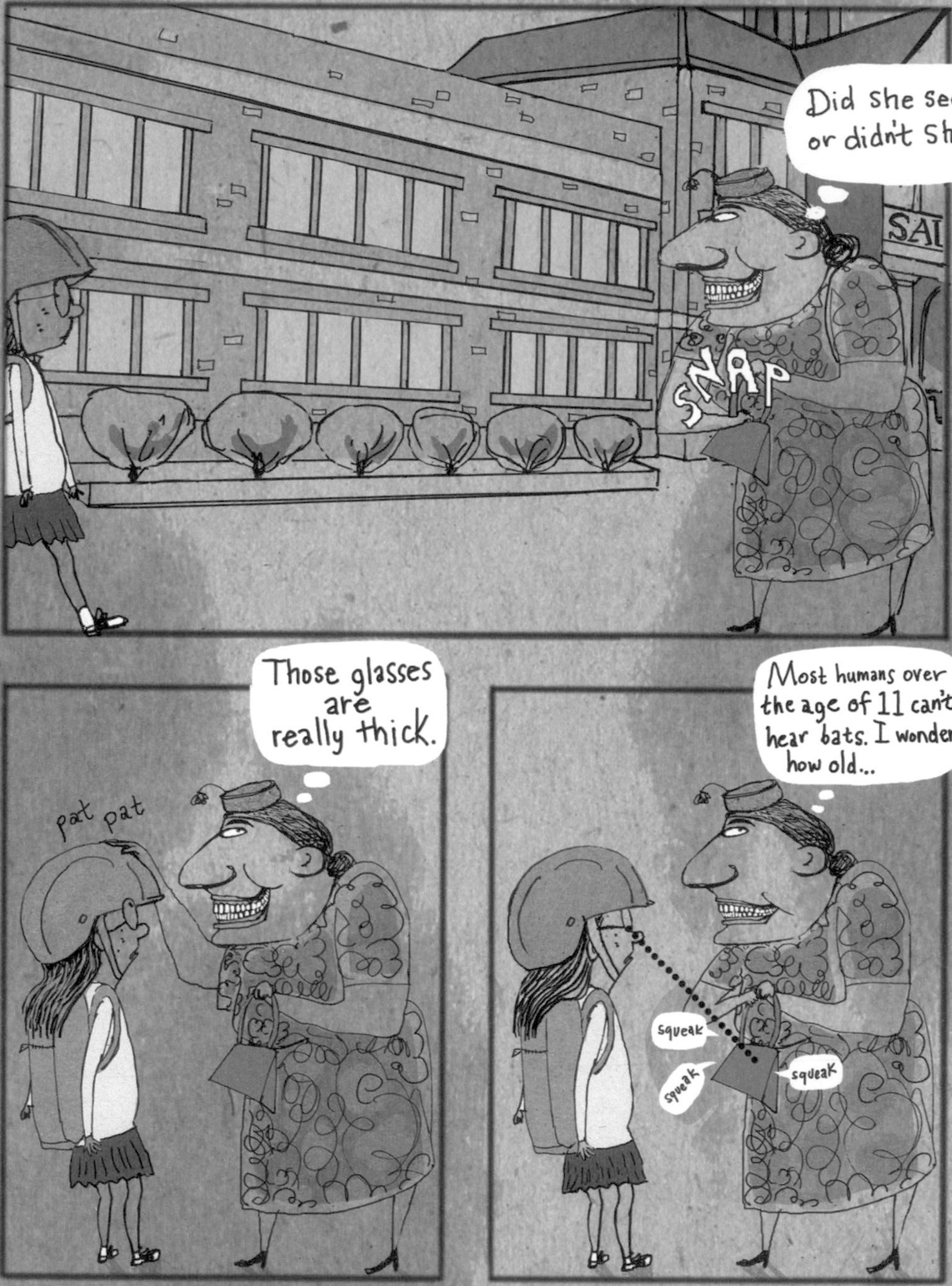
SNAP
Did she see or didn't she?
pat pat
Those glasses are really thick.
Most humans over the age of 11 can't hear bats. I wonder how old...
squeak
squeak
squeak

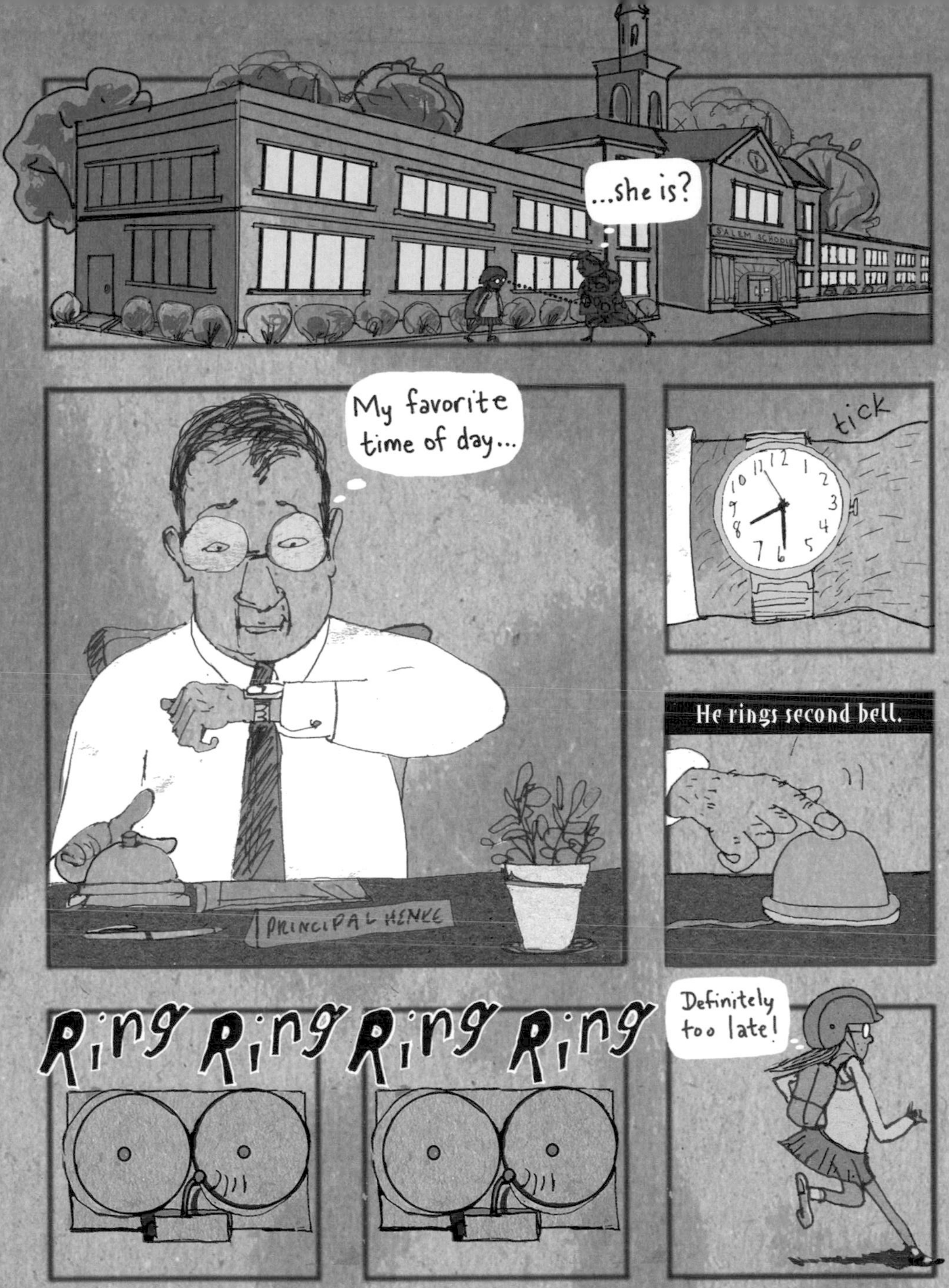

...she is?
SALEM SCHOOL
My favorite time of day...
tick
PRINCIPAL HENKE
He rings second bell.
Ring Ring Ring Ring
Definitely too late!

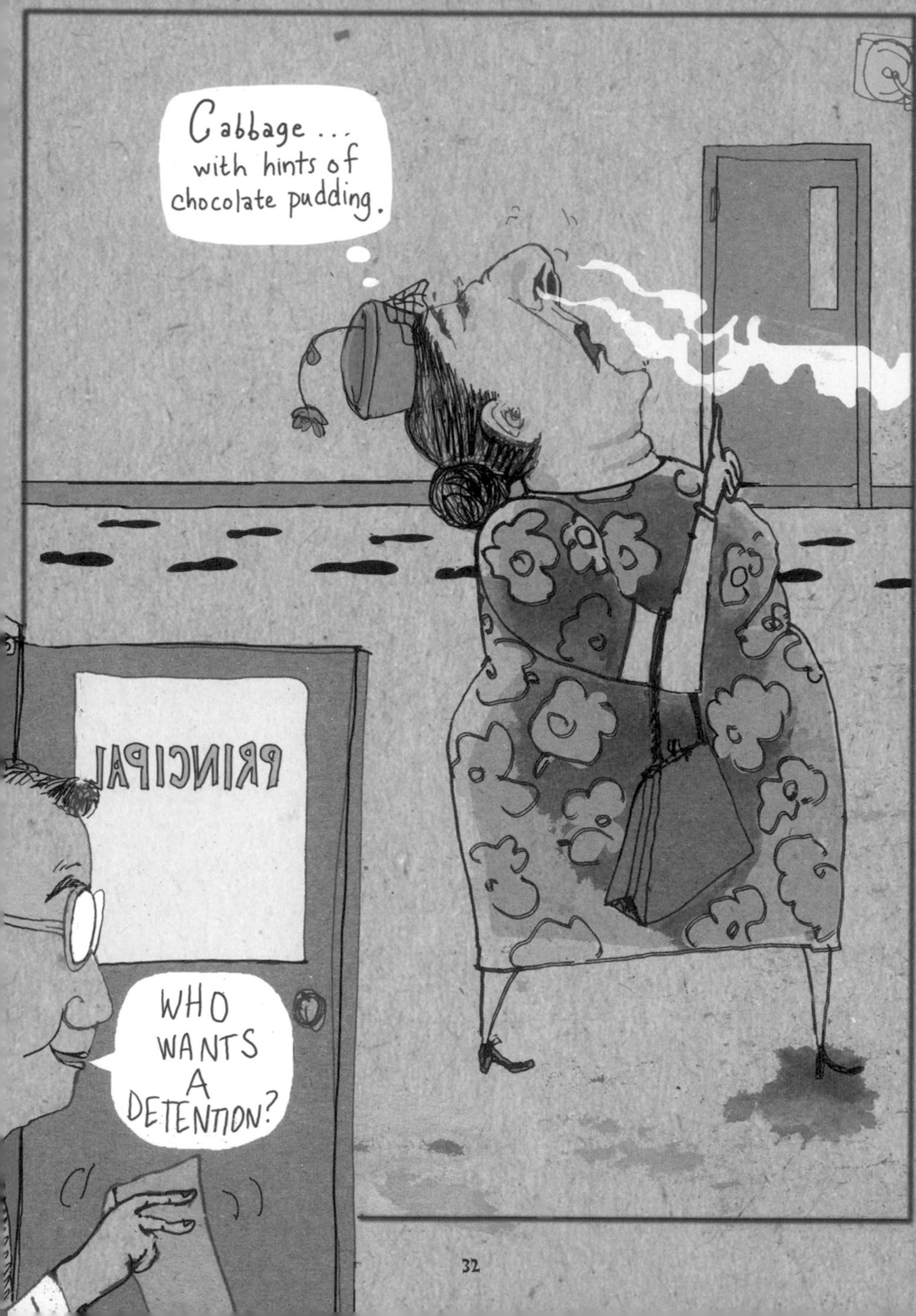
Cabbage ... with hints of chocolate pudding.
PRINCIPAL
WHO WANTS A DETENTION?

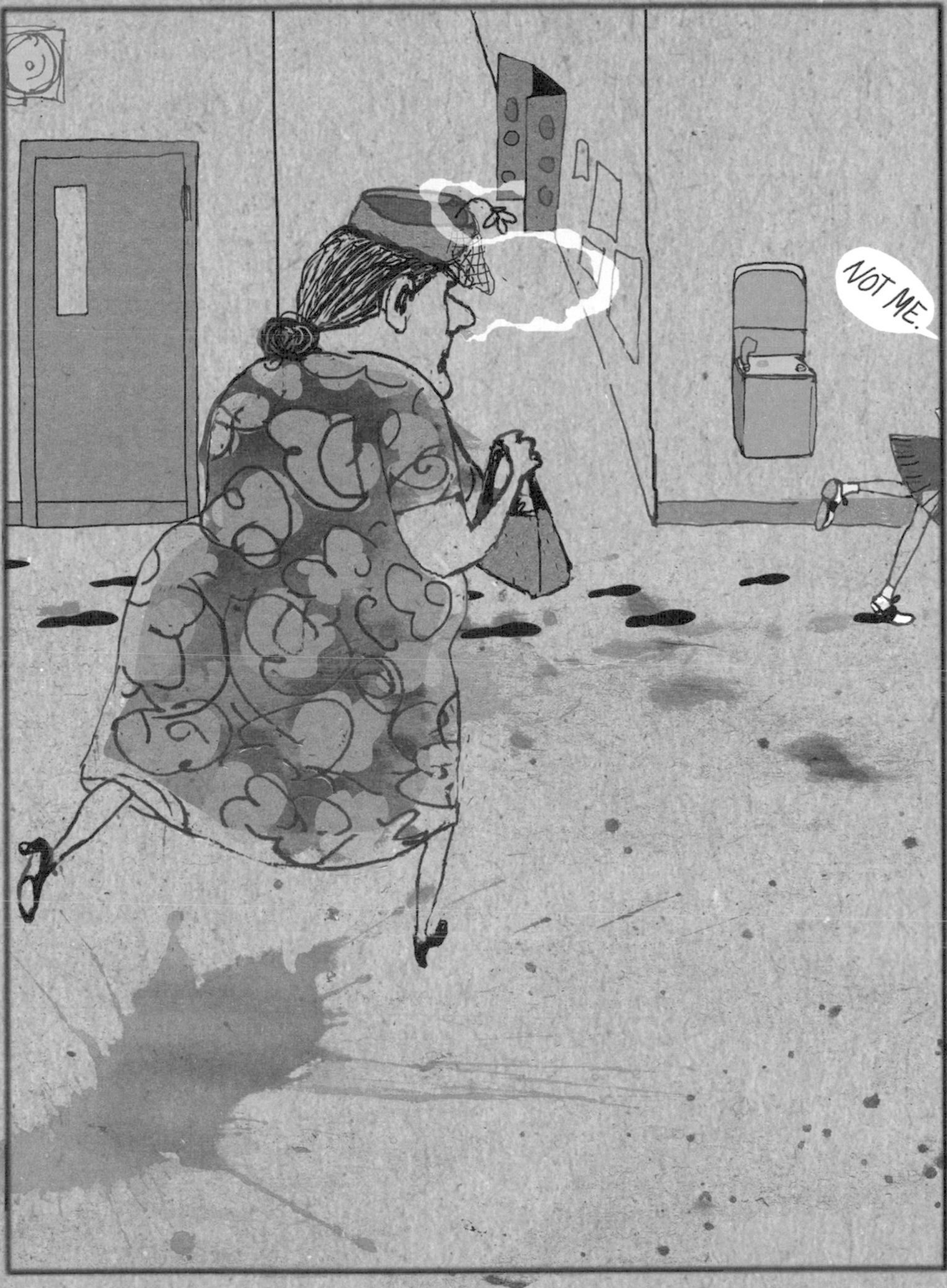
NOT ME.

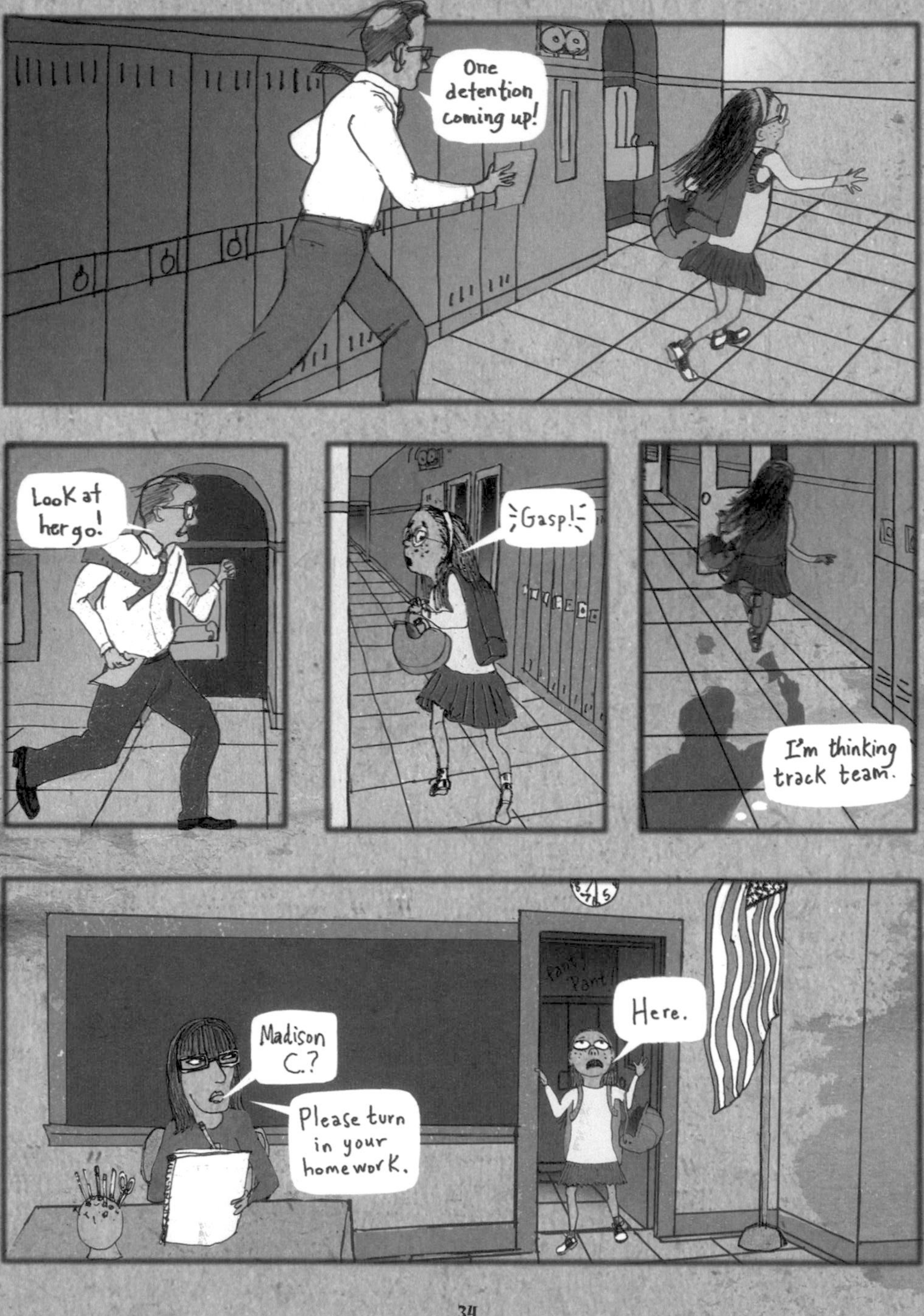
One detention coming up!
Look at her go!
Gasp!
I'm thinking track team.
Pant! Pant!
Madison C.?
Here.
Please turn in your homework.

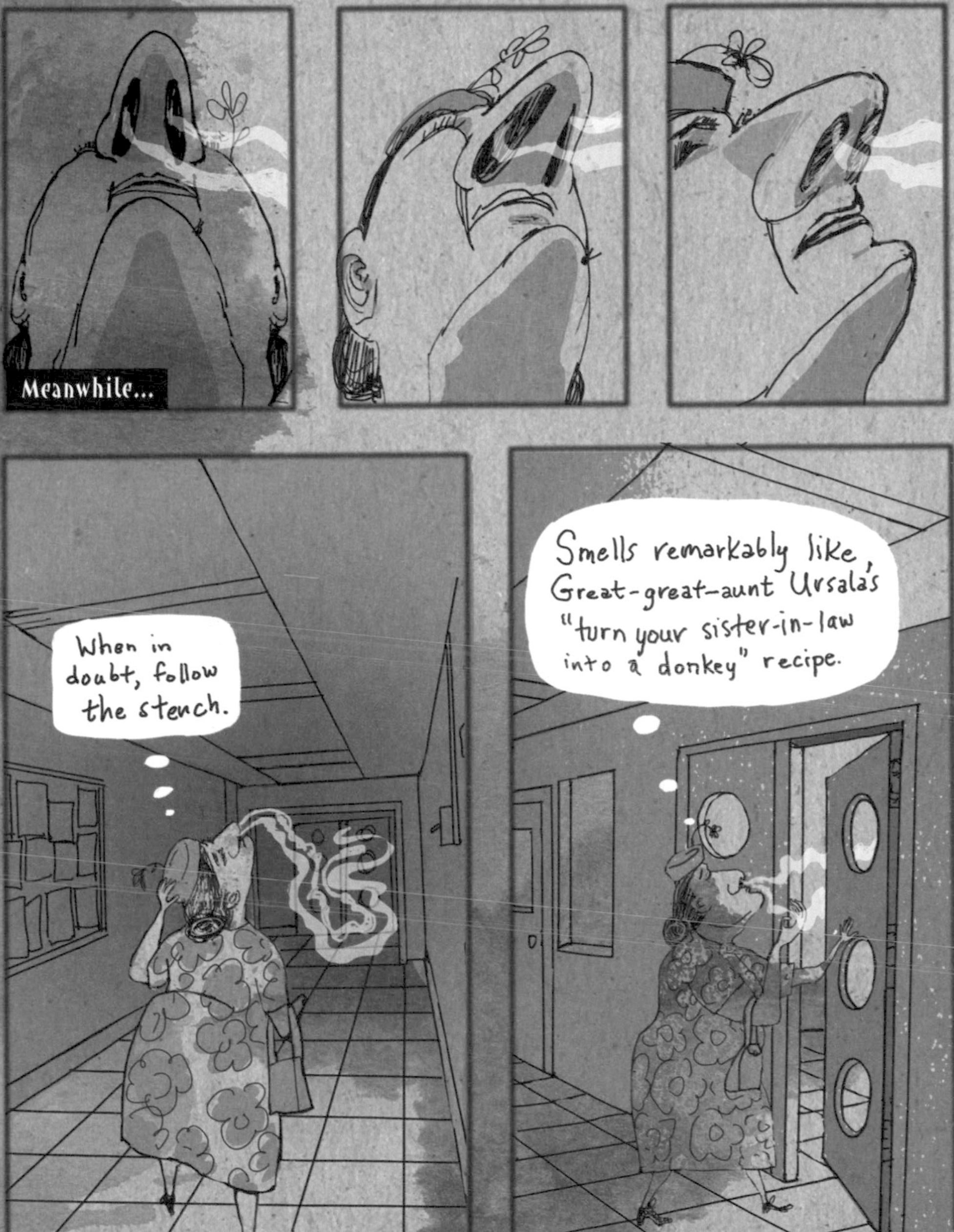
Meanwhile...
When in doubt, follow the stench.
Smells remarkably like, Great-great-aunt Ursala's "turn your sister-in-law into a donkey" recipe.

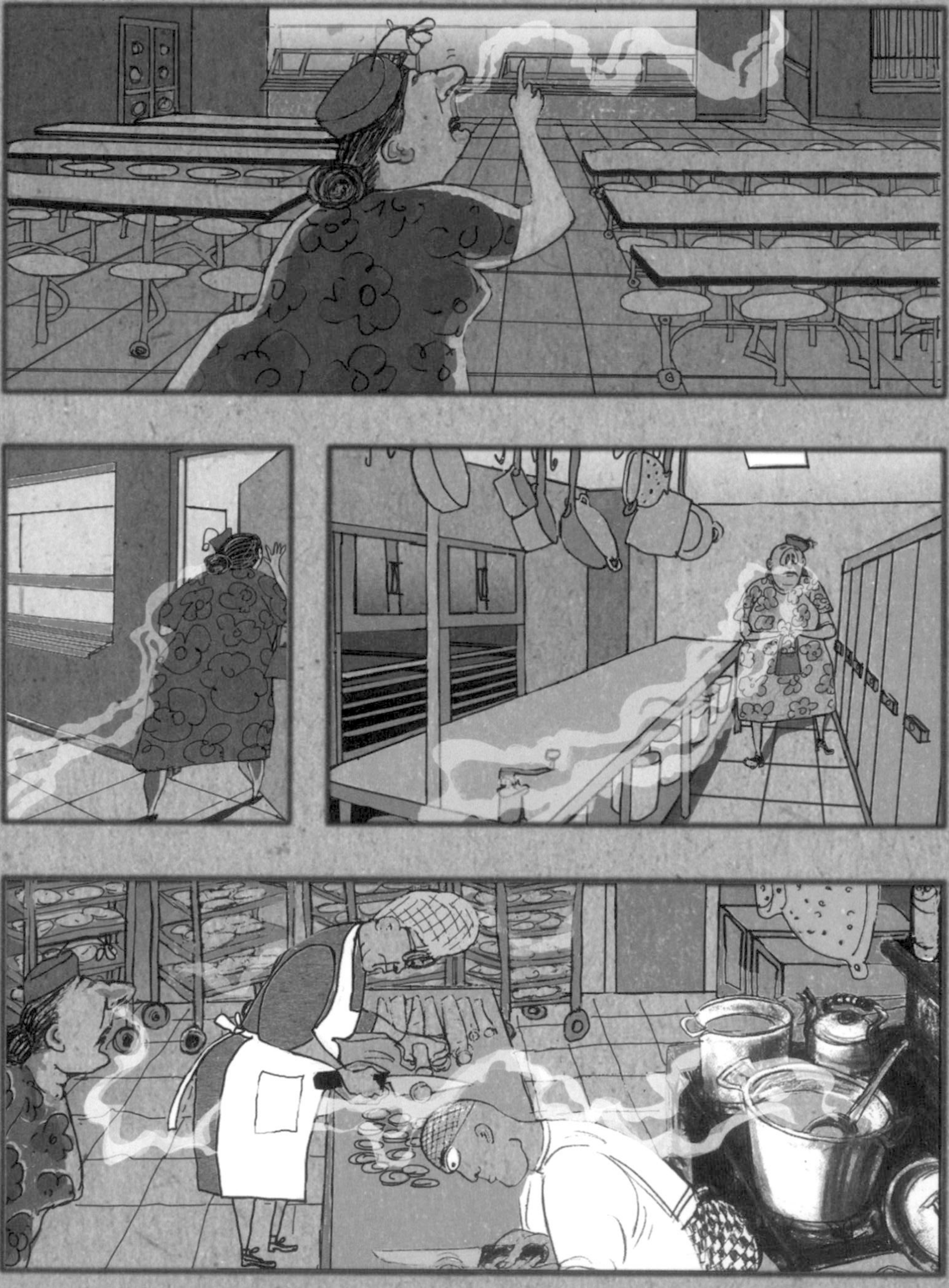

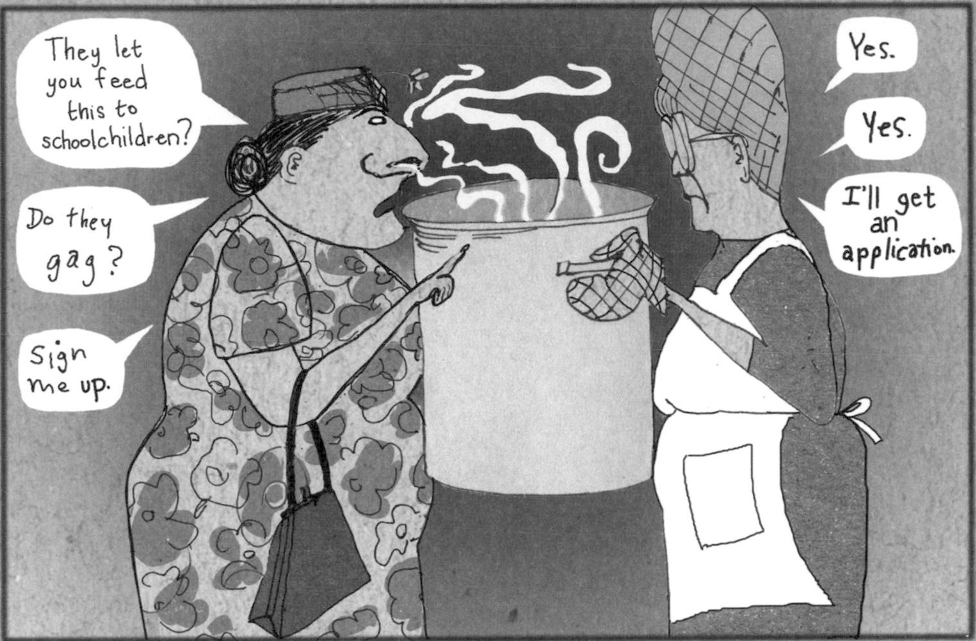
They let you feed this to schoolchildren?
Do they gag?
Sign me up.
Yes.
Yes.
I'll get an application.

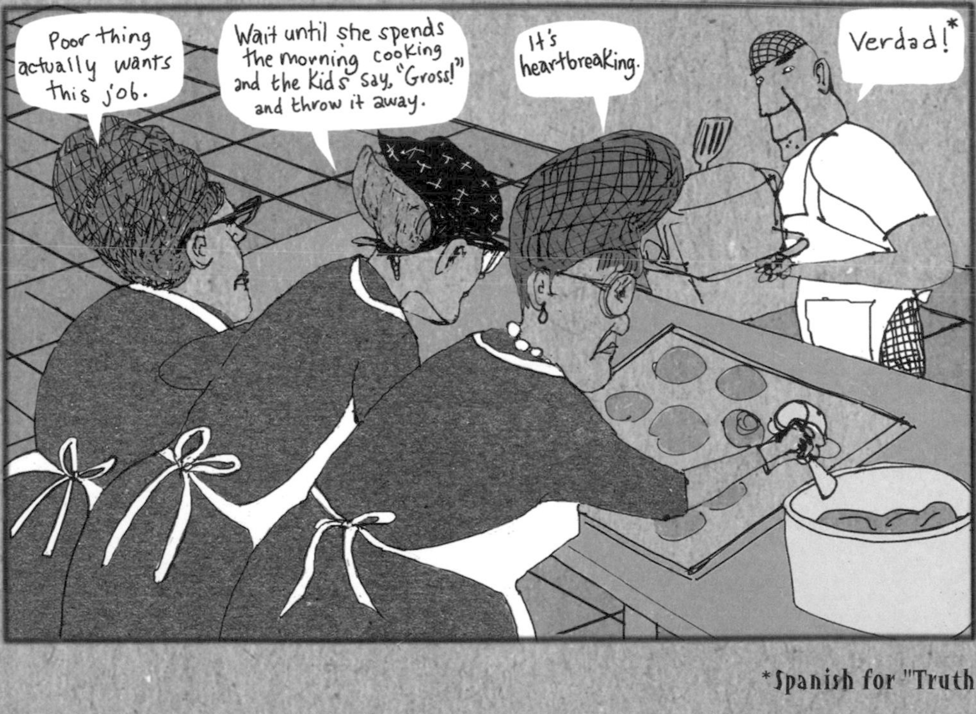
Poor thing actually wants this job.
Wait until she spends the morning cooking and the kids say, "Gross!" and throw it away.
It's heartbreaking.
Verdad!*

*Spanish for "Truth"

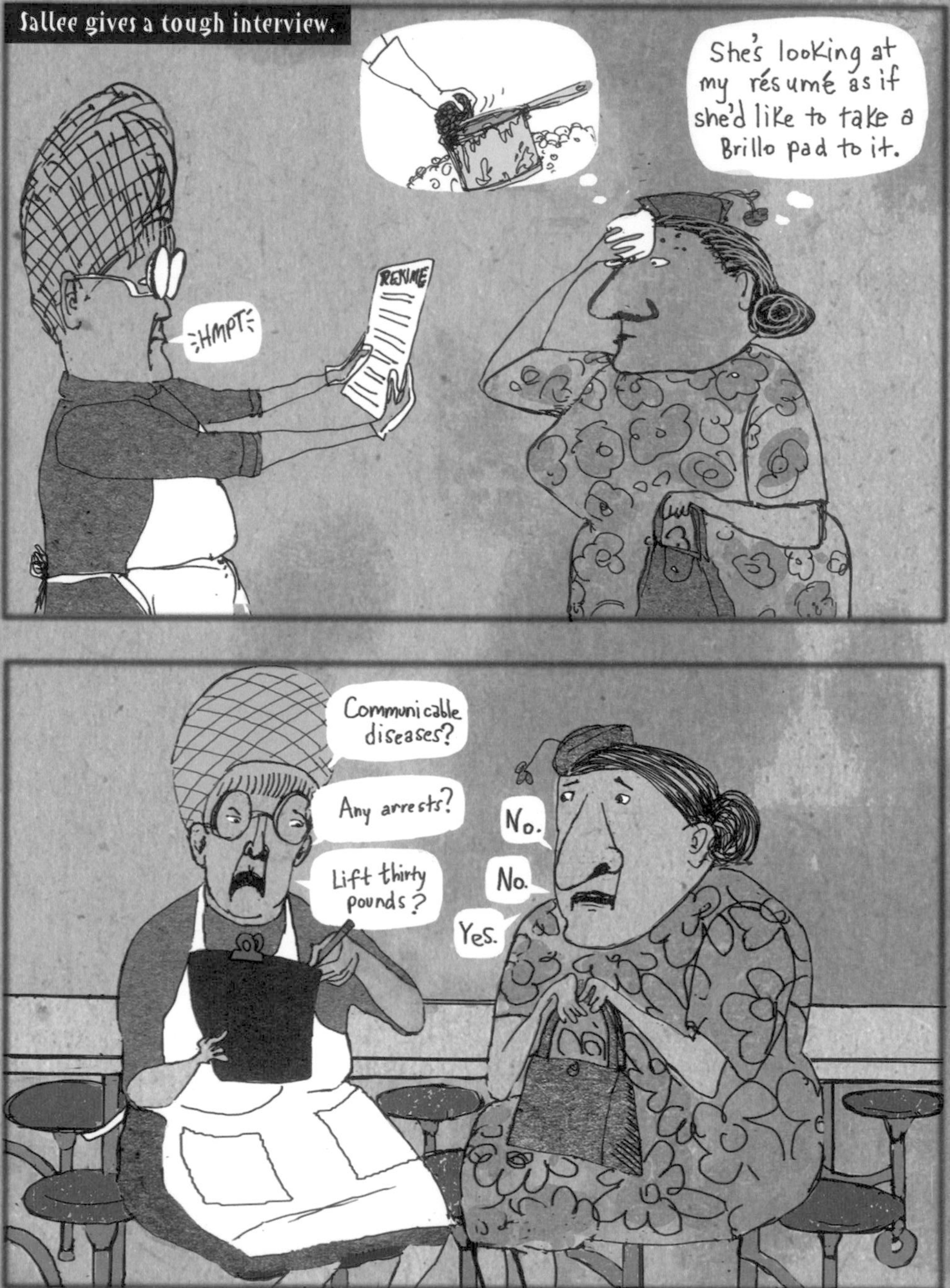
Sallee gives a tough interview.
RESUME
HMPT
She's looking at my résumé as if she'd like to take a Brillo pad to it.
Communicable diseases?
No.
Any arrests?
No.
Lift thirty pounds?
Yes.

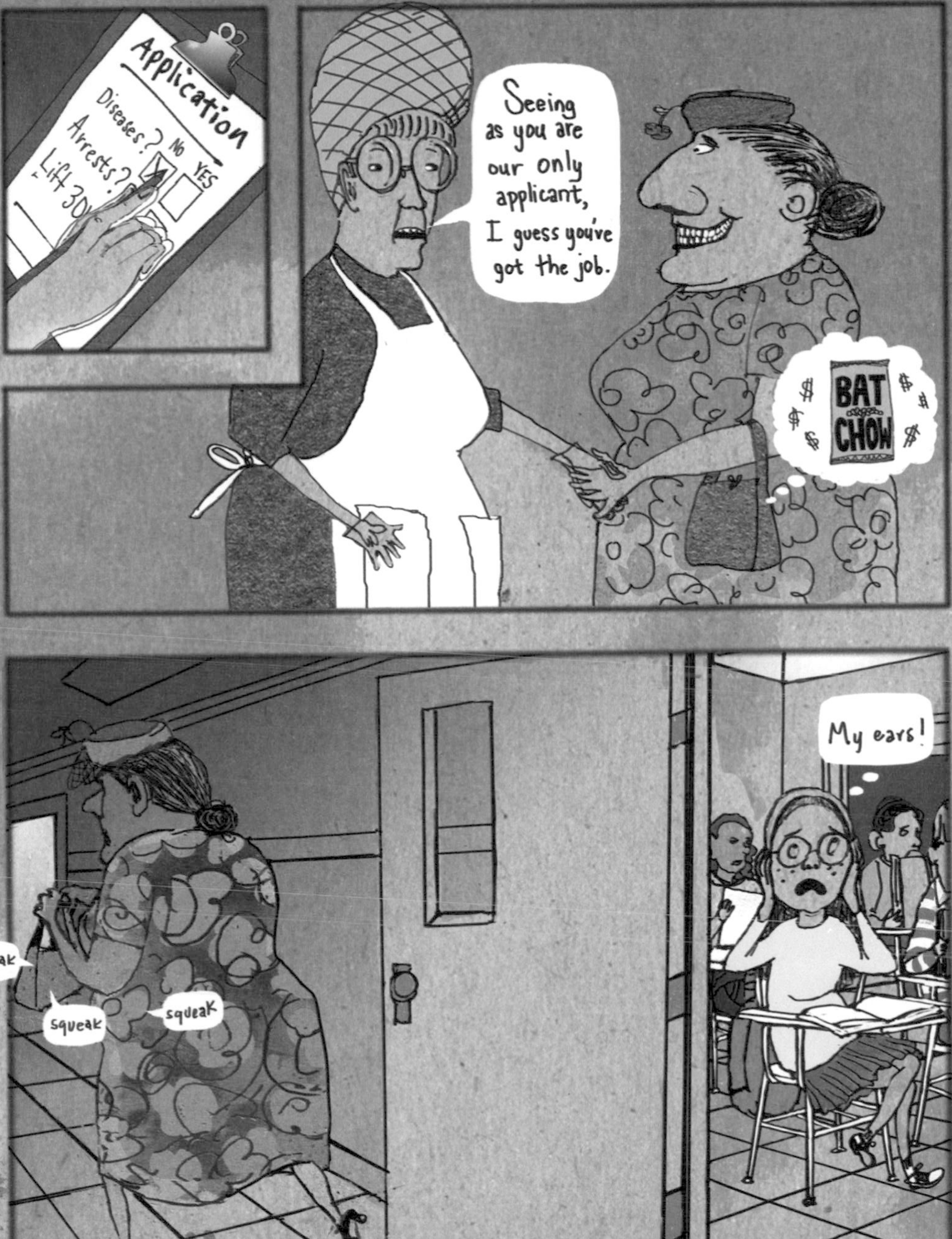
Application
Diseases?
Arrests?
Lift 30
NO
YES
Seeing as you are our only applicant, I guess you've got the job.
BAT CHOW
squeak
squeak
squeak
My ears!

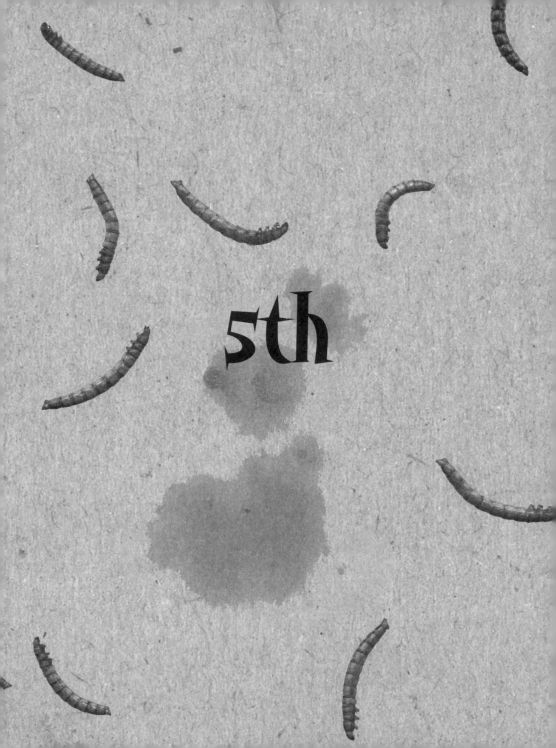

5th

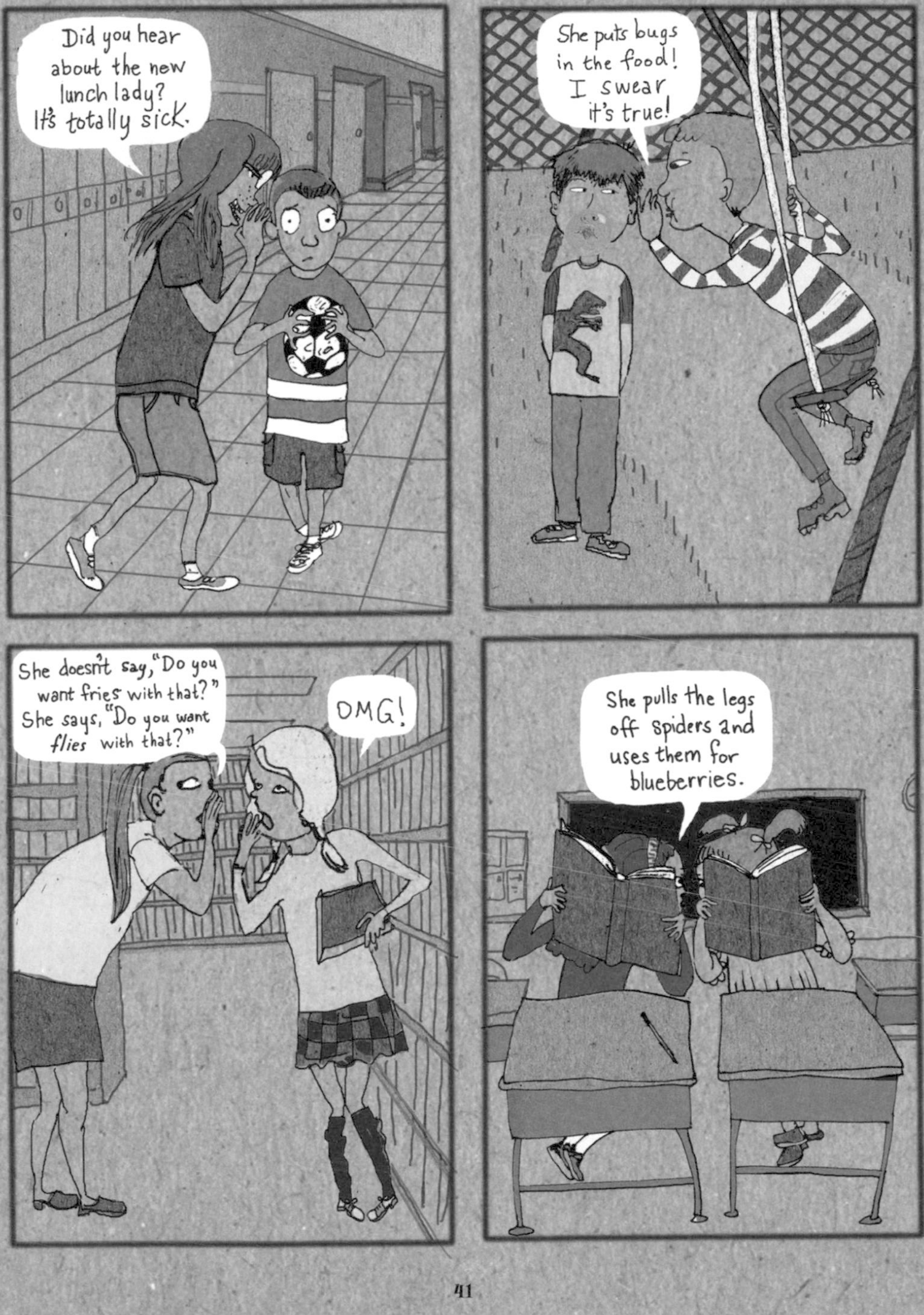
Did you hear about the new lunch lady? It's totally sick.
She puts bugs in the food! I swear it's true!
She doesn't say, "Do you want fries with that?" She says, "Do you want *flies* with that?"
OMG!
She pulls the legs off spiders and uses them for blueberries.

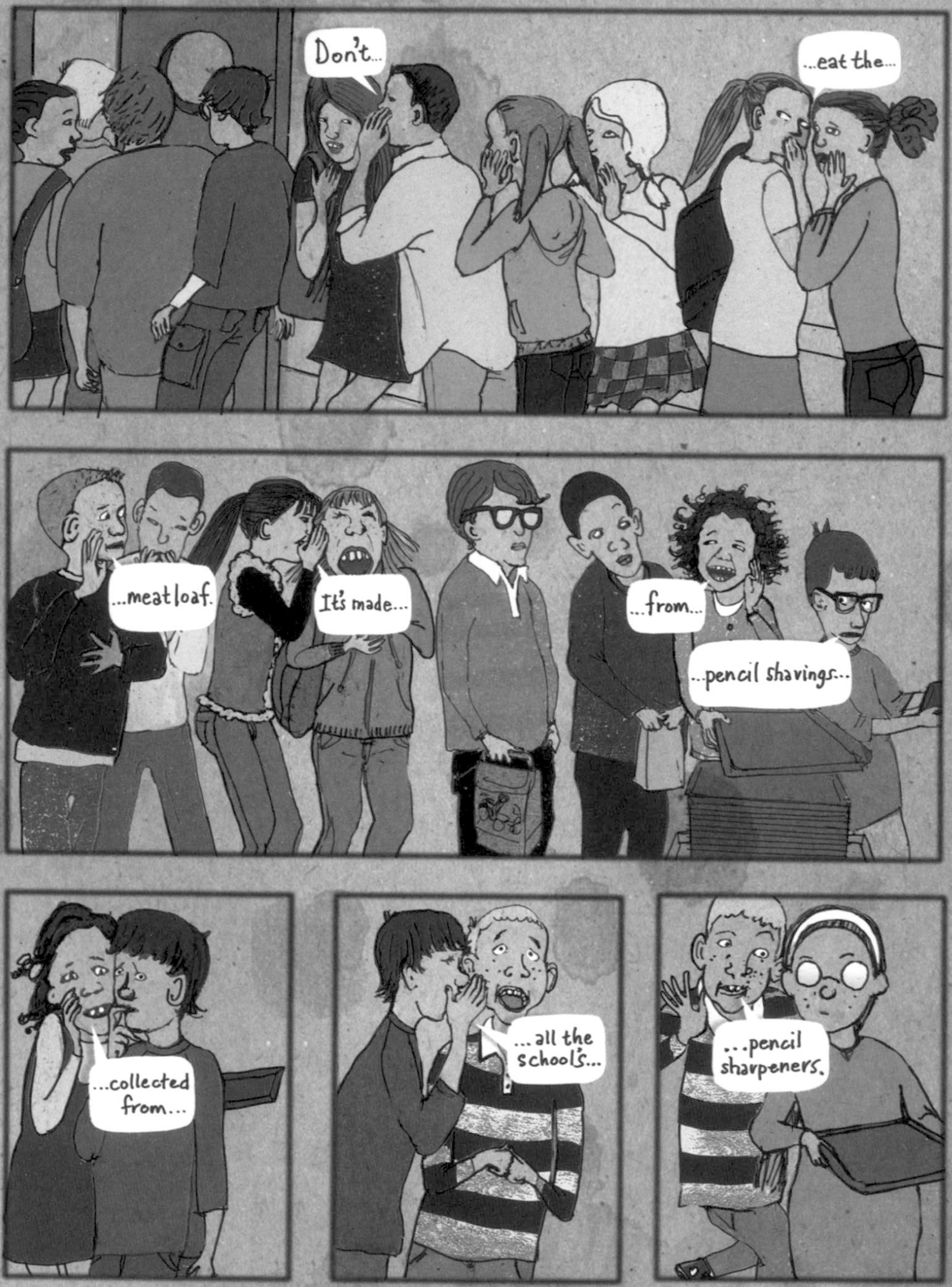
Don't...
...eat the...
...meatloaf.
It's made...
...from...
...pencil shavings...
...collected from...
...all the school's...
...pencil sharpeners.

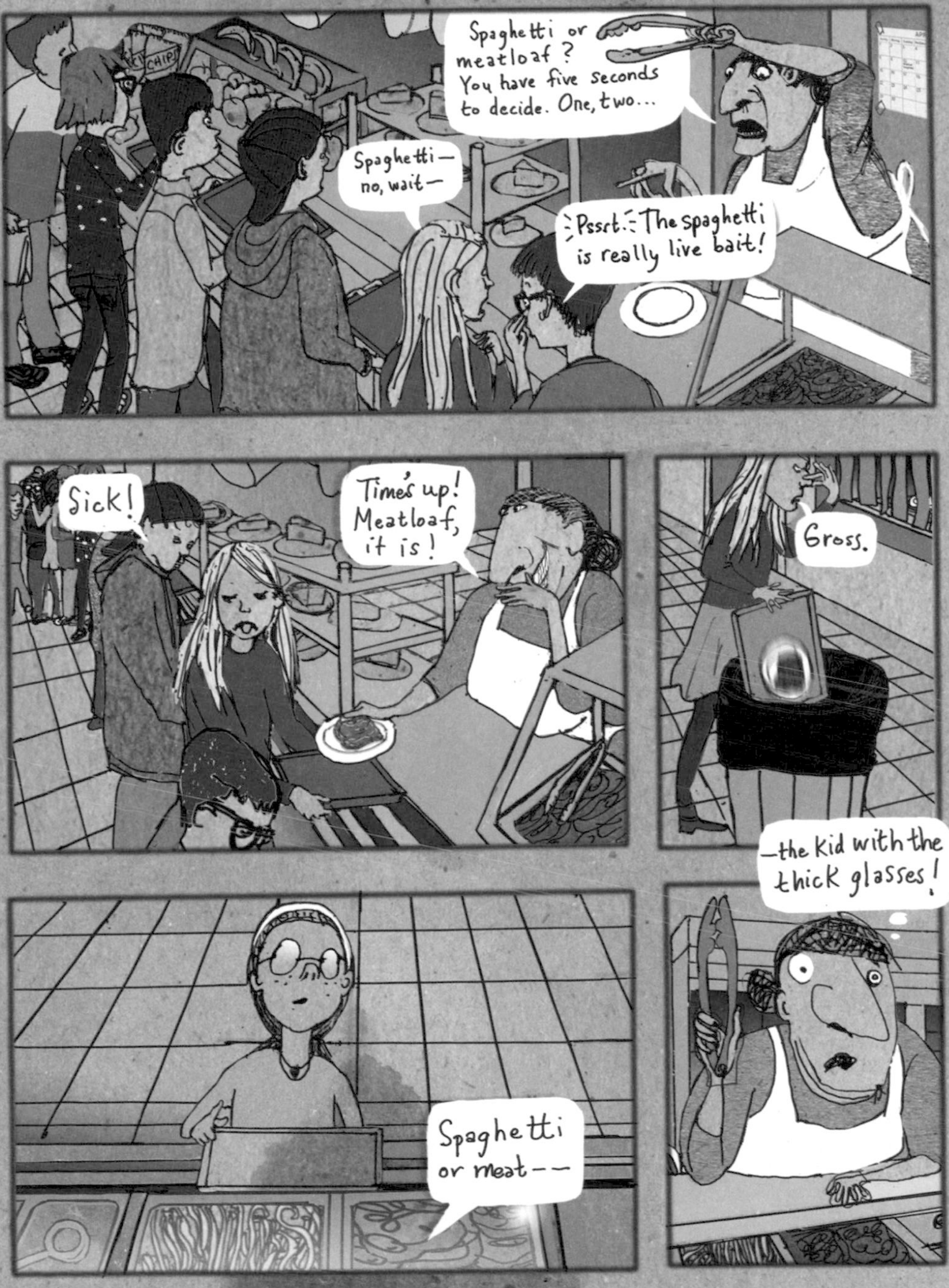
CHIPS
Spaghetti or meatloaf? You have five seconds to decide. One, two...
Spaghetti— no, wait—
Pssrt. The spaghetti is really live bait!
Sick!
Time's up! Meatloaf, it is!
Gross.
—the kid with the thick glasses!
Spaghetti or meat——

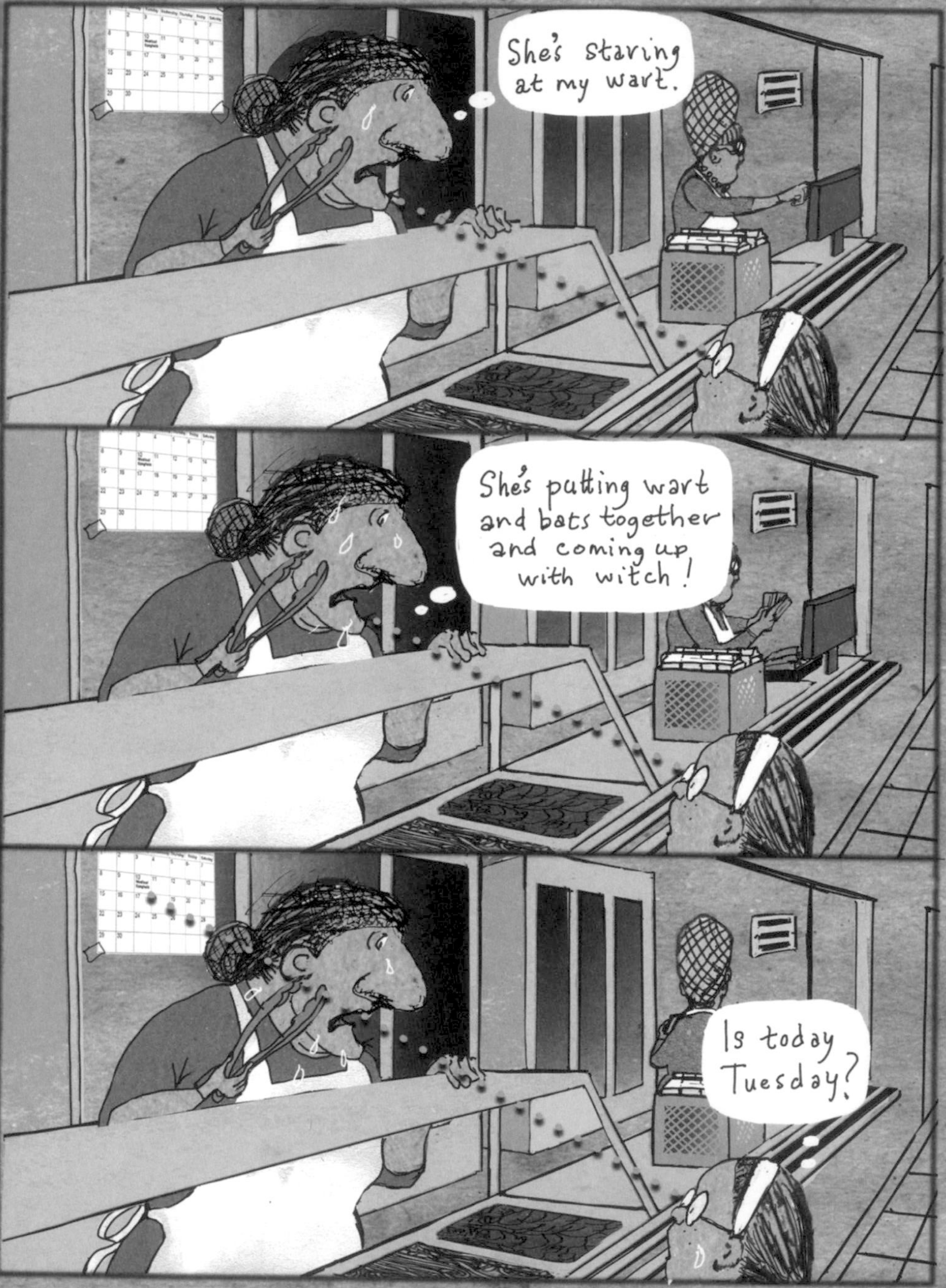
She's staring at my wart.
She's putting wart and bats together and coming up with witch!
Is today Tuesday?

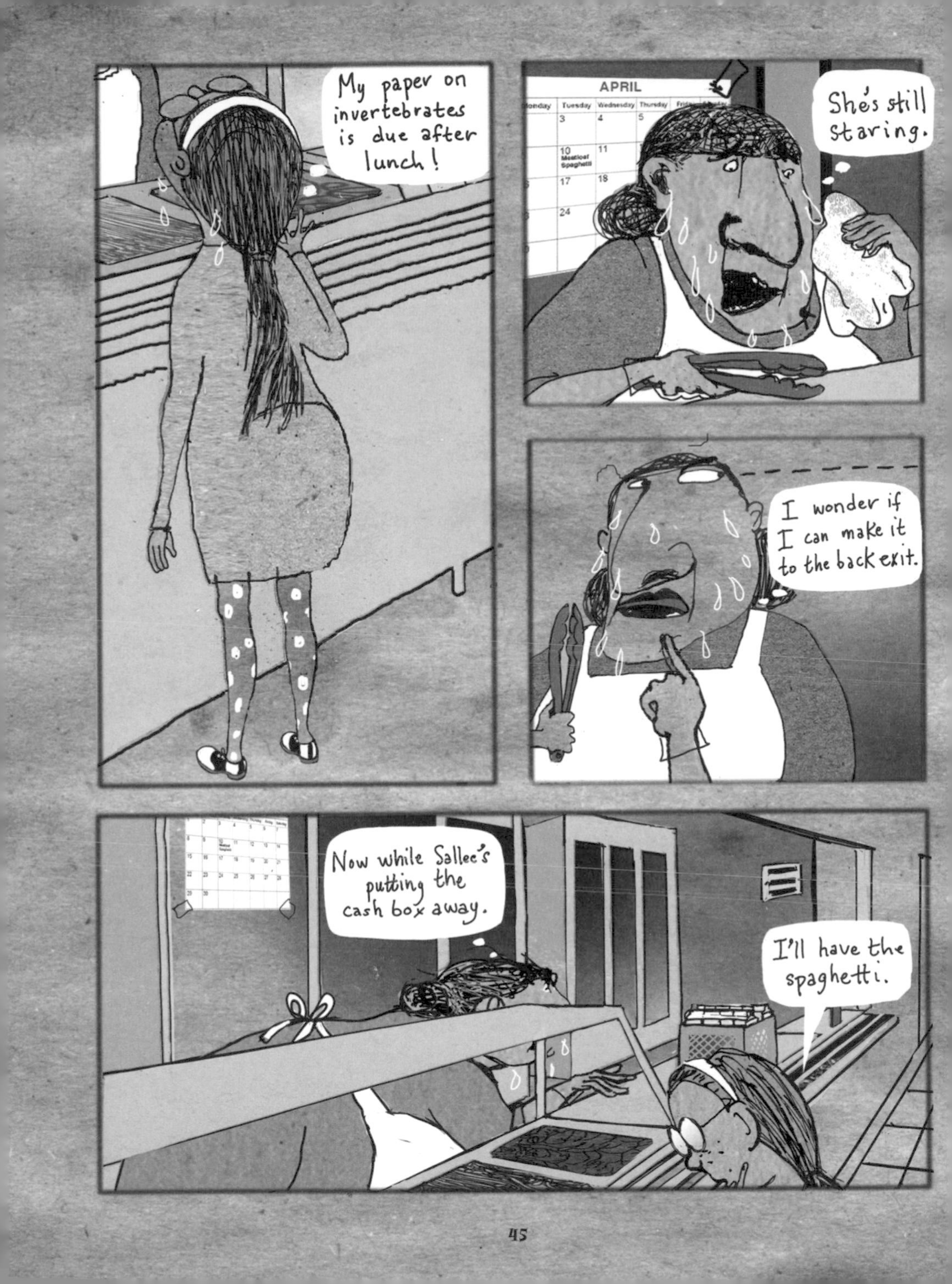

My paper on invertebrates is due after lunch!
APRIL
She's still staring.
I wonder if I can make it to the back exit.
Now while Sallee's putting the cash box away.
I'll have the spaghetti.

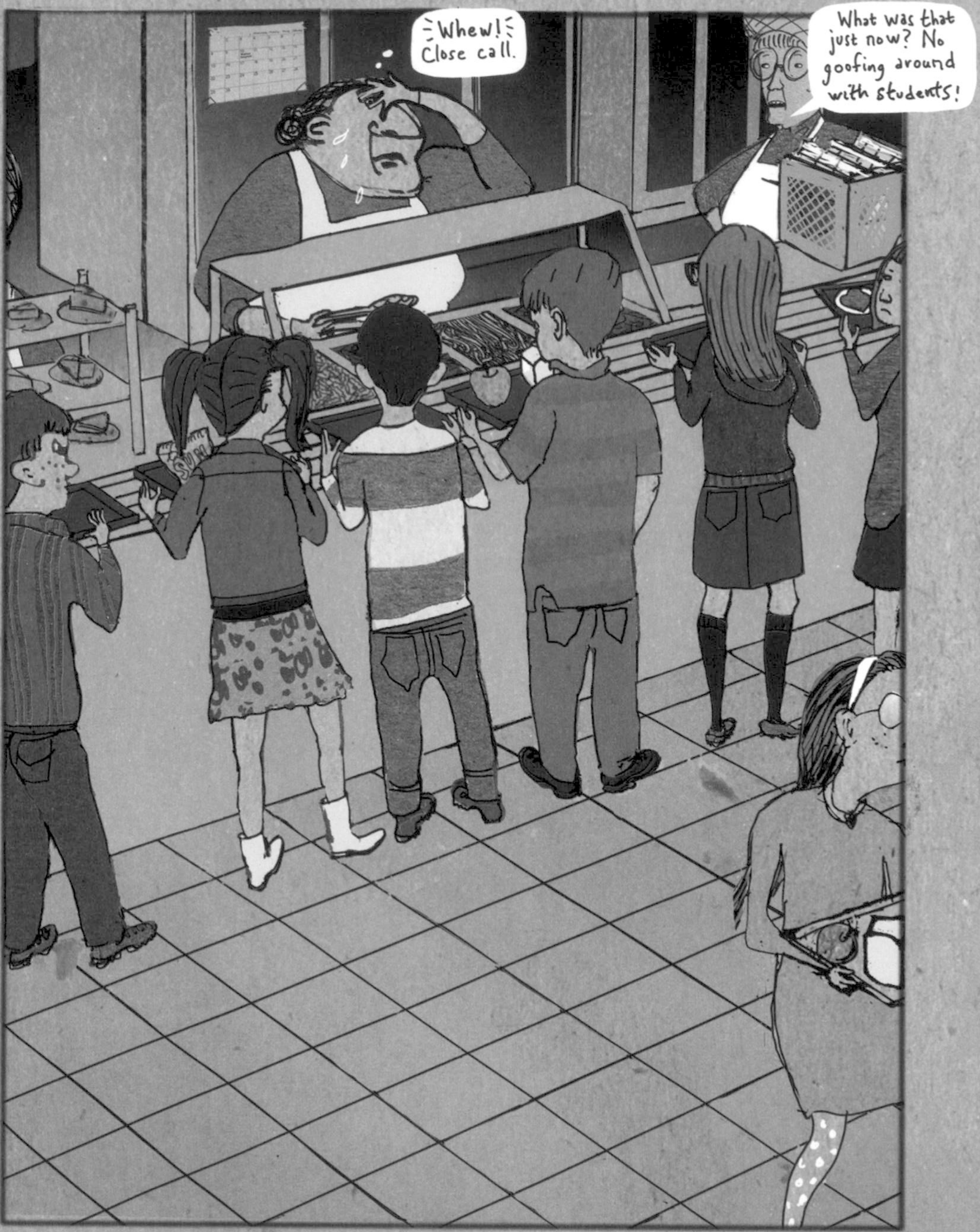
Whew! Close call.
What was that just now? No goofing around with students!

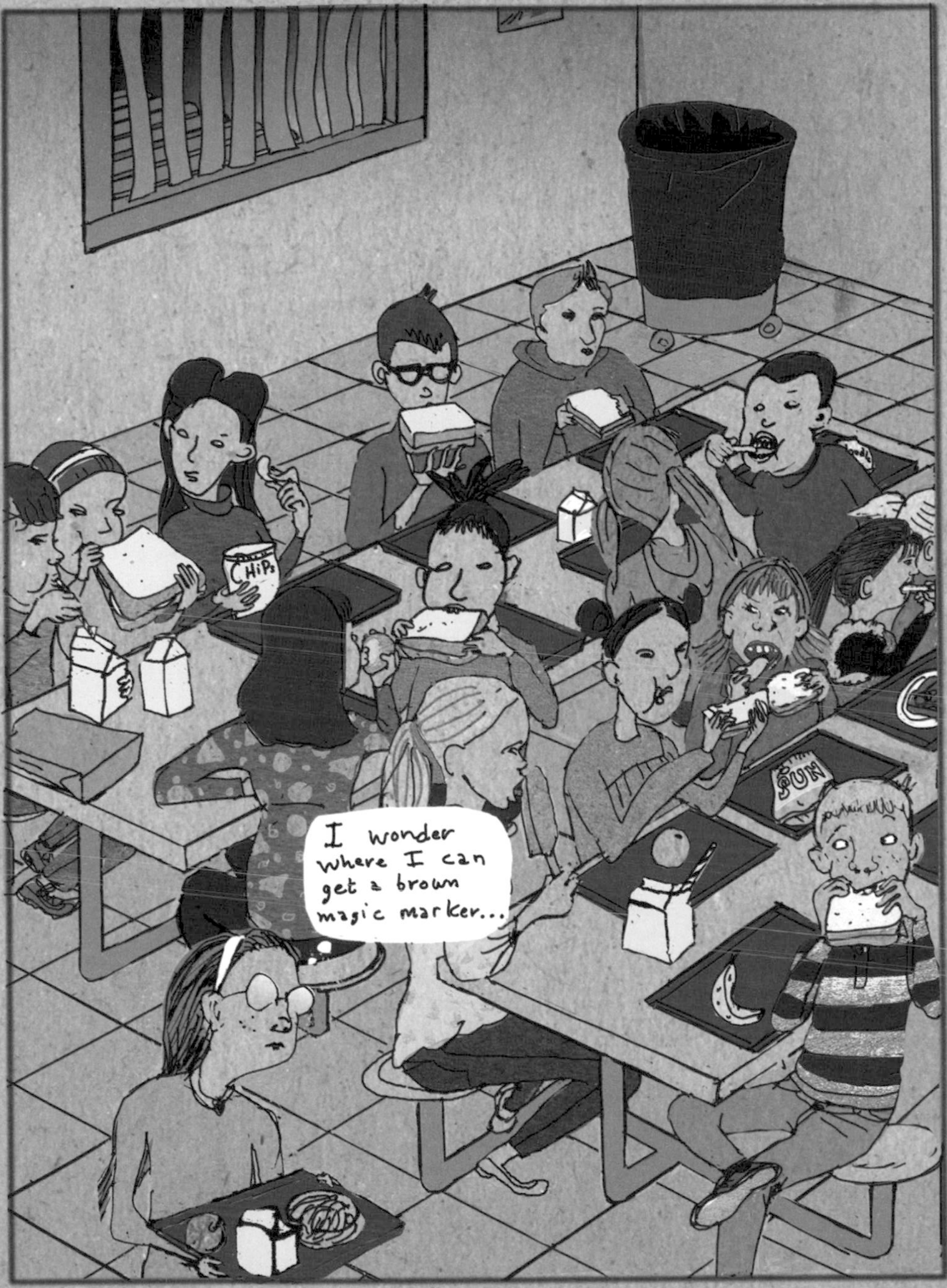
I wonder where I can get a brown magic marker...
CHIPS
SUN

6th

The earthworm is NOT a small snake!
The Earthworm
by Madison C.
The earthworm is a very small snake. It lives in the ground.
Tail ← Head
Tail
The earth worm

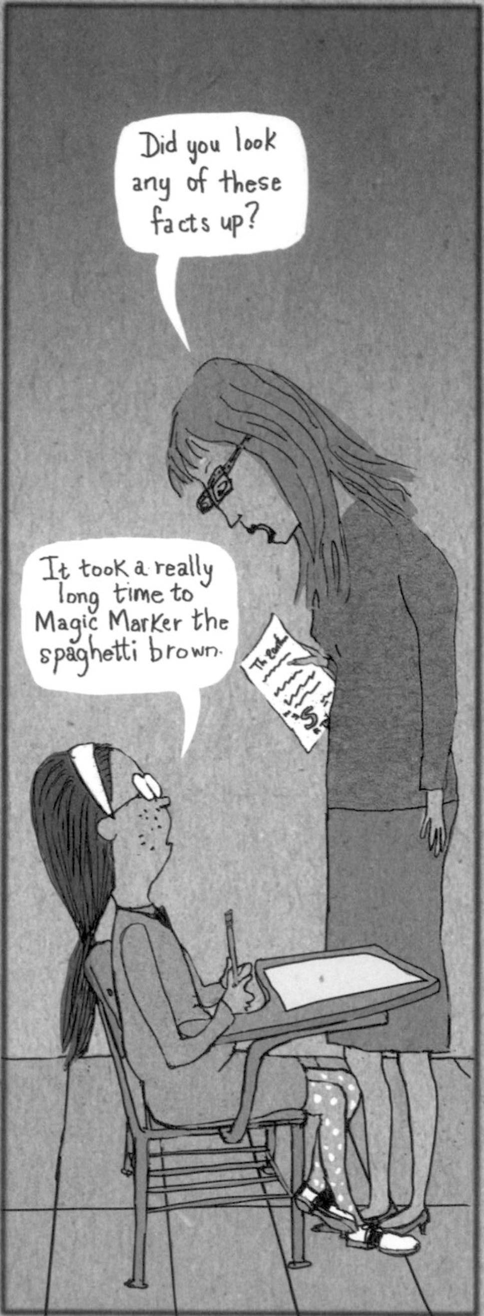
Did you look any of these facts up?
It took a really long time to Magic Marker the spaghetti brown.

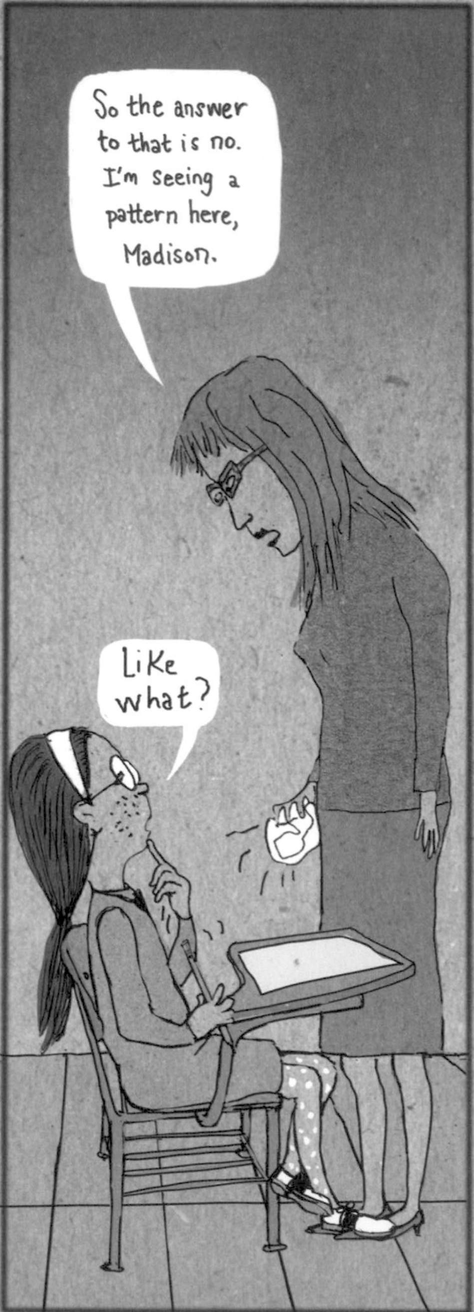
So the answer to that is no. I'm seeing a pattern here, Madison.
Like what?

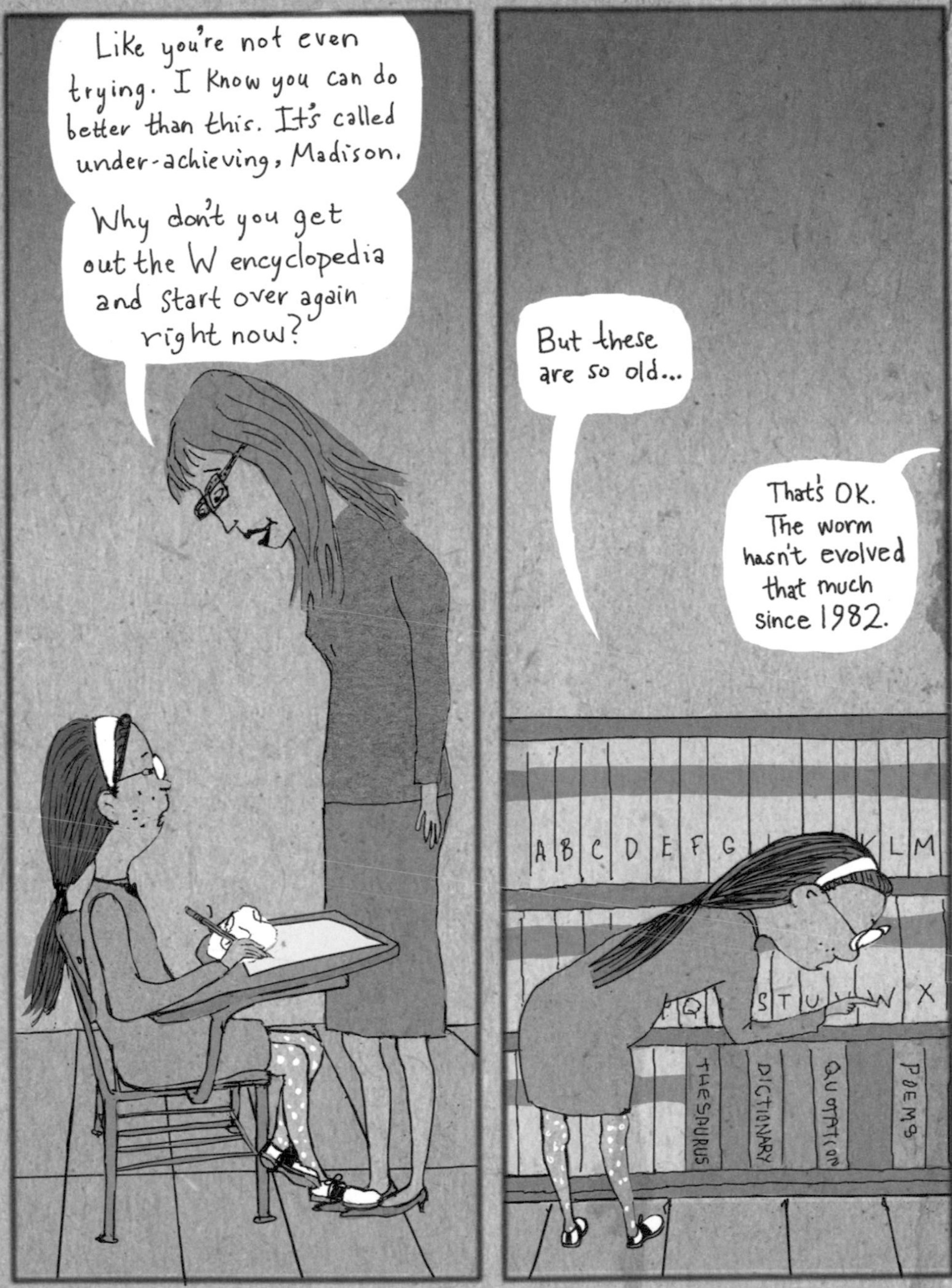
Like you're not even trying. I know you can do better than this. It's called under-achieving, Madison.
Why don't you get out the W encyclopedia and start over again right now?
But these are so old...
That's OK. The worm hasn't evolved that much since 1982.
A B C D E F G
K L M
Q
S T U
W X
THESAURUS
DICTIONARY
QUOTATIONS
POEMS

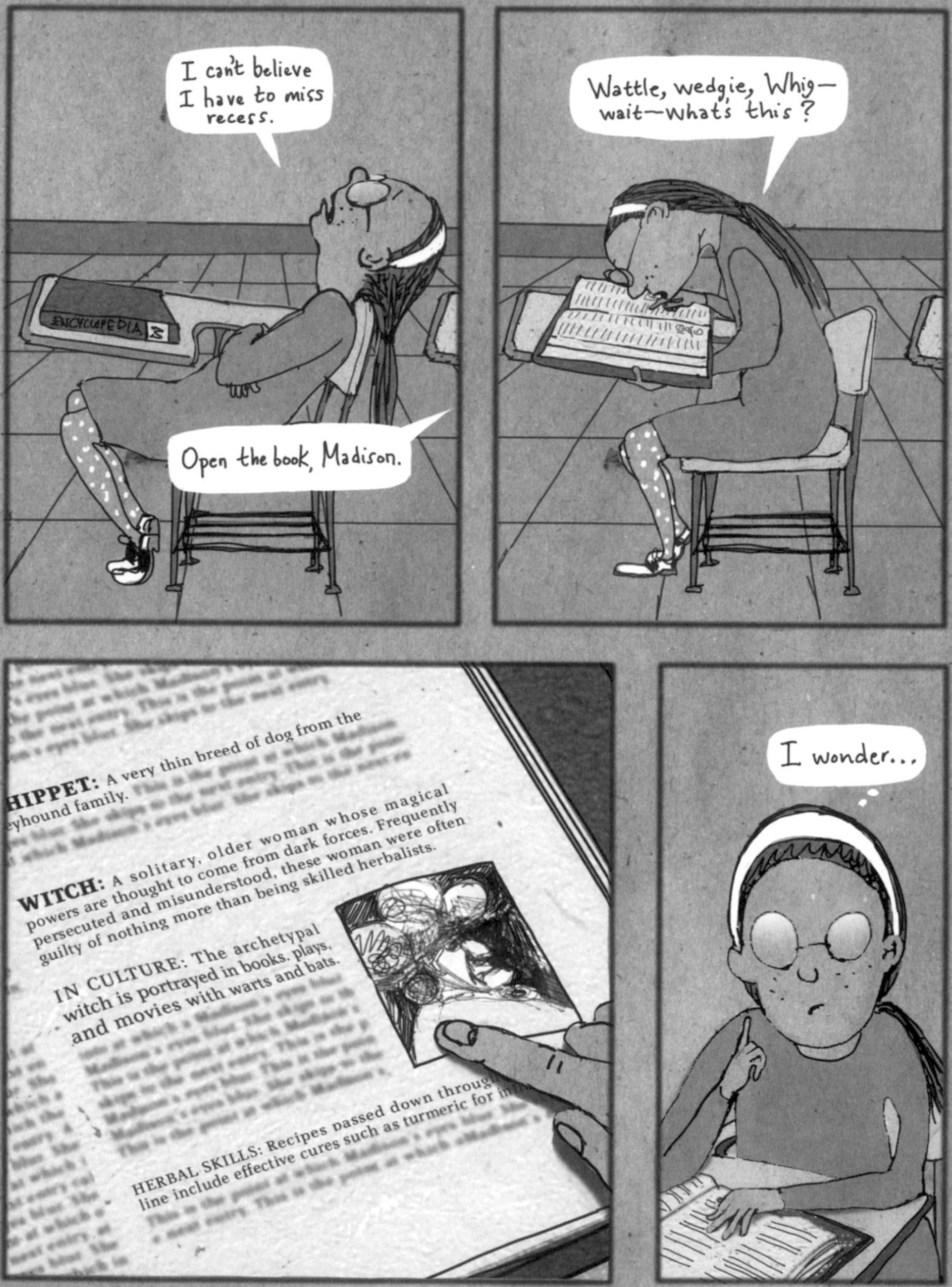
I can't believe I have to miss recess.
Open the book, Madison.
Wattle, wedgie, Whig— wait—what's this?
ENCYCLOPEDIA W
HIPPET: A very thin breed of dog from the
eyhound family.
WITCH: A solitary, older woman whose magical powers are thought to come from dark forces. Frequently persecuted and misunderstood, these woman were often guilty of nothing more than being skilled herbalists.
IN CULTURE: The archetypal witch is portrayed in books, plays, and movies with warts and bats.
HERBAL SKILLS: Recipes passed down throug
line include effective cures such as turmeric for in
I wonder...

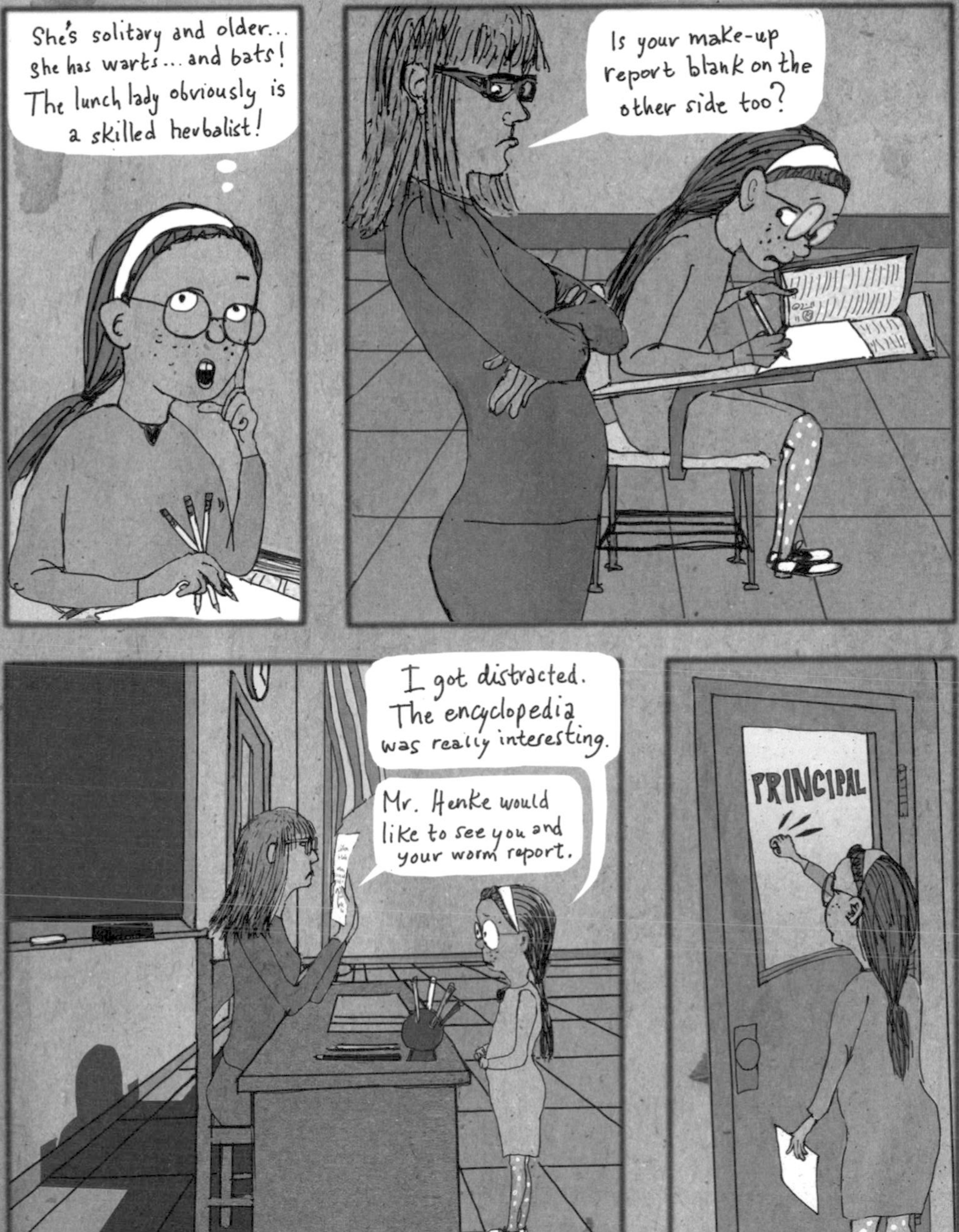
She's solitary and older... she has warts... and bats! The lunch lady obviously is a skilled herbalist!
Is your make-up report blank on the other side too?
I got distracted. The encyclopedia was really interesting.
Mr. Henke would like to see you and your worm report.
PRINCIPAL

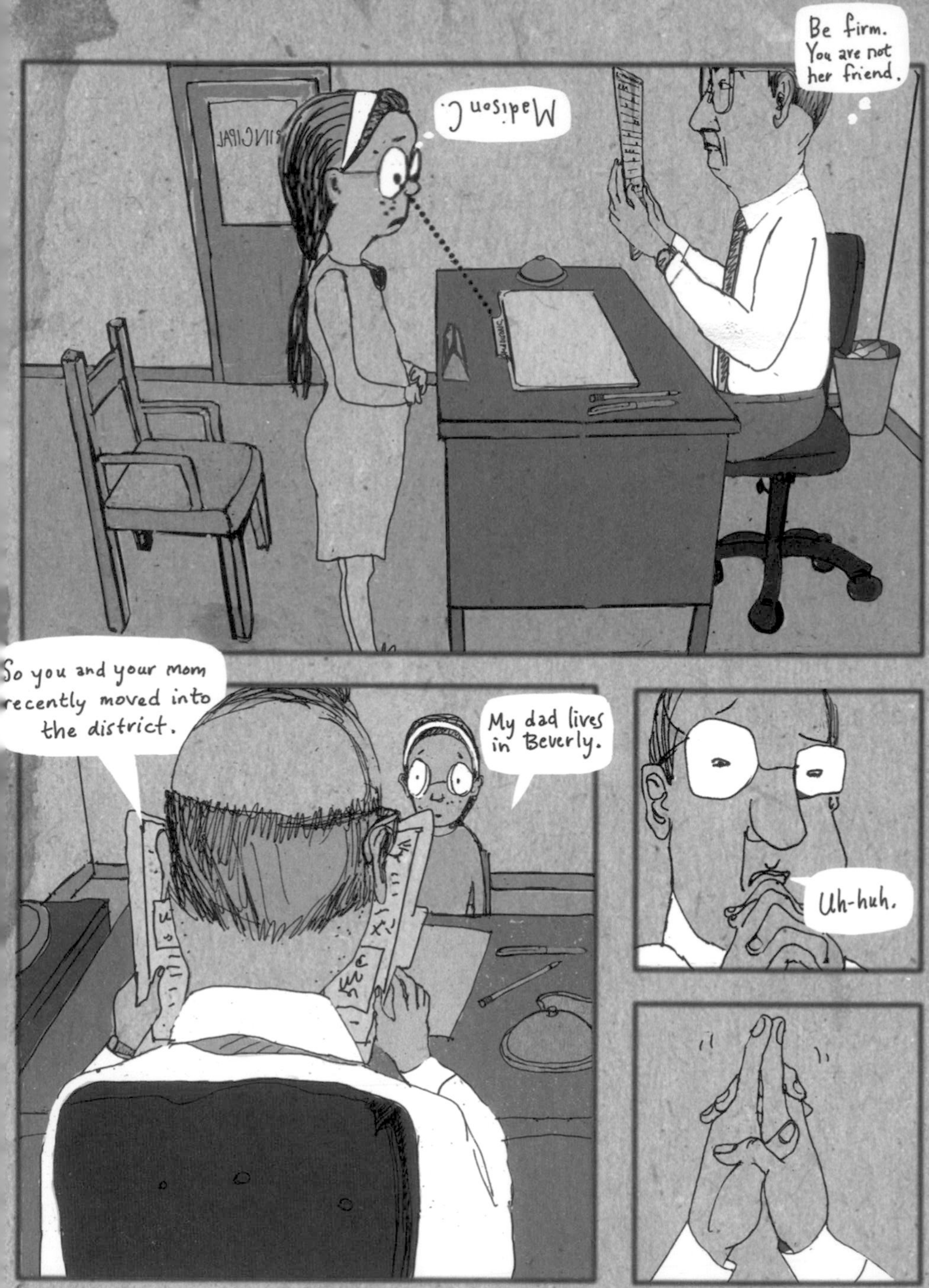

Madison C.
Be firm. You are not her friend.
So you and your mom recently moved into the district.
My dad lives in Beverly.
Uh-huh.

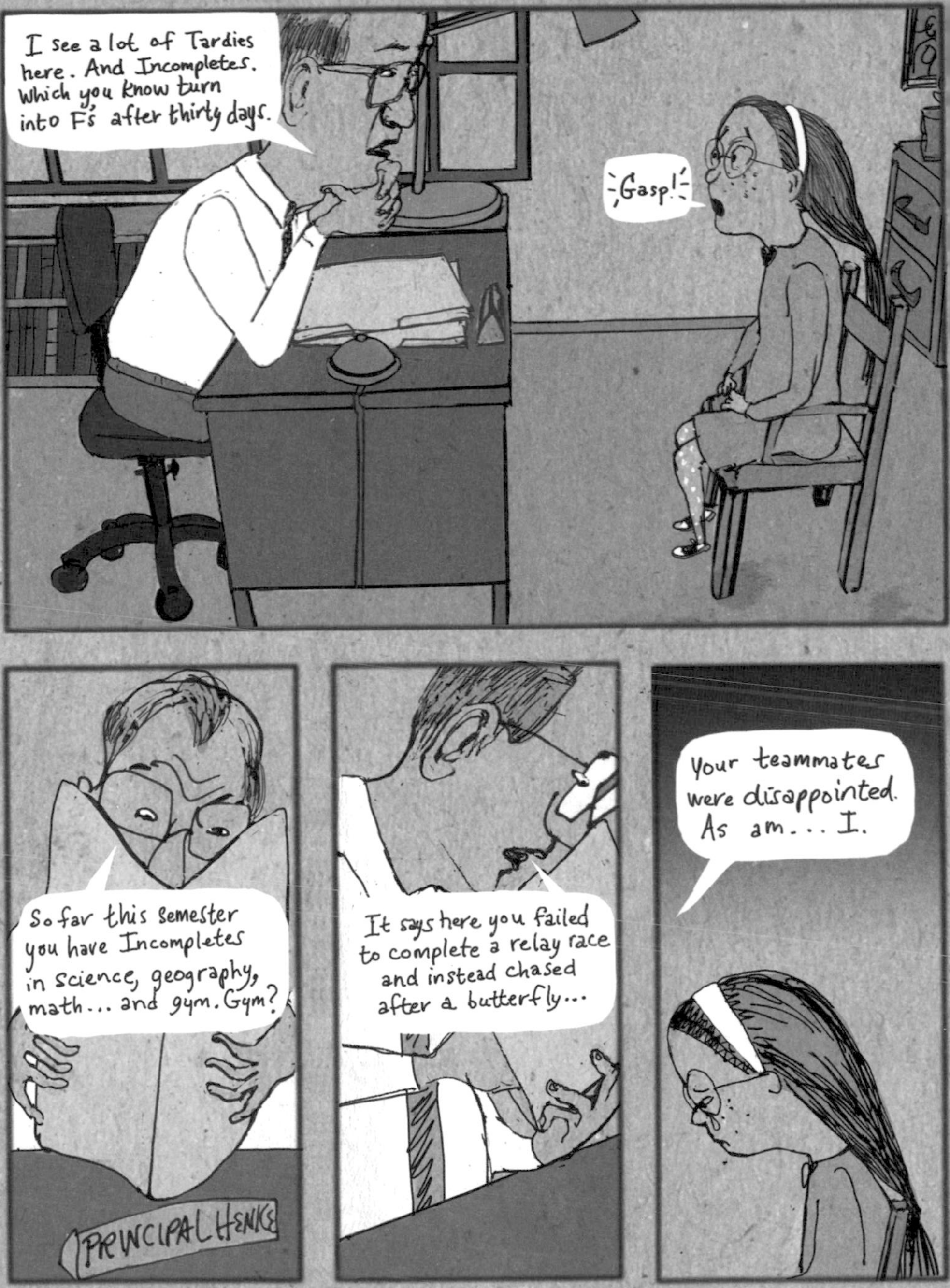
I see a lot of Tardies here. And Incompletes. Which you know turn into F's after thirty days.
Gasp!
So far this semester you have Incompletes in science, geography, math... and gym. Gym?
PRINCIPAL HENKE
It says here you failed to complete a relay race and instead chased after a butterfly...
Your teammates were disappointed. As am... I.

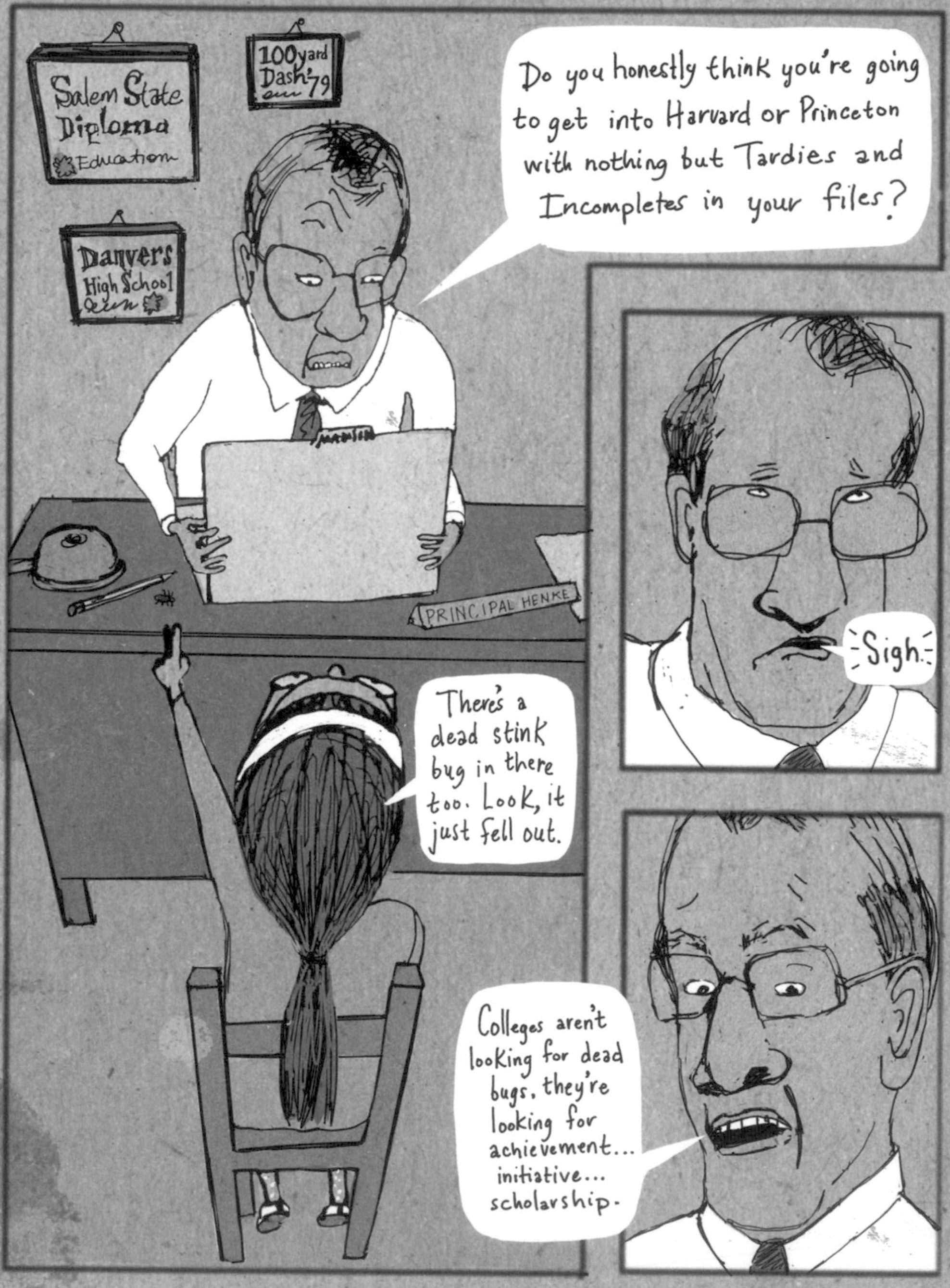
Salem State Diploma Education
100 yard Dash '79
Danvers High School
Do you honestly think you're going to get into Harvard or Princeton with nothing but Tardies and Incompletes in your files?
PRINCIPAL HENKE
There's a dead stink bug in there too. Look, it just fell out.
Sigh.
Colleges aren't looking for dead bugs, they're looking for achievement... initiative... scholarship.

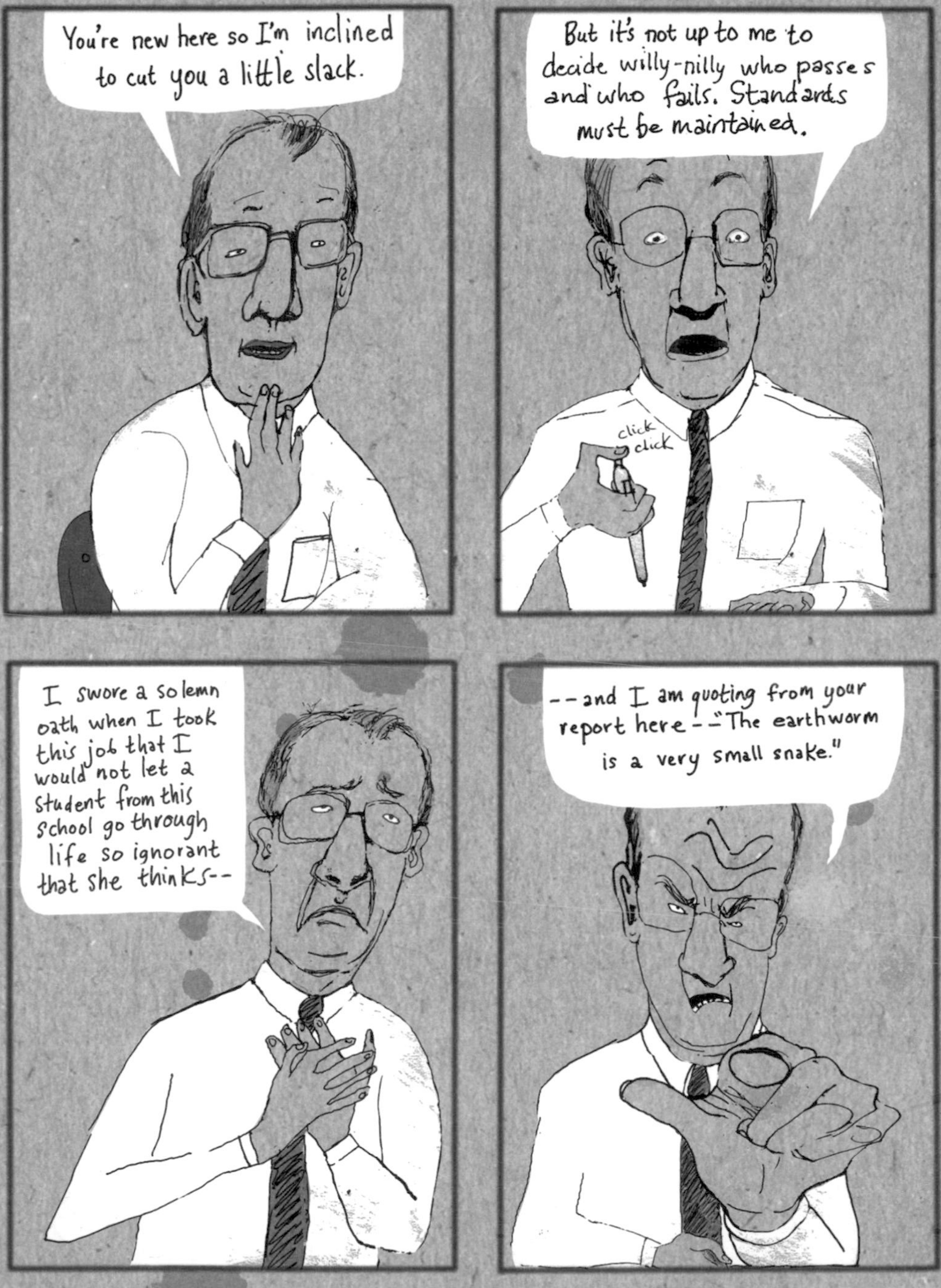
You're new here so I'm inclined to cut you a little slack.
But it's not up to me to decide willy-nilly who passes and who fails. Standards must be maintained.
click click
I swore a solemn oath when I took this job that I would not let a student from this school go through life so ignorant that she thinks--
--and I am quoting from your report here--"The earthworm is a very small snake."

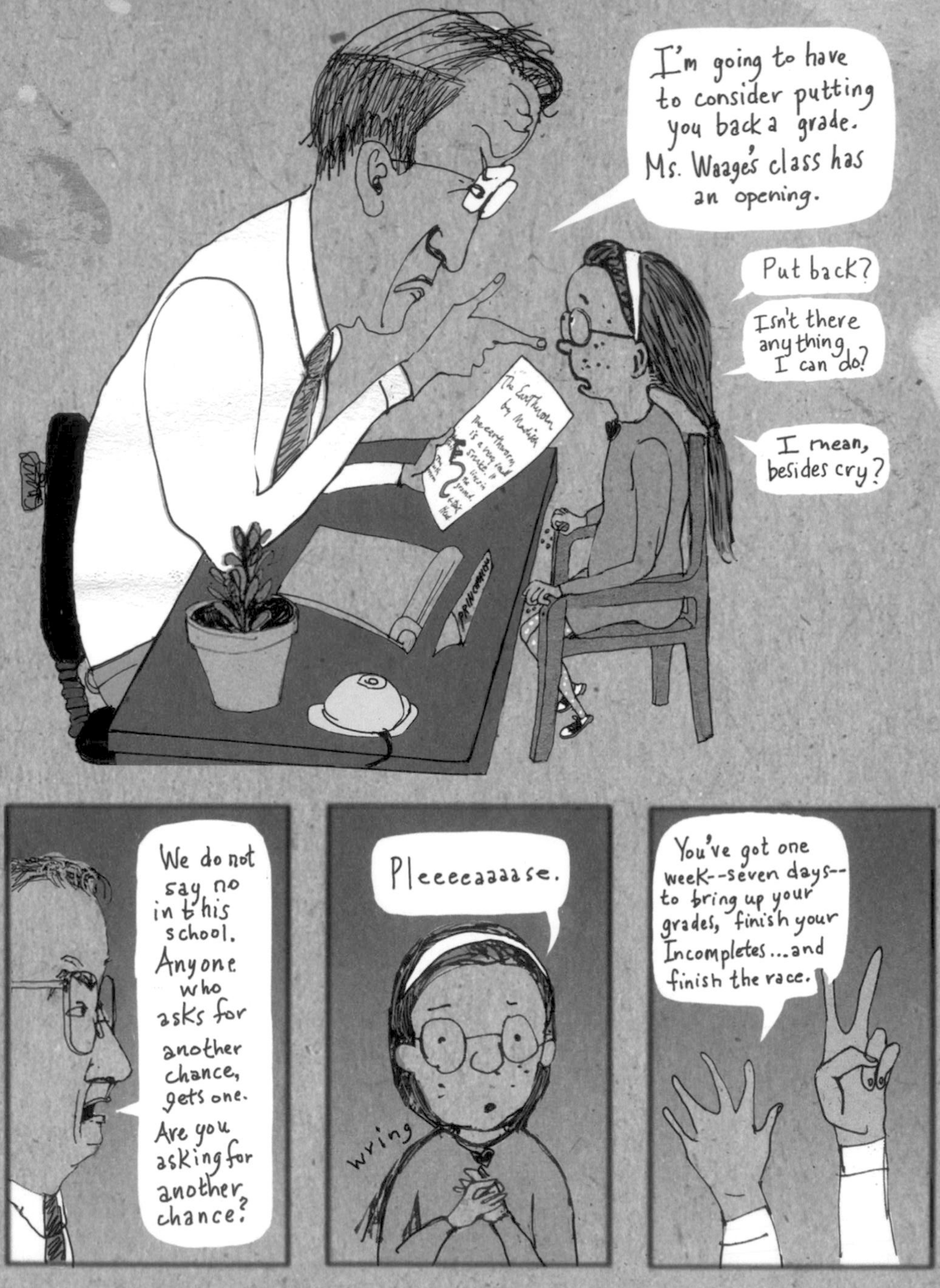
I'm going to have to consider putting you back a grade. Ms. Waage's class has an opening.
Put back?
Isn't there anything I can do?
I mean, besides cry?
We do not say no in this school. Anyone who asks for another chance, gets one. Are you asking for another chance?
Pleeeeaaaase.
wring
You've got one week--seven days--to bring up your grades, finish your Incompletes...and finish the race.

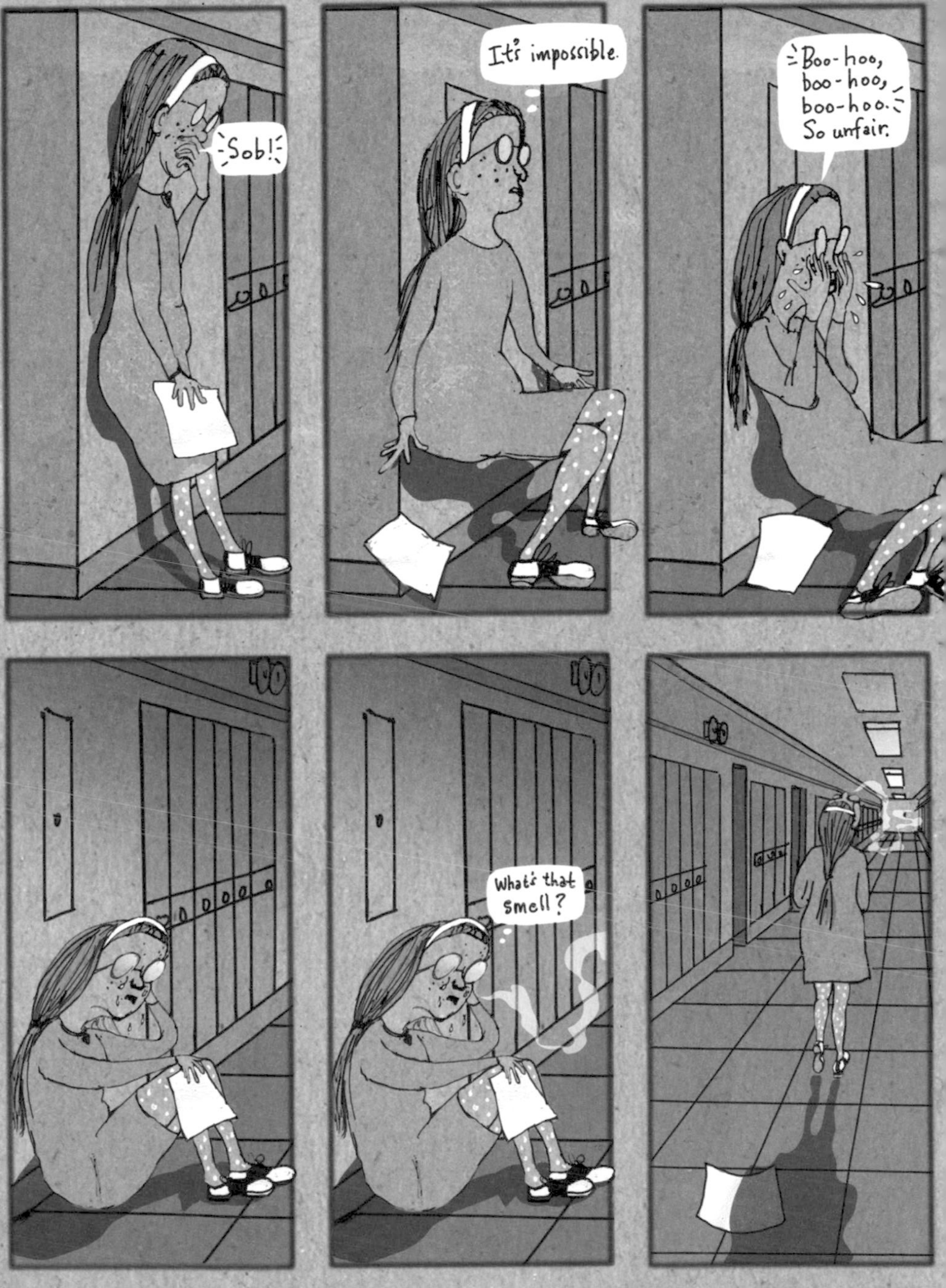
Sob!
It's impossible.
Boo-hoo, boo-hoo, boo-hoo. So unfair.
What's that smell?

7th

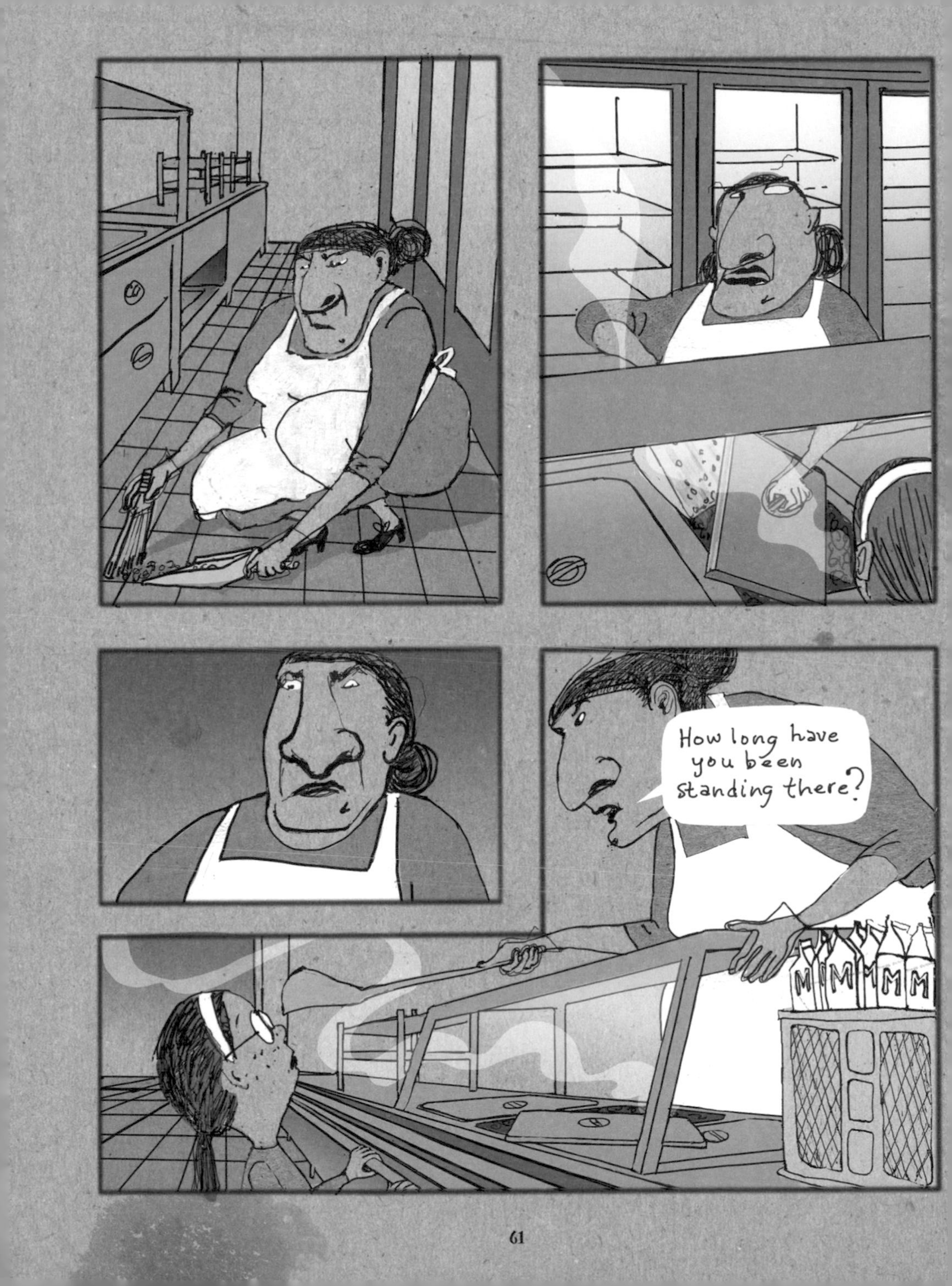
How long have you been standing there?

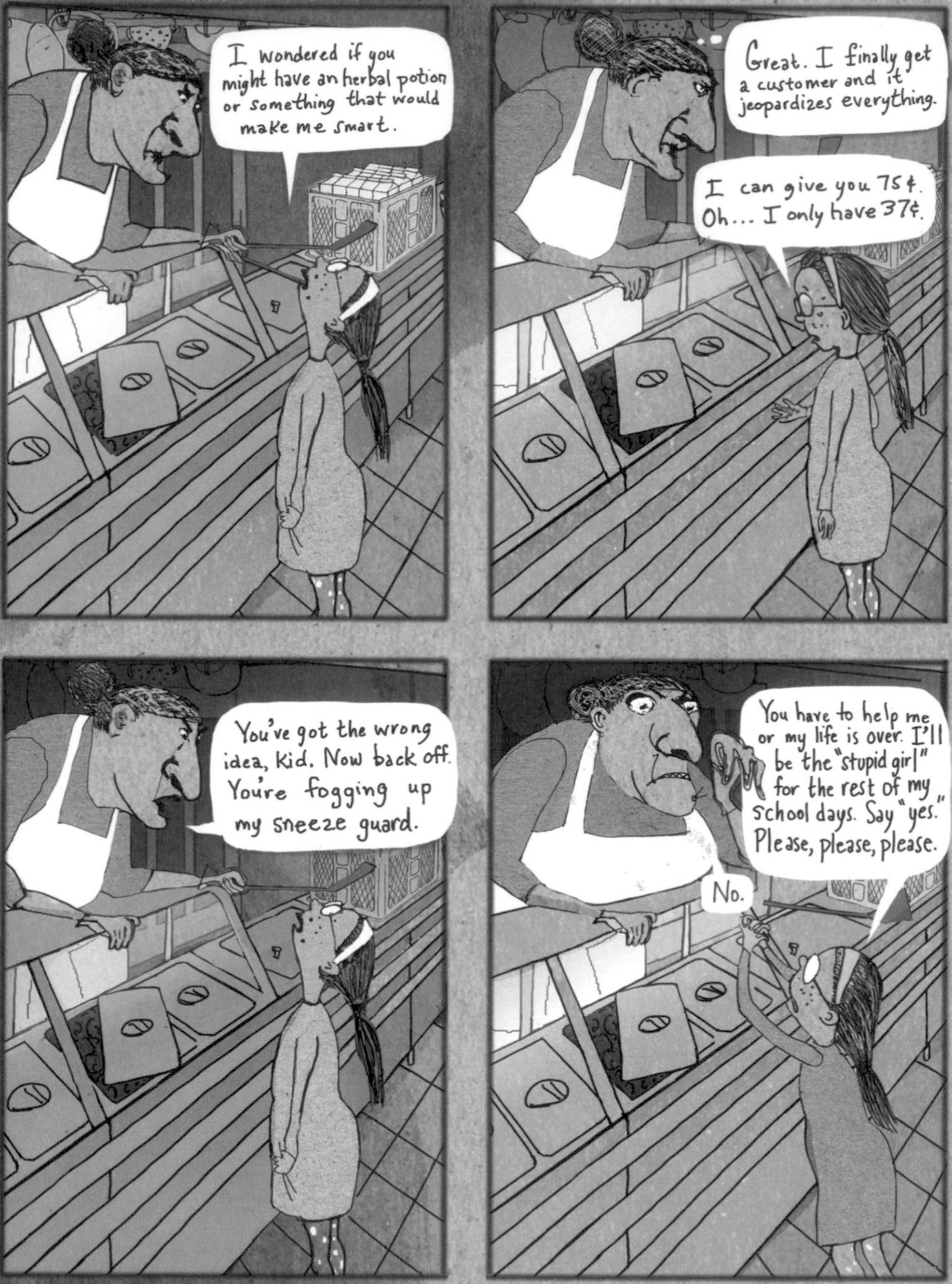
I wondered if you might have an herbal potion or something that would make me smart.
Great. I finally get a customer and it jeopardizes everything.
I can give you 75¢. Oh... I only have 37¢.
You've got the wrong idea, kid. Now back off. You're fogging up my sneeze guard.
You have to help me or my life is over. I'll be the "stupid girl" for the rest of my school days. Say "yes." Please, please, please.
No.

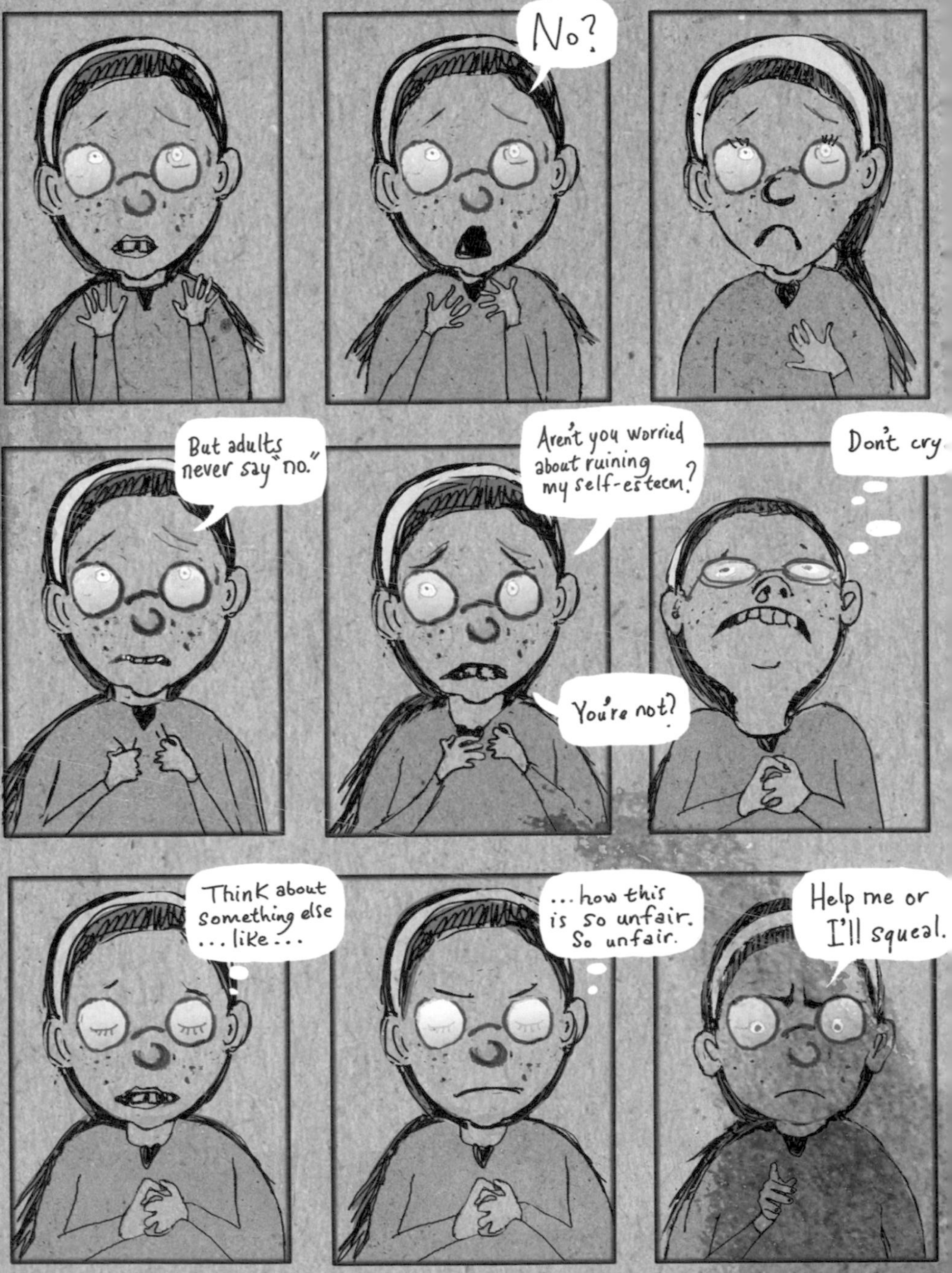
No?
But adults never say "no."
Aren't you worried about ruining my self-esteem?
You're not?
Don't cry.
Think about something else . . . like . . .
. . . how this is so unfair. So unfair.
Help me or I'll squeal.

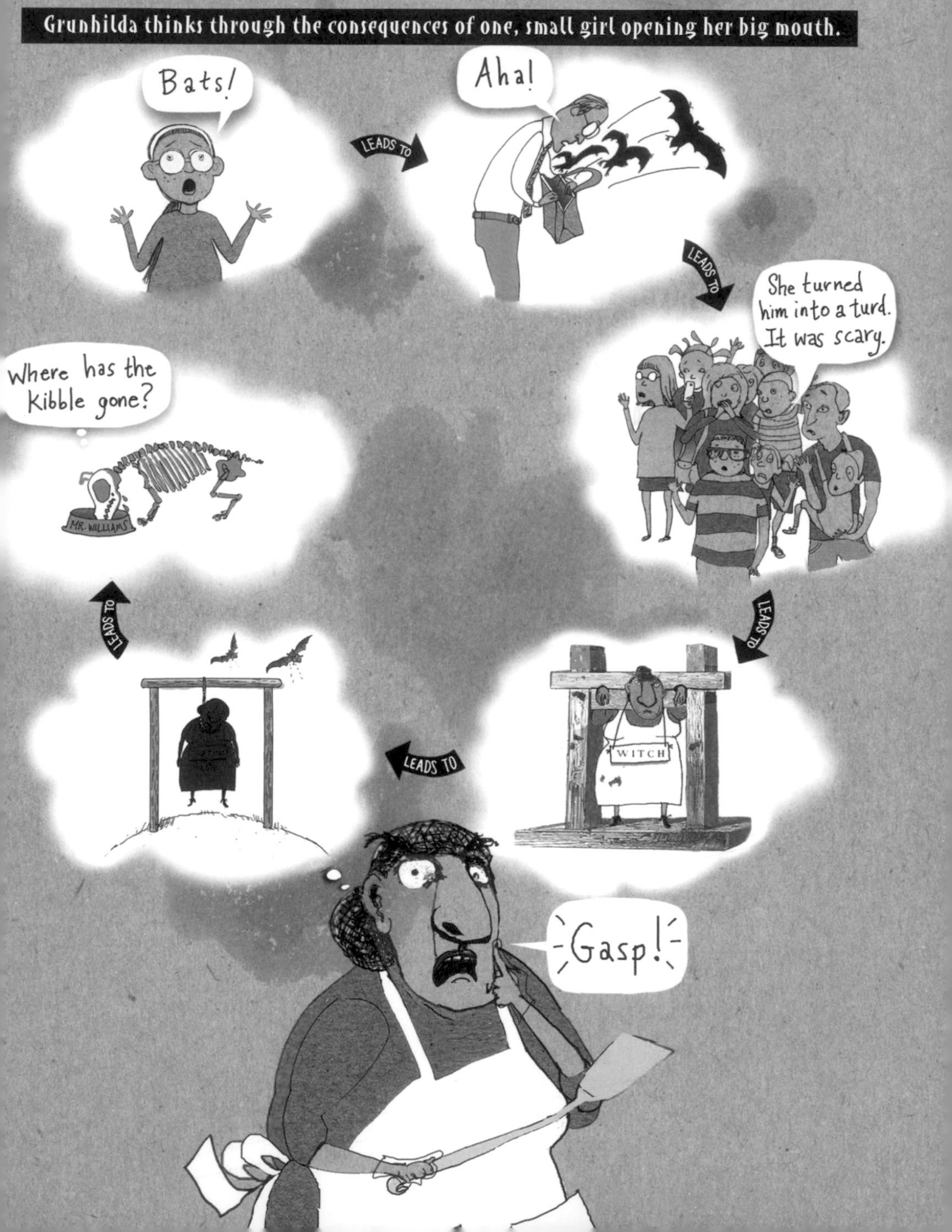
Grunhilda thinks through the consequences of one, small girl opening her big mouth.
Bats!
LEADS TO
Aha!
LEADS TO
She turned him into a turd. It was scary.
LEADS TO
WITCH
LEADS TO
LEADS TO
MR. WILLIAMS
Where has the Kibble gone?
Gasp!

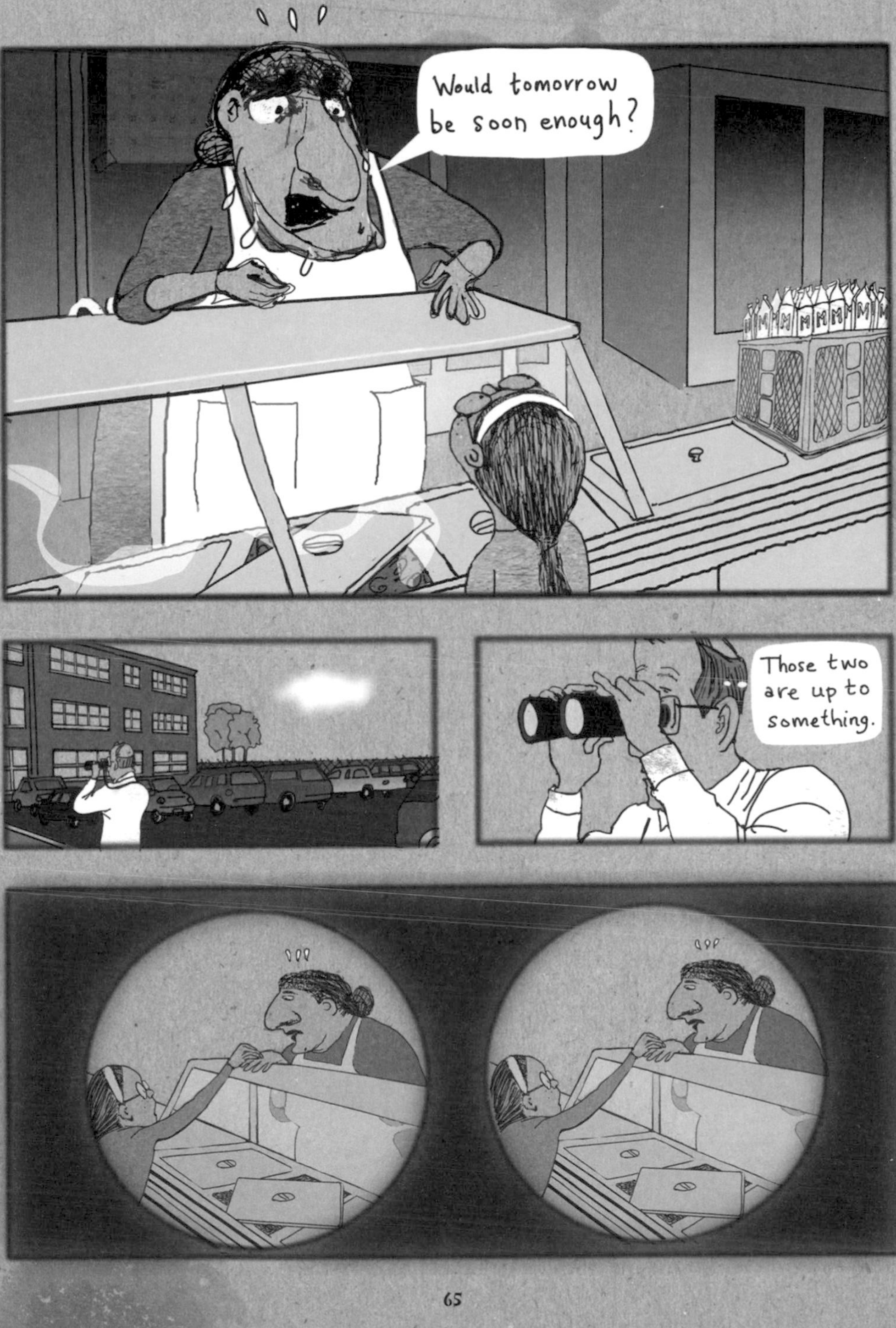
Would tomorrow be soon enough?
Those two are up to something.

8th

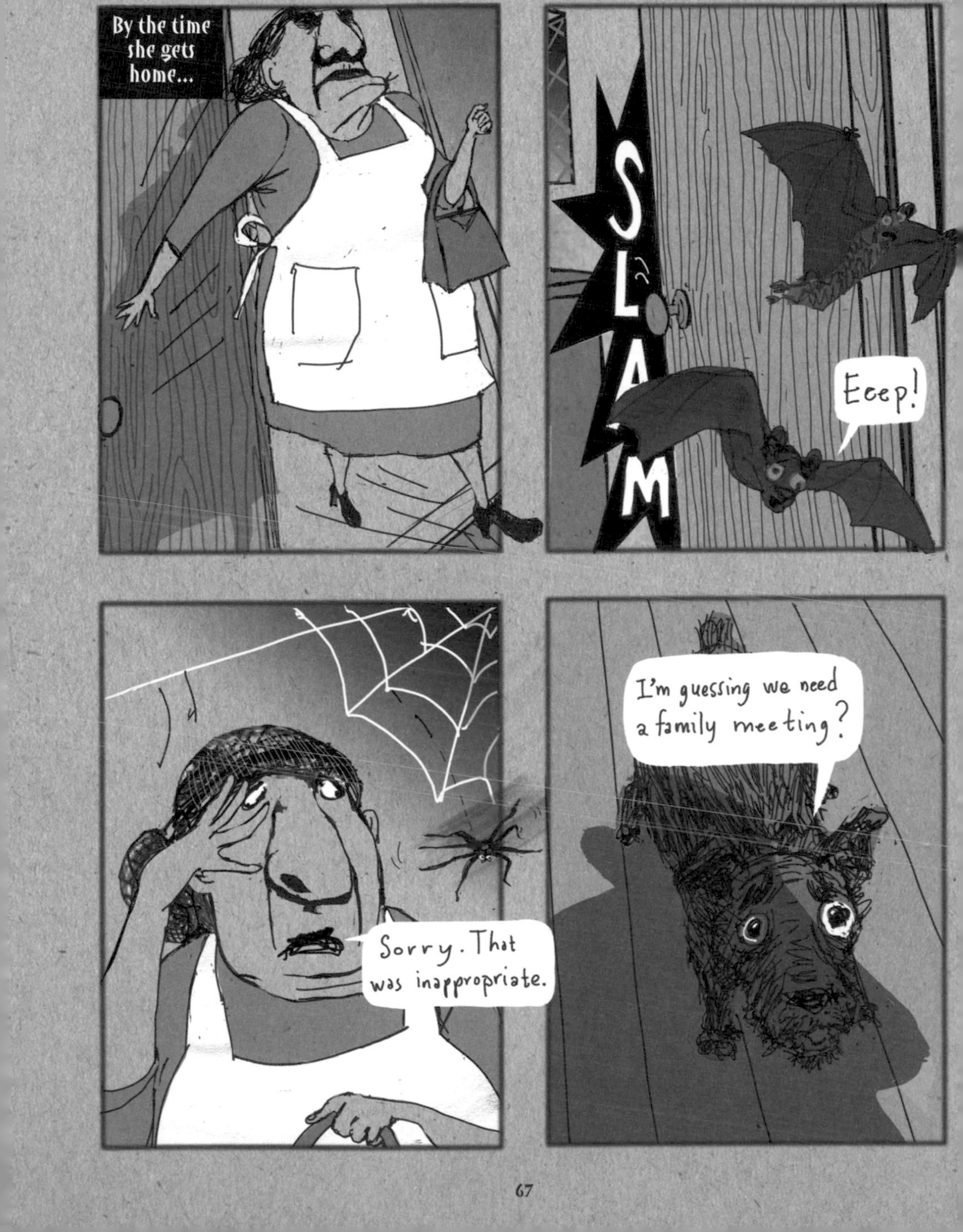
By the time she gets home...
SLAM
Eeep!
Sorry. That was inappropriate.
I'm guessing we need a family meeting?

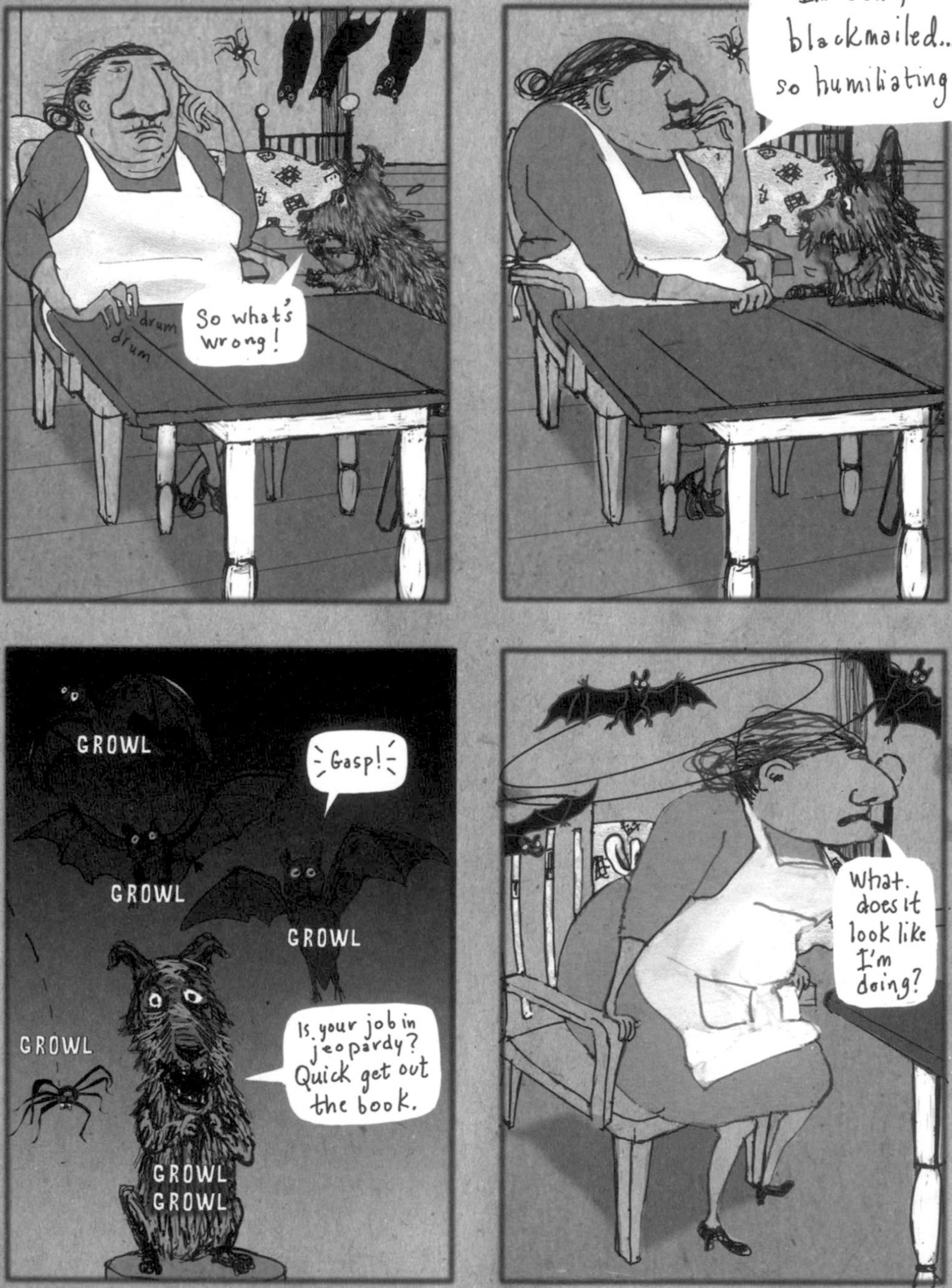
drum drum
So what's wrong!
I'm being blackmailed... so humiliating.
GROWL
Gasp!
GROWL
GROWL
GROWL
Is your job in jeopardy? Quick get out the book.
GROWL GROWL
What. does it look like I'm doing?

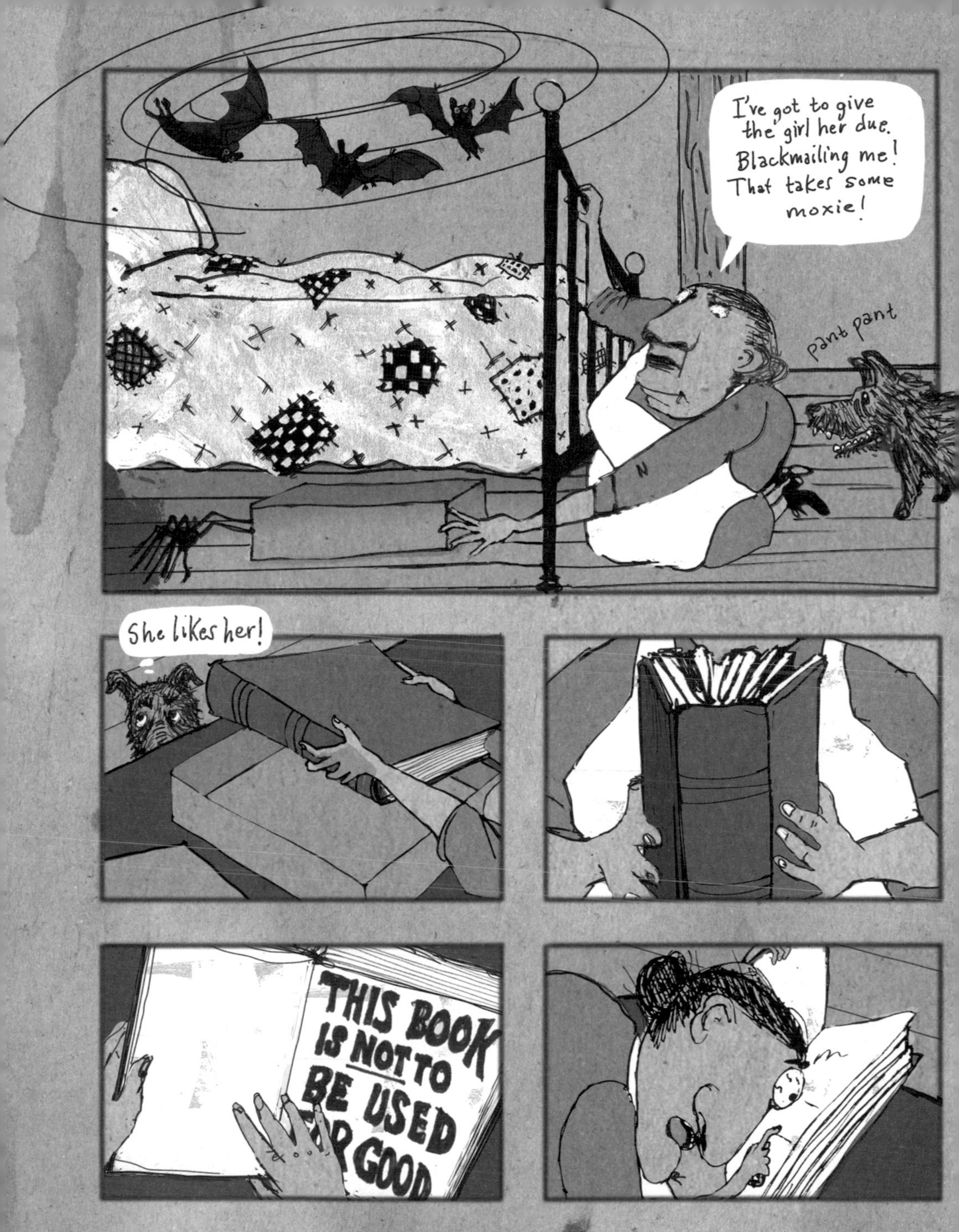
I've got to give the girl her due. Blackmailing me! That takes some moxie!
pant pant
She likes her!
THIS BOOK IS NOT TO BE USED FOR GOOD

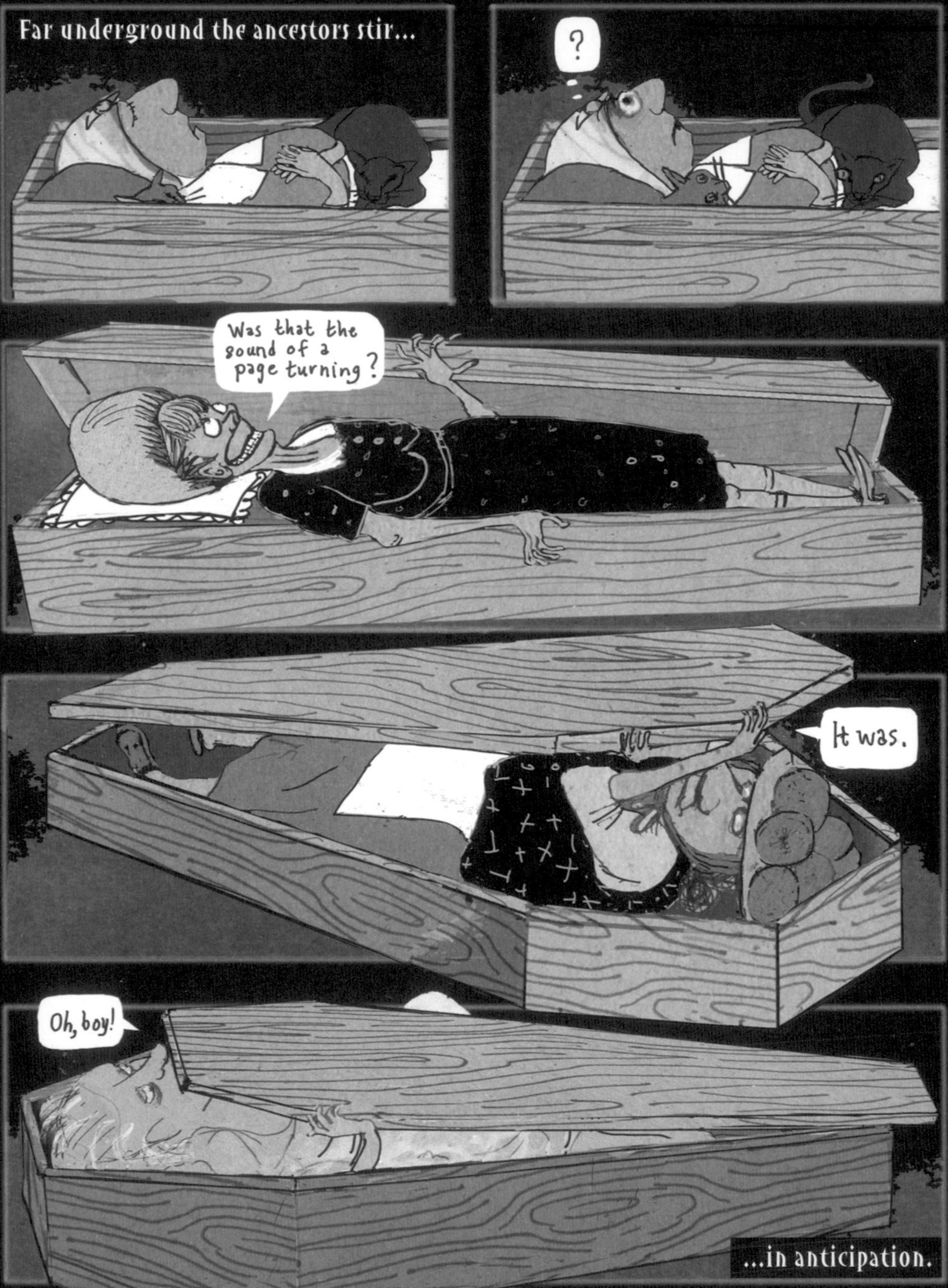

Far underground the ancestors stir...
?
Was that the sound of a page turning?
It was.
Oh, boy!
...in anticipation.

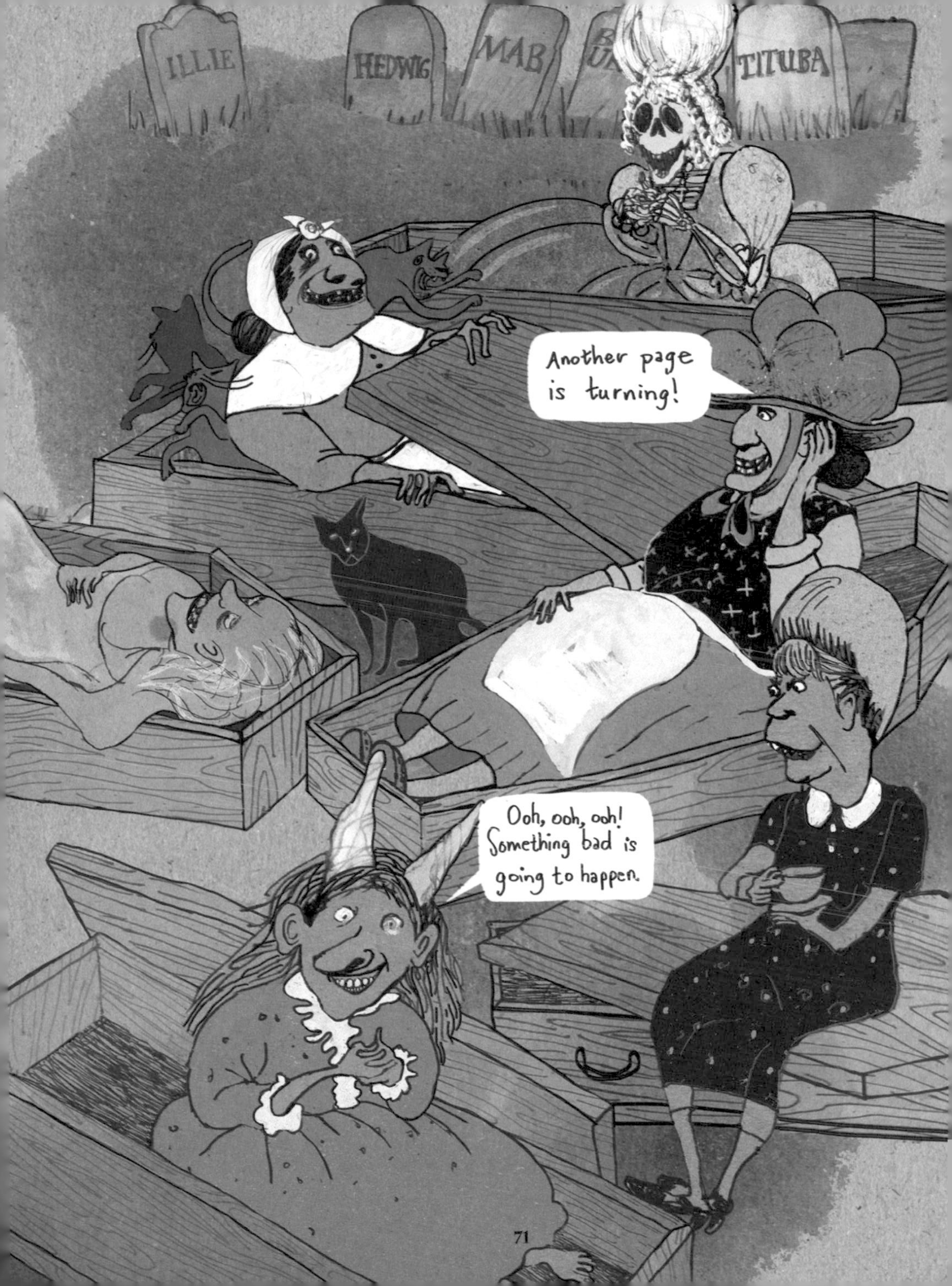
ILLIE
HEDWIG
MAB
TITUBA
Another page is turning!
Ooh, ooh, ooh! Something bad is going to happen.

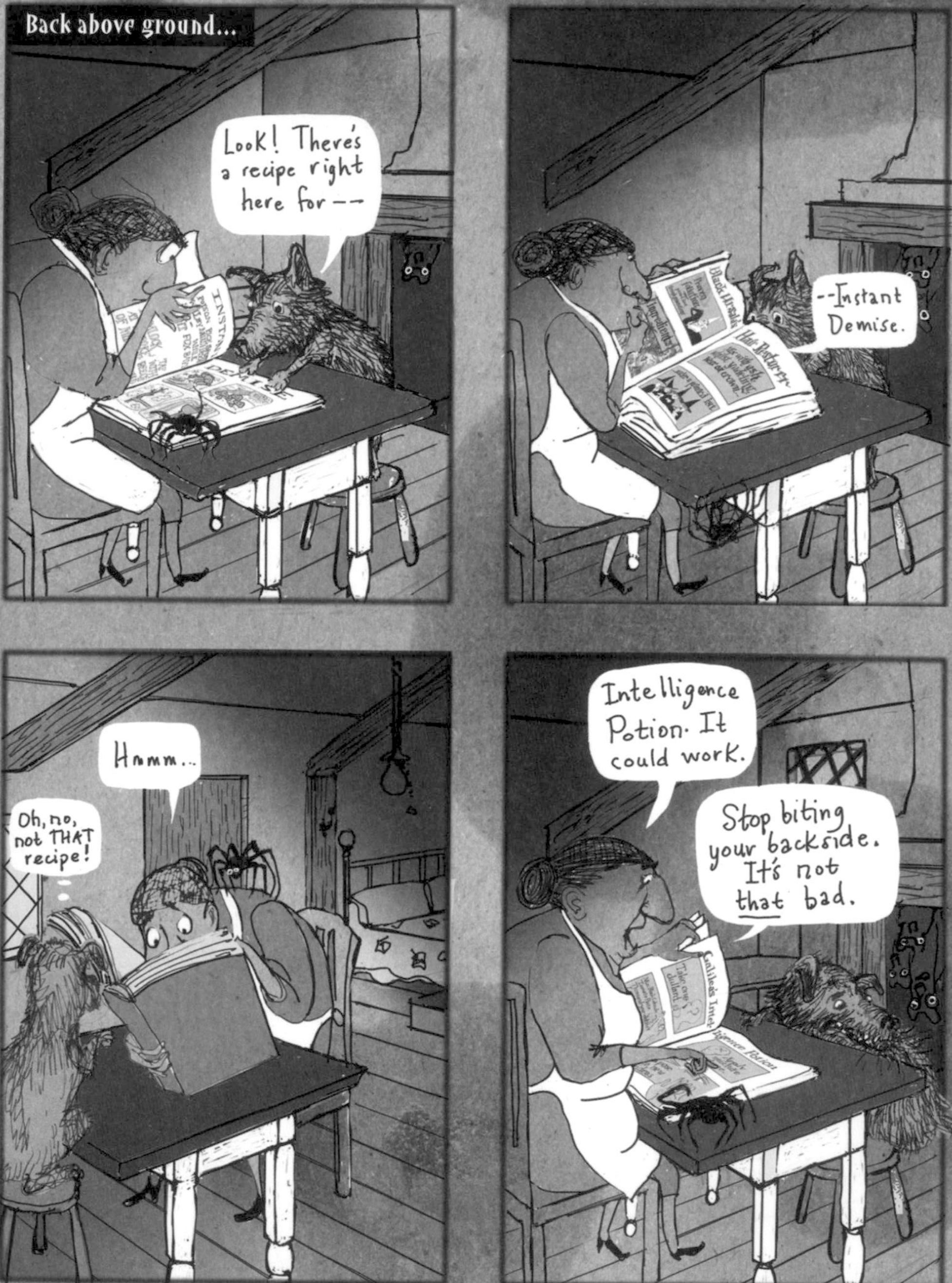

Back above ground...
Look! There's a recipe right here for --
--Instant Demise.
Hmmm...
Oh, no, not THAT recipe!
Intelligence Potion. It could work.
Stop biting your backside. It's not that bad.

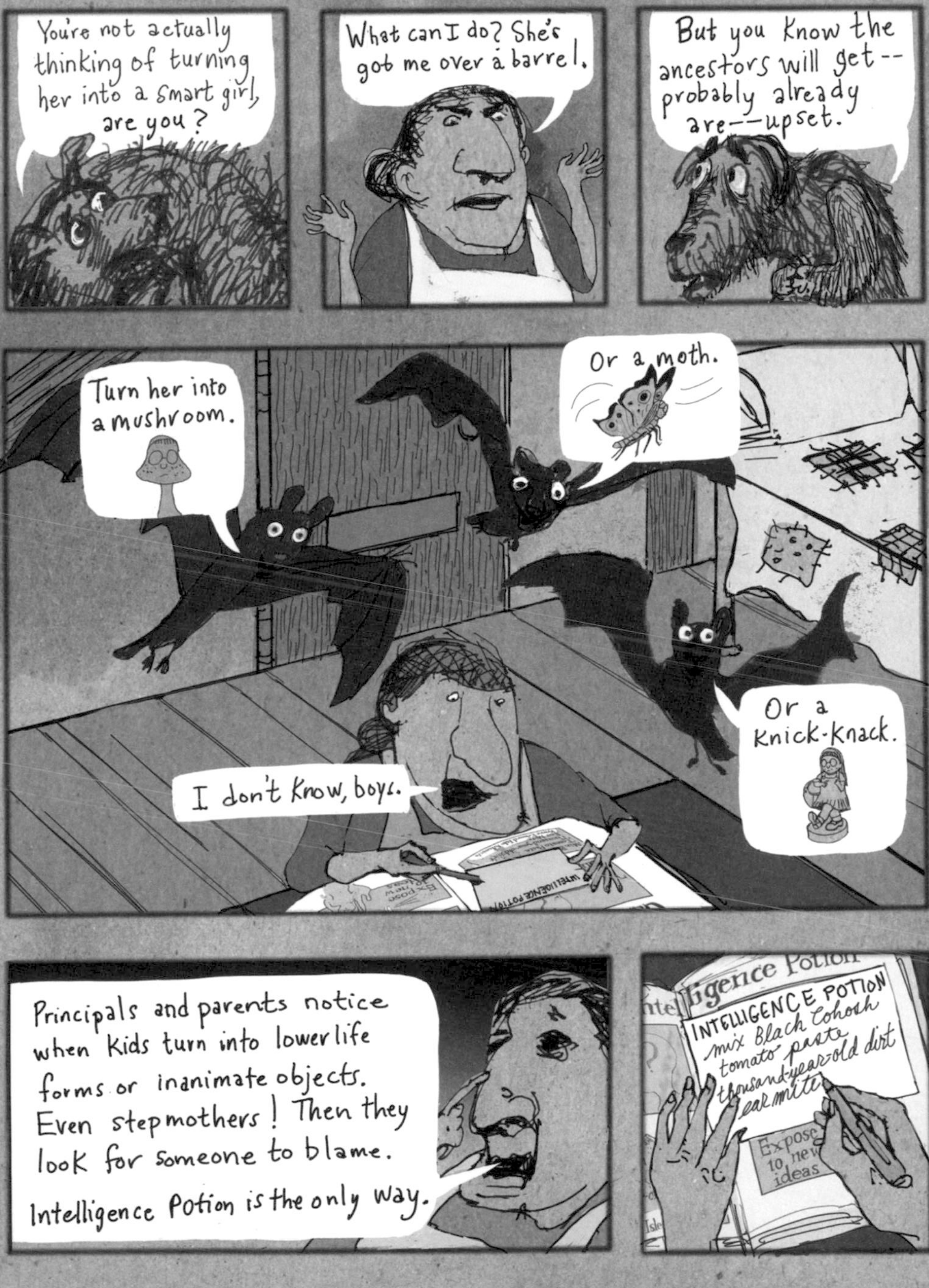
You're not actually thinking of turning her into a smart girl, are you?
What can I do? She's got me over a barrel.
But you know the ancestors will get-- probably already are--upset.
Turn her into a mushroom.
Or a moth.
Or a knick-knack.
I don't know, boys.
Principals and parents notice when kids turn into lower life forms or inanimate objects. Even stepmothers! Then they look for someone to blame.
Intelligence Potion is the only way.
INTELLIGENCE POTION
mix Black Cohosh
tomato paste
thousand-year-old dirt
ear mites
Expose to new ideas

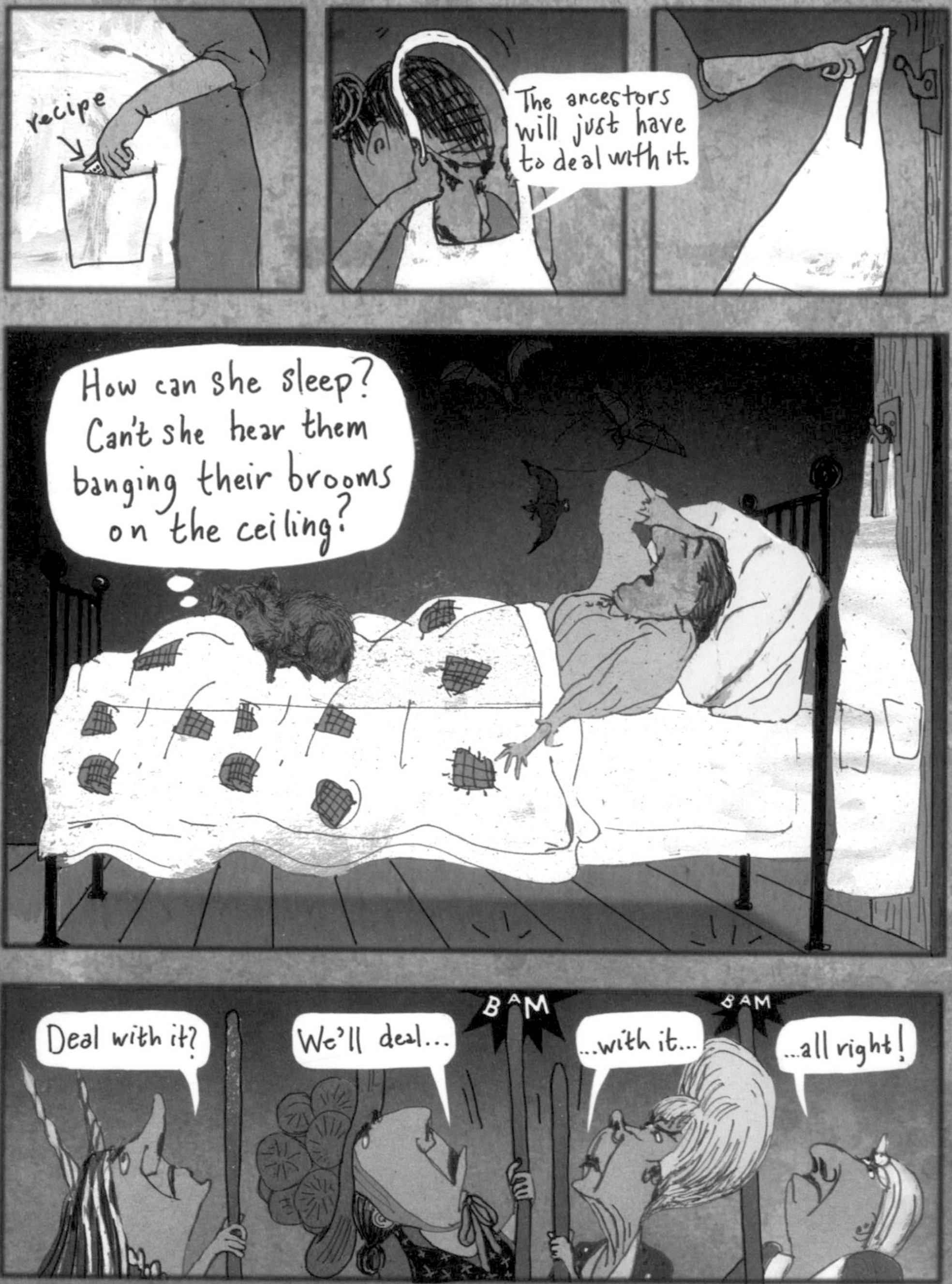
recipe
The ancestors will just have to deal with it.
How can she sleep? Can't she hear them banging their brooms on the ceiling?
Deal with it?
We'll deal...
BAM
...with it...
BAM
...all right!

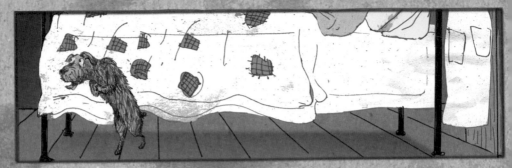

Here's one with similar ingredients the hags will love.

SNORE

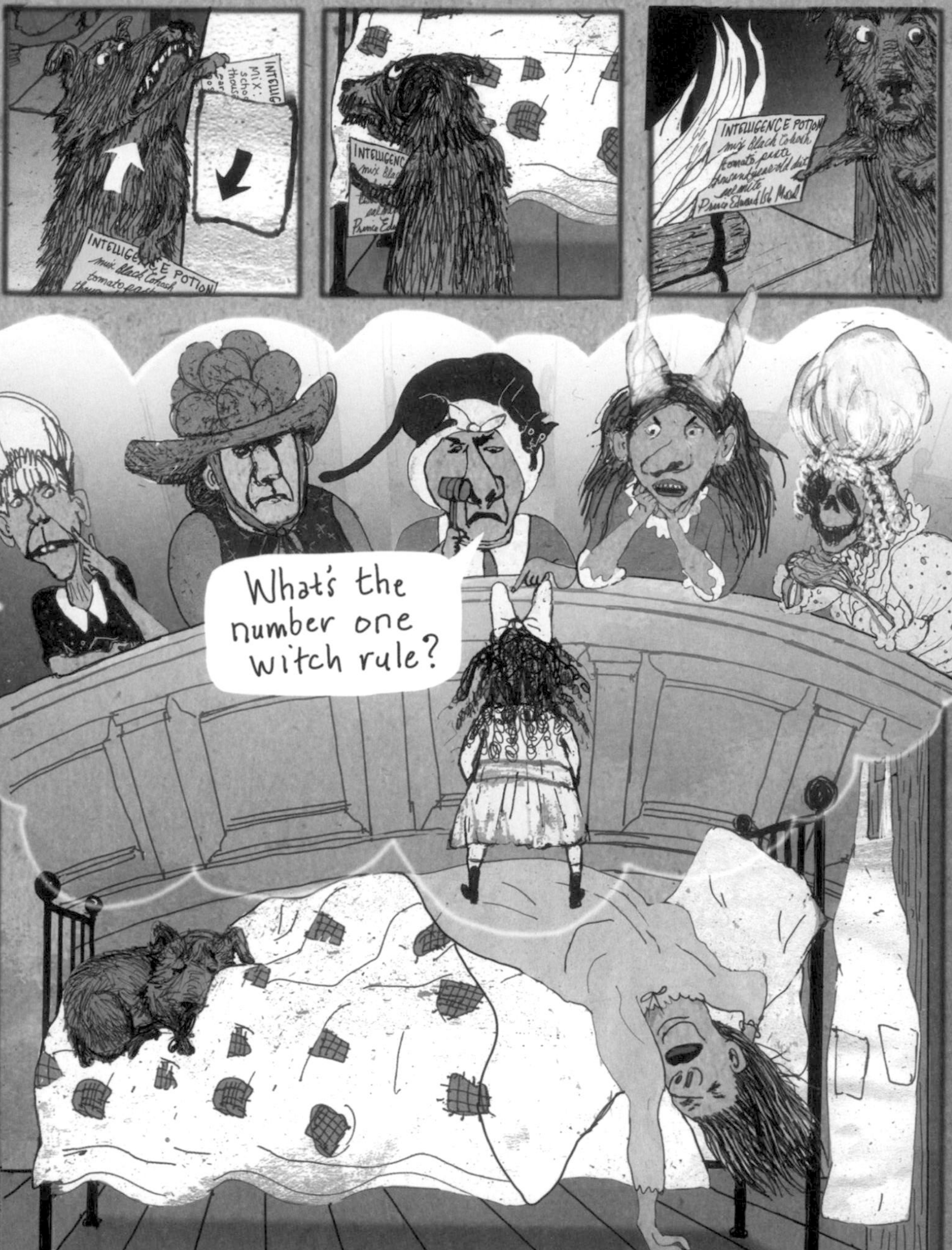
INTELLIGENCE POTION
INTELLIGENCE POTION
What's the number one witch rule?

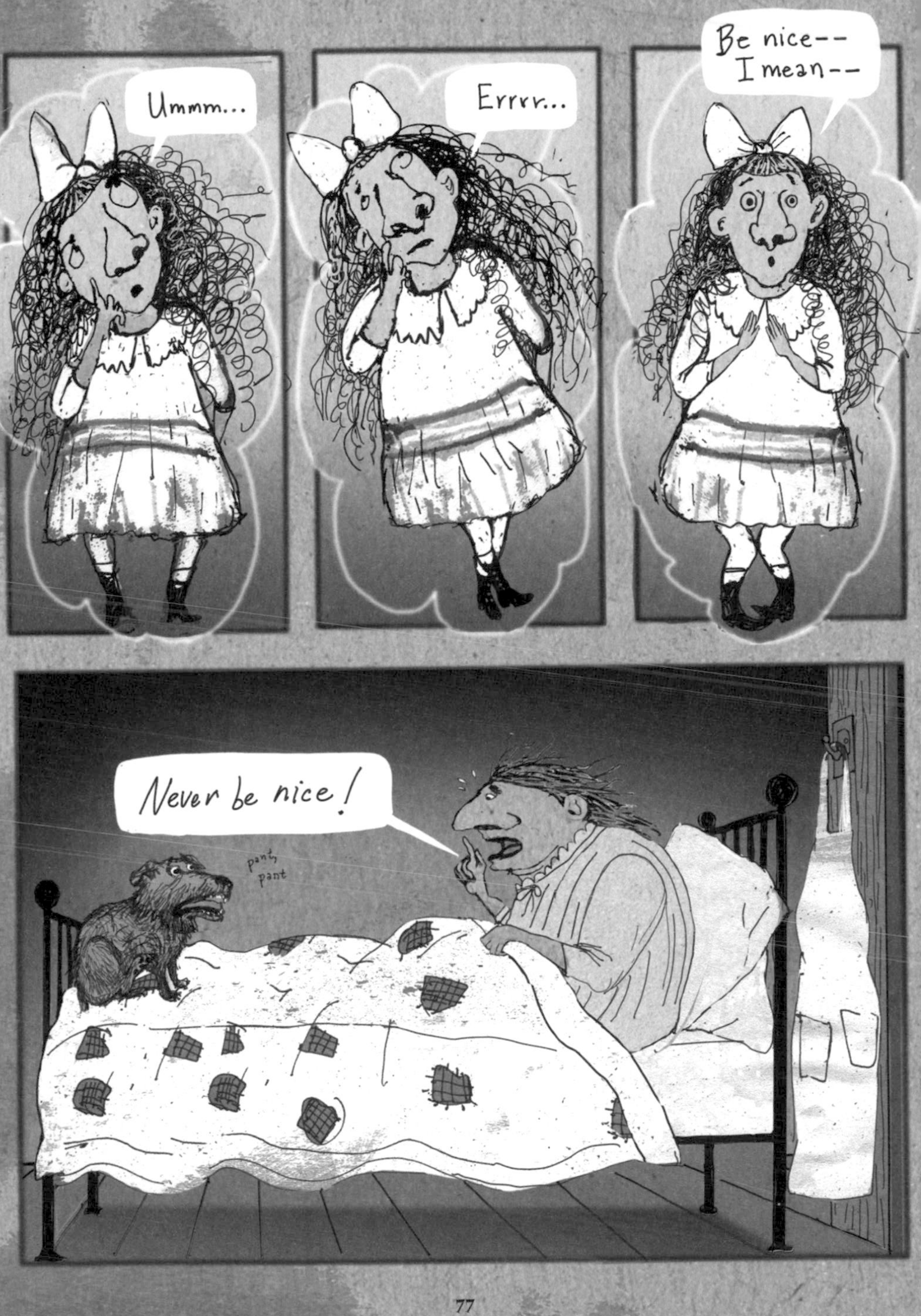
Ummm...
Errrr...
Be nice-- I mean--
Never be nice!
pant, pant

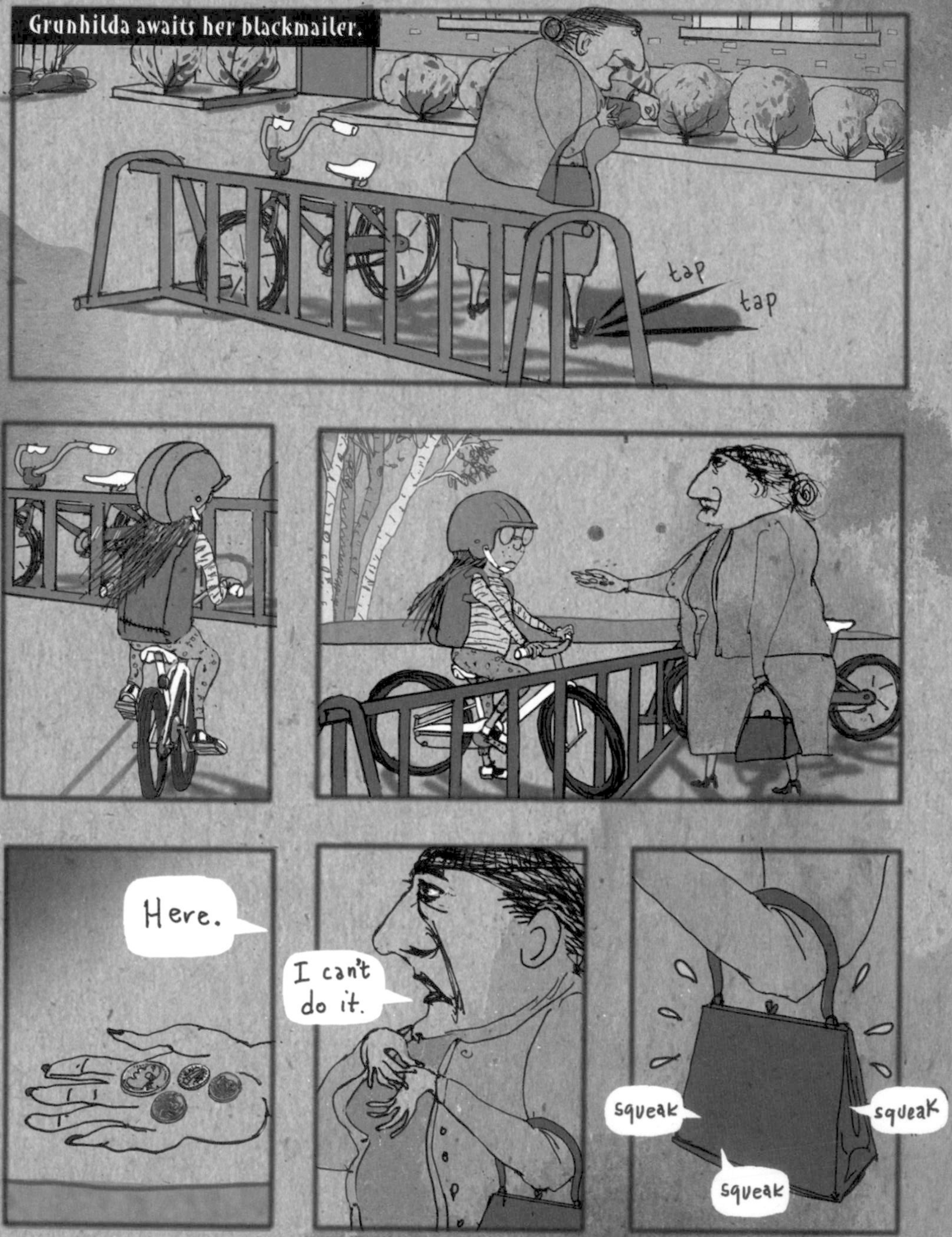
Grunhilda awaits her blackmailer.
tap
tap
Here.
I can't do it.
squeak
squeak
squeak

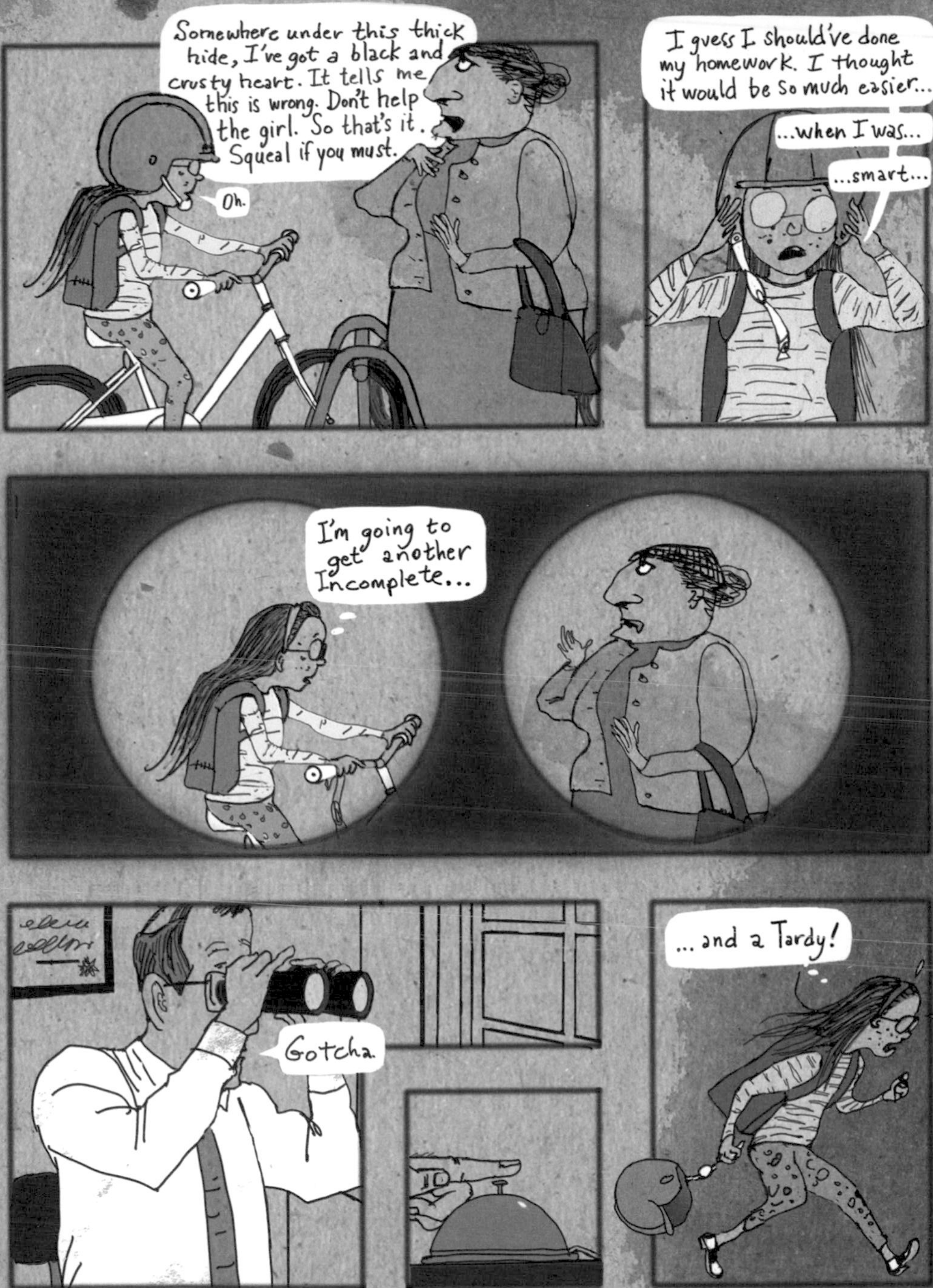

Somewhere under this thick hide, I've got a black and crusty heart. It tells me this is wrong. Don't help the girl. So that's it. Squeal if you must.
Oh.
I guess I should've done my homework. I thought it would be so much easier...
...when I was...
...smart...
I'm going to get another Incomplete...
Gotcha.
... and a Tardy!

9th

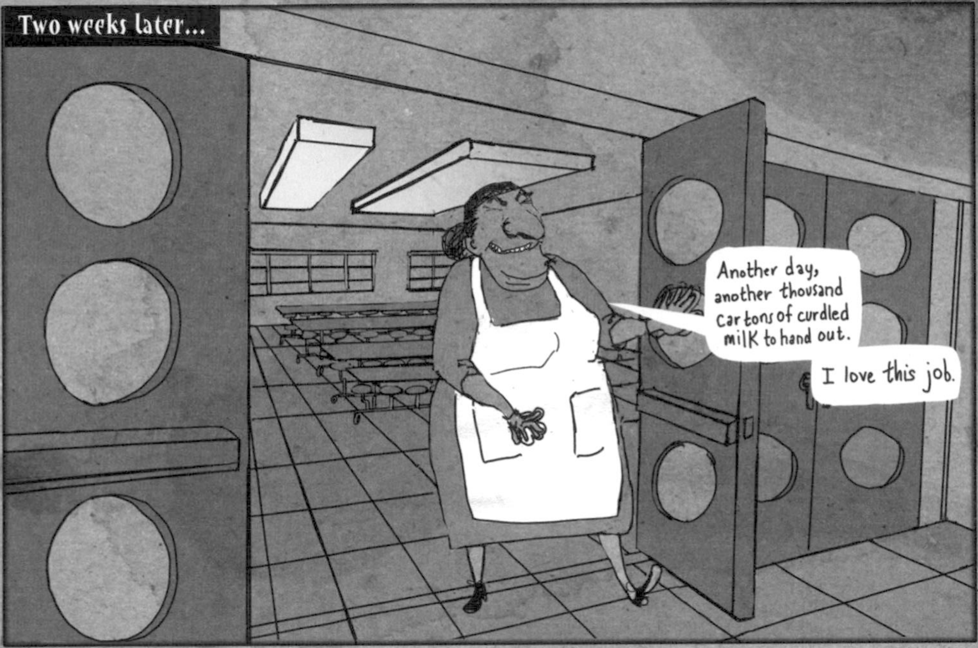
Two weeks later...
Another day, another thousand cartons of curdled milk to hand out.
I love this job.

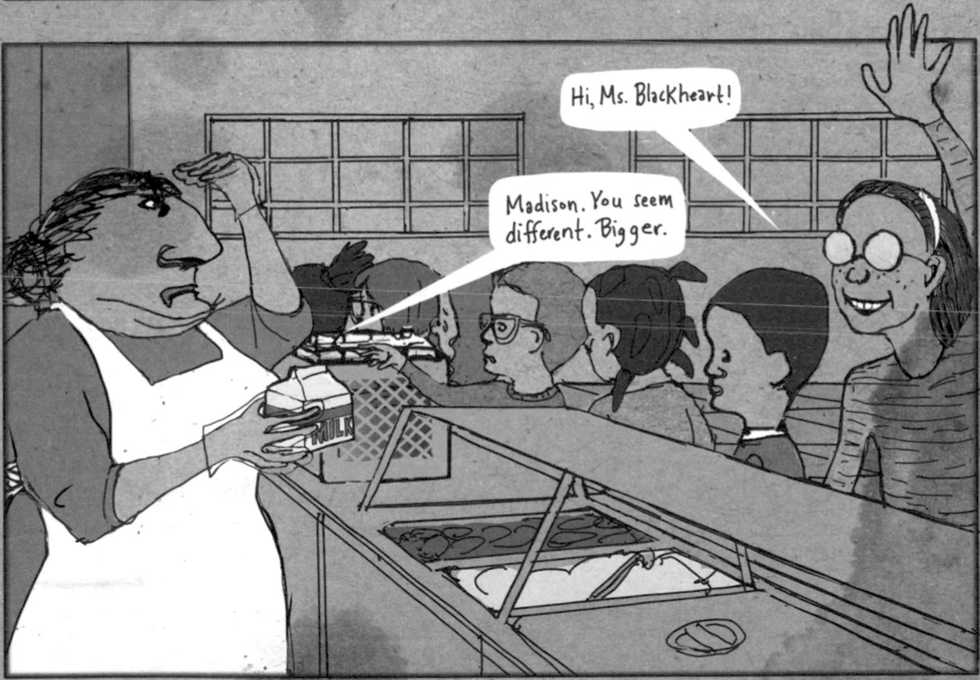
Hi, Ms. Blackheart!
Madison. You seem different. Bigger.
MILK

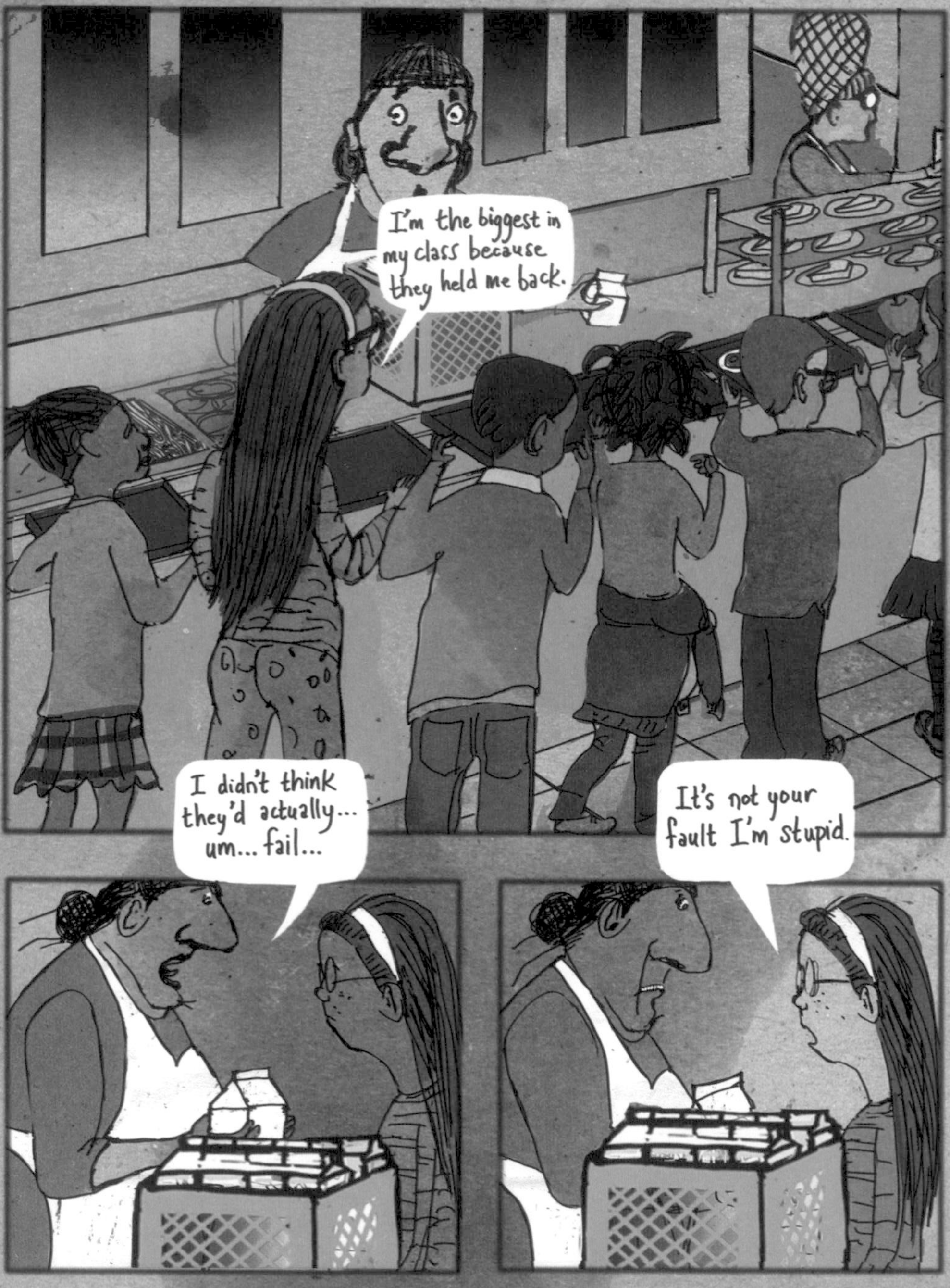
I'm the biggest in my class because they held me back.
I didn't think they'd actually... um... fail...
It's not your fault I'm stupid.

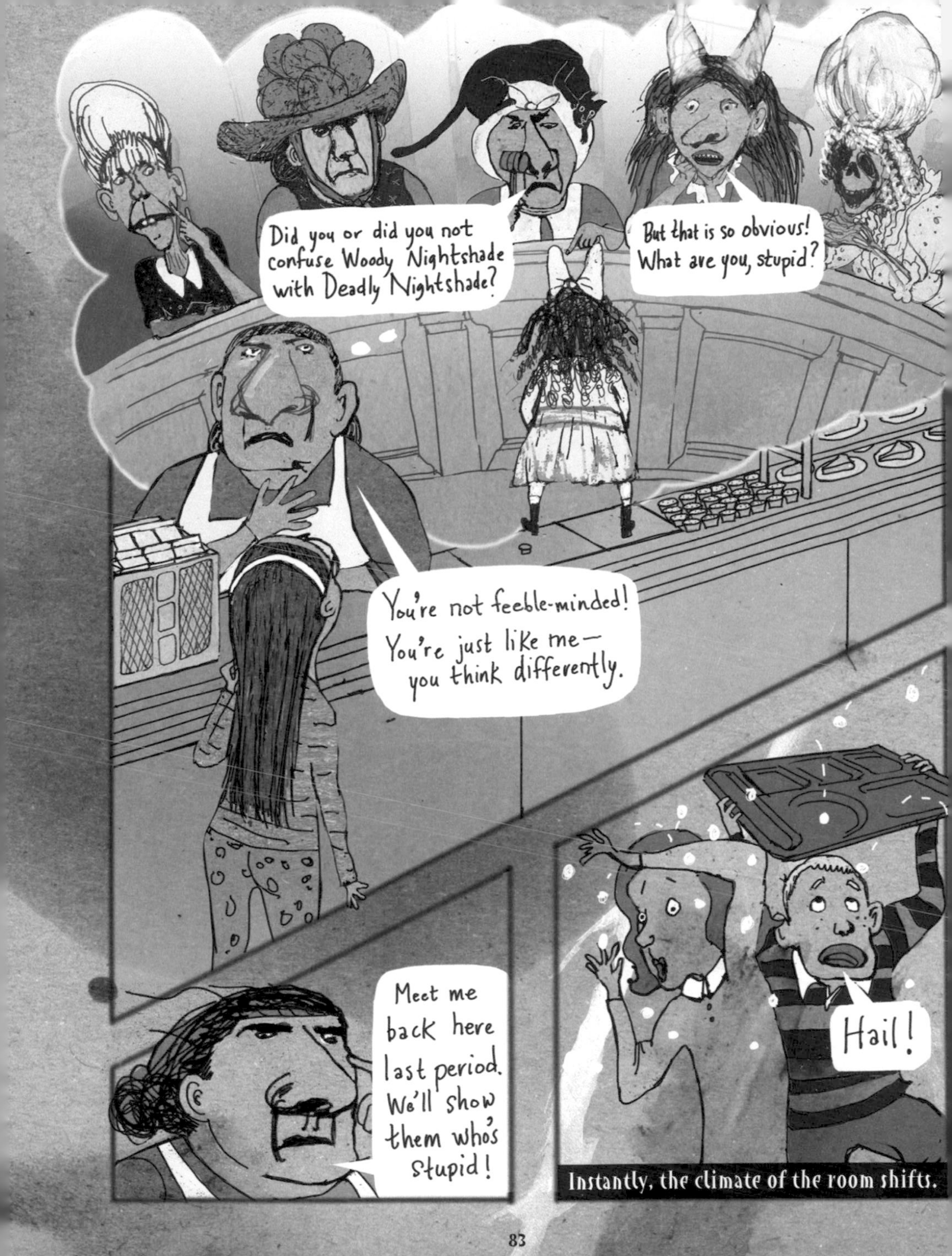

Did you or did you not confuse Woody Nightshade with Deadly Nightshade?
But that is so obvious! What are you, stupid?
You're not feeble-minded! You're just like me— you think differently.
Meet me back here last period. We'll show them who's stupid!
Hail!
Instantly, the climate of the room shifts.

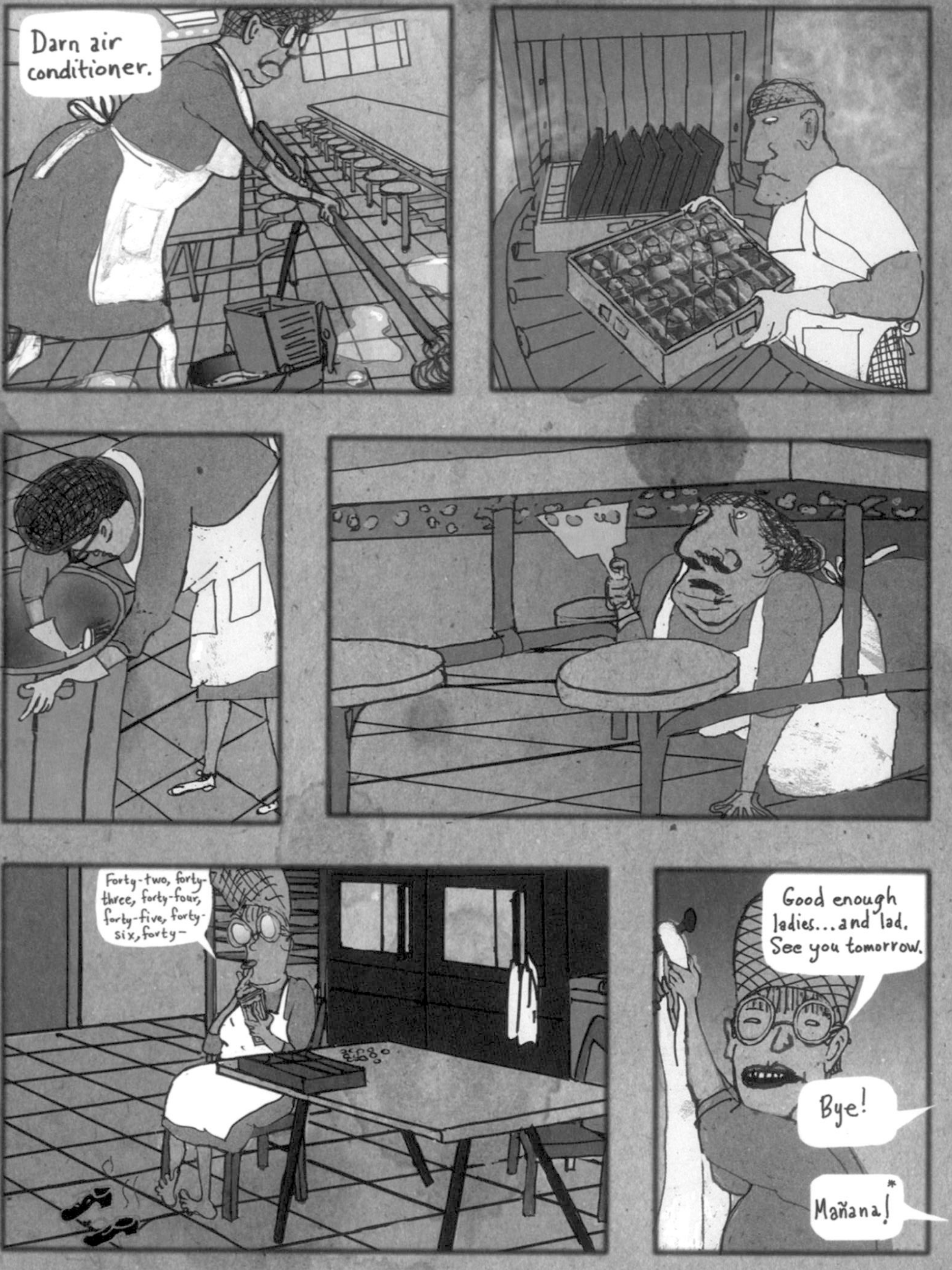
Darn air conditioner.
Forty-two, forty-three, forty-four, forty-five, forty-six, forty-
Good enough ladies...and lad. See you tomorrow.
Bye!
Mañana!*

*Spanish for "Tomorrow"

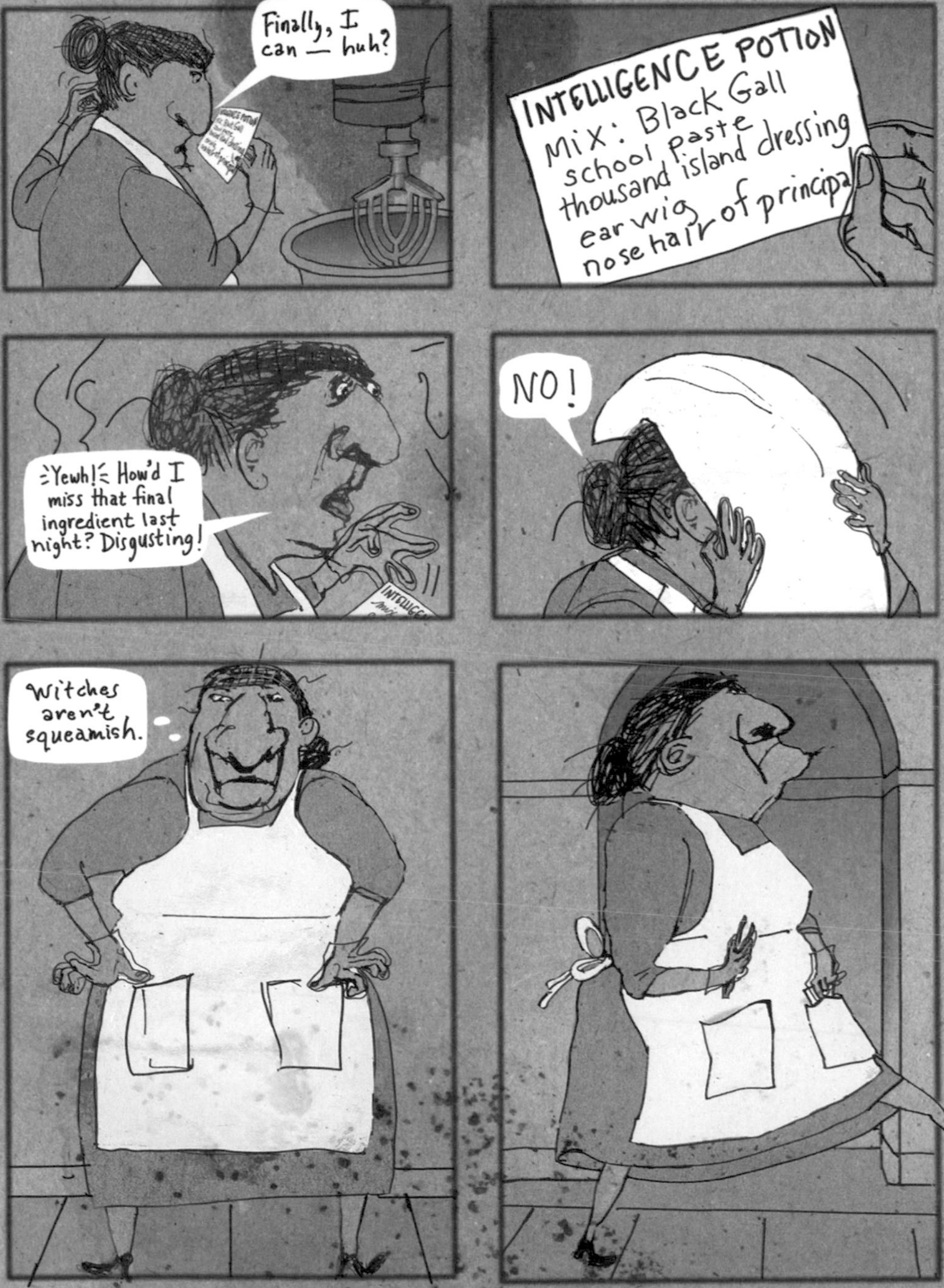
Finally, I can — huh?
INTELLIGENCE POTION
Mix: Black Gall
school paste
thousand island dressing
ear wig
nose hair of principal
=Yewh!= How'd I miss that final ingredient last night? Disgusting!
NO!
Witches aren't squeamish.

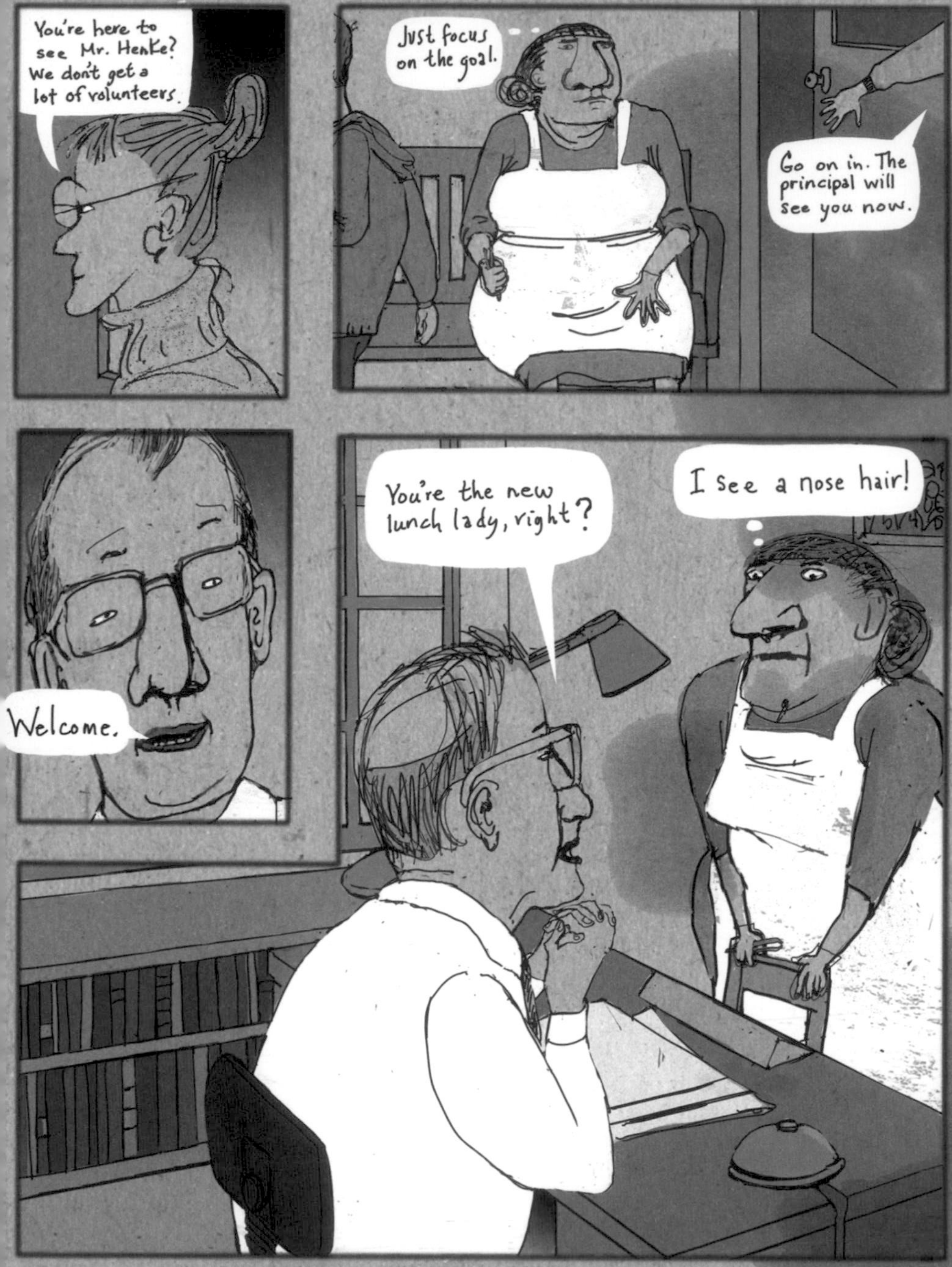

You're here to see Mr. Henke? We don't get a lot of volunteers.
Just focus on the goal.
Go on in. The principal will see you now.
Welcome.
You're the new lunch lady, right?
I see a nose hair!

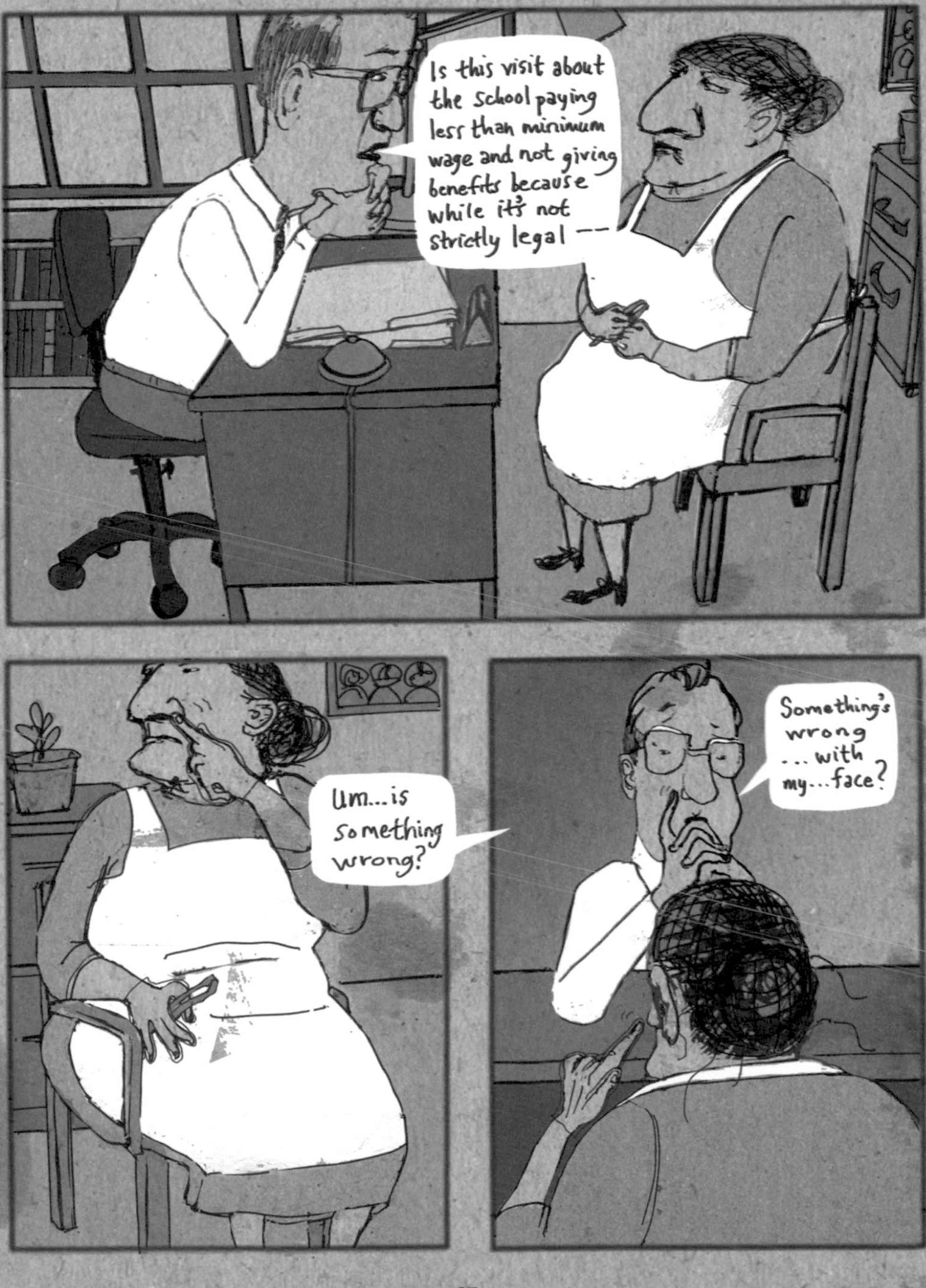
Is this visit about the school paying less than minimum wage and not giving benefits because while it's not strictly legal --
Um...is something wrong?
Something's wrong ...with my...face?

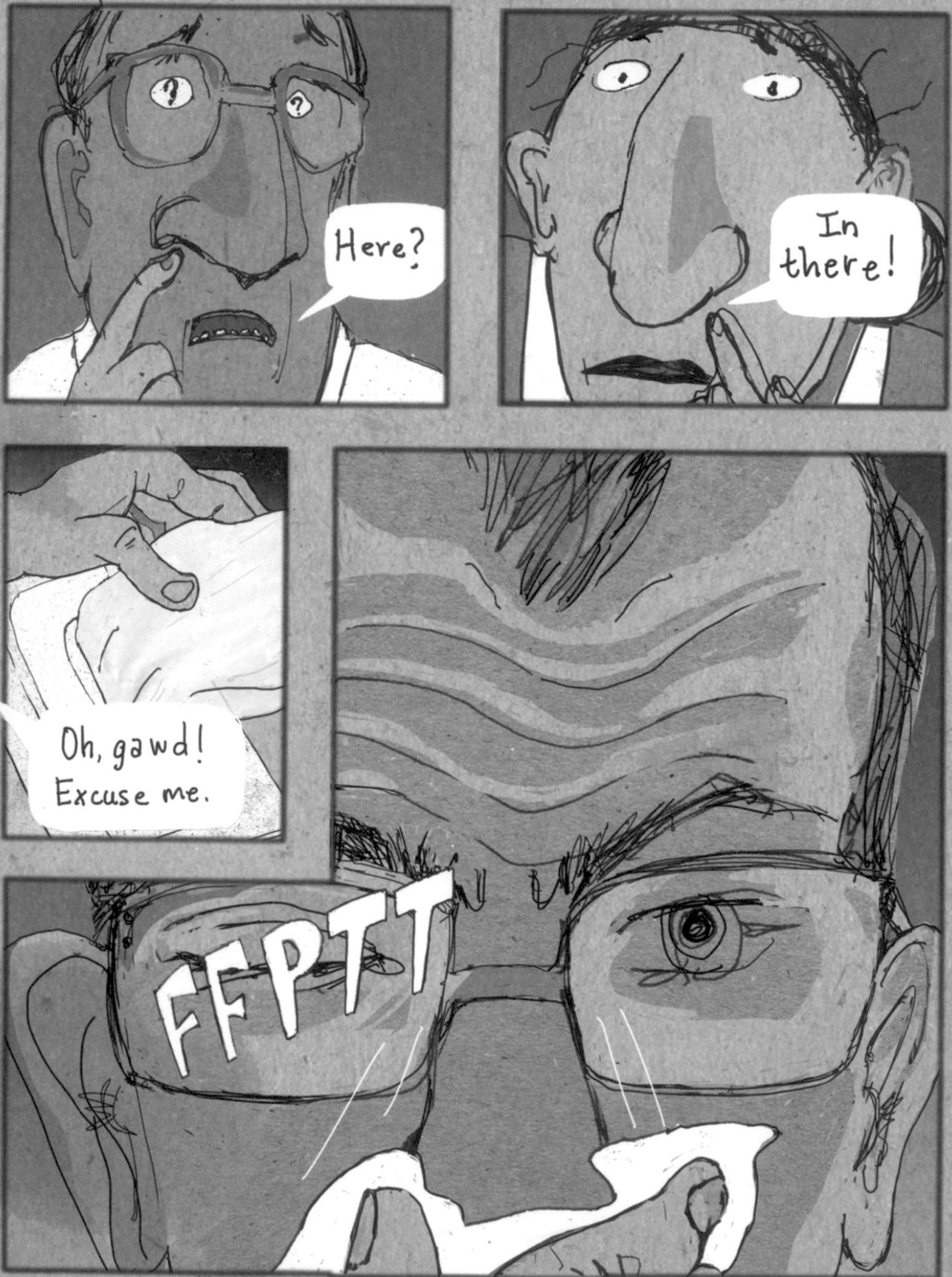
Here?
In there!
Oh, gawd! Excuse me.
FFPTT

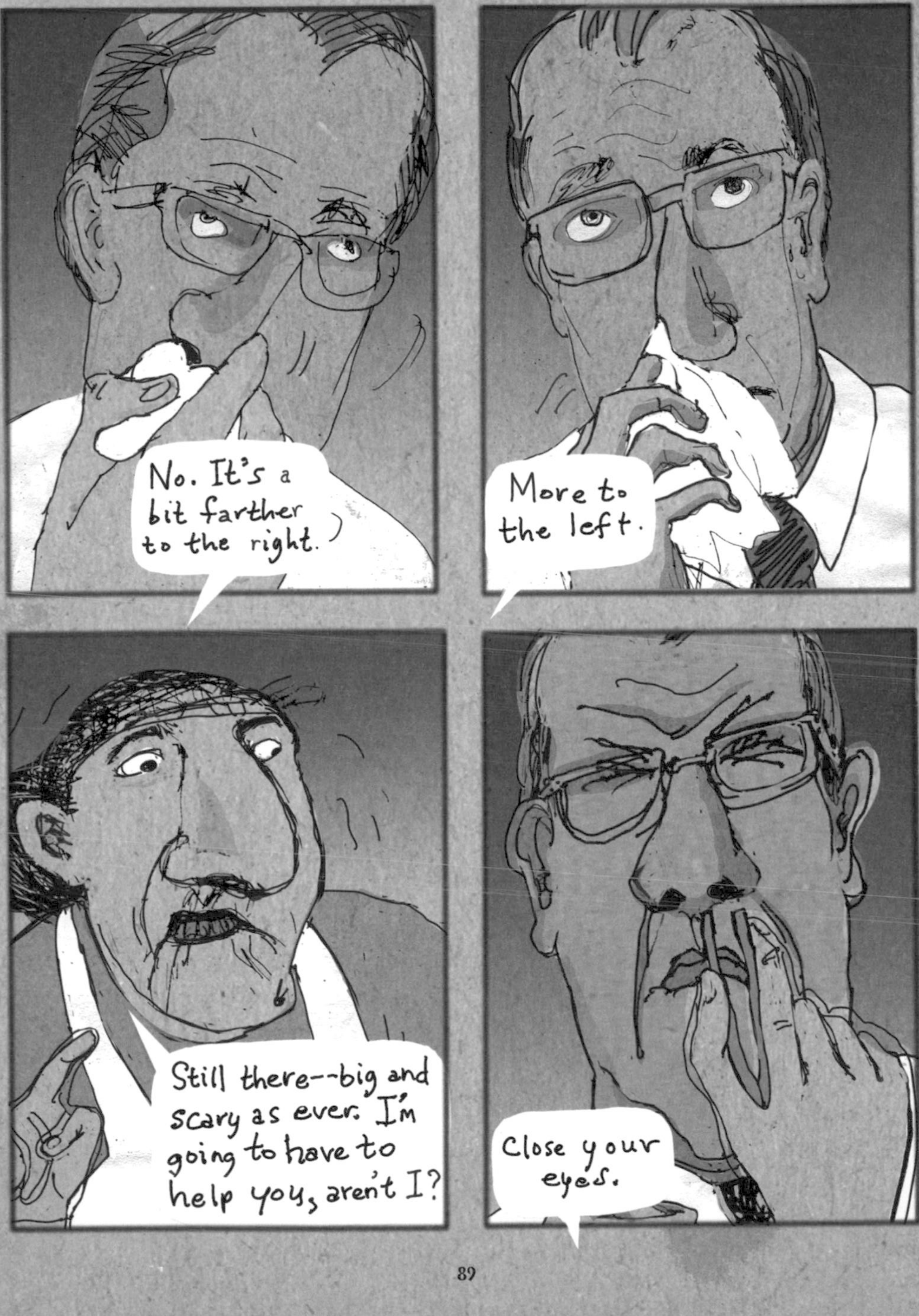
No. It's a bit farther to the right.
More to the left.
Still there--big and scary as ever. I'm going to have to help you, aren't I?
Close your eyes.

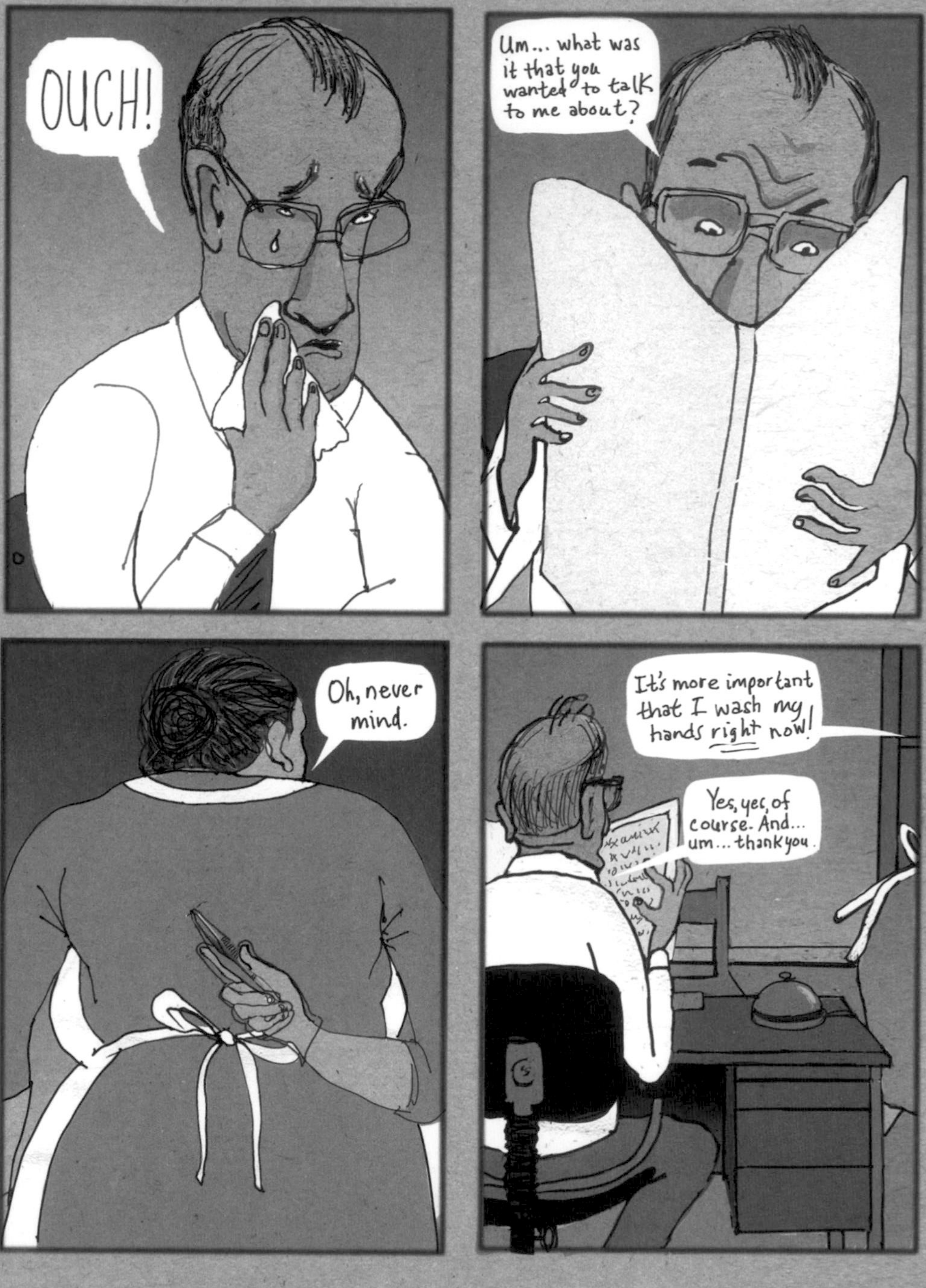
OUCH!
Um... what was it that you wanted to talk to me about?
Oh, never mind.
It's more important that I wash my hands right now!
Yes, yes, of course. And... um... thank you.

10th

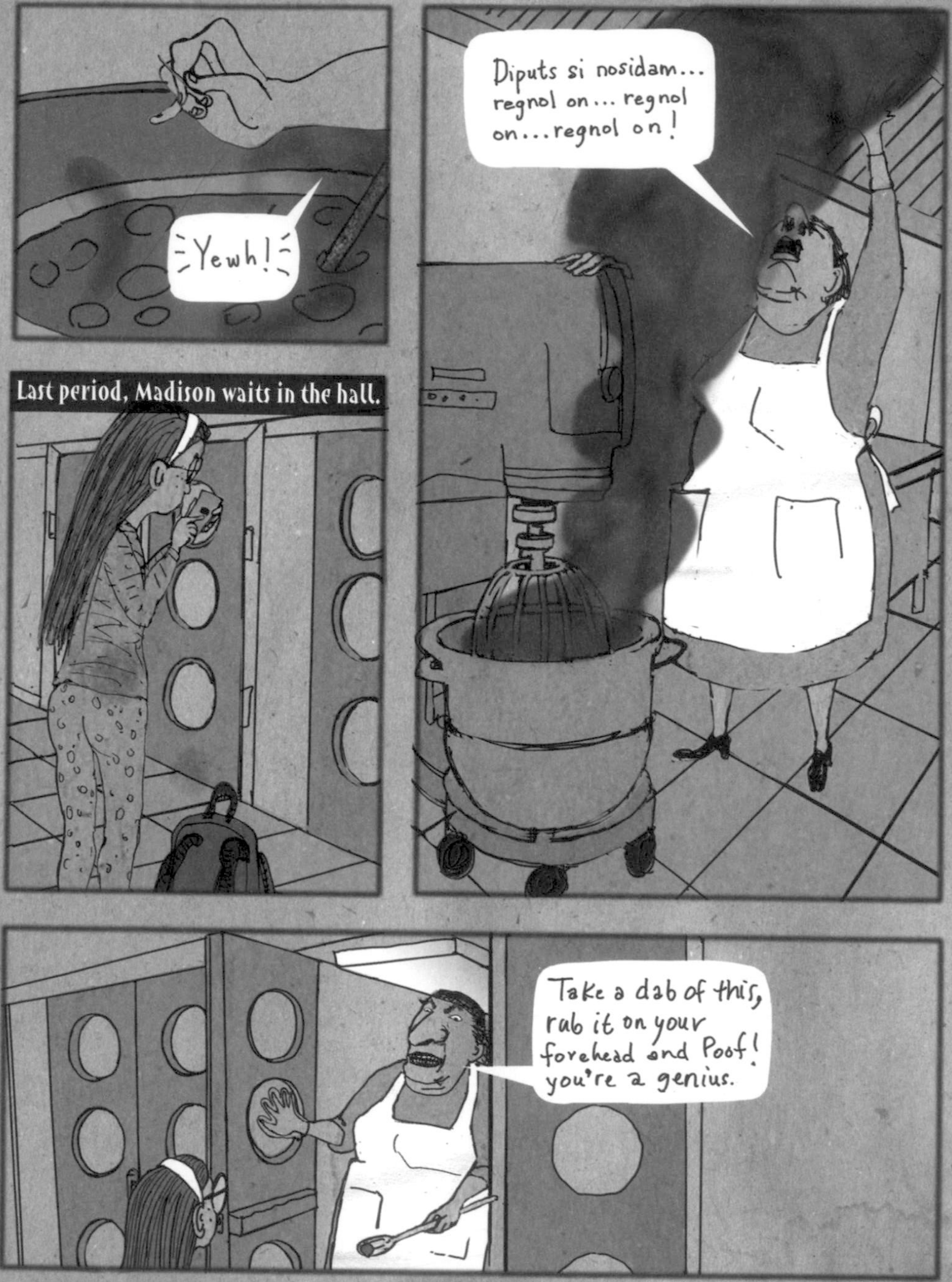
Yewh!
Diputs si nosidam... regnol on... regnol on...regnol on!
Last period, Madison waits in the hall.
Take a dab of this, rab it on your forehead and Poof! you're a genius.

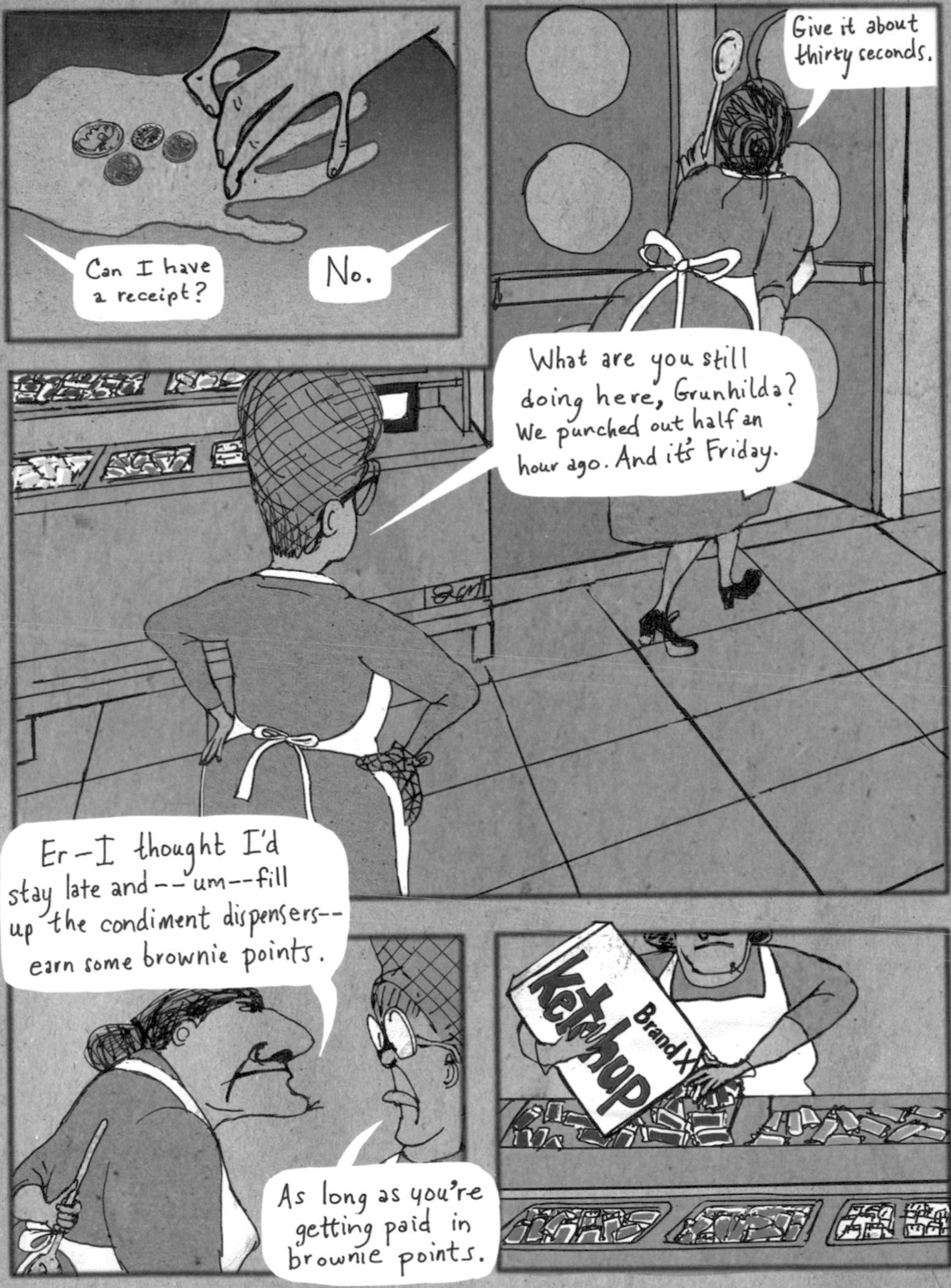
Can I have a receipt?
No.
Give it about thirty seconds.
What are you still doing here, Grunhilda? We punched out half an hour ago. And it's Friday.
Er—I thought I'd stay late and — — um — — fill up the condiment dispensers— — earn some brownie points.
As long as you're getting paid in brownie points.
Brand X Ketchup

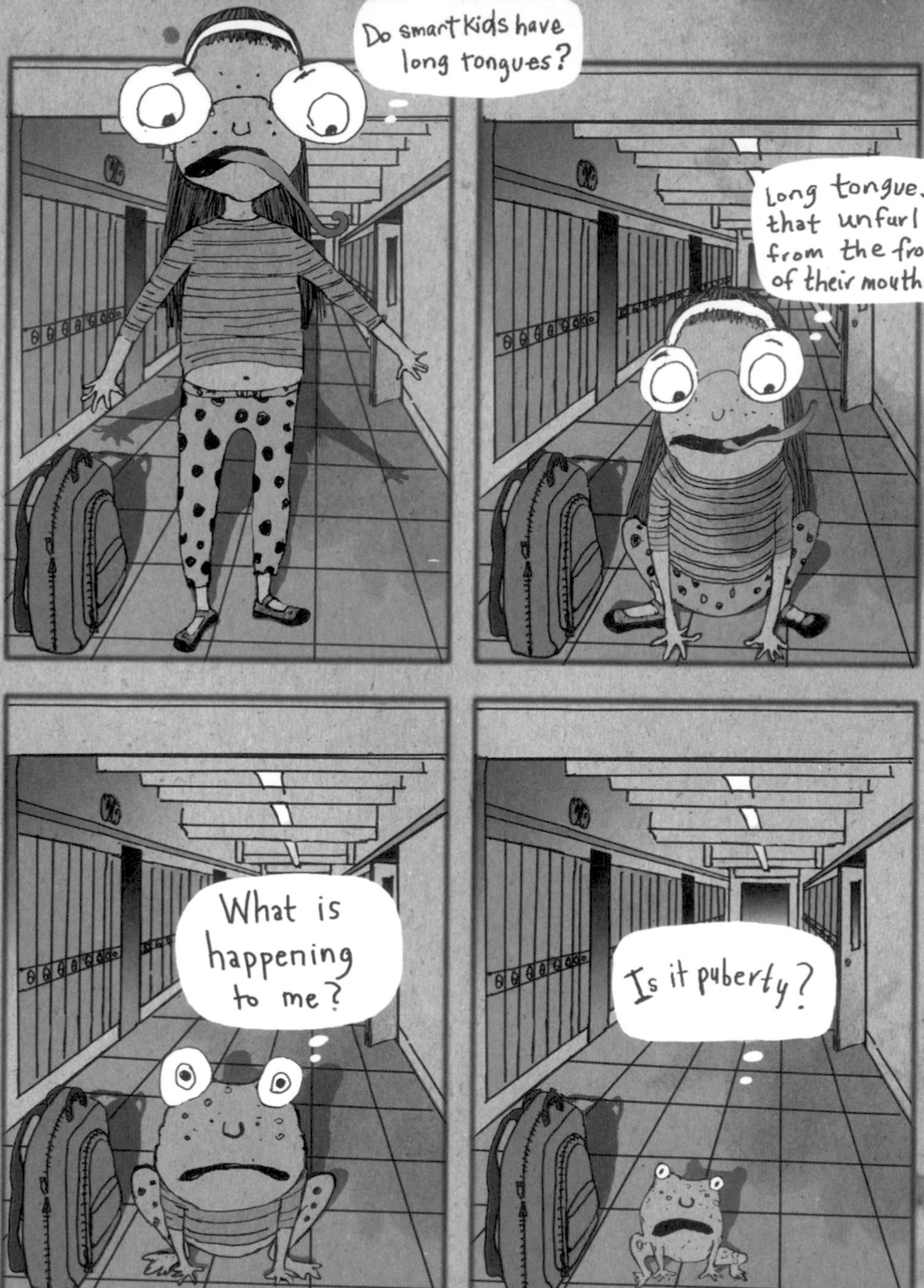
Do smart kids have long tongues?
Long tongues that unfurl from the front of their mouths?
What is happening to me?
Is it puberty?

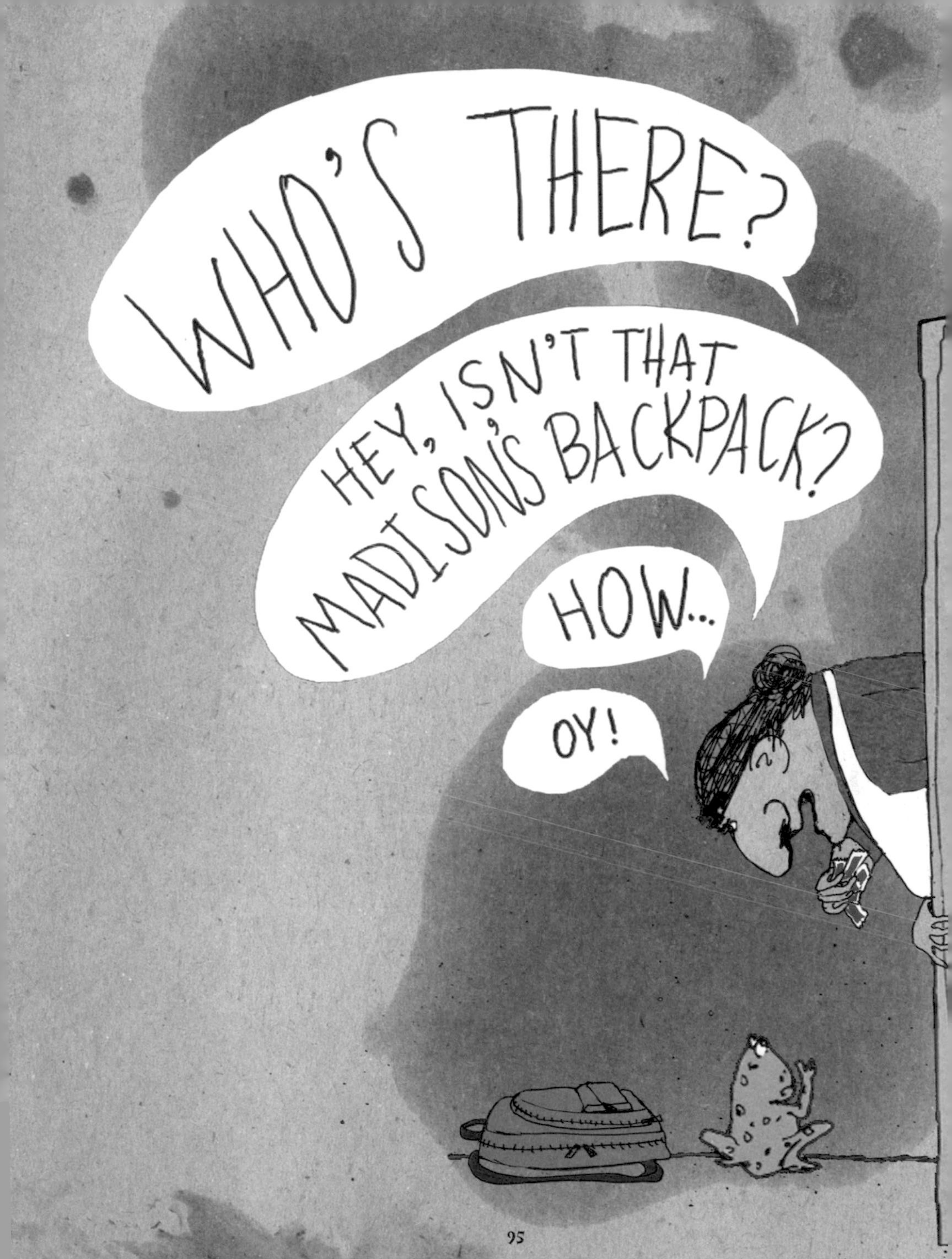
WHO'S THERE?
HEY, ISN'T THAT MADISON'S BACKPACK?
HOW...
OY!

Before Grunhilda can pick Madison up, the bell rings...

Bwrrrppt!

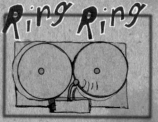

Ring Ring

Watch it!

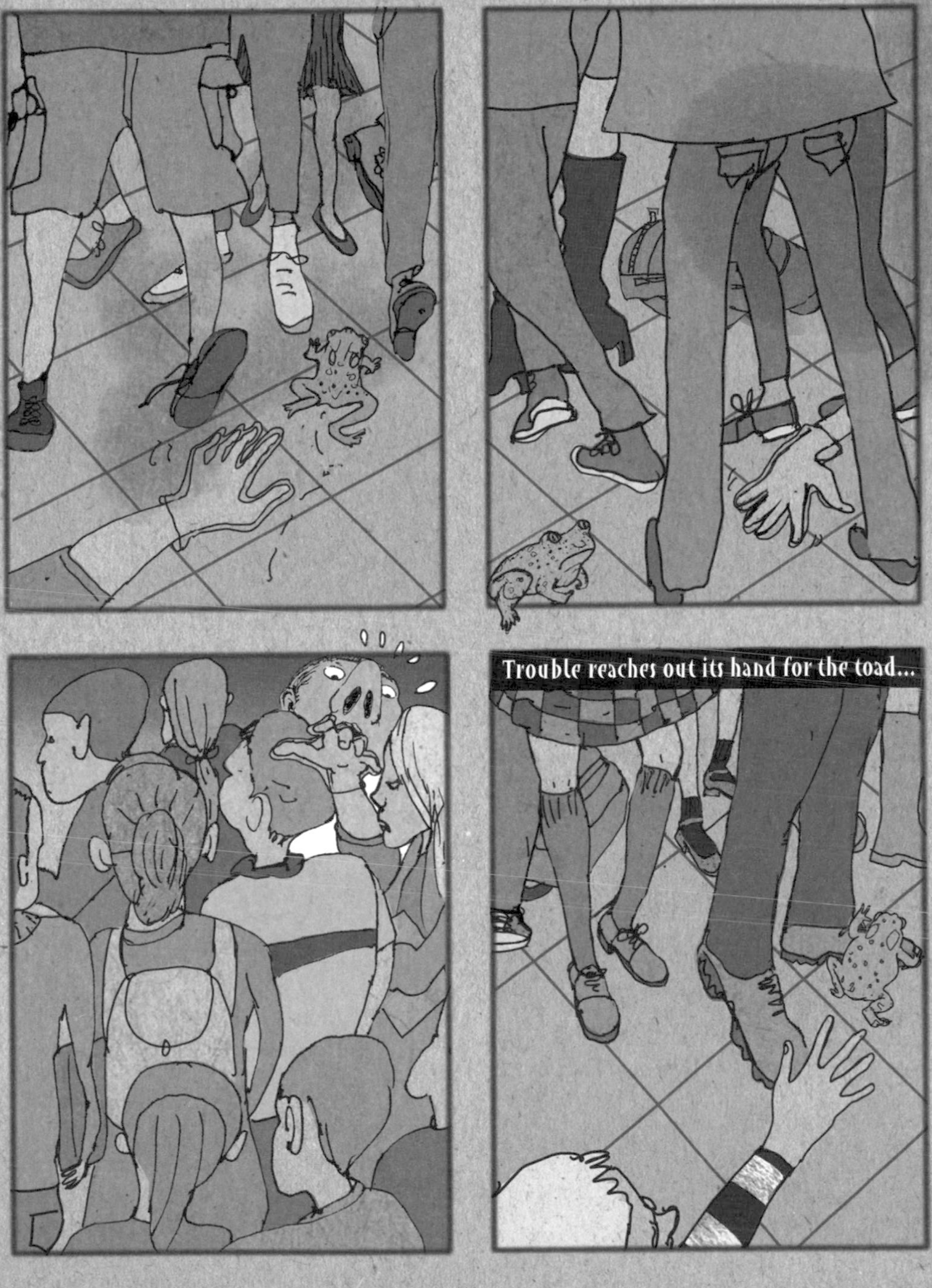
Trouble reaches out its hand for the toad...

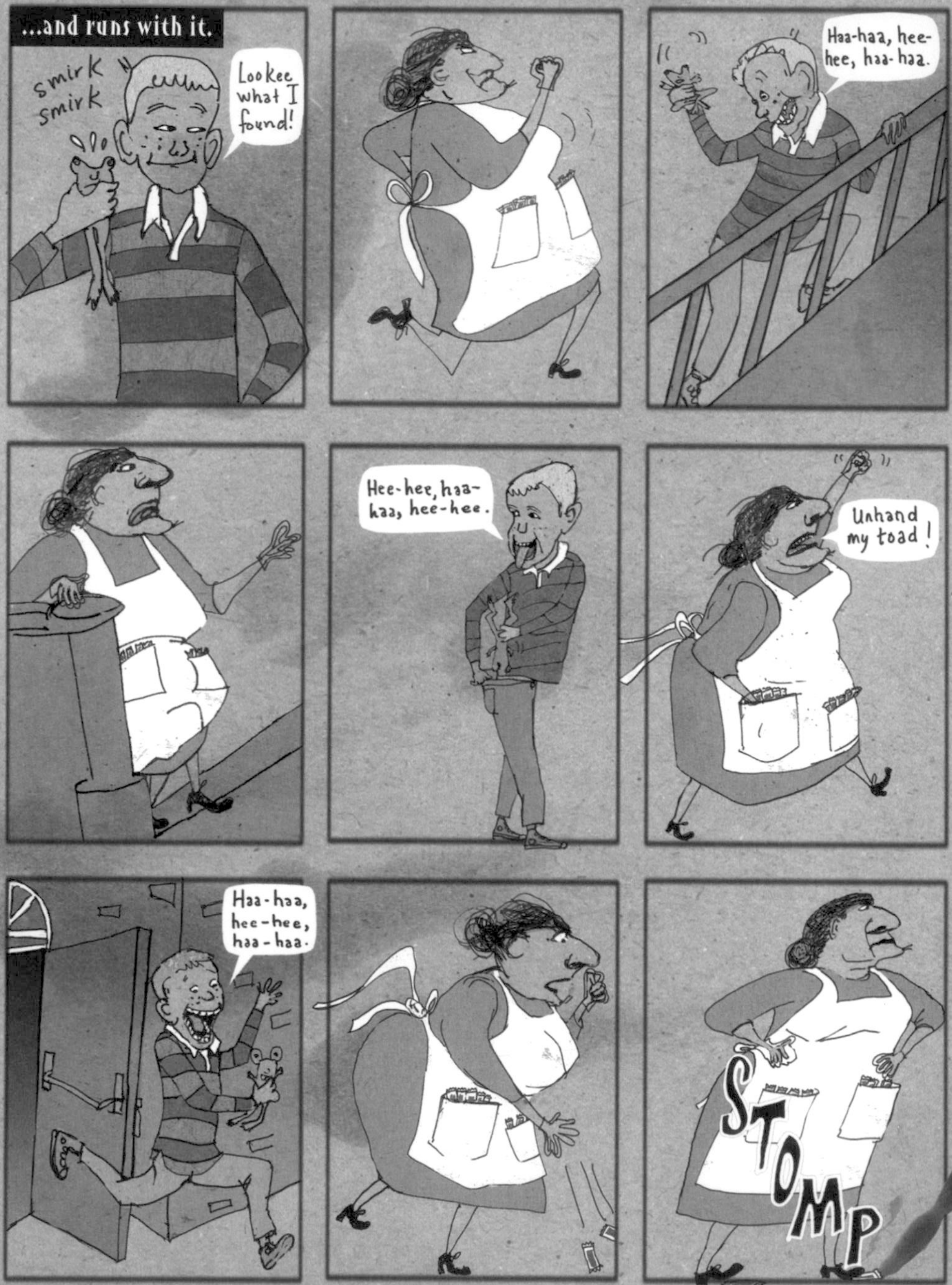
...and runs with it.
smirk smirk
Lookee what I found!
Haa-haa, hee-hee, haa-haa.
Hee-hee, haa-haa, hee-hee.
Unhand my toad!
Haa-haa, hee-hee, haa-haa.
STOMP

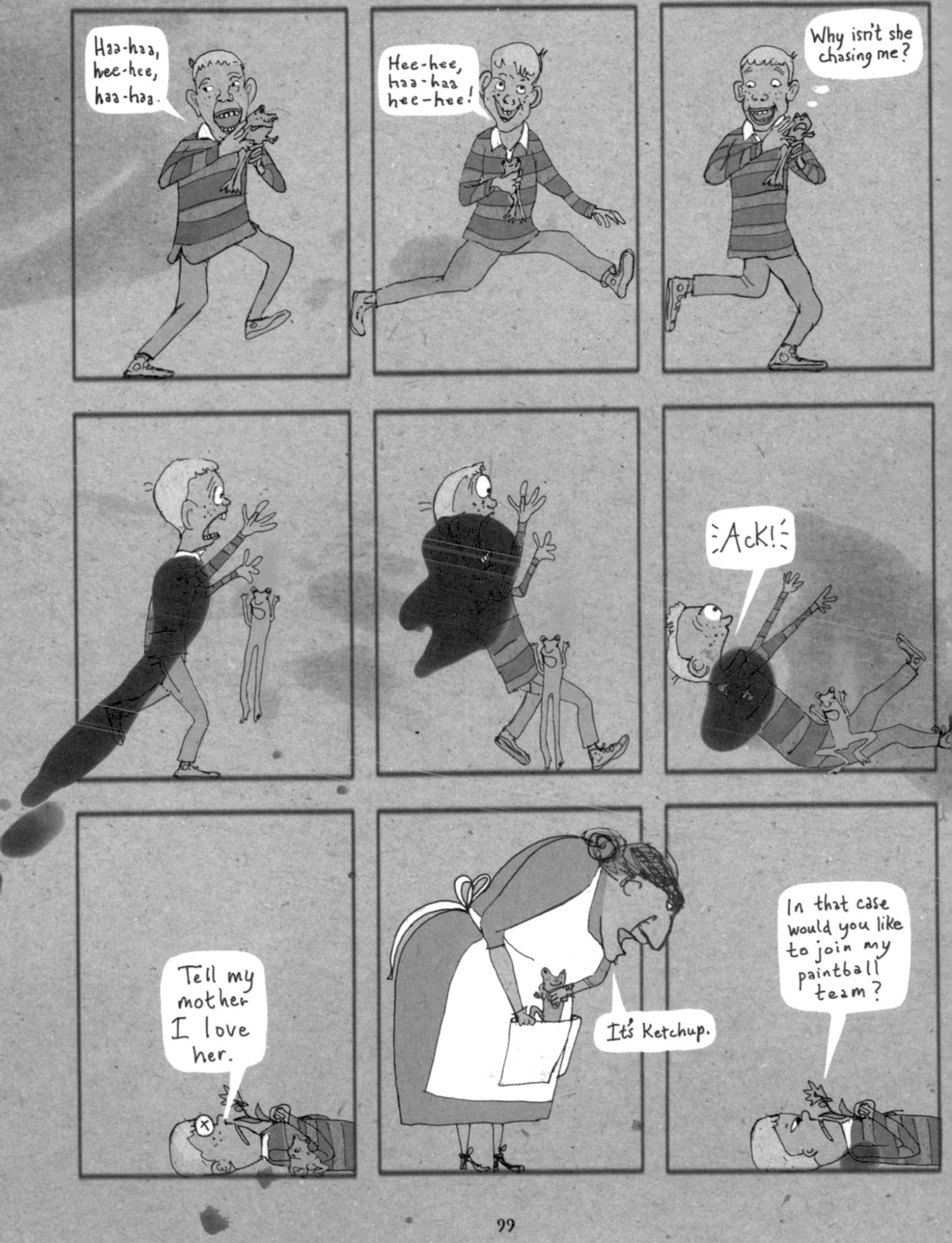
Haa-haa, hee-hee, haa-haa.
Hee-hee, haa-haa hee-hee!
Why isn't she chasing me?
Ack!
Tell my mother I love her.
It's Ketchup.
In that case would you like to join my paintball team?

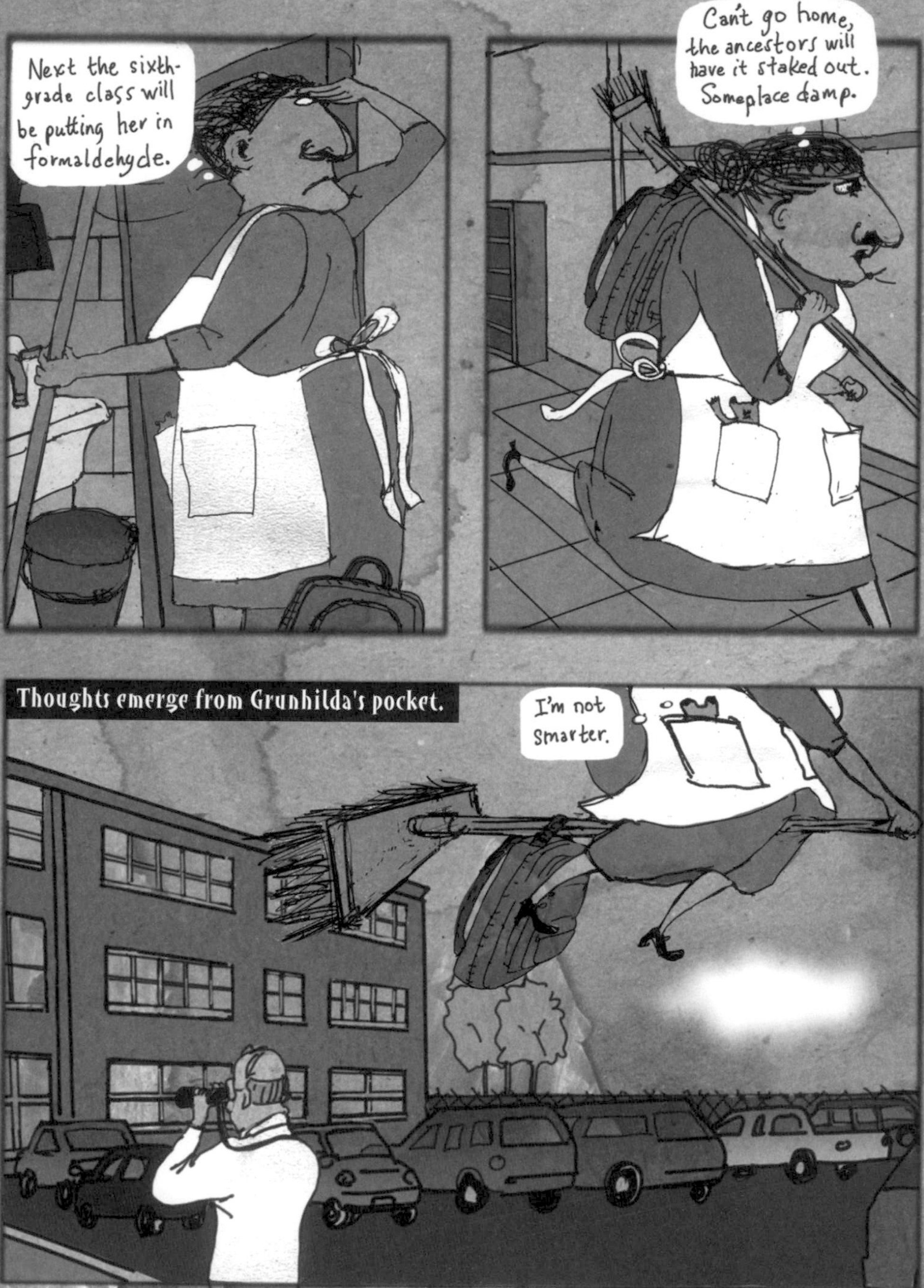
Next the sixth-grade class will be putting her in formaldehyde.
Can't go home, the ancestors will have it staked out. Someplace damp.
Thoughts emerge from Grunhilda's pocket.
I'm not smarter.

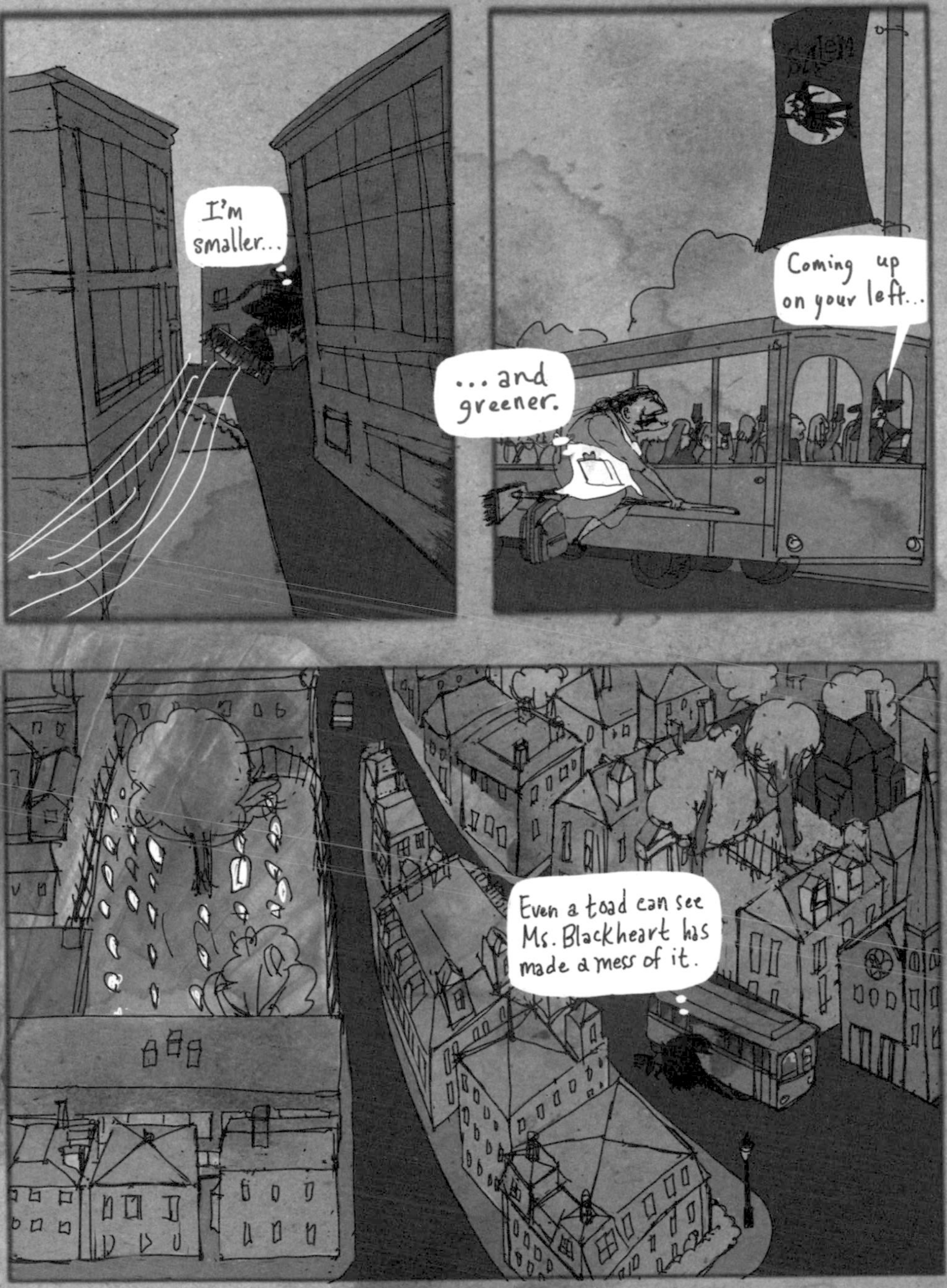
I'm smaller...
Coming up on your left...
...and greener.
Even a toad can see Ms. Blackheart has made a mess of it.

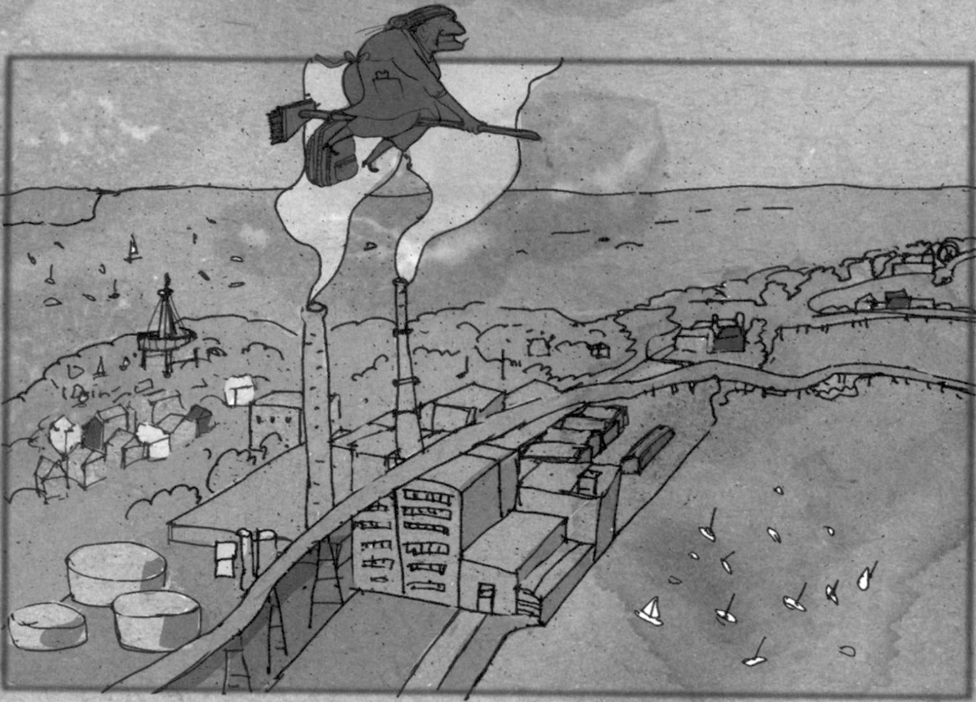

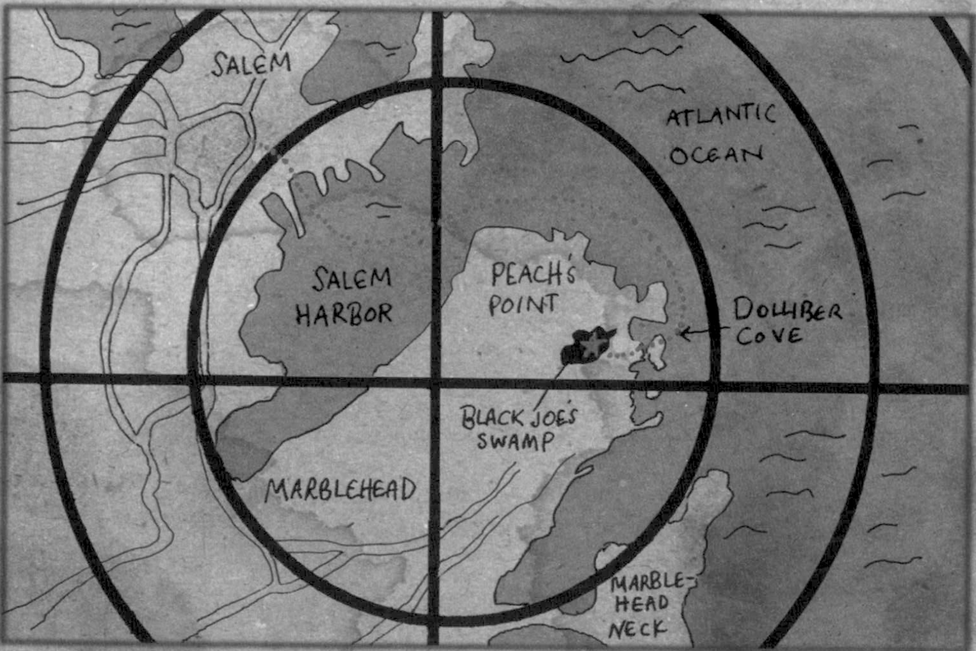
SALEM
ATLANTIC OCEAN
SALEM HARBOR
PEACH'S POINT
DOLLIBER COVE
BLACK JOE'S SWAMP
MARBLEHEAD
MARBLEHEAD NECK

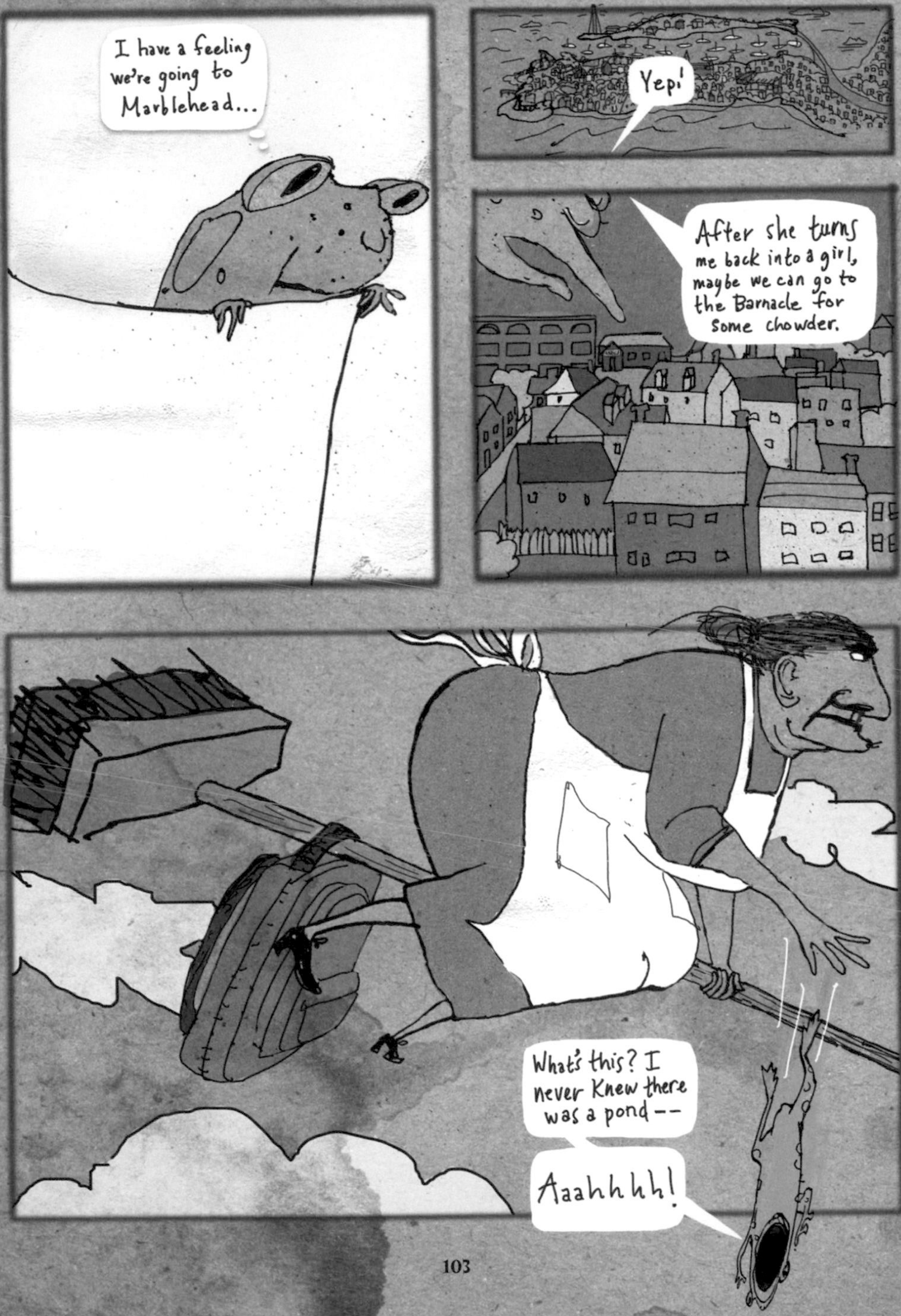
I have a feeling we're going to Marblehead...
Yep!
After she turns me back into a girl, maybe we can go to the Barnacle for some chowder.
What's this? I never Knew there was a pond --
Aaahhhh!

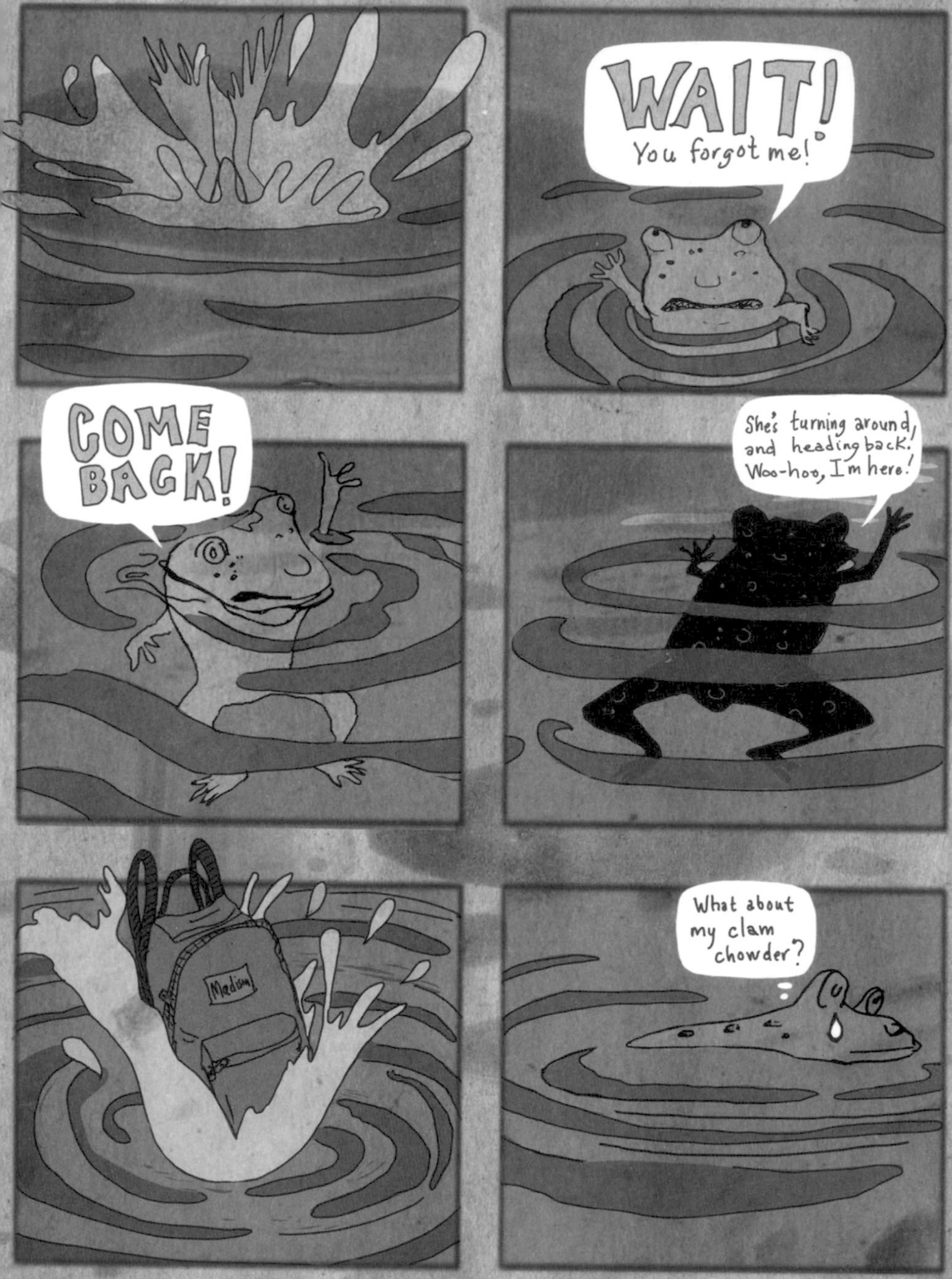
WAIT! You forgot me!
COME BACK!
She's turning around, and heading back! Woo-hoo, I'm here!
Madison
What about my clam chowder?

11th

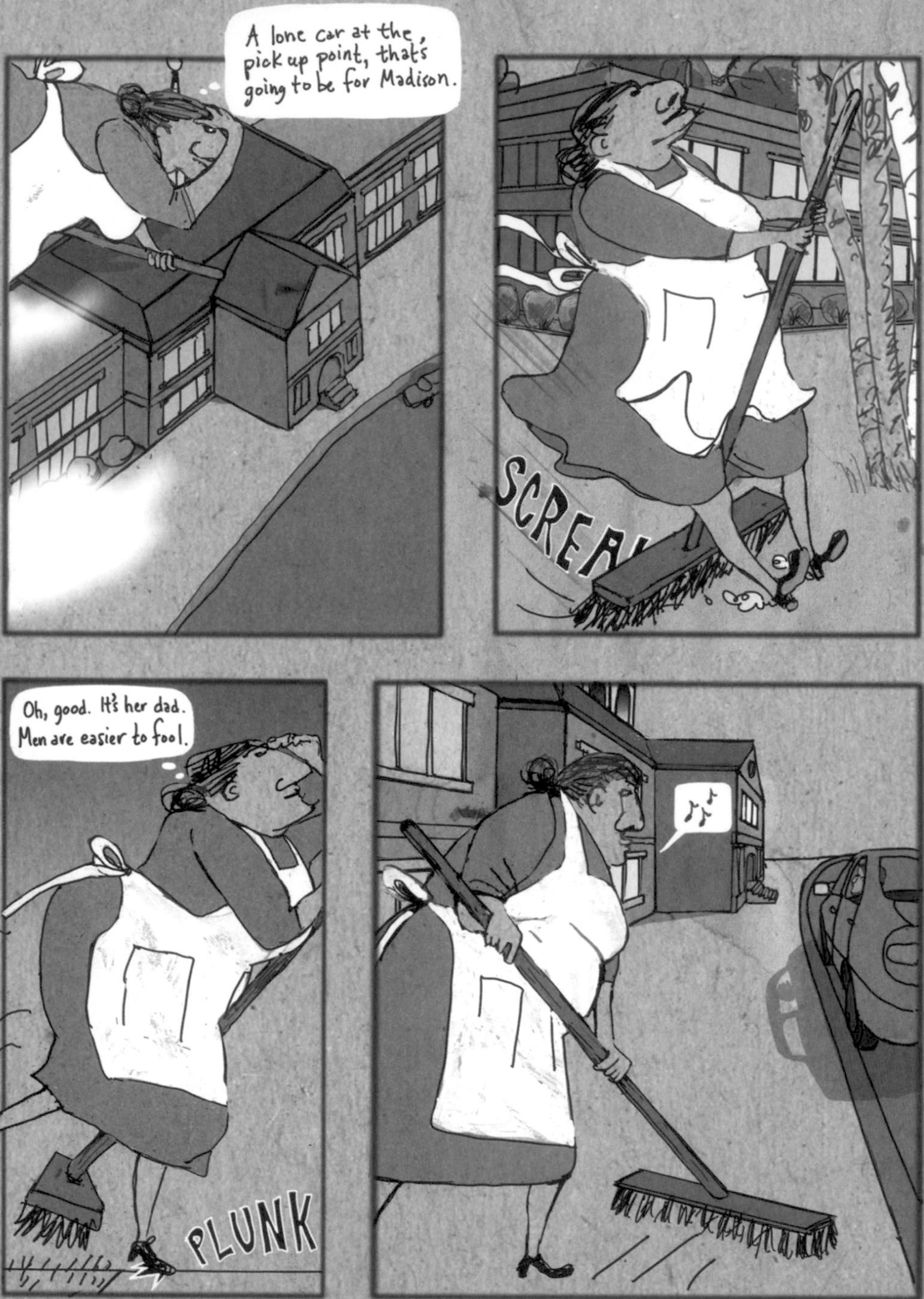
A lone car at the pick up point, that's going to be for Madison.
SCREA
Oh, good. It's her dad. Men are easier to fool.
PLUNK

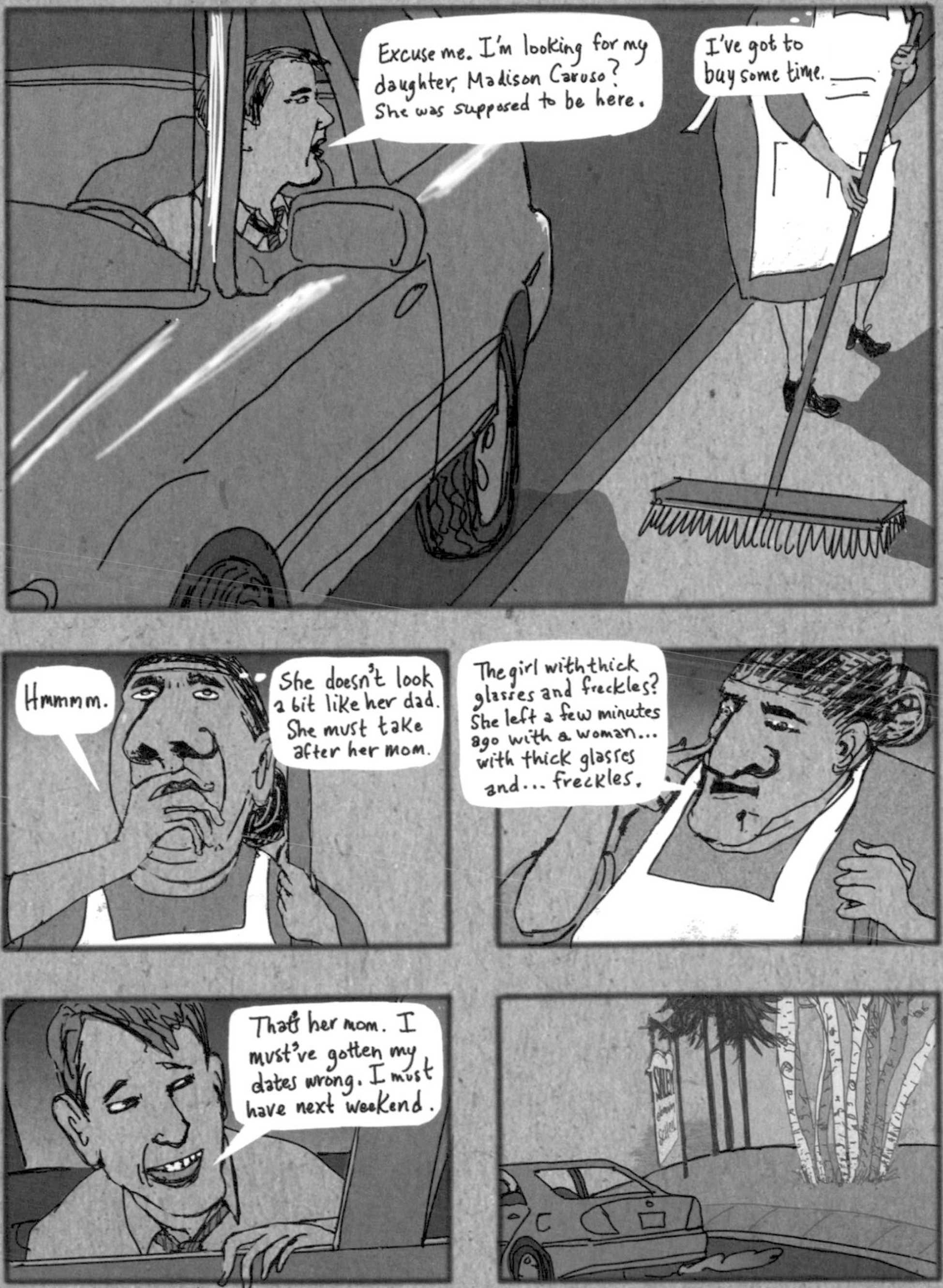
Excuse me. I'm looking for my daughter, Madison Caruso? She was supposed to be here.
I've got to buy some time.
Hmmmm.
She doesn't look a bit like her dad. She must take after her mom.
The girl with thick glasses and freckles? She left a few minutes ago with a woman... with thick glasses and... freckles.
That's her mom. I must've gotten my dates wrong. I must have next weekend.

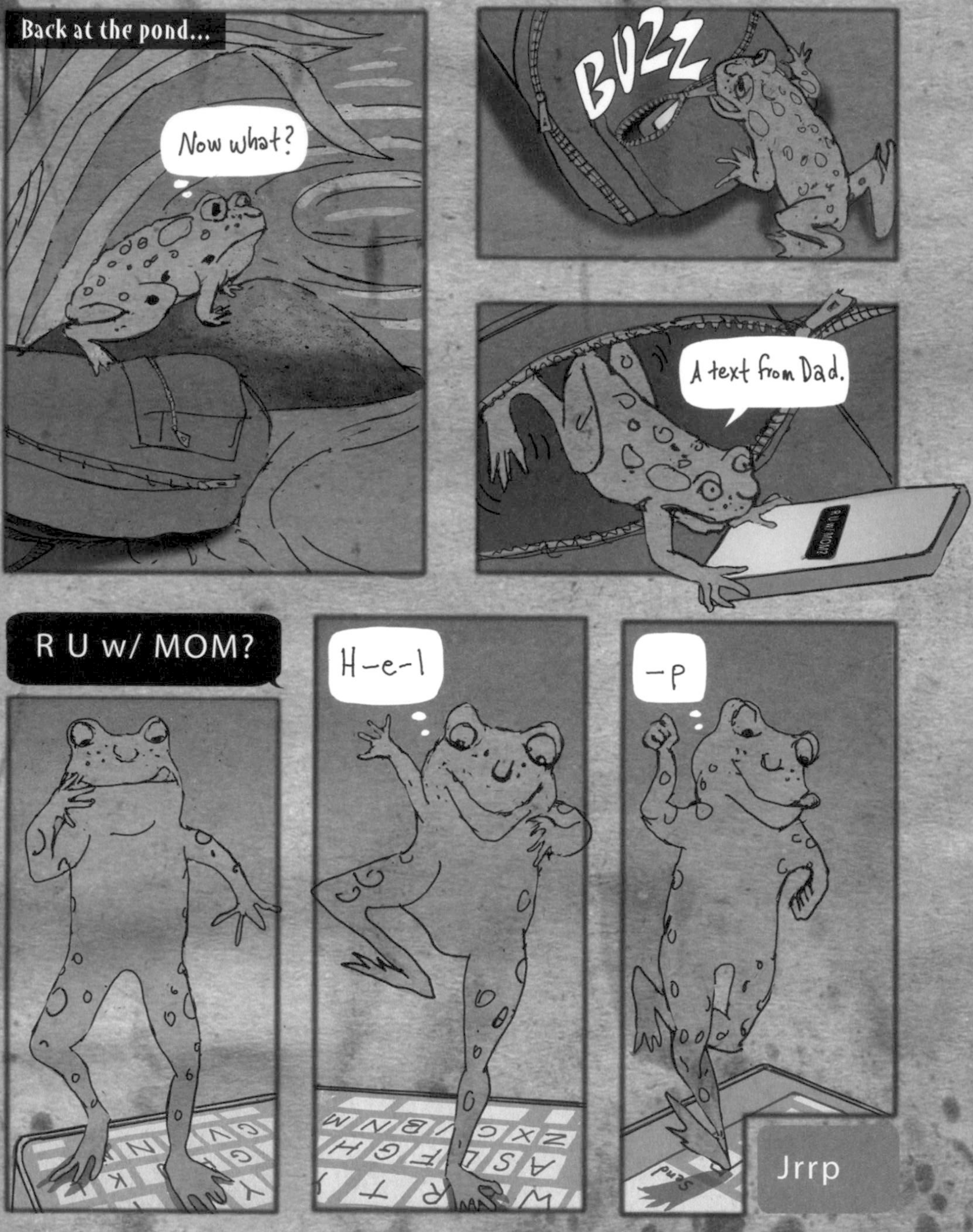
Back at the pond...
Now what?
BUZZ
A text from Dad.
R U w/ MOM?
H-e-l
-p
Jrrp

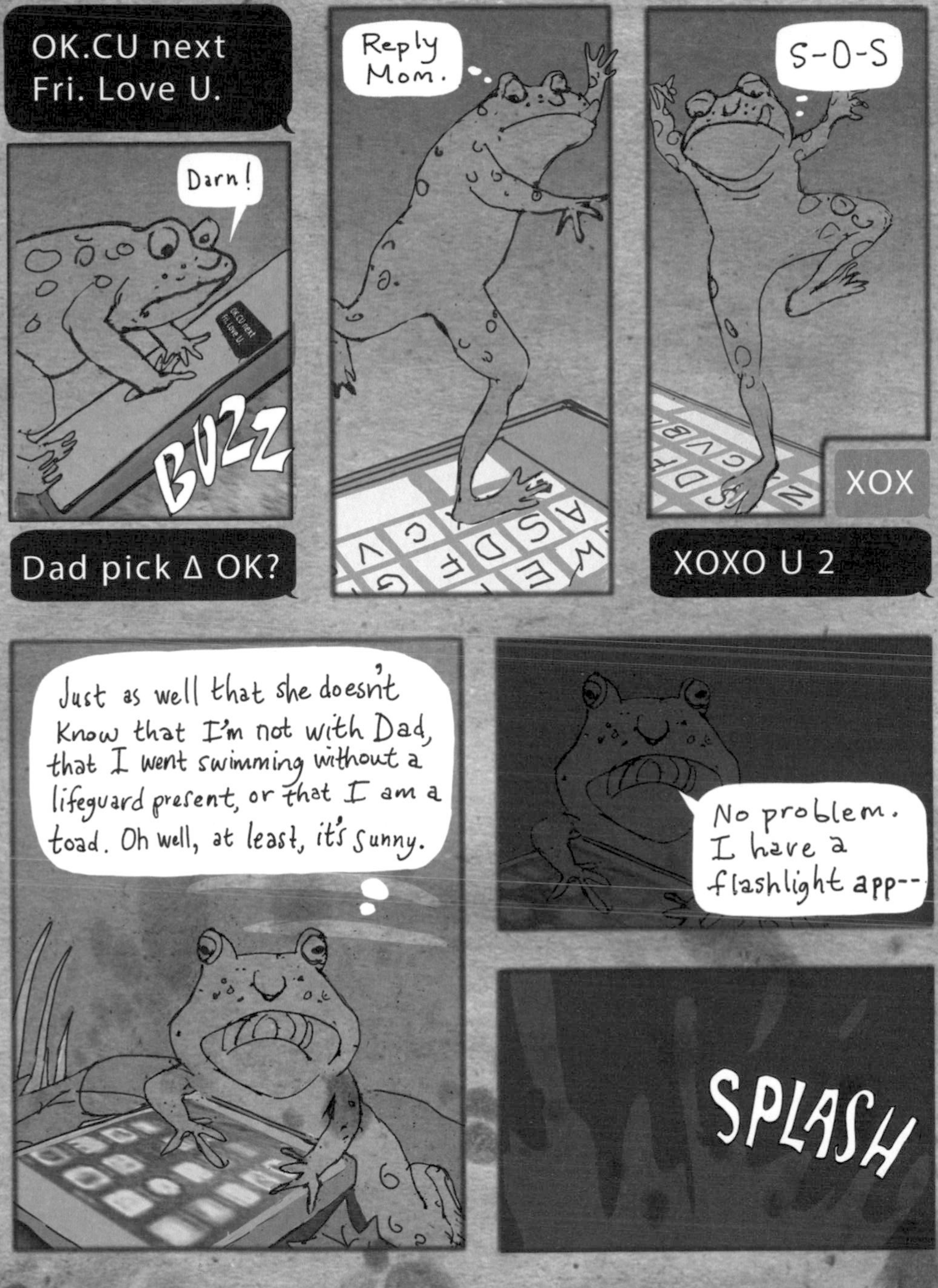
OK.CU next Fri. Love U.
Darn!
BUZZ
Dad pick Δ OK?
Reply Mom.
S-O-S
XOX
XOXO U 2
Just as well that she doesn't know that I'm not with Dad, that I went swimming without a lifeguard present, or that I am a toad. Oh well, at least, it's sunny.
No problem. I have a flashlight app--
SPLASH

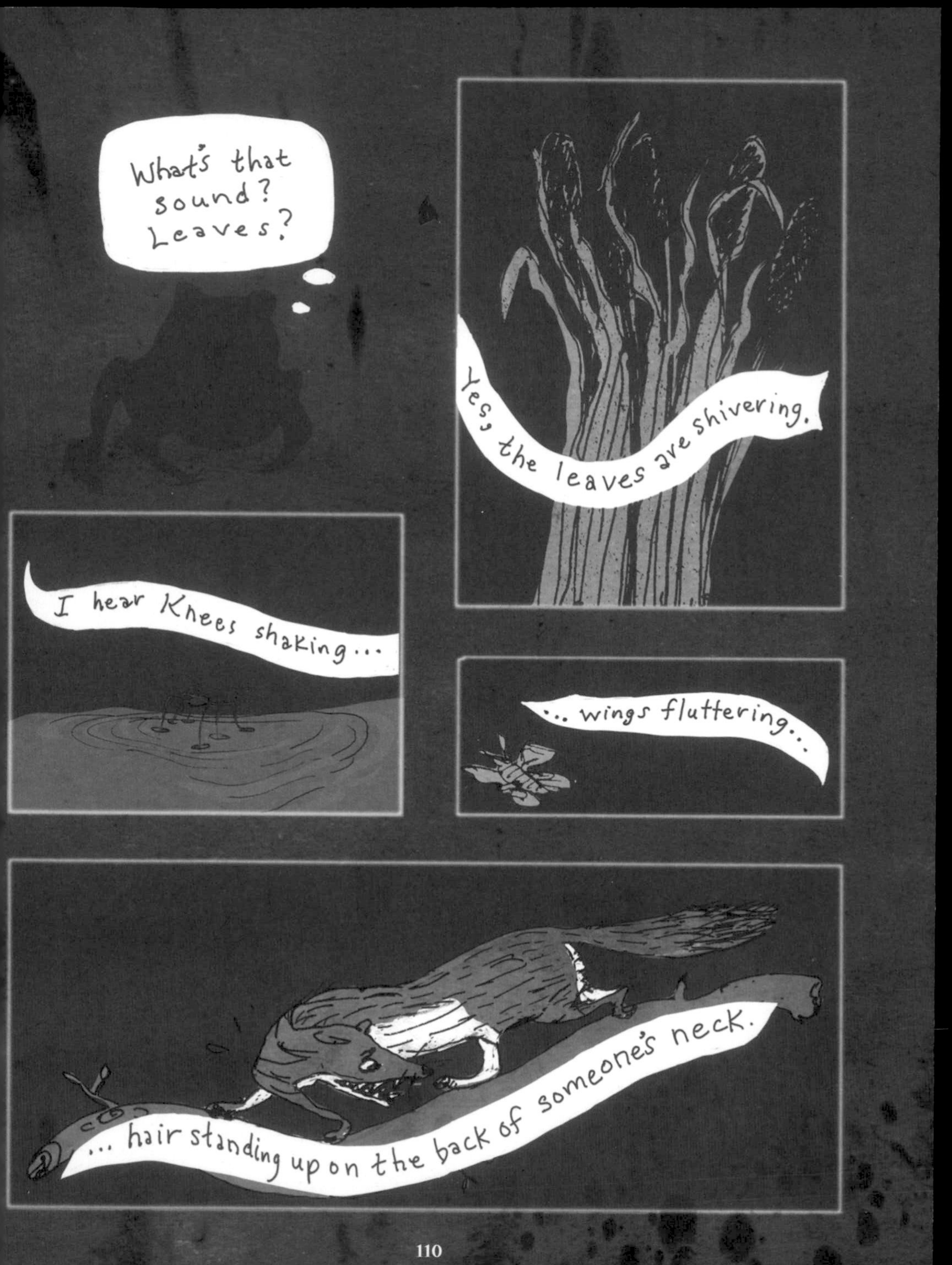
What's that sound? Leaves?
Yes, the leaves are shivering.
I hear knees shaking...
... wings fluttering...
... hair standing up on the back of someone's neck.

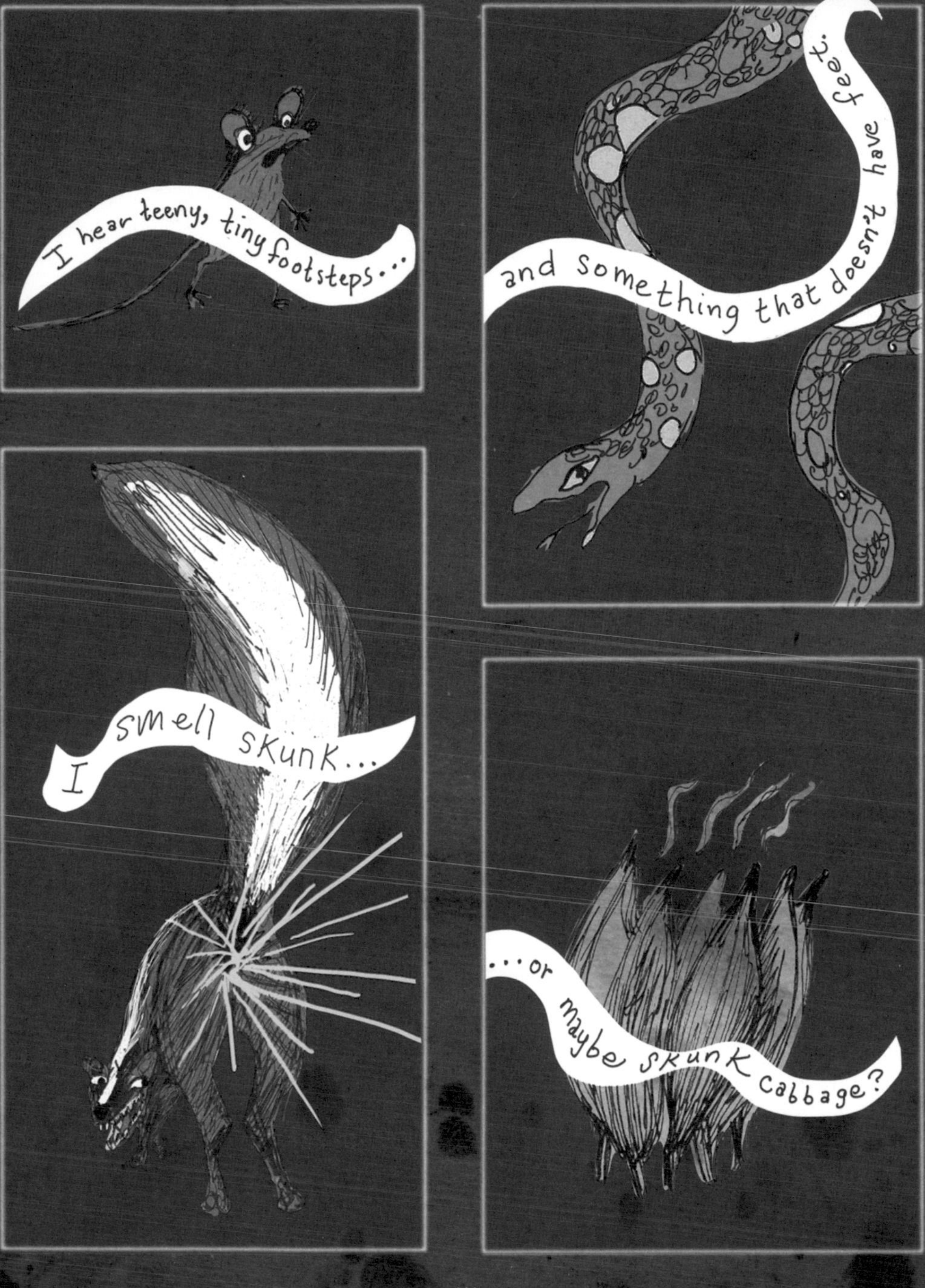
I hear teeny, tiny footsteps...
and something that doesn't have feet.
I smell skunk...
...or maybe skunk cabbage?

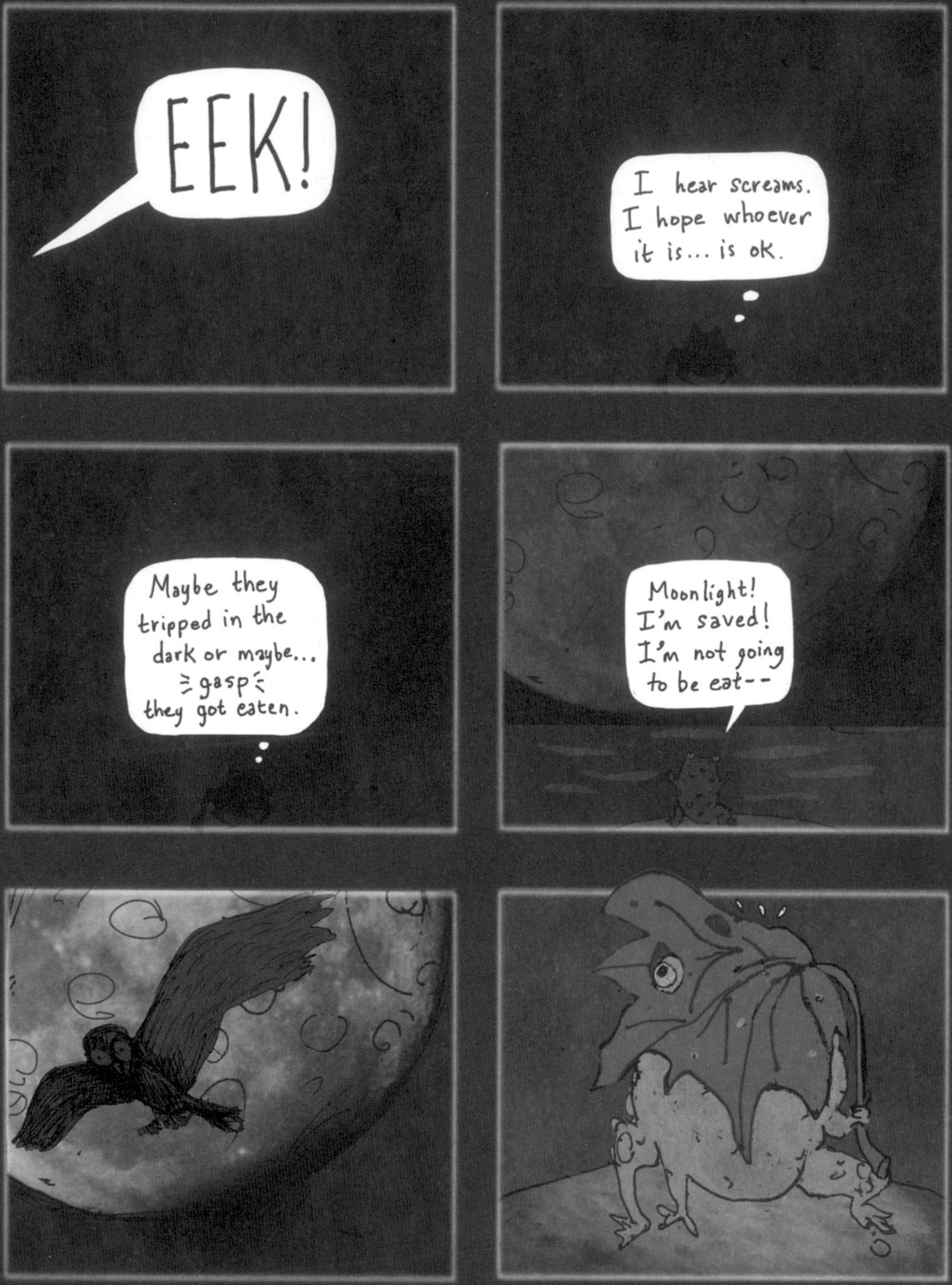
EEK!
I hear screams. I hope whoever it is... is ok.
Maybe they tripped in the dark or maybe... gasp they got eaten.
Moonlight! I'm saved! I'm not going to be eat--

12th

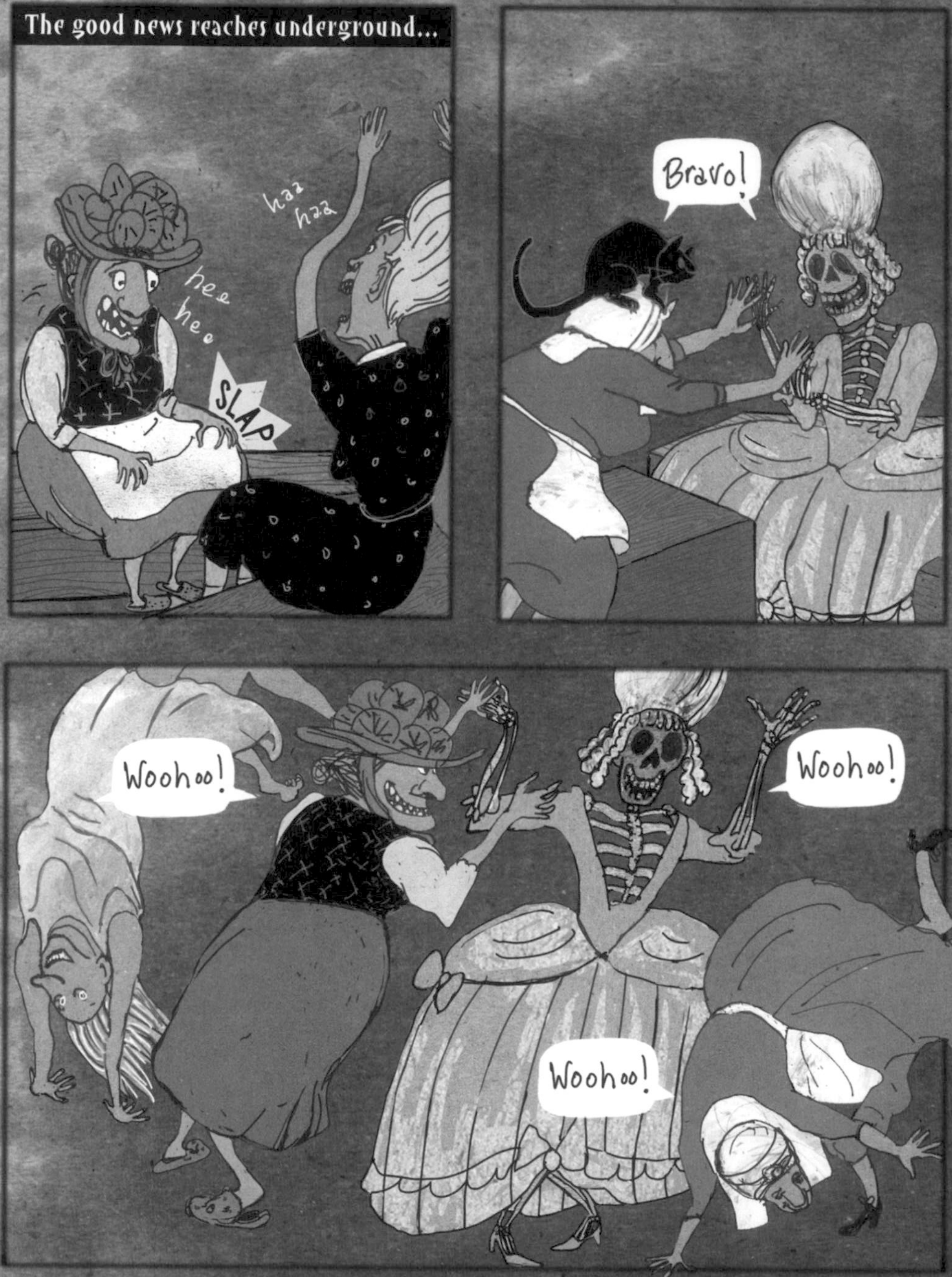
The good news reaches underground...
haa haa
hee hee
SLAP
Bravo!
Woohoo!
Woohoo!
Woohoo!

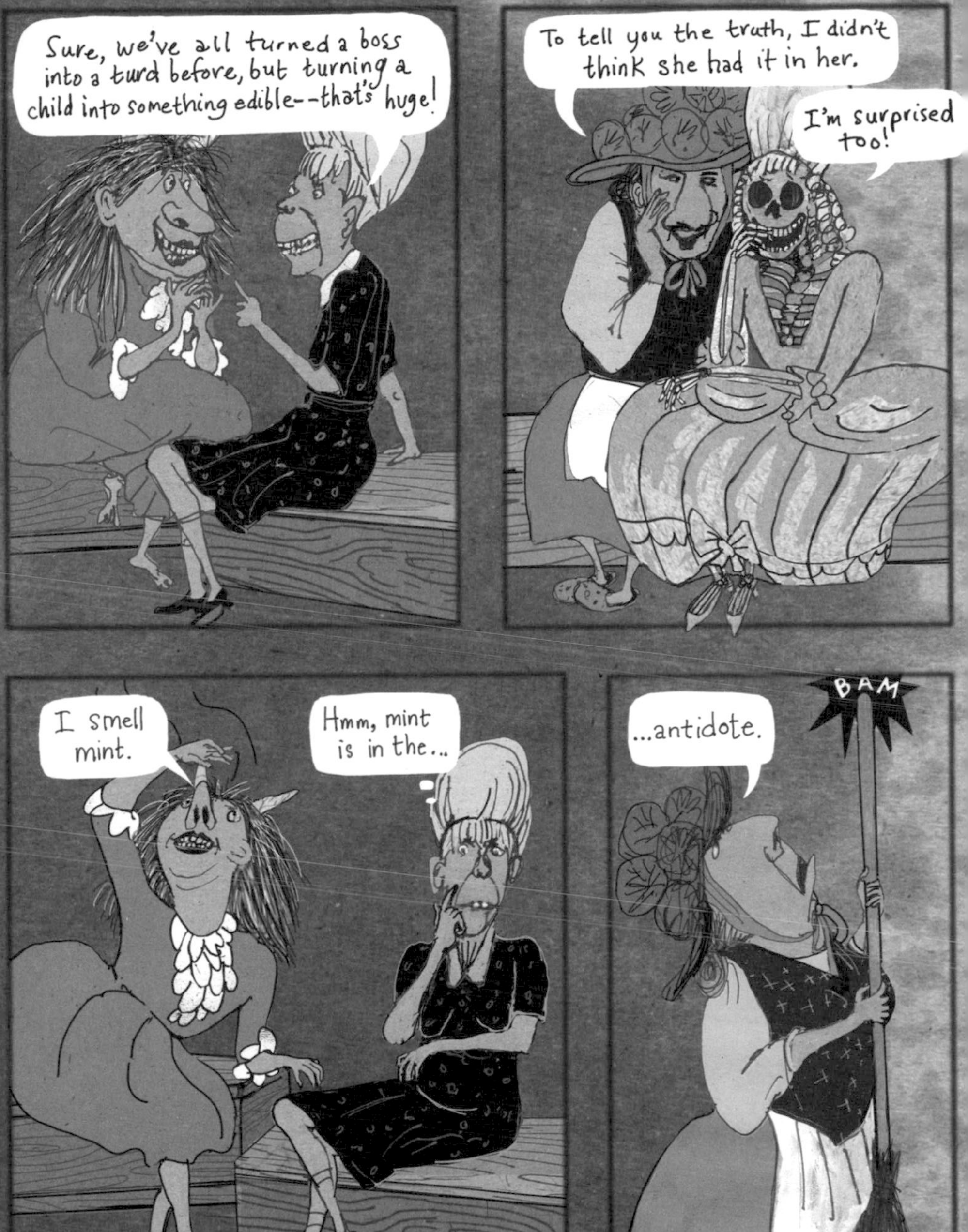

Sure, we've all turned a boss into a turd before, but turning a child into something edible--that's huge!
To tell you the truth, I didn't think she had it in her.
I'm surprised too!
I smell mint.
Hmm, mint is in the...
...antidote.
BAM

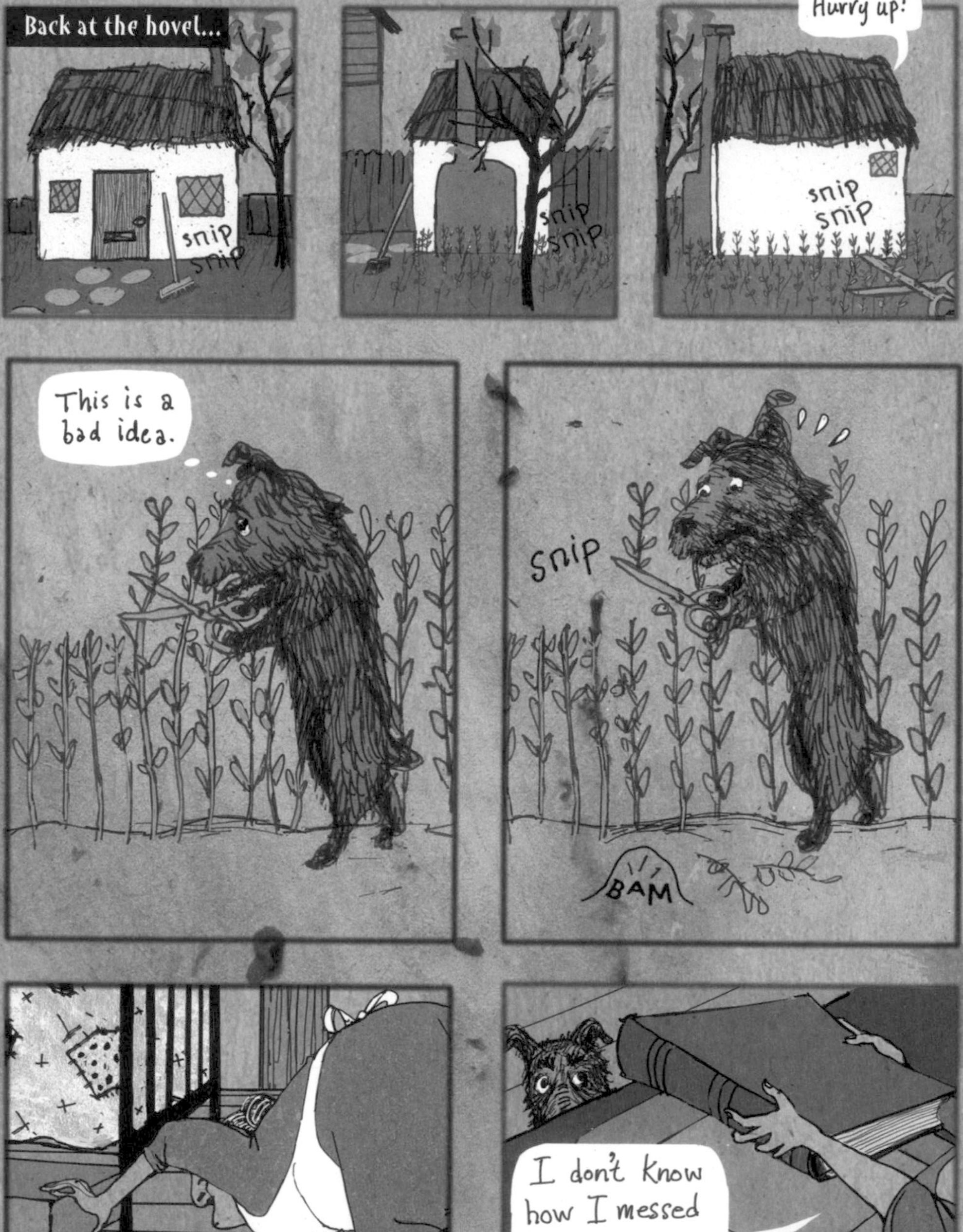
Back at the hovel...
snip snip
snip snip
Hurry up!
snip snip
This is a bad idea.
snip
BAM
I don't know how I messed that recipe up.

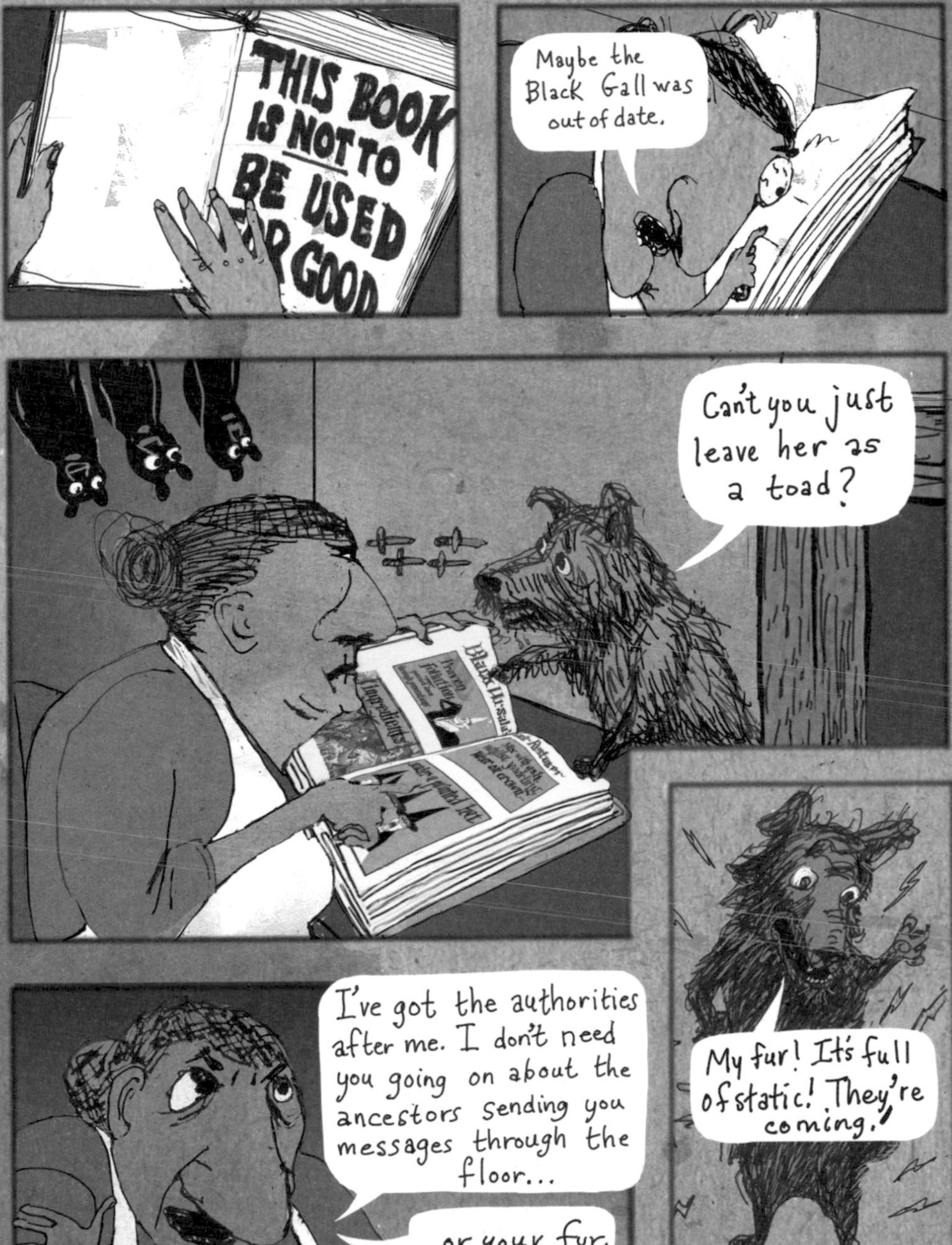
THIS BOOK IS NOT TO BE USED FOR GOOD
Maybe the Black Gall was out of date.
Can't you just leave her as a toad?
I've got the authorities after me. I don't need you going on about the ancestors sending you messages through the floor...
...or your fur.
My fur! It's full of static! They're coming!

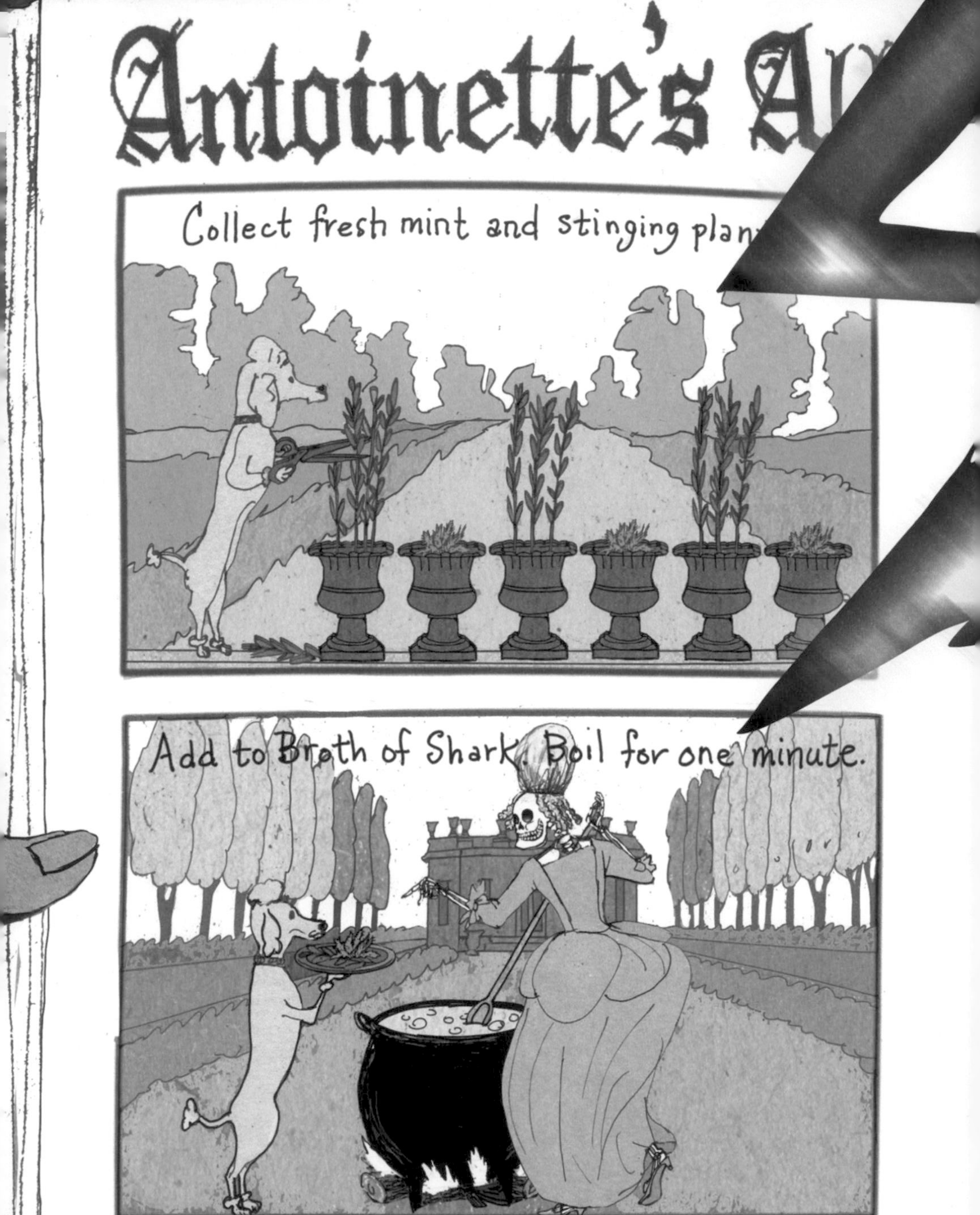
Antoinette's A
Collect fresh mint and stinging plan
Add to Broth of Shark. Boil for one minute.

Purpose Antidote

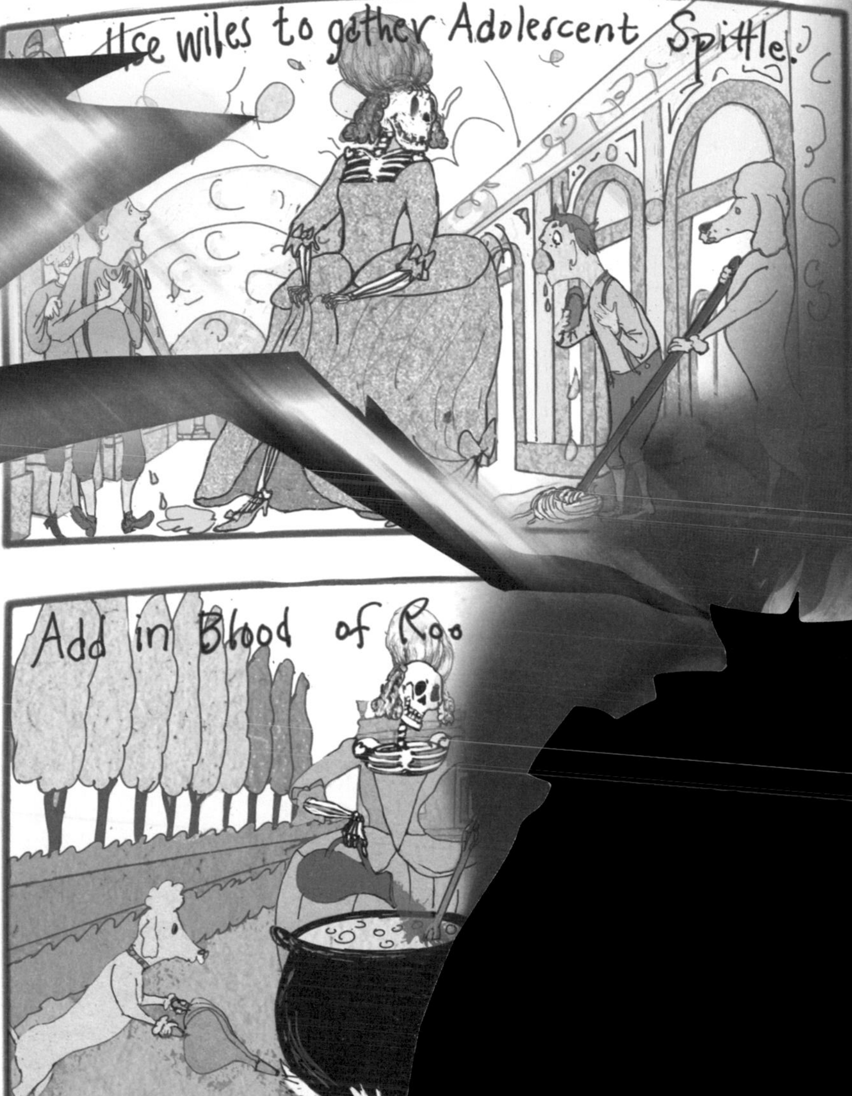
Use wiles to gather Adolescent Spittle.
Add in Blood of

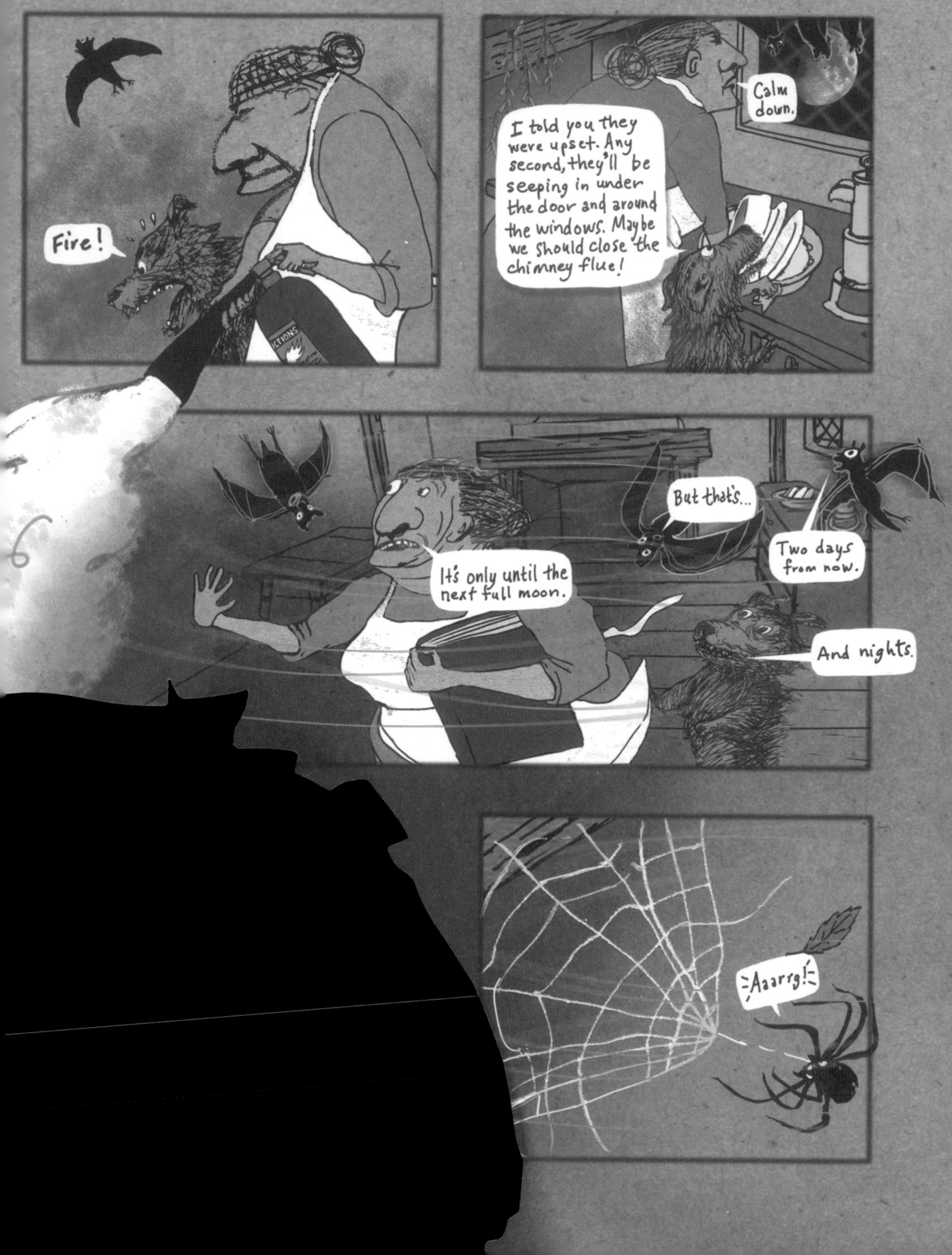
Fire!
I told you they were upset. Any second, they'll be seeping in under the door and around the windows. Maybe we should close the chimney flue!
Calm down.
It's only until the next full moon.
But that's...
Two days from now.
And nights.
Aaarrg!

13th

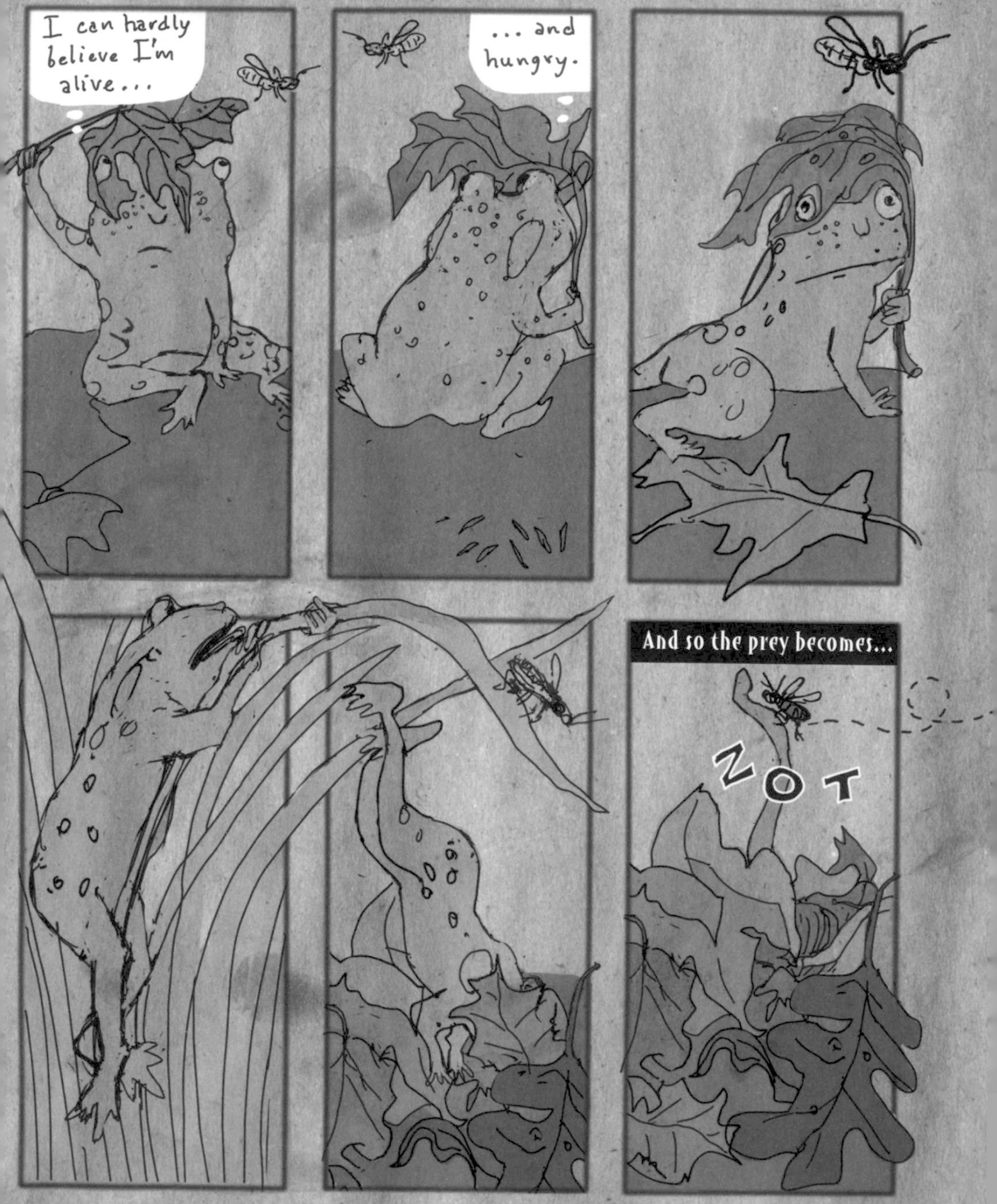
I can hardly believe I'm alive...
... and hungry.
And so the prey becomes...
ZOT

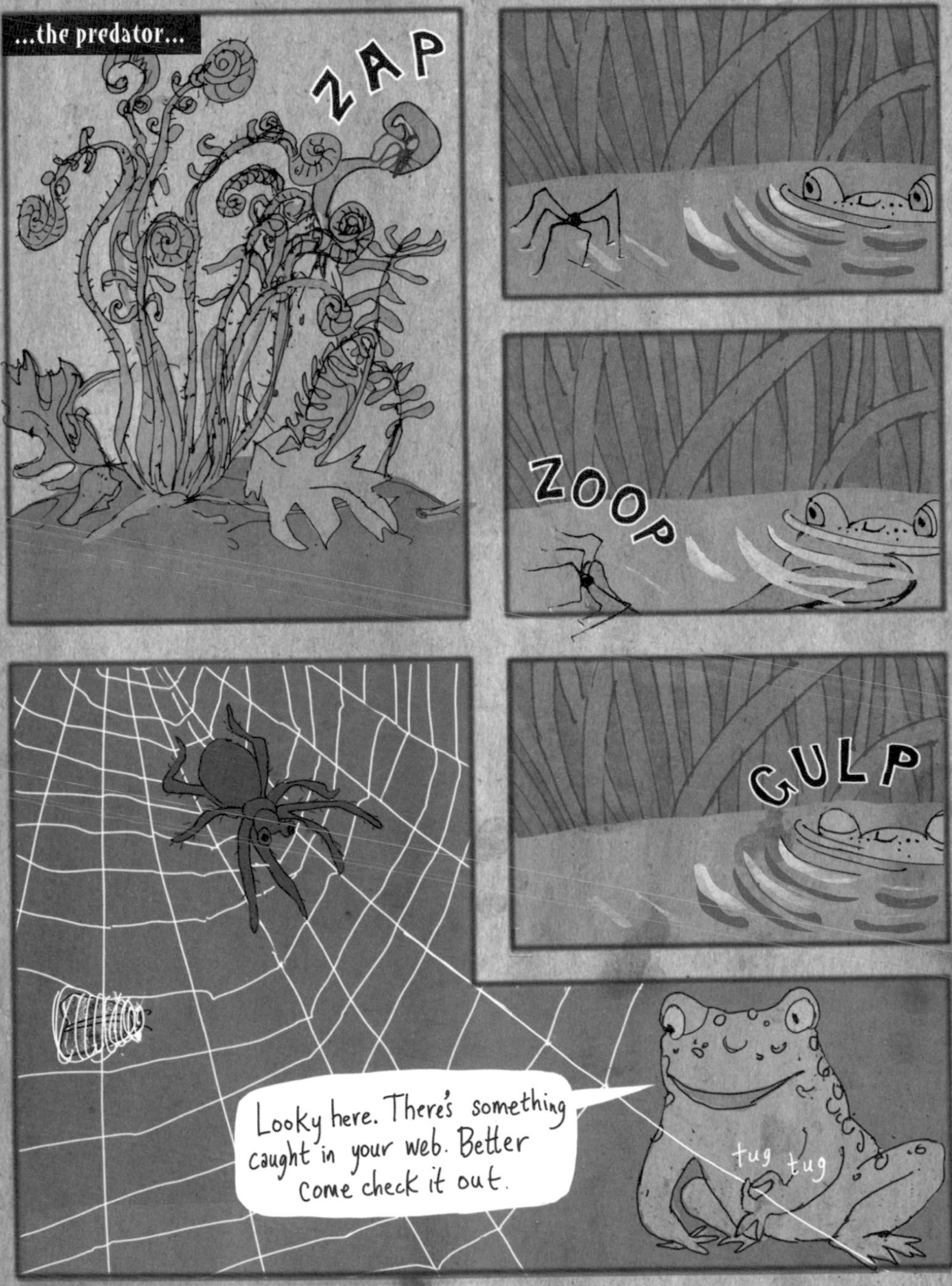
...the predator...
ZAP
ZOOP
GULP
Looky here. There's something caught in your web. Better come check it out.
tug tug

14th

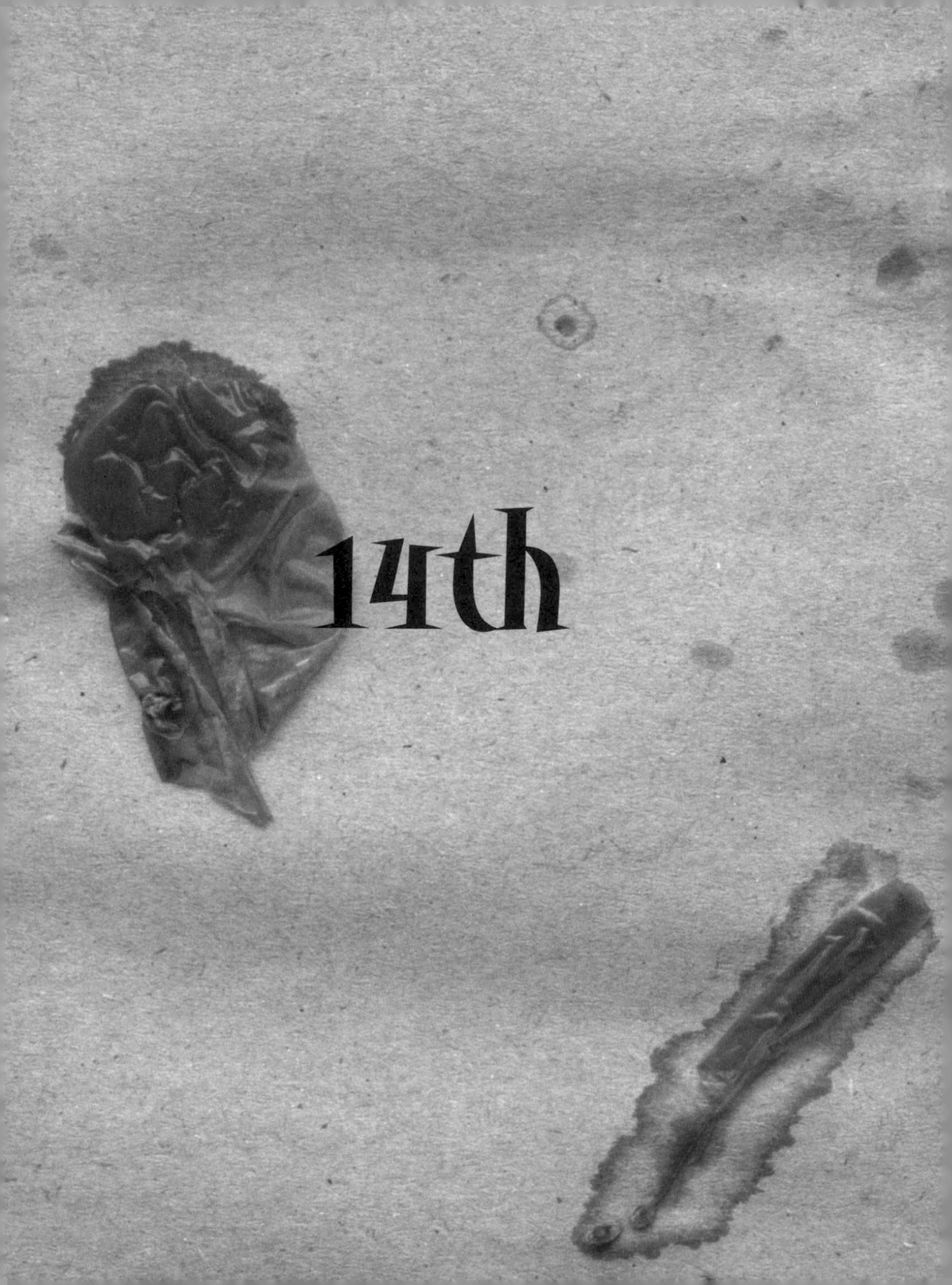

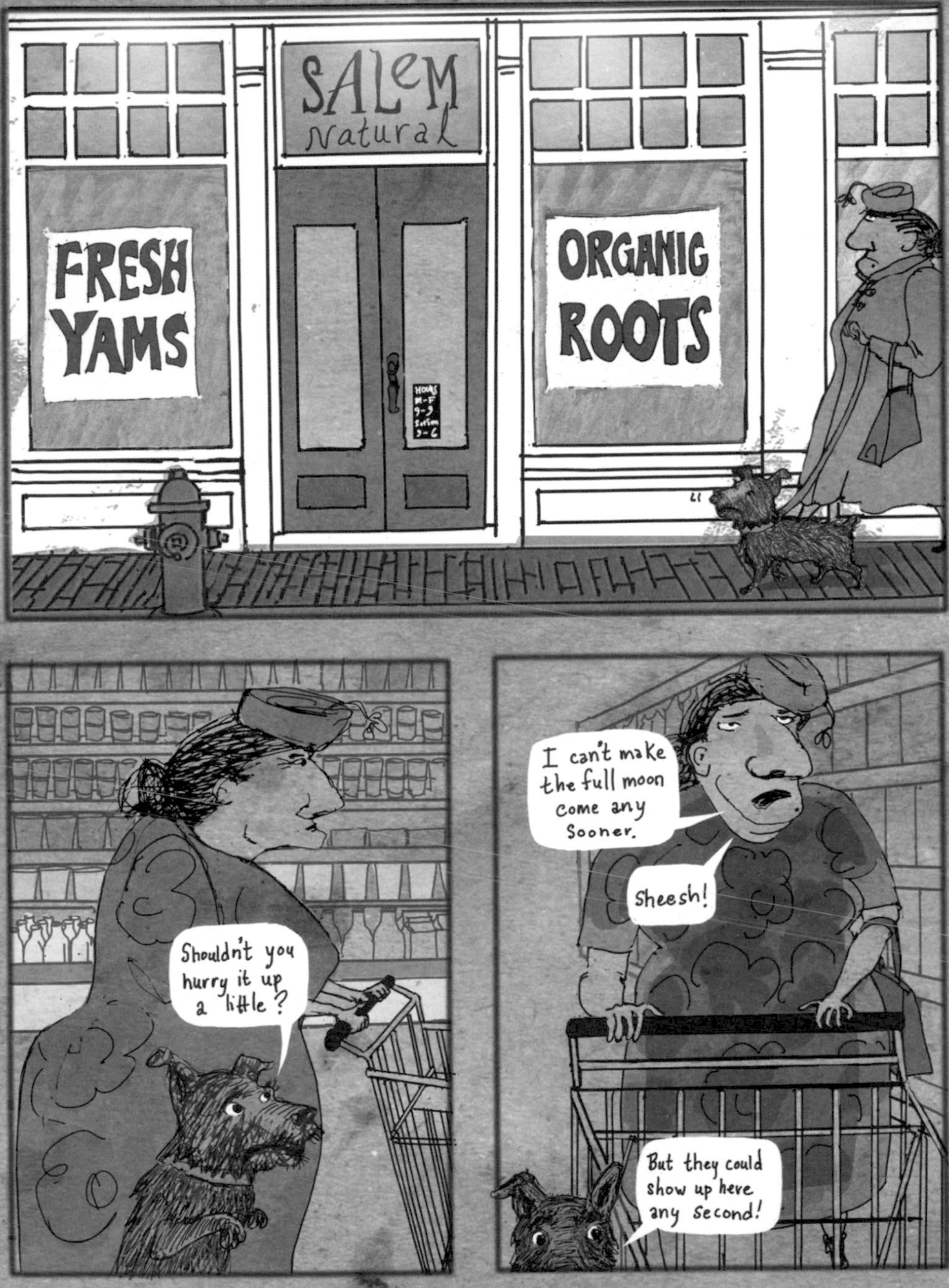
SALEM
Natural
FRESH YAMS
ORGANIC ROOTS
Shouldn't you hurry it up a little?
I can't make the full moon come any sooner.
Sheesh!
But they could show up here any second!

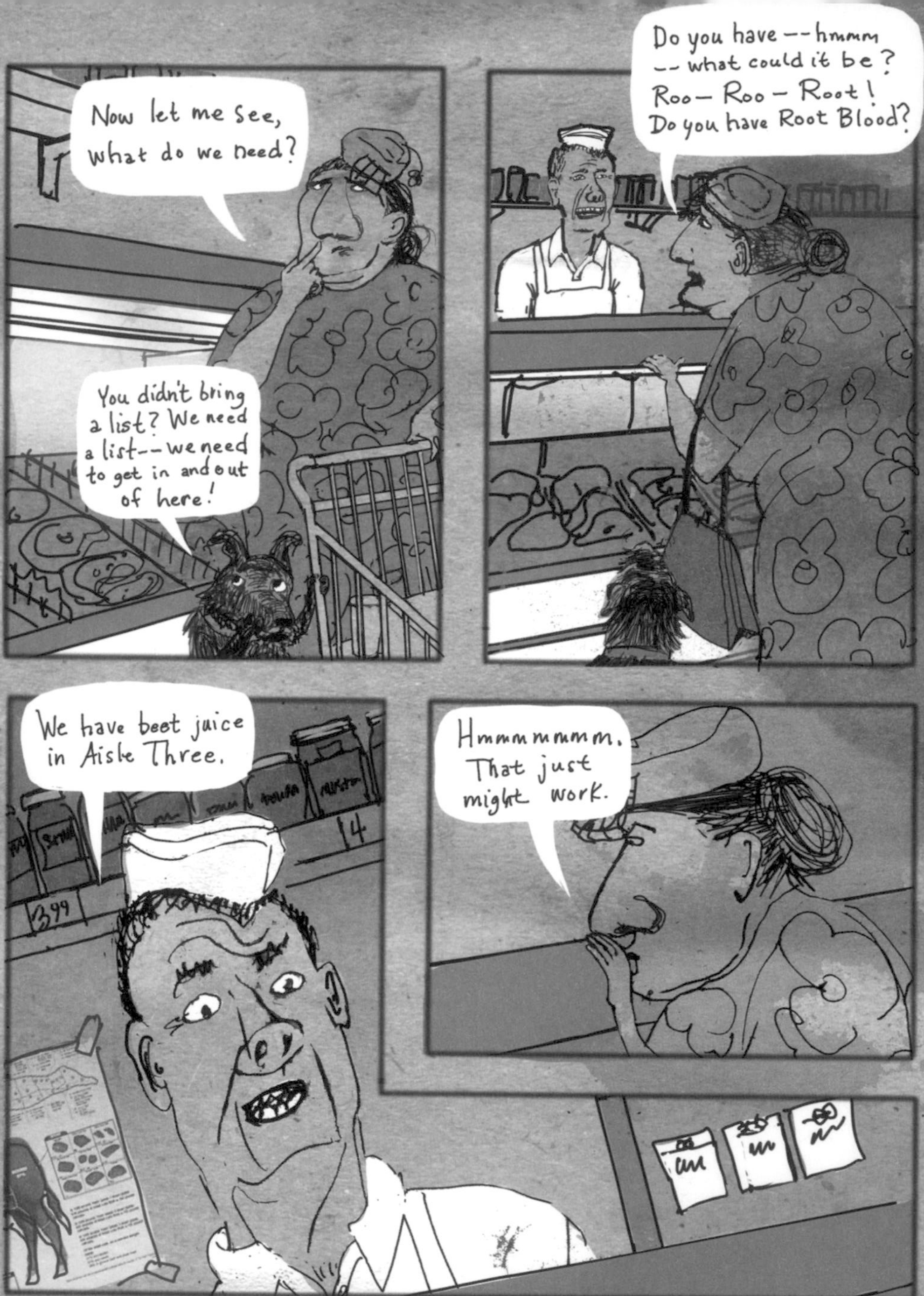
Now let me see, what do we need?
You didn't bring a list? We need a list-- we need to get in and out of here!
Do you have -- hmmm -- what could it be? Roo- Roo- Root! Do you have Root Blood?
We have beet juice in Aisle Three.
Hmmmmmmm. That just might work.

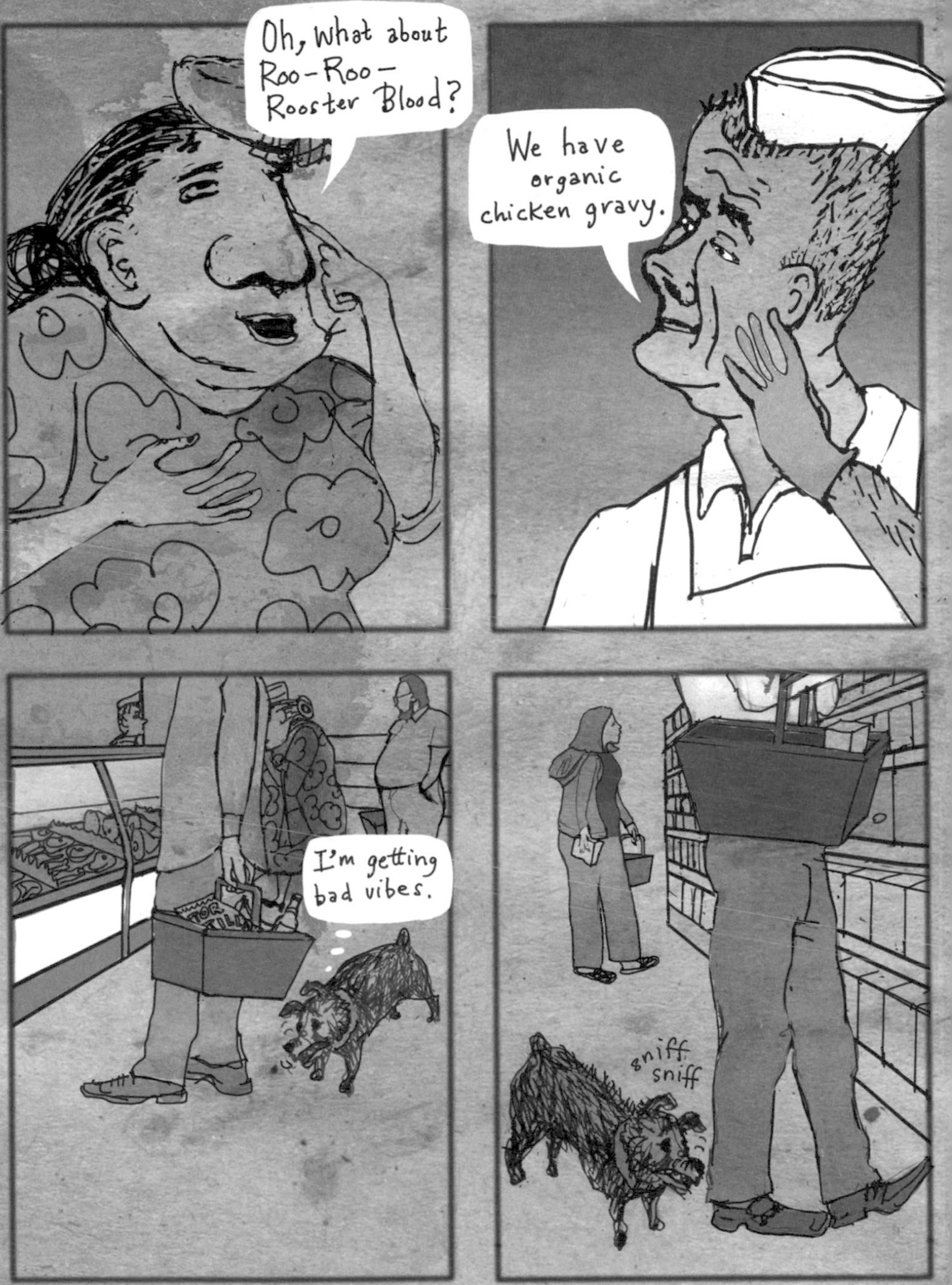
Oh, what about Roo-Roo-Rooster Blood?
We have organic chicken gravy.
I'm getting bad vibes.
sniff sniff

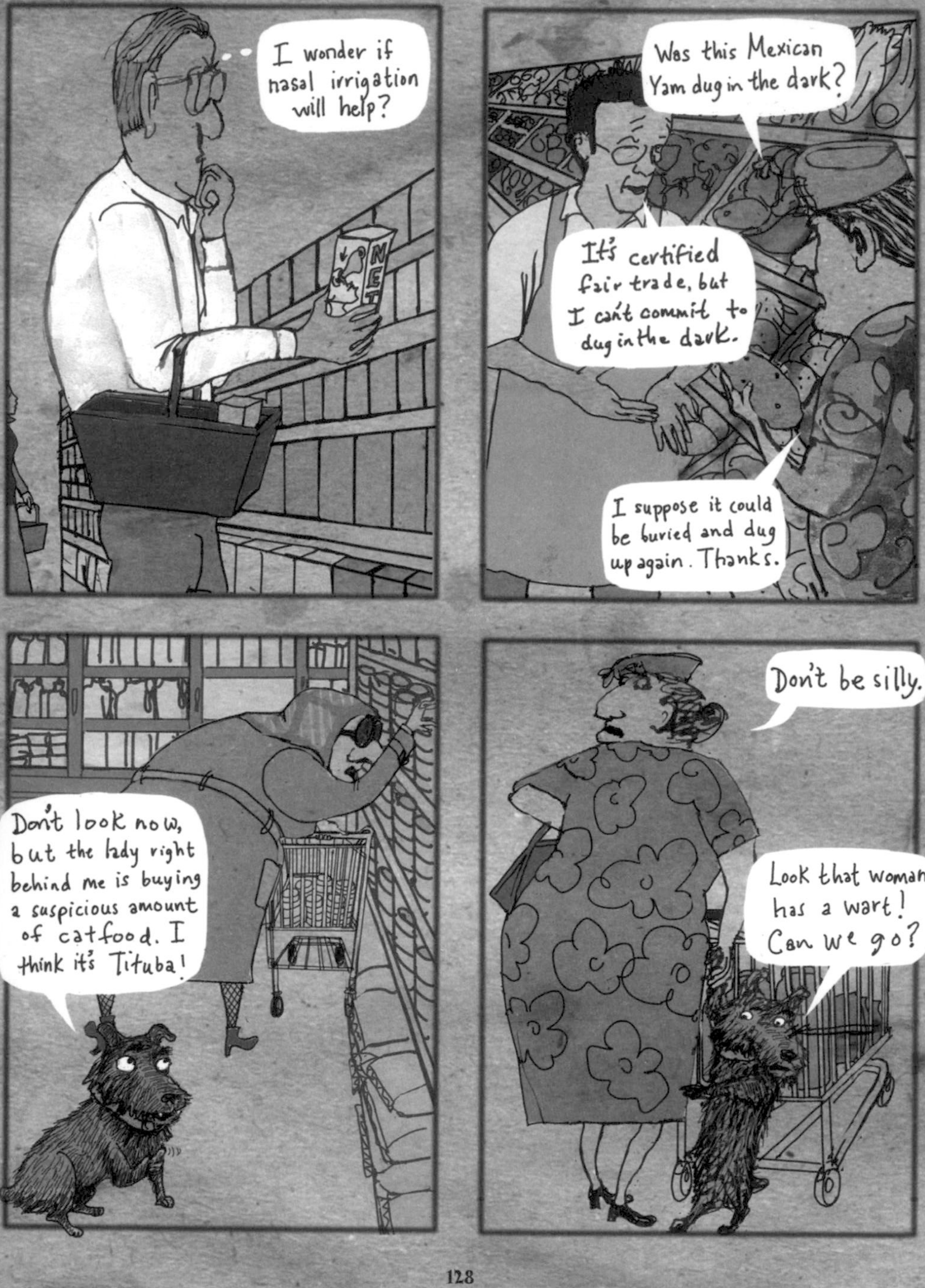
I wonder if nasal irrigation will help?
Was this Mexican Yam dug in the dark?
It's certified fair trade, but I can't commit to dug in the dark.
I suppose it could be buried and dug up again. Thanks.
Don't look now, but the lady right behind me is buying a suspicious amount of catfood. I think it's Tituba!
Don't be silly.
Look that woman has a wart! Can we go?

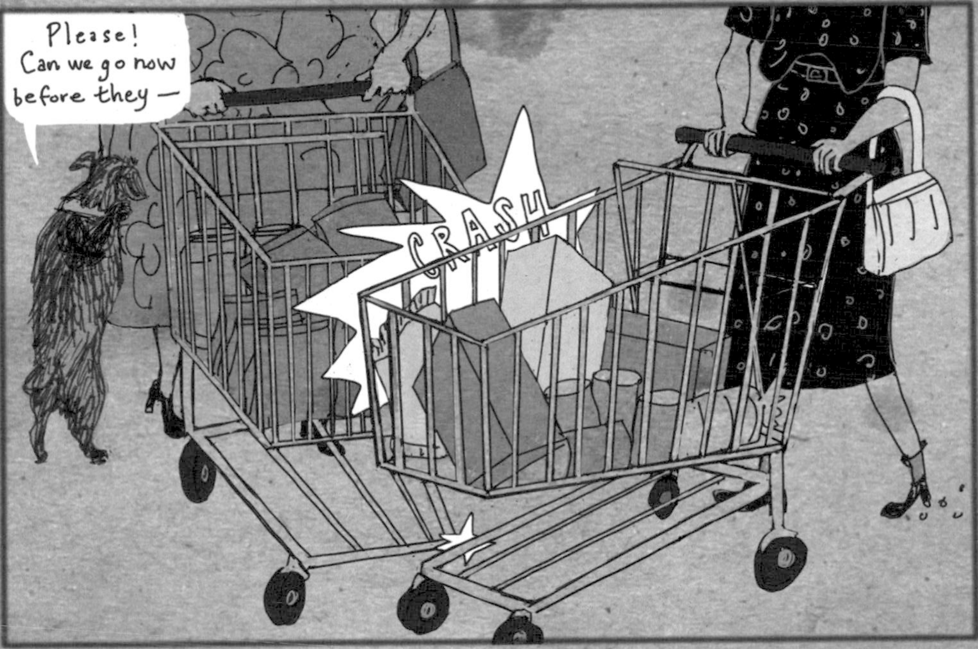
Please! Can we go now before they —
CRASH

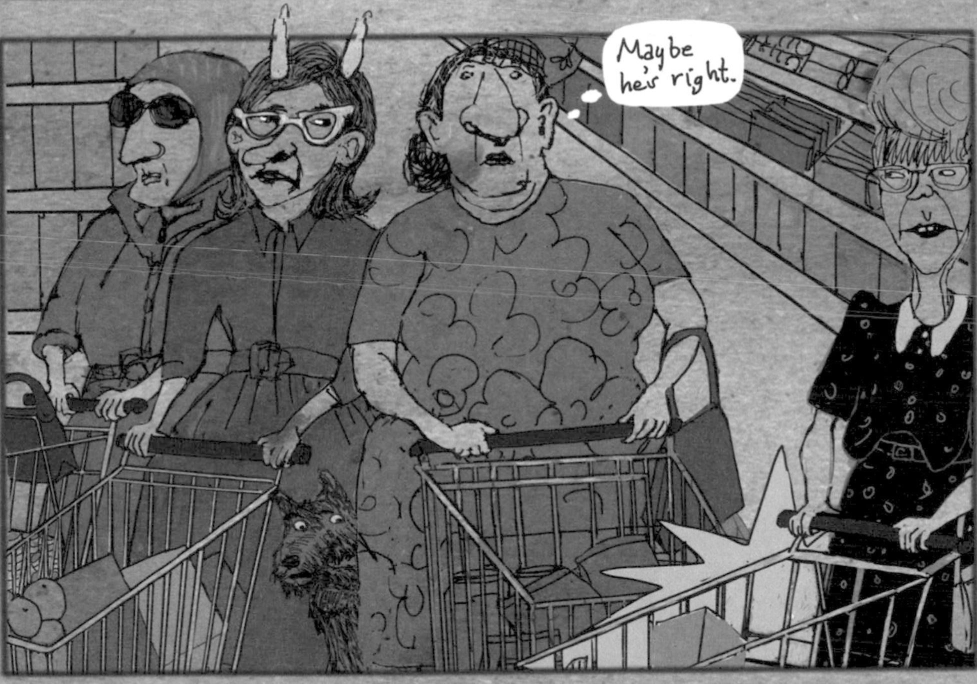
Maybe he's right.

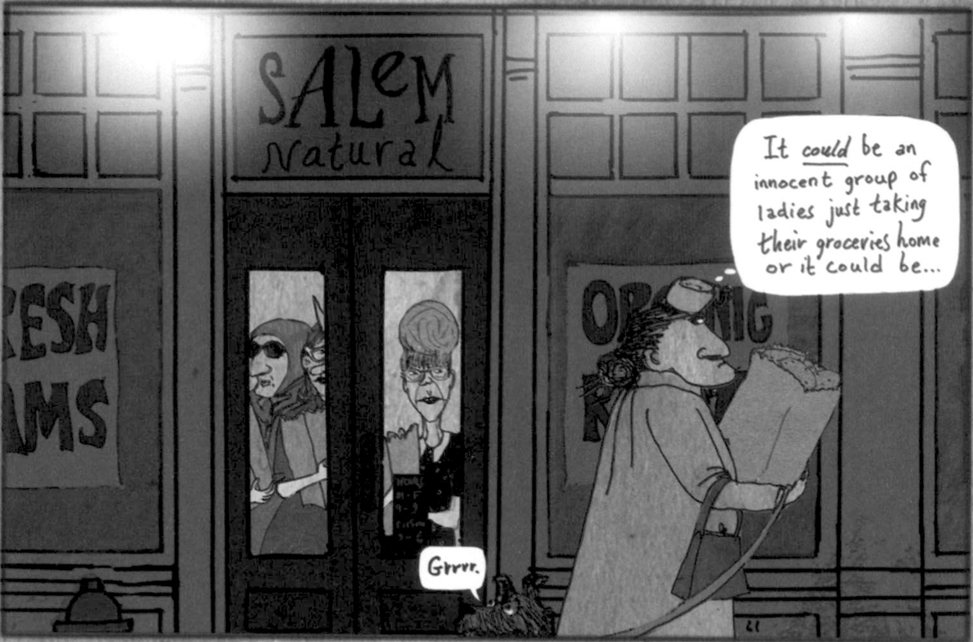
SALEM Natural
It could be an innocent group of ladies just taking their groceries home or it could be...
Grrrr.

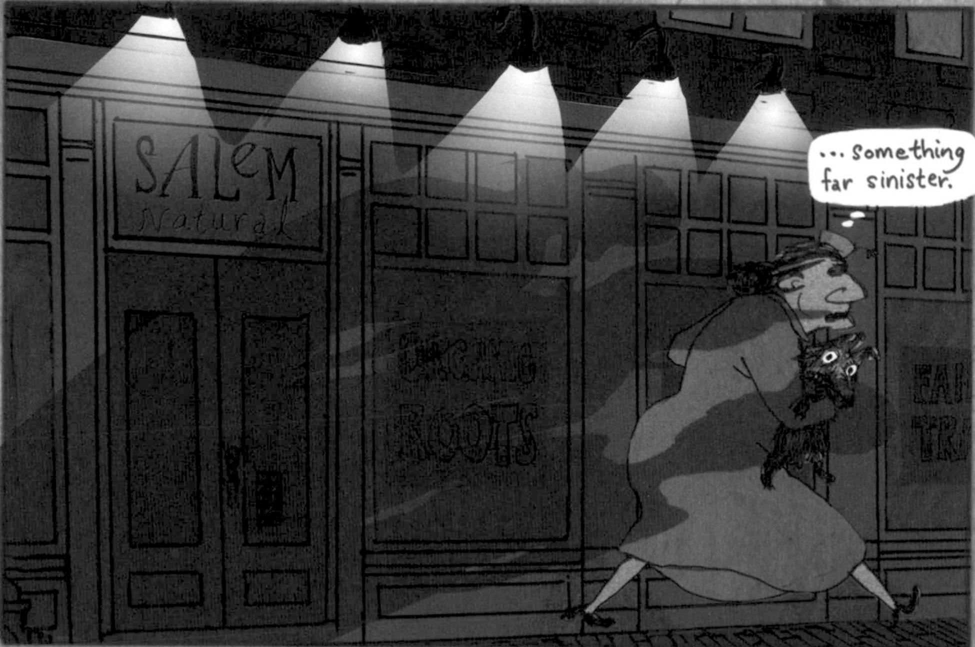
SALEM Natural
ROOTS
...something far sinister.

15th

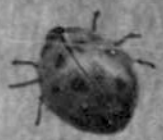

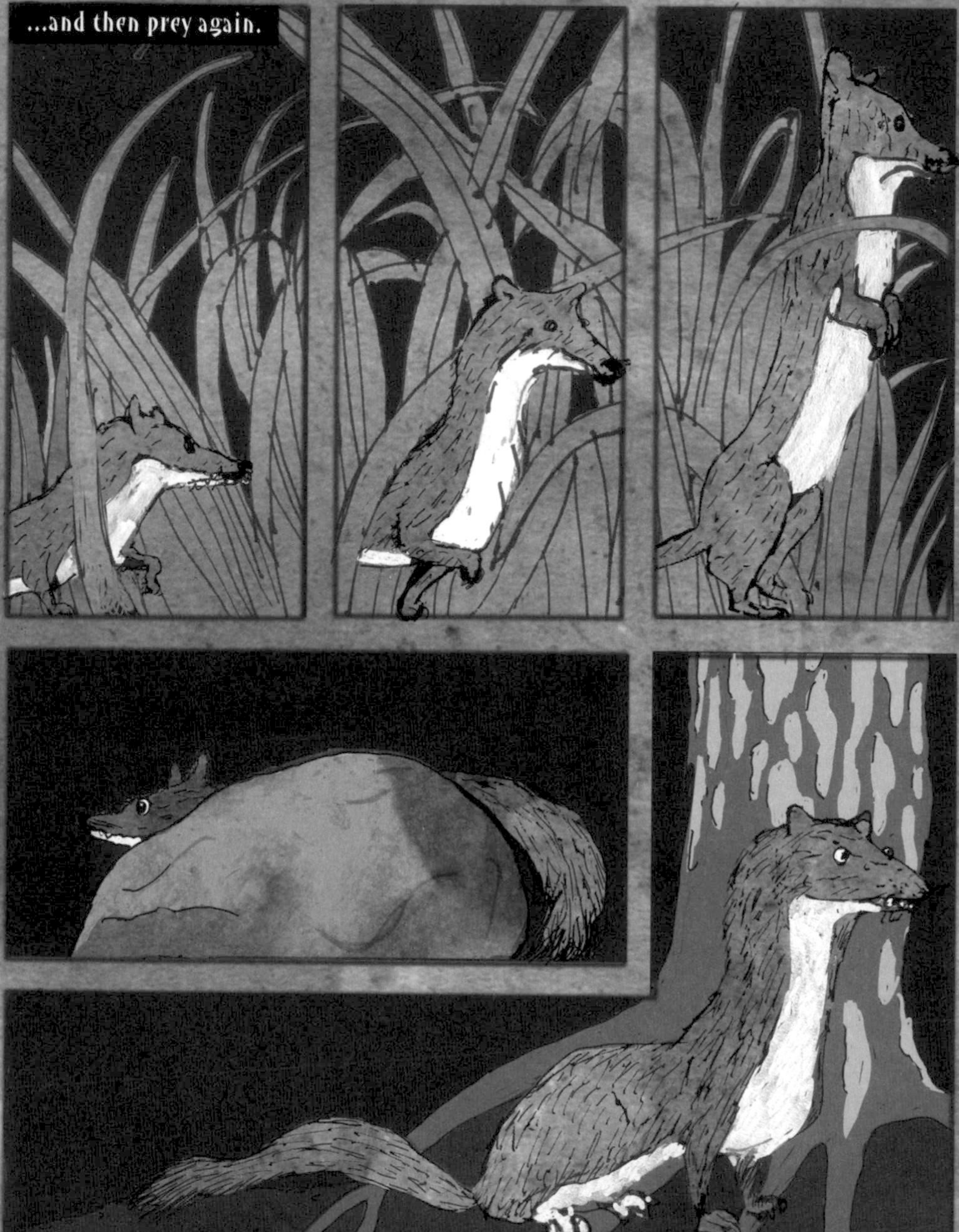
...and then prey again.

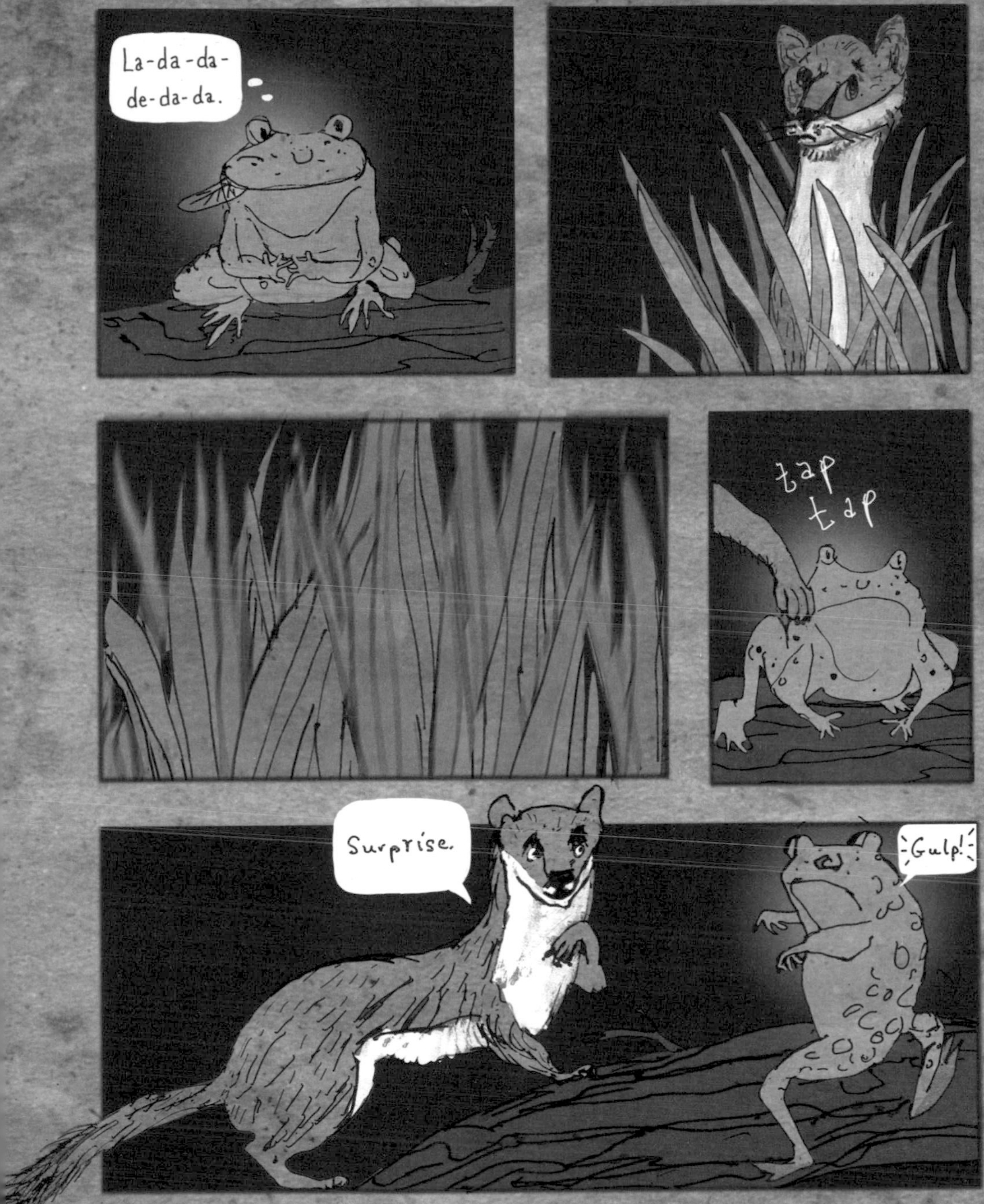
La-da-da-
de-da-da.
tap
tap
Surprise.
Gulp!

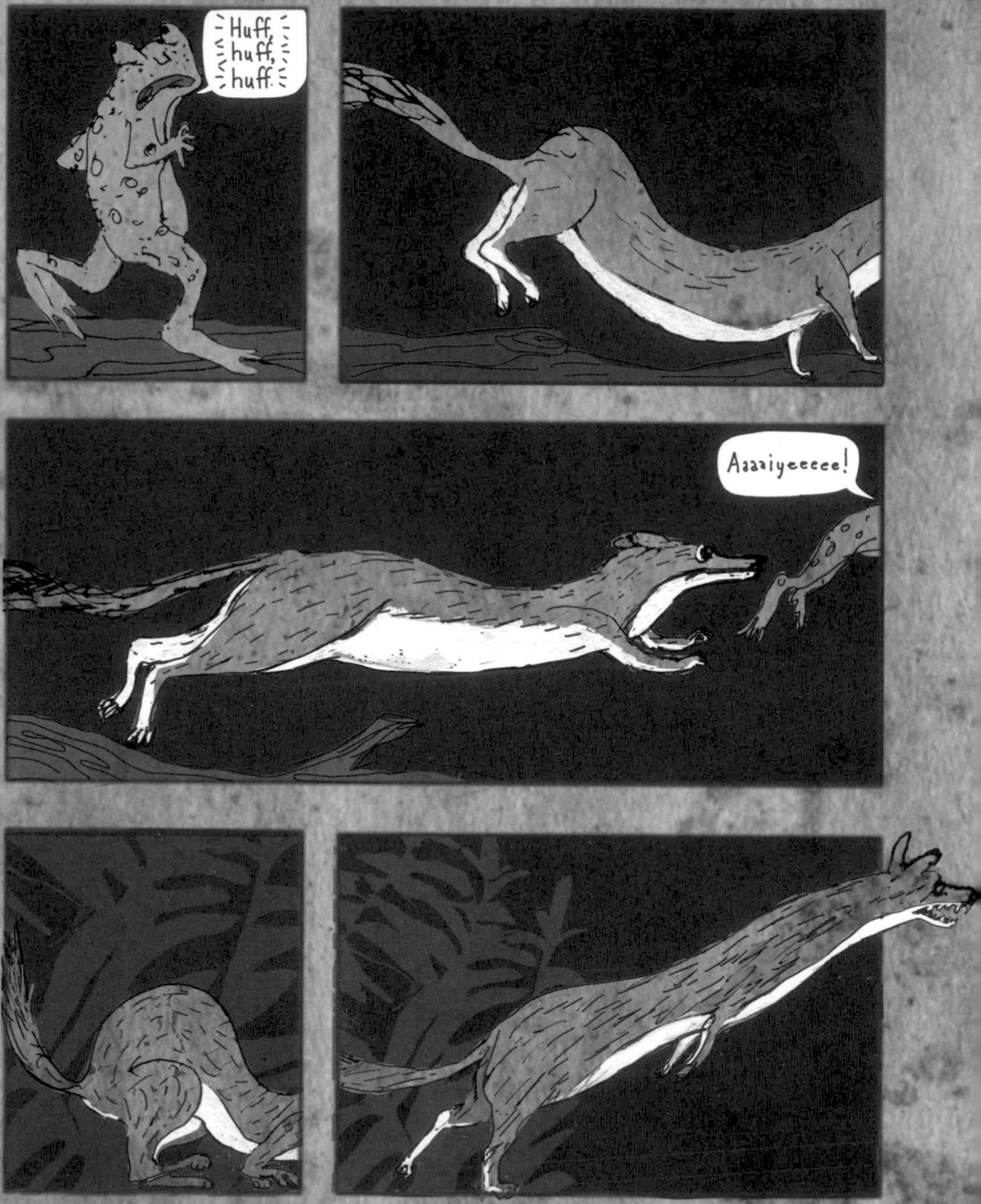
Huff, huff, huff.
Aaaaiyeeeee!

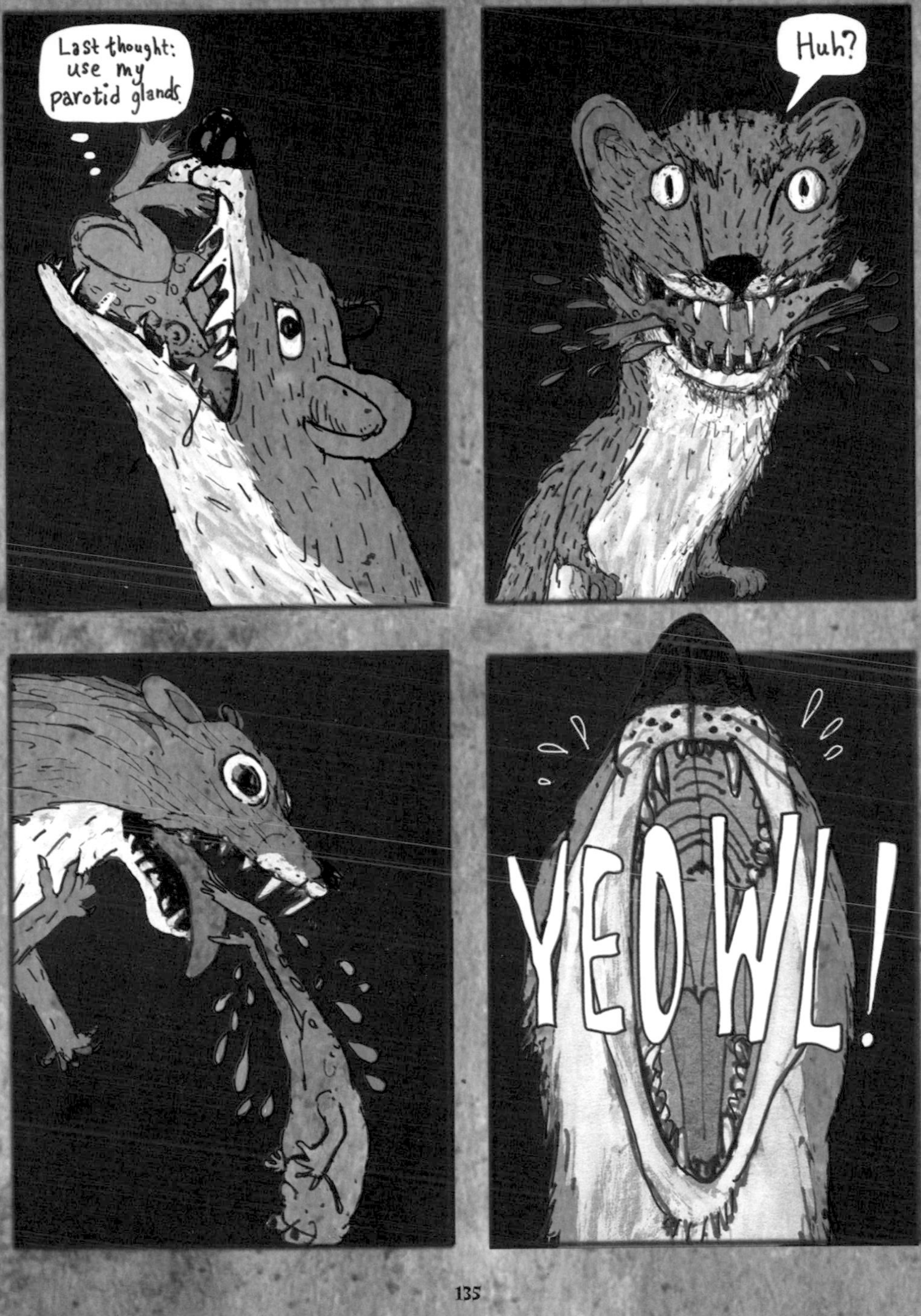
Last thought: use my parotid glands.
Huh?
YEOWL!

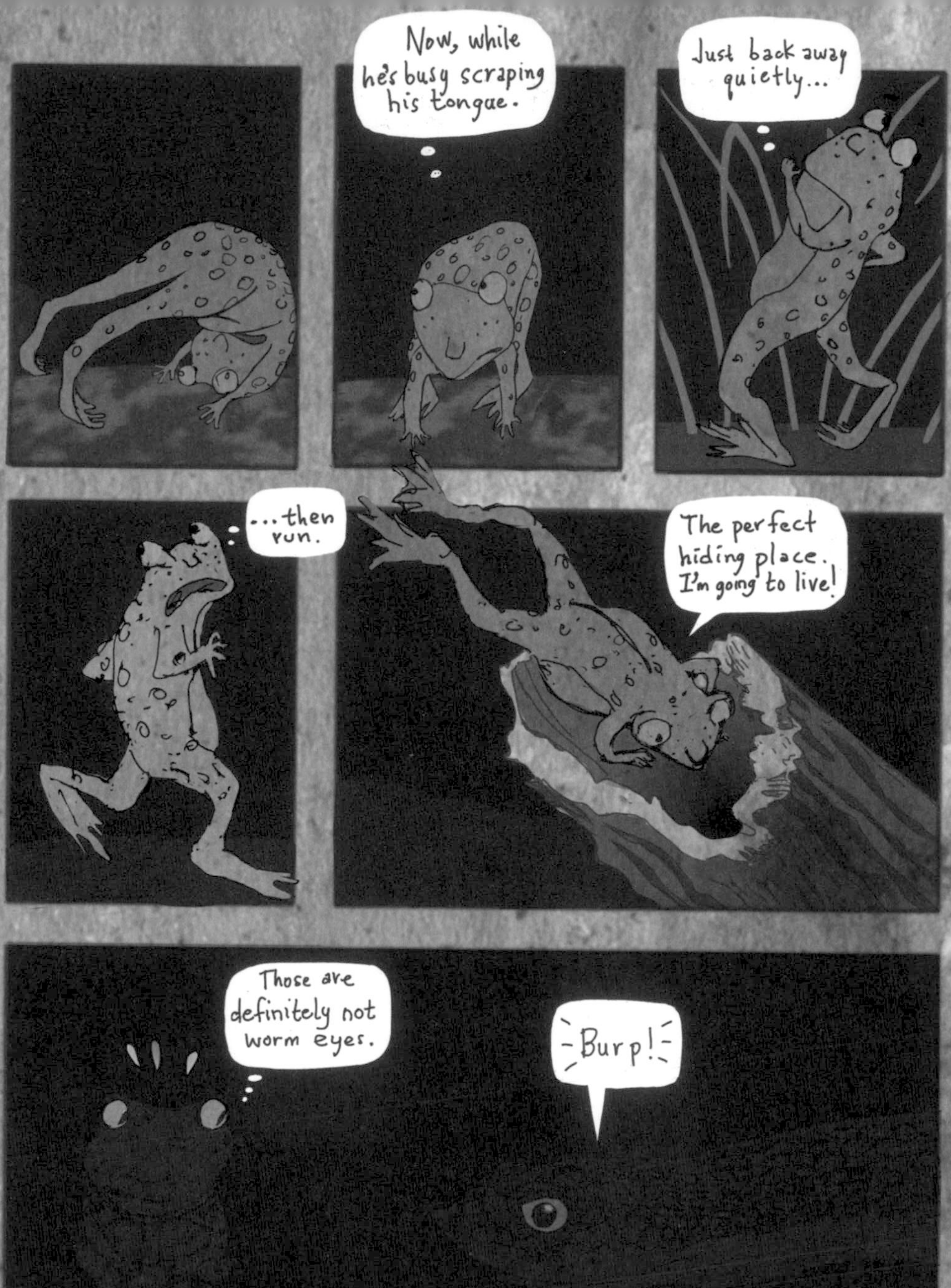

Now, while he's busy scraping his tongue.
Just back away quietly...
...then run.
The perfect hiding place. I'm going to live!
Those are definitely not worm eyes.
Burp!

16th

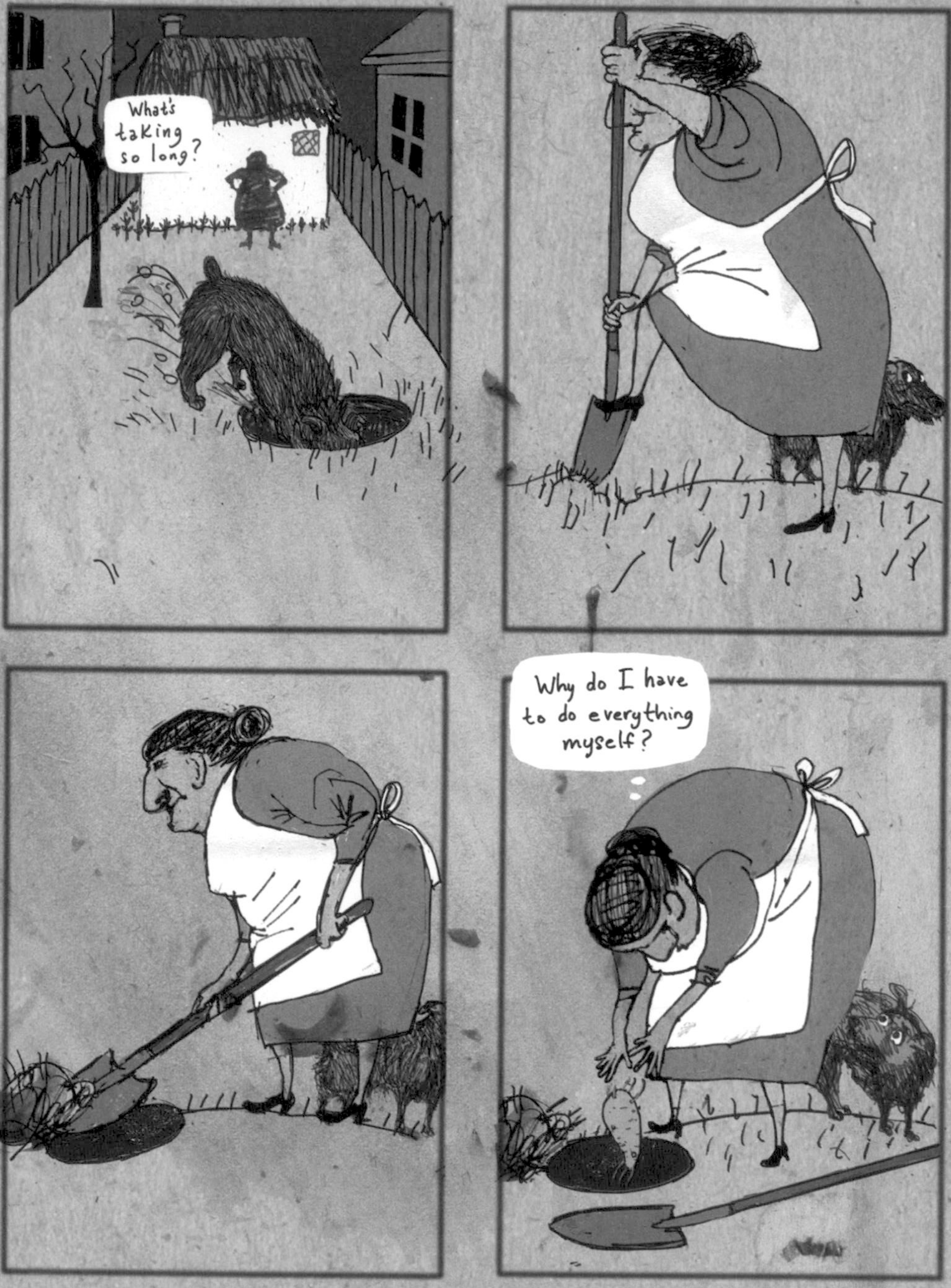
What's taking so long?
Why do I have to do everything myself?

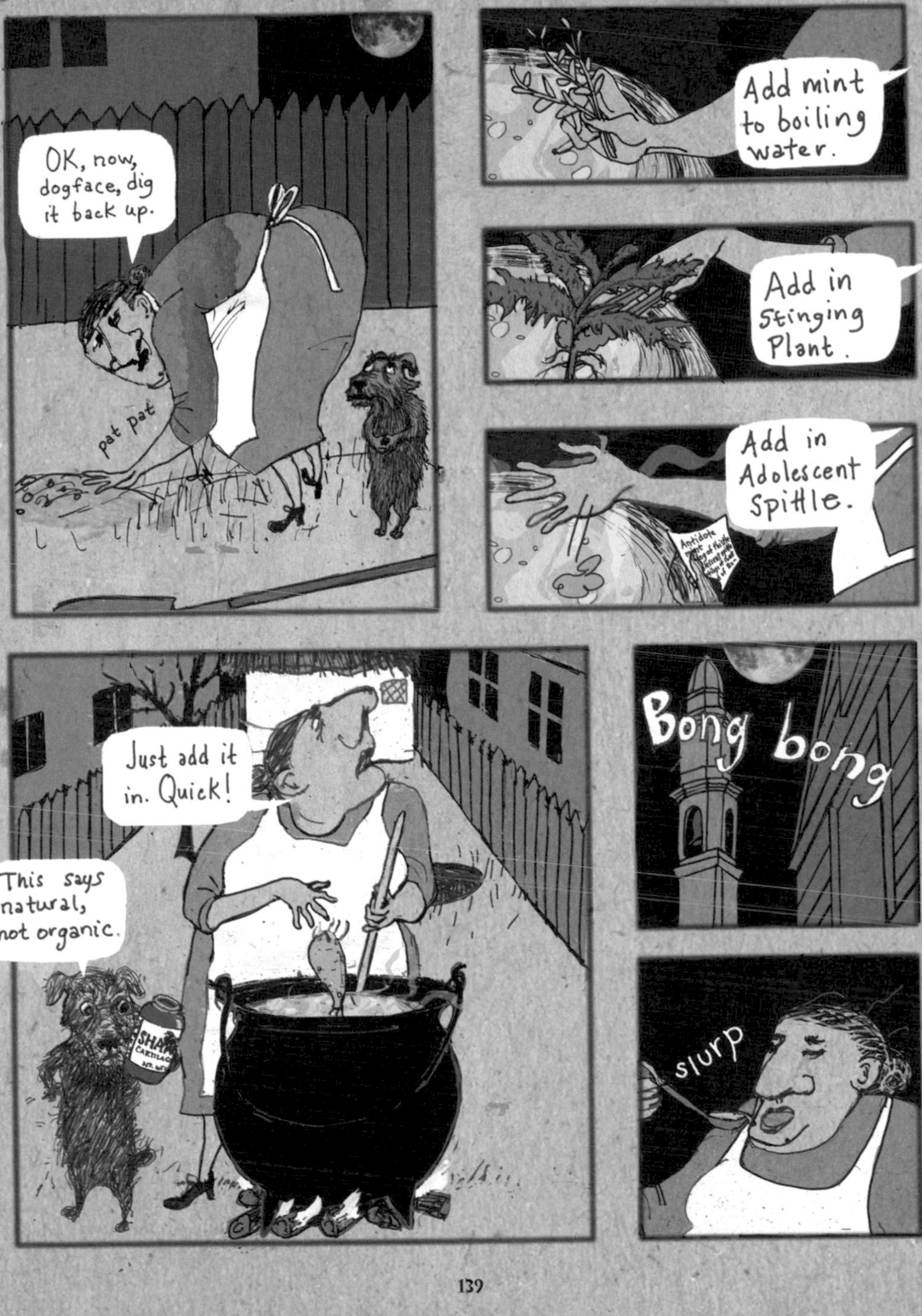
OK, now, dogface, dig it back up.
pat pat
Add mint to boiling water.
Add in Stinging Plant.
Add in Adolescent Spittle.
Just add it in. Quick!
This says natural, not organic.
Bong bong
slurp

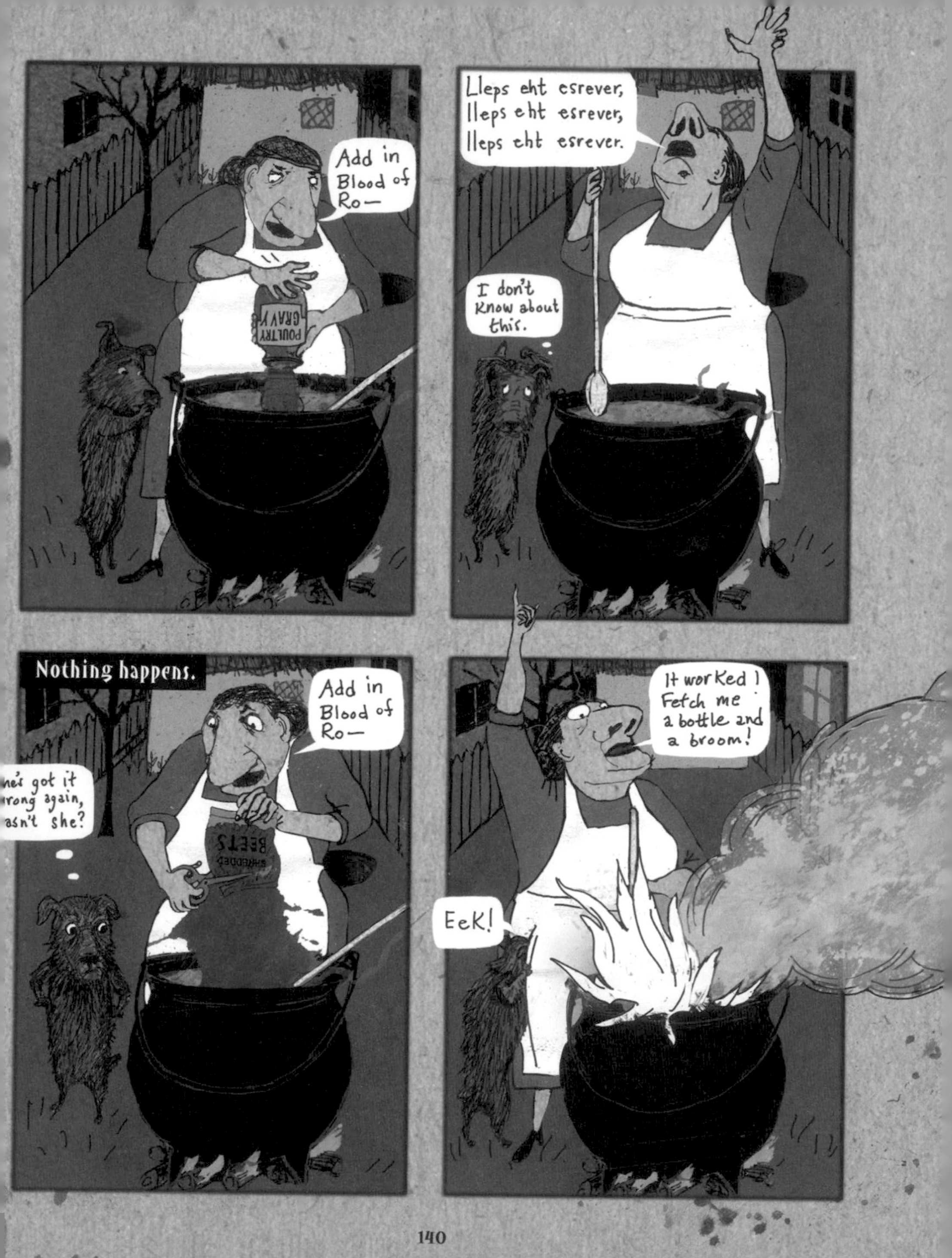
Add in Blood of Ro—
Lleps eht esrever, lleps eht esrever, lleps eht esrever.
I don't know about this.
Nothing happens.
Add in Blood of Ro—
ne's got it rong again, asn't she?
It worked! Fetch me a bottle and a broom!
EeK!

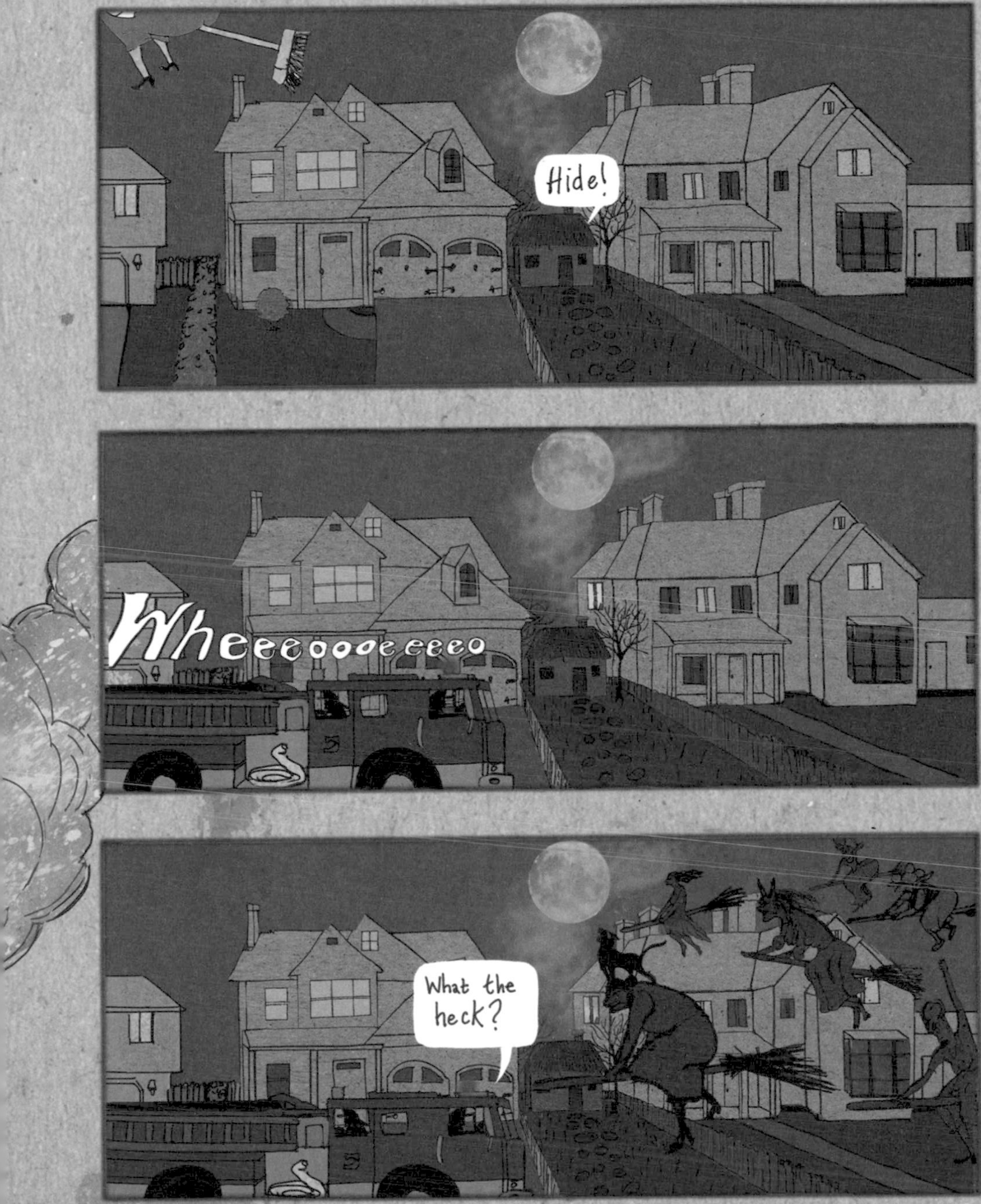
Hide!
Wheeeoooeeeeo
What the heck?

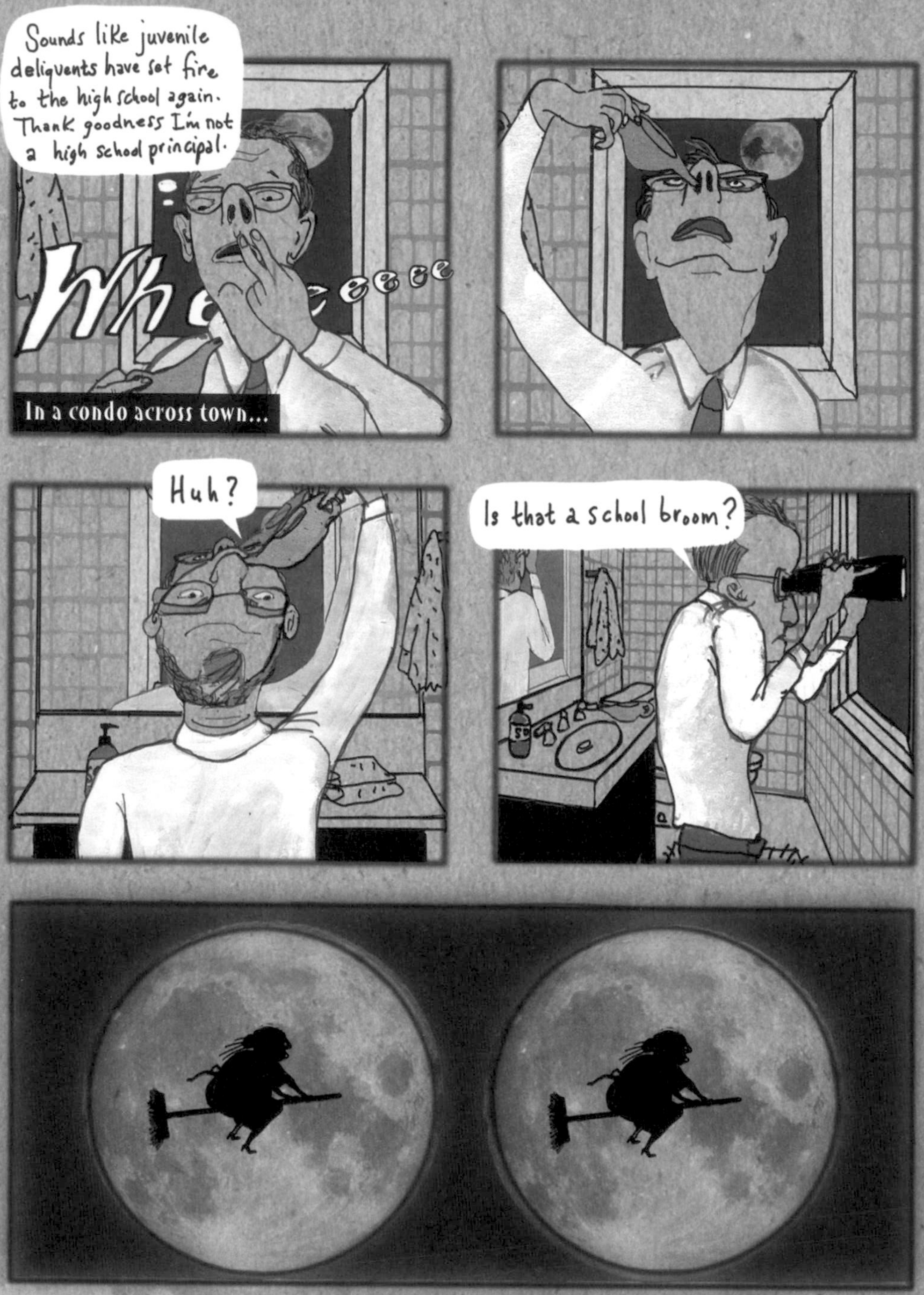
Sounds like juvenile deliquents have set fire to the high school again. Thank goodness I'm not a high school principal.
Wheeeeee
In a condo across town...
Huh?
Is that a school broom?

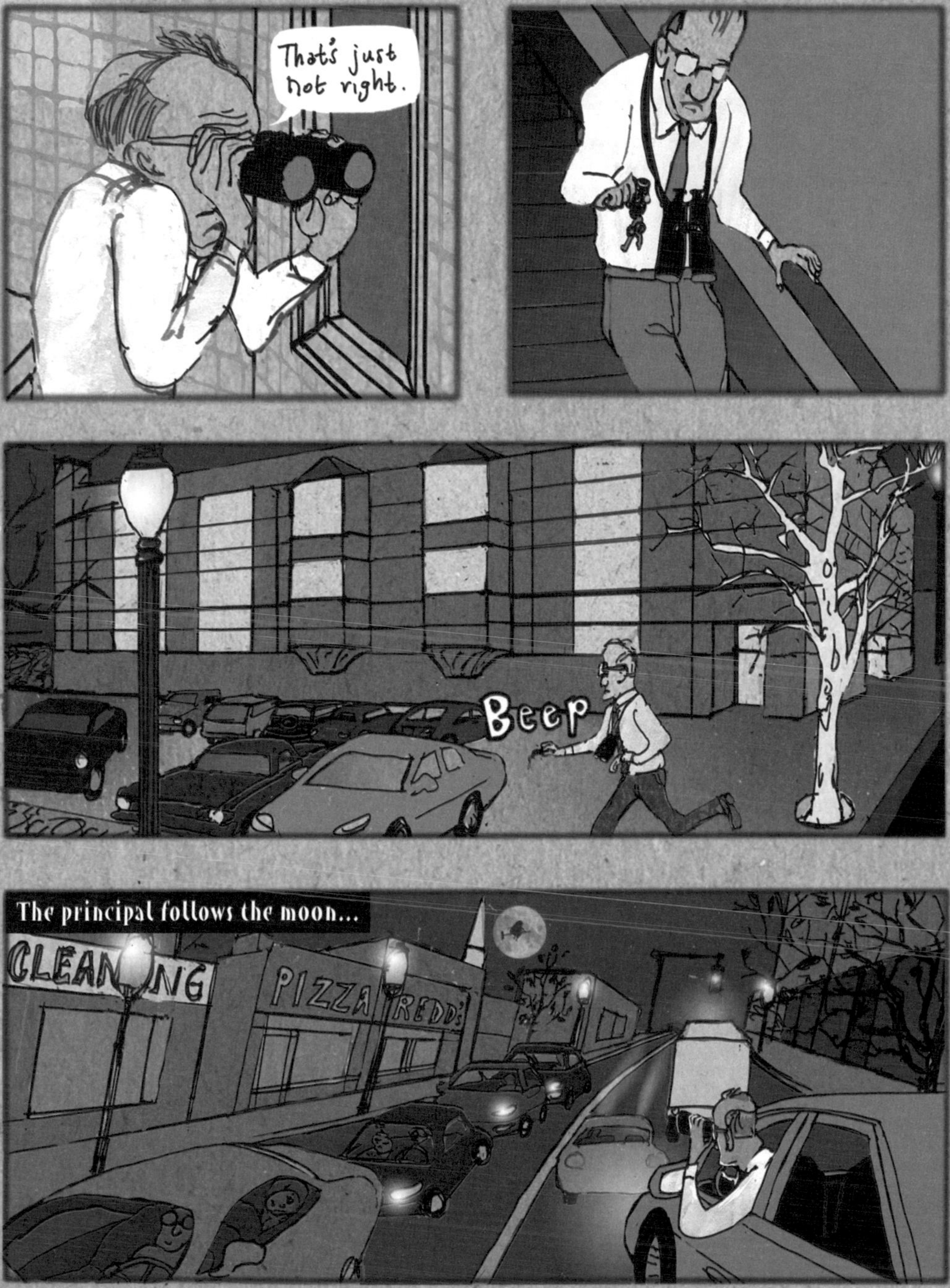
That's just not right.
Beep
The principal follows the moon...
CLEANING
PIZZA
REDD's

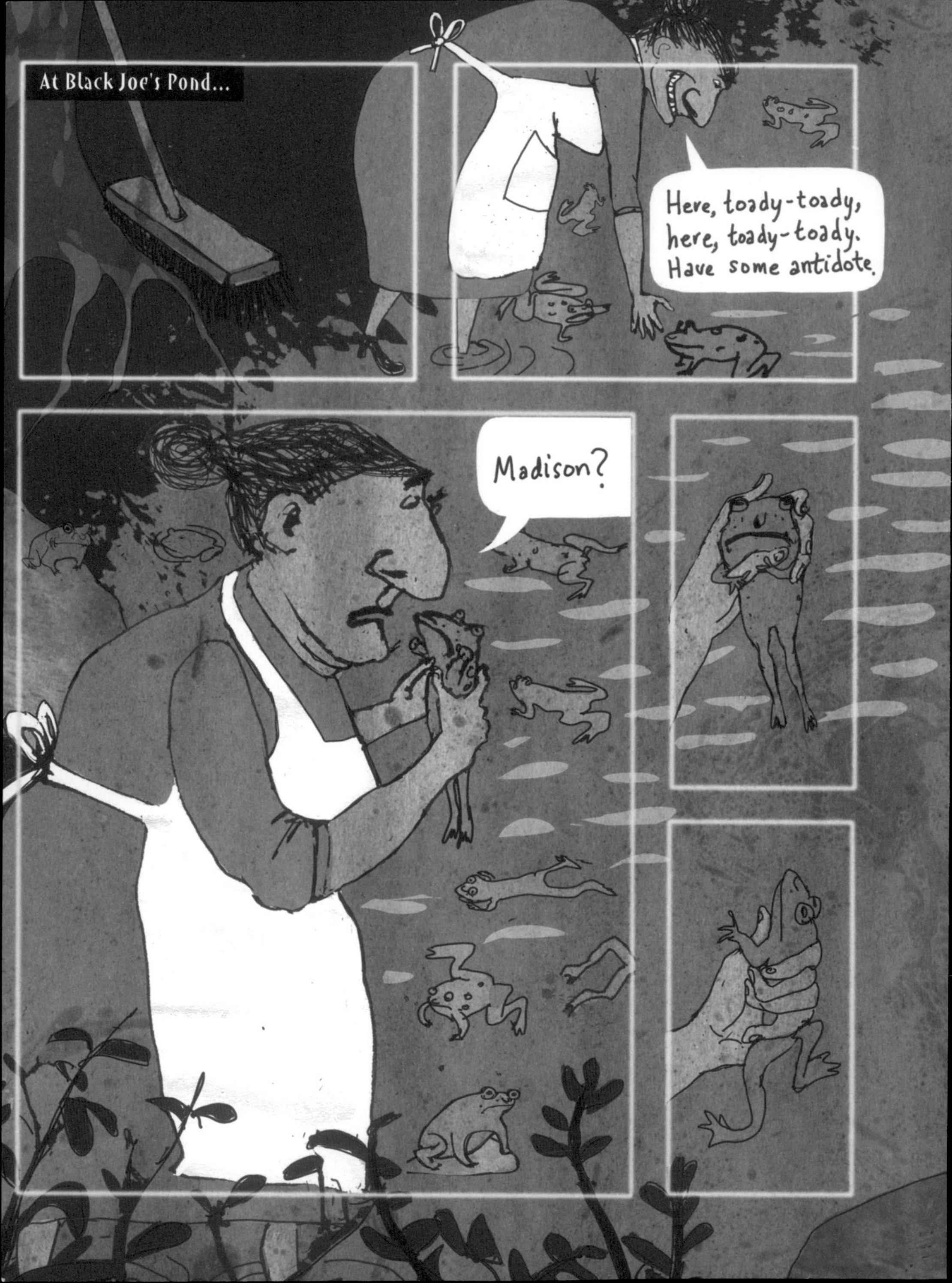
At Black Joe's Pond...
Here, toady-toady, here, toady-toady. Have some antidote.
Madison?

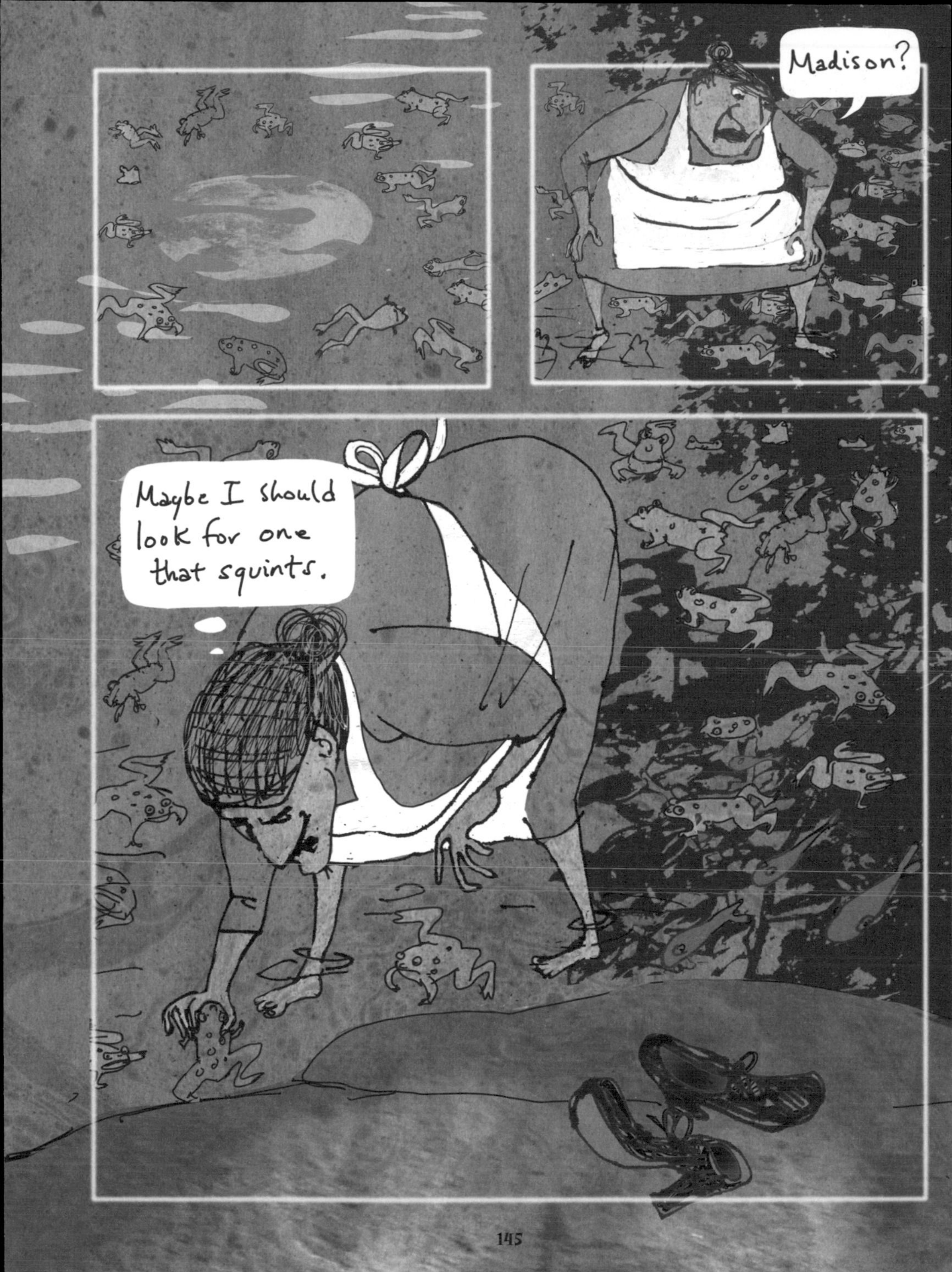
Madison?
Maybe I should look for one that squints.

How about you? Are you named Madison?
Gulp!
Open wide.

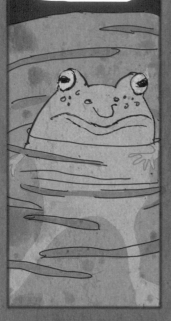

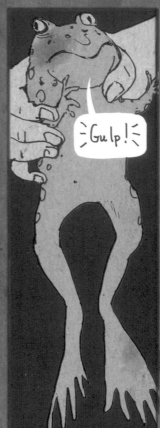

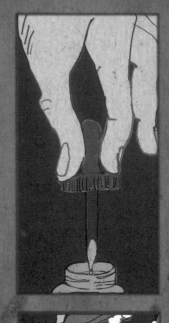

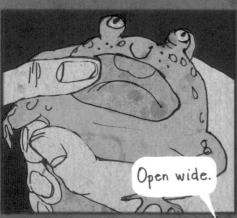

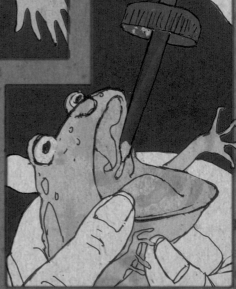

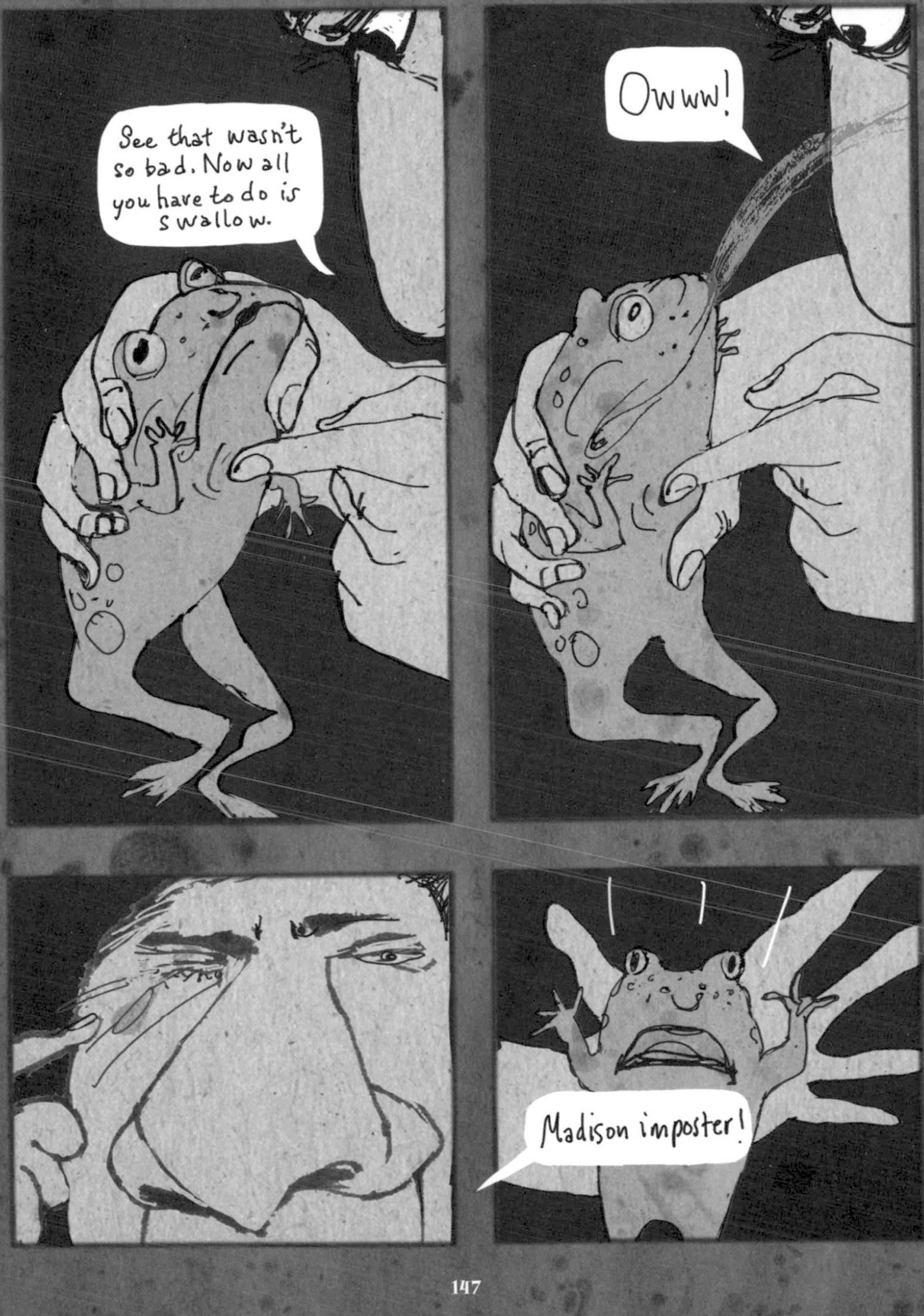
See that wasn't so bad. Now all you have to do is swallow.
Owww!
Madison imposter!

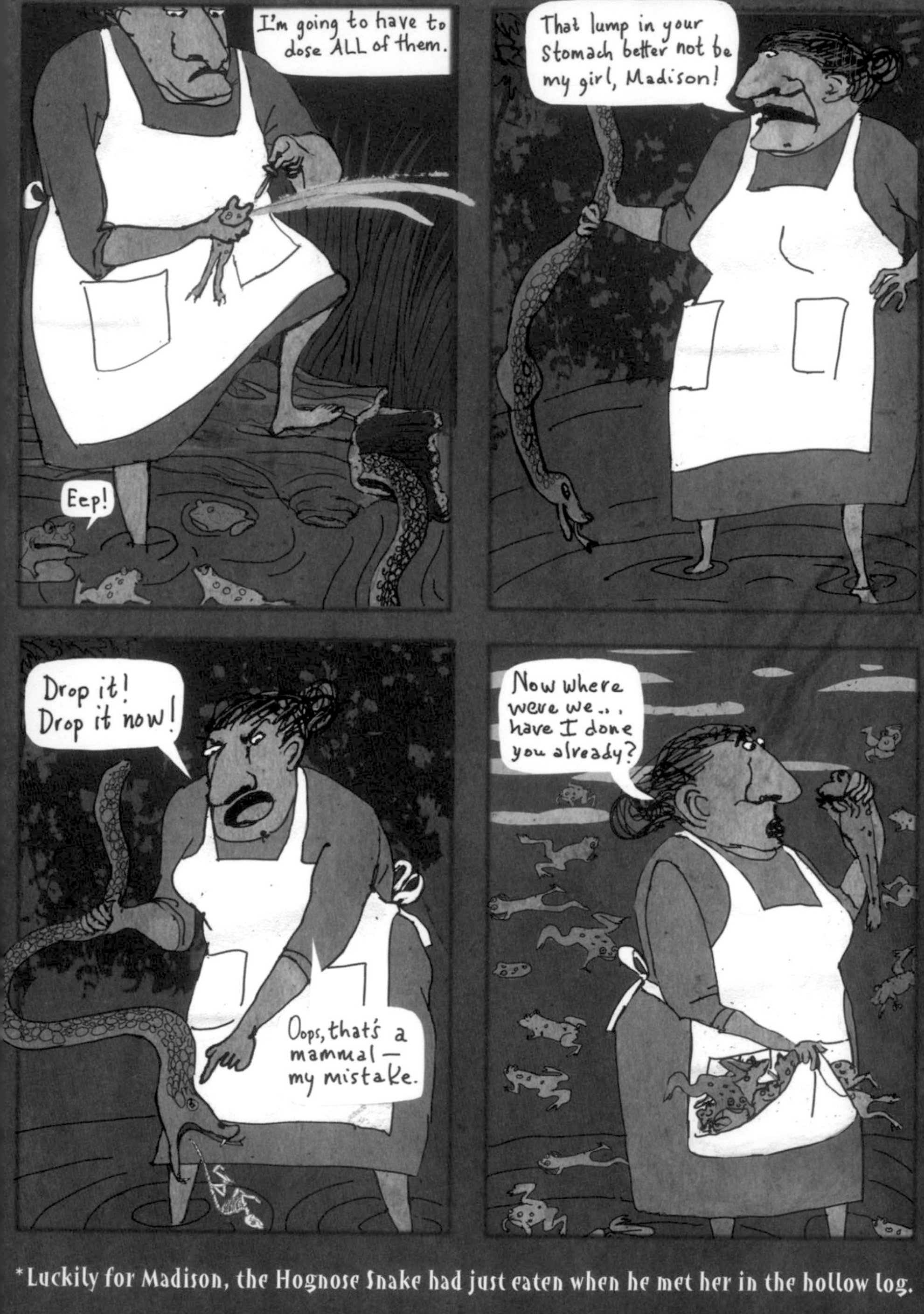
I'm going to have to dose ALL of them.
Eep!
That lump in your stomach better not be my girl, Madison!
Drop it! Drop it now!
Oops, that's a mammal— my mistake.
Now where were we... have I done you already?

*Luckily for Madison, the Hognose Snake had just eaten when he met her in the hollow log.

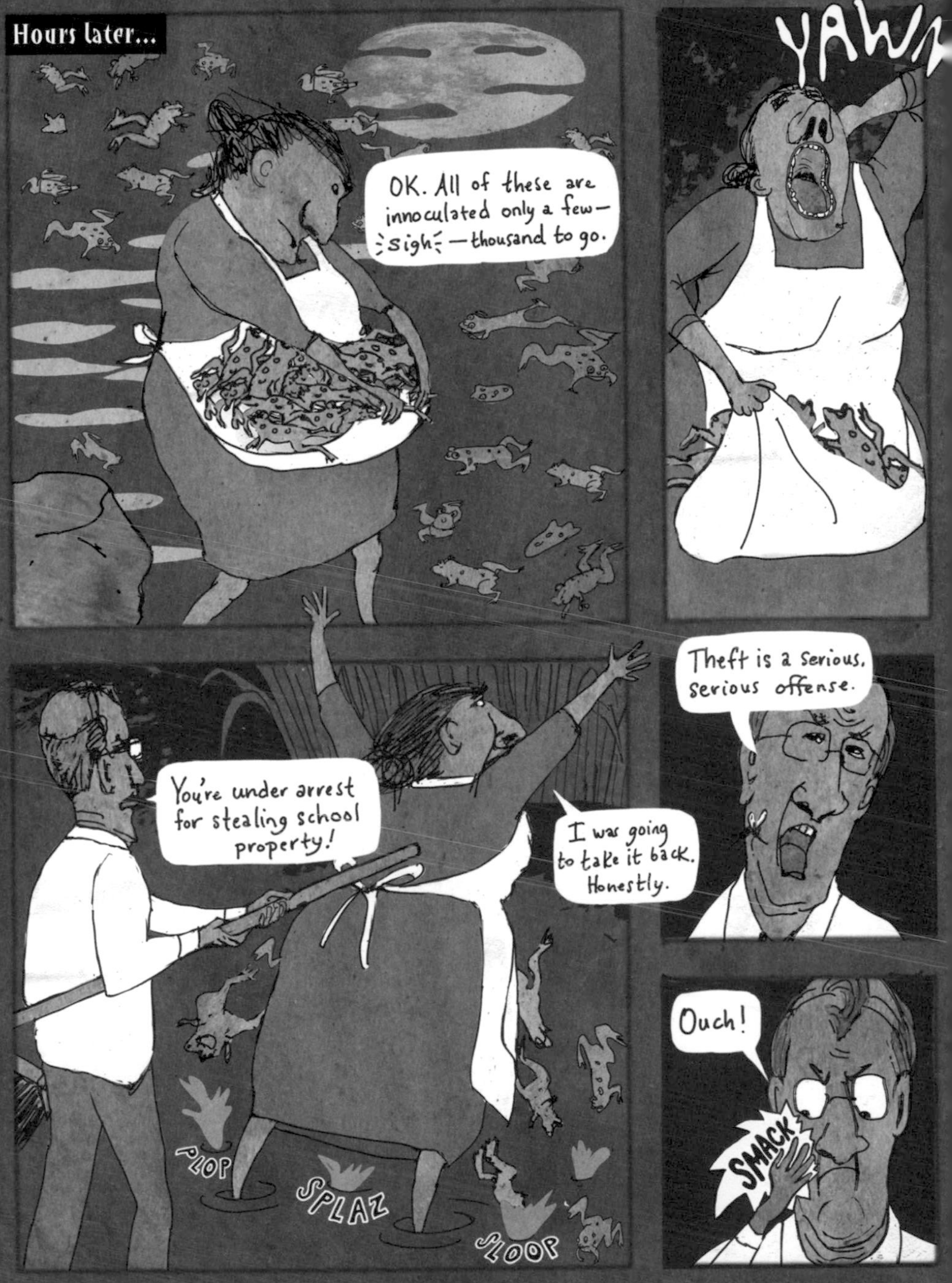
Hours later...
OK. All of these are innoculated only a few— sigh —thousand to go.
YAWN
You're under arrest for stealing school property!
I was going to take it back. Honestly.
PLOP
SPLAZ
SLOOP
Theft is a serious, serious offense.
Ouch!
SMACK

Look, a rare Swamp Milkweed Beetle!

SWIIISSH

SWIIJS

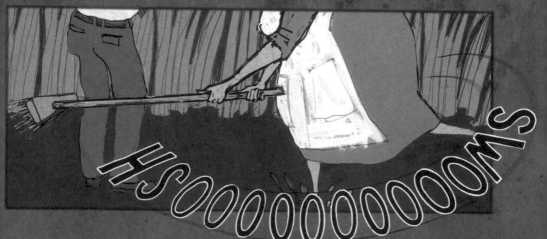

HSOOOOOOOOOOOMS

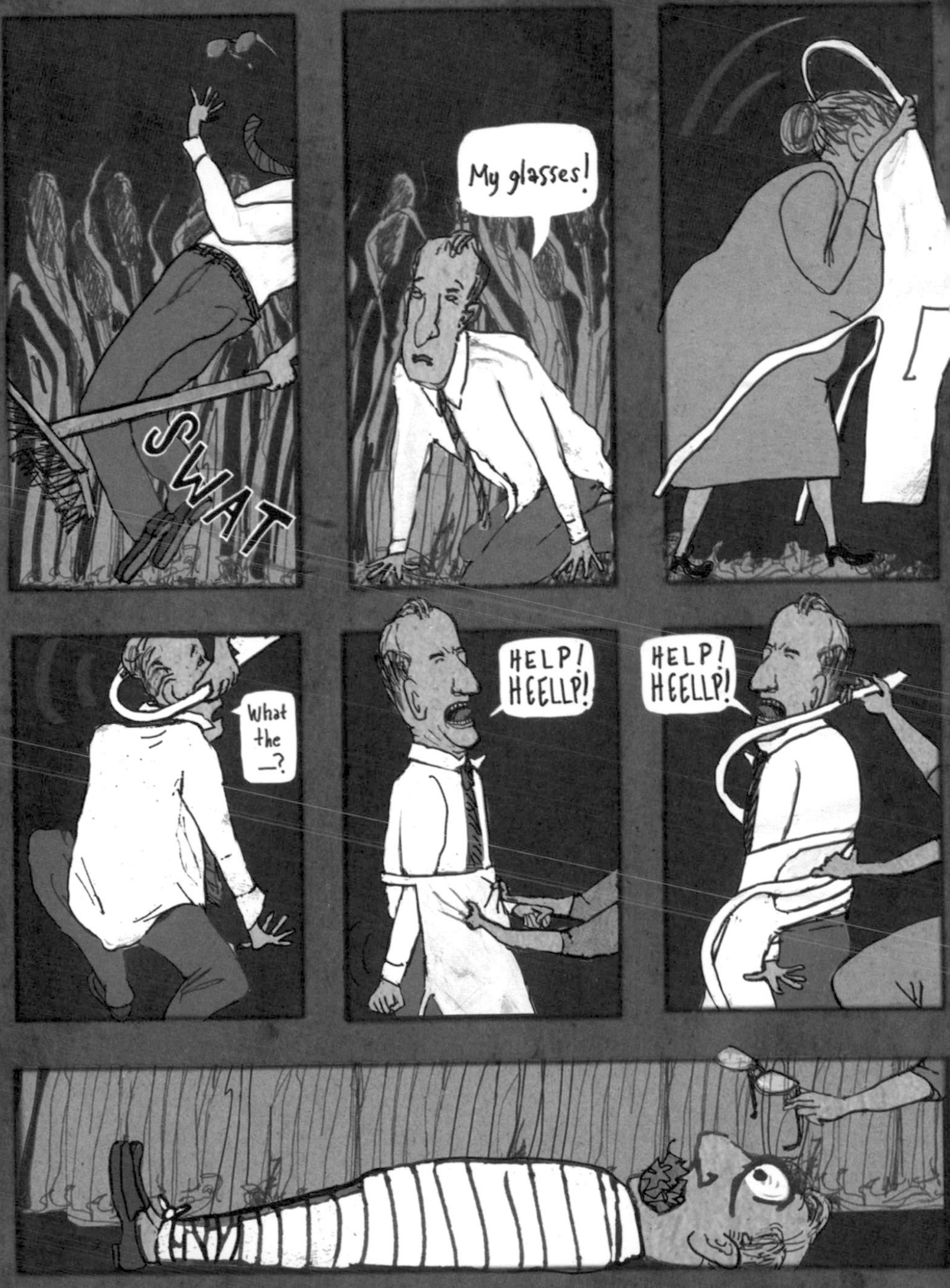
SWAT
My glasses!
What the —?
HELP! HEELLP!
HELP! HEELLP!

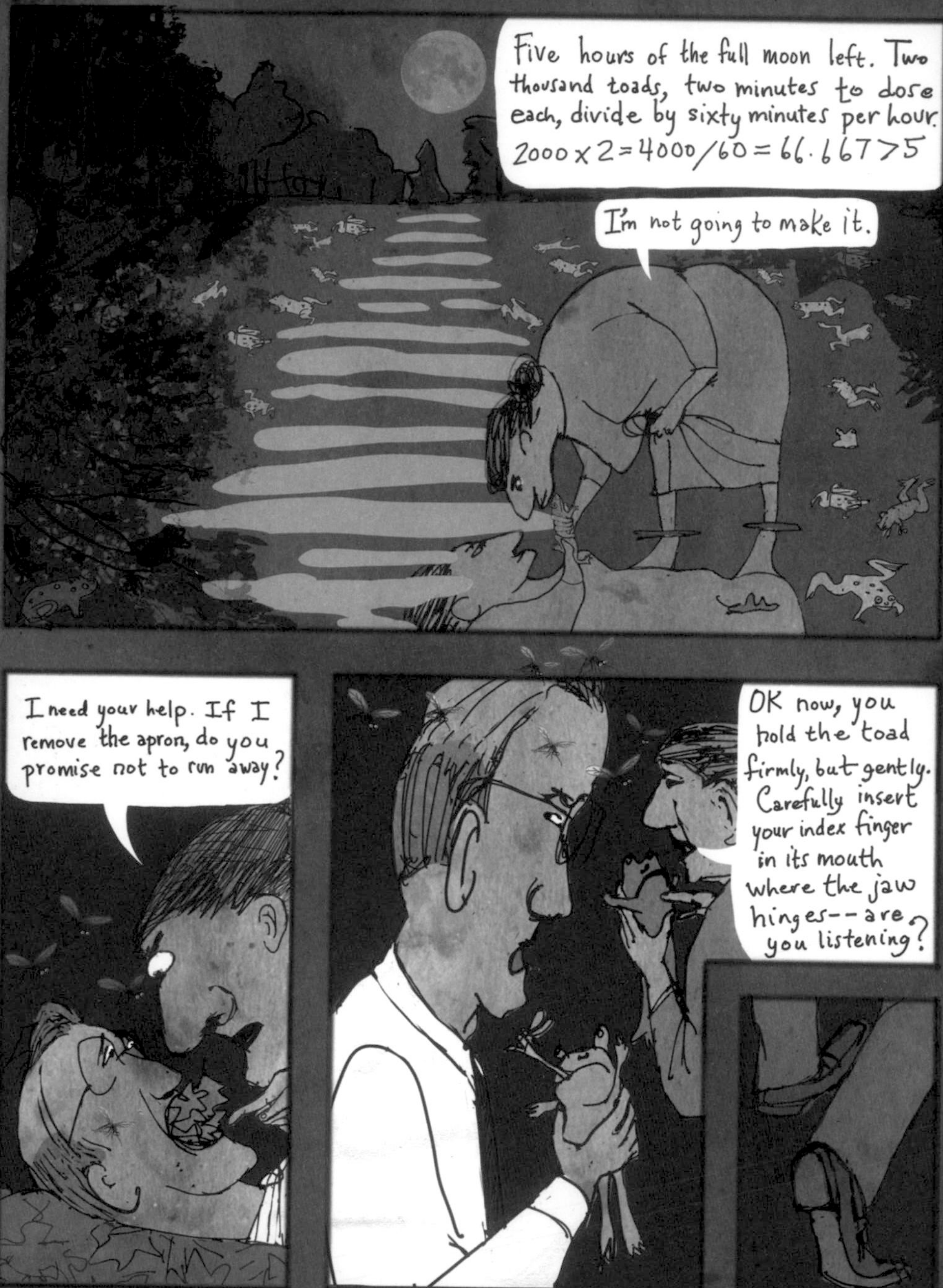
Five hours of the full moon left. Two thousand toads, two minutes to dose each, divide by sixty minutes per hour. 2000 x 2 = 4000/60 = 66.667 > 5
I'm not going to make it.
I need your help. If I remove the apron, do you promise not to run away?
OK now, you hold the toad firmly, but gently. Carefully insert your index finger in its mouth where the jaw hinges-- are you listening?

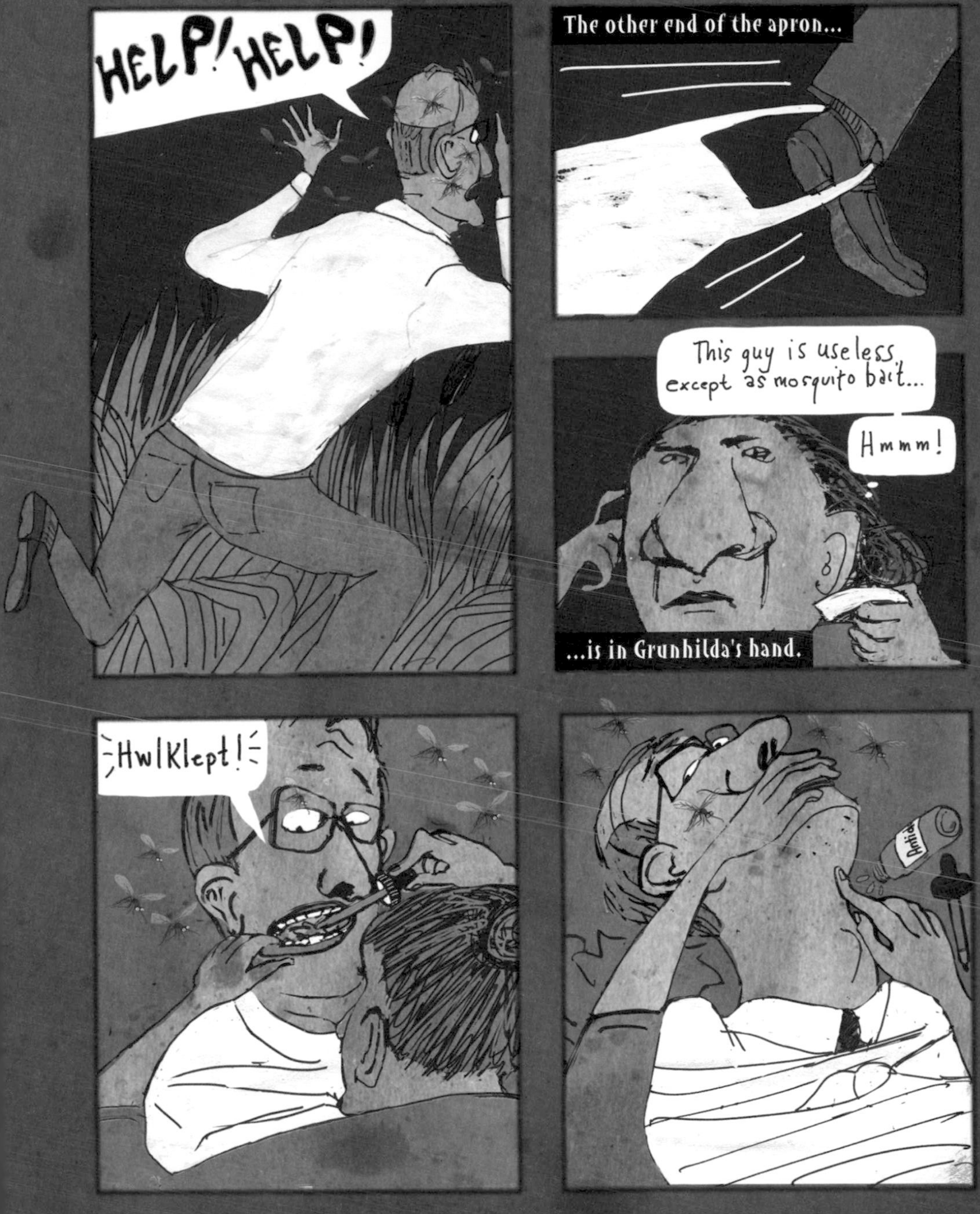
HELP! HELP!
The other end of the apron...
This guy is useless except as mosquito bait...
Hmmm!
...is in Grunhilda's hand.
Hwlklept!

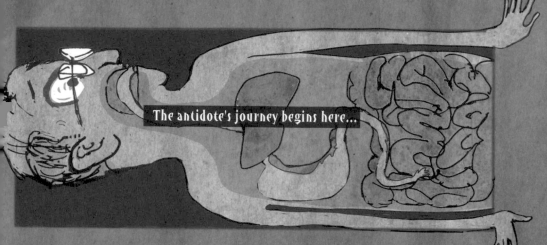

The antidote's journey begins here...

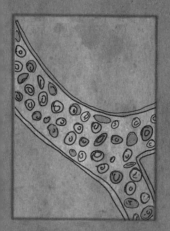

Minty!

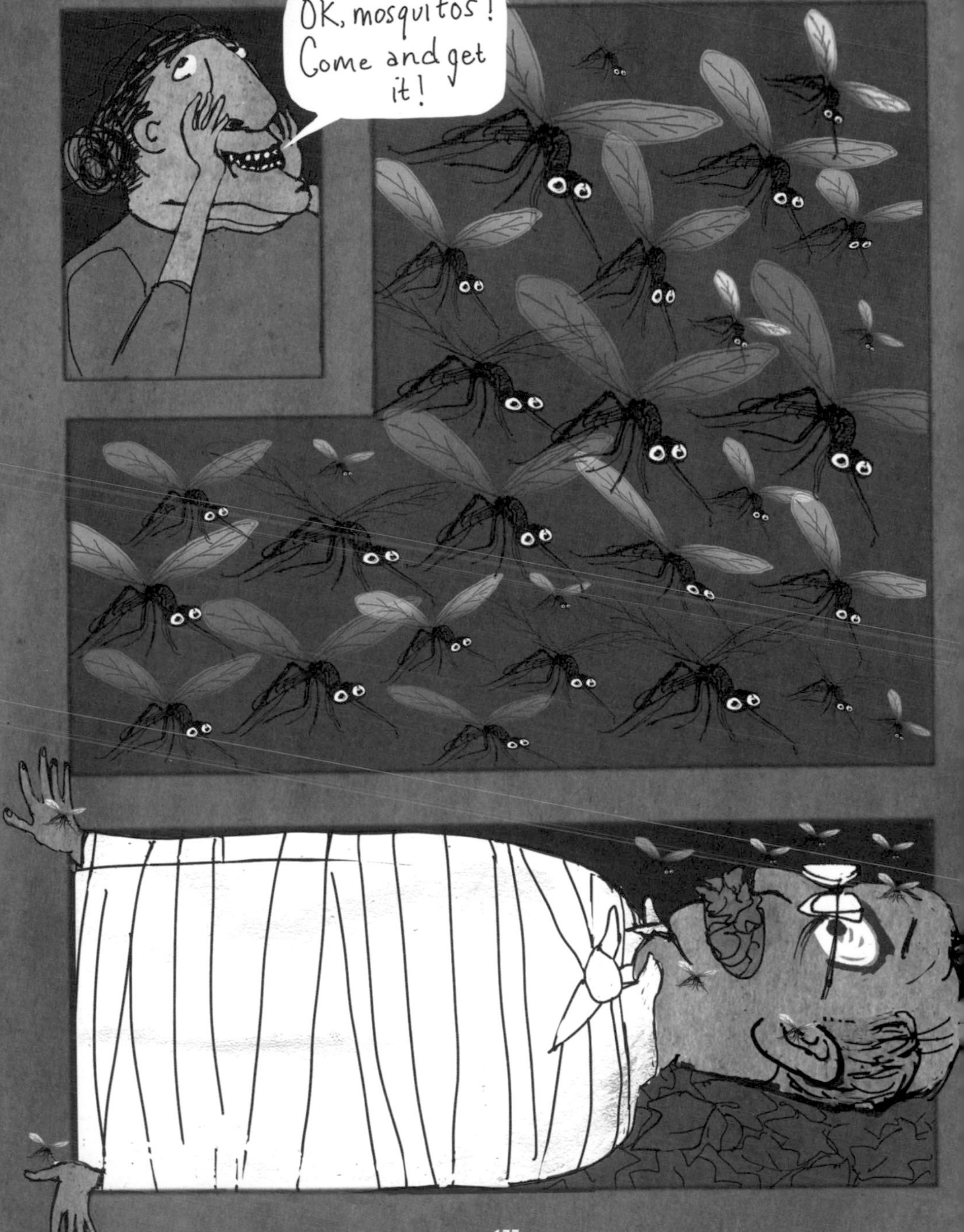
OK, mosquitos! Come and get it!

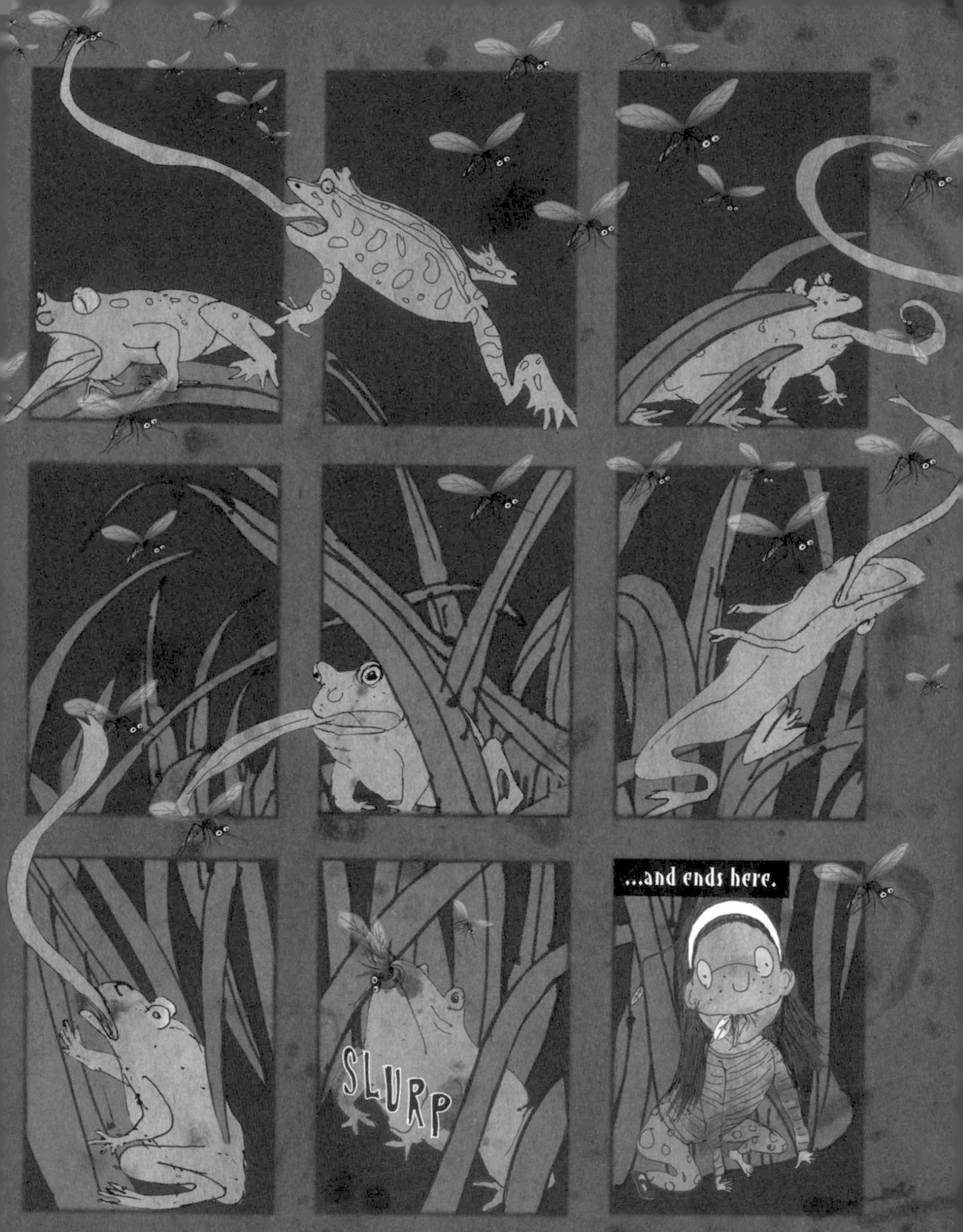
SLURP
...and ends here.

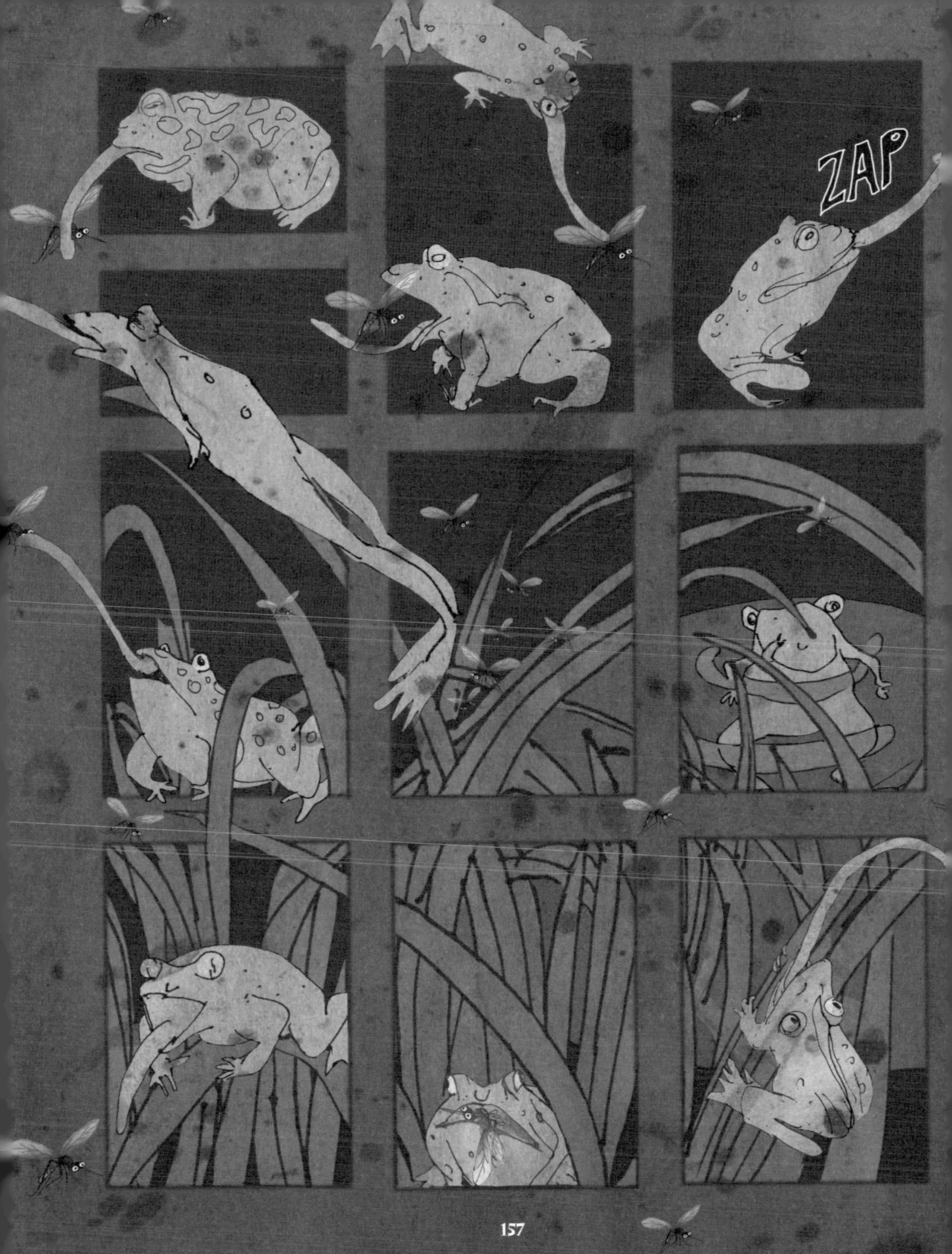
ZAP

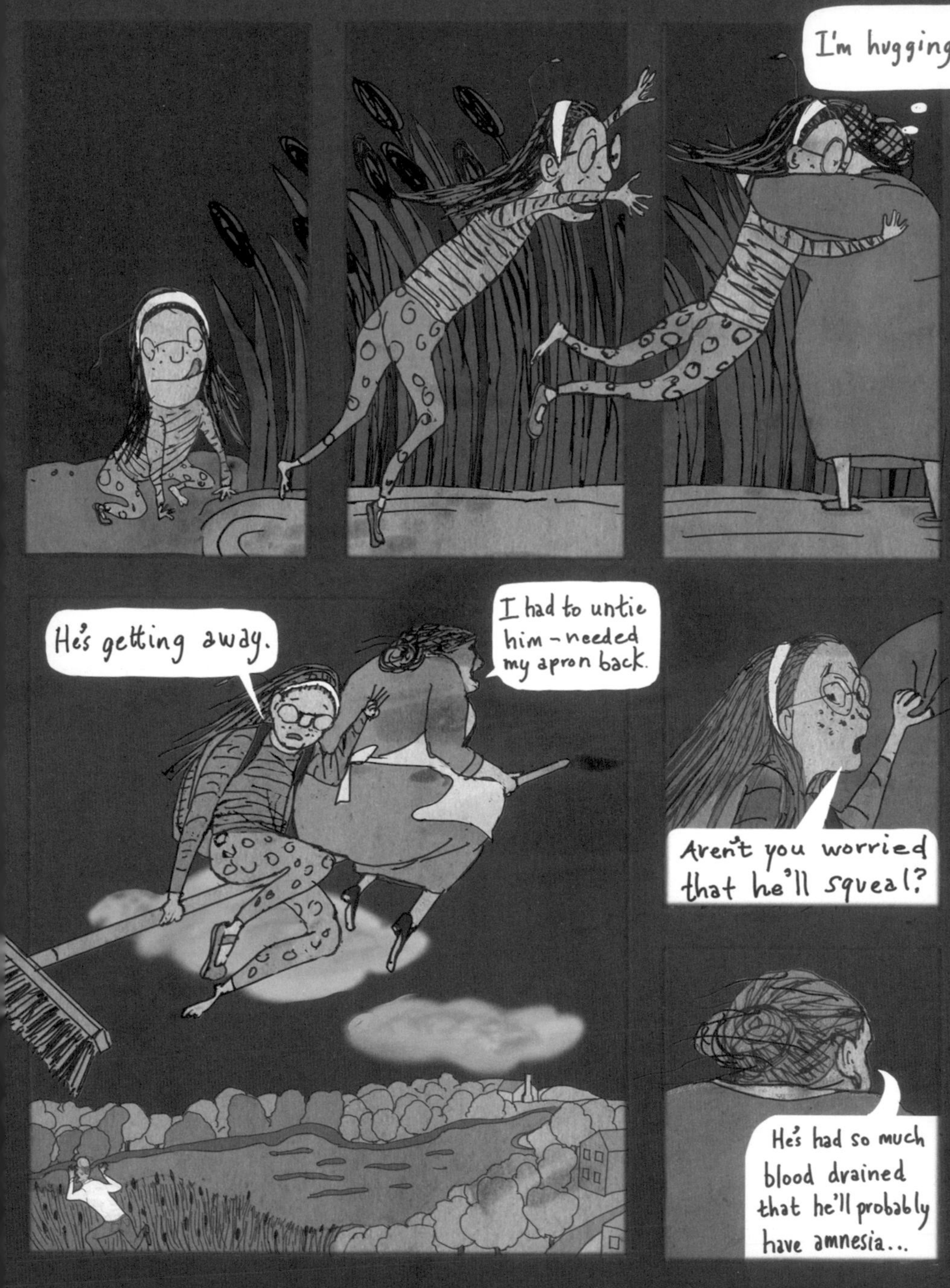
I'm hugging!?
He's getting away.
I had to untie him - needed my apron back.
Aren't you worried that he'll squeal?
He's had so much blood drained that he'll probably have amnesia...

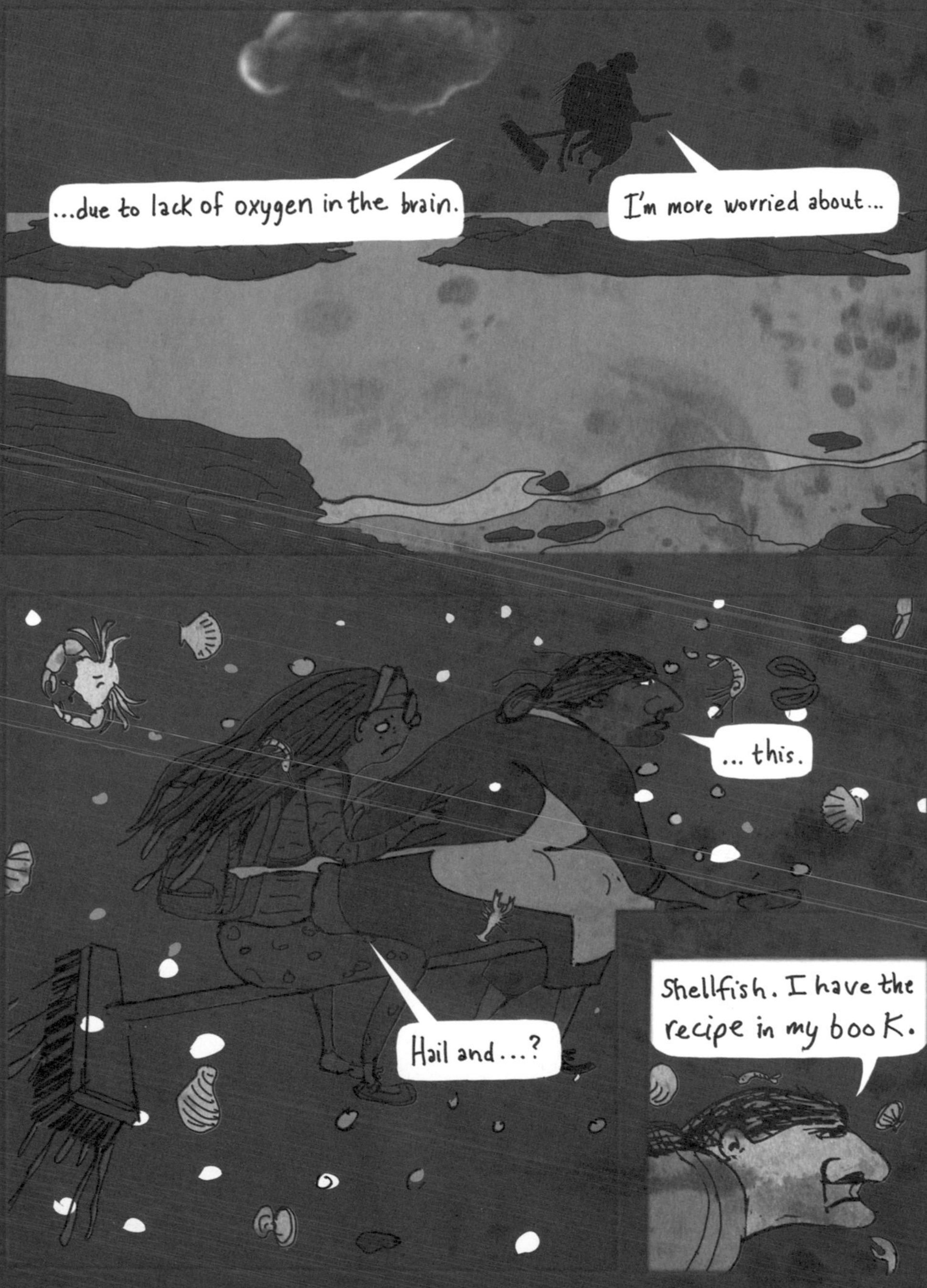
...due to lack of oxygen in the brain.
I'm more worried about...
... this.
Hail and...?
Shellfish. I have the recipe in my book.

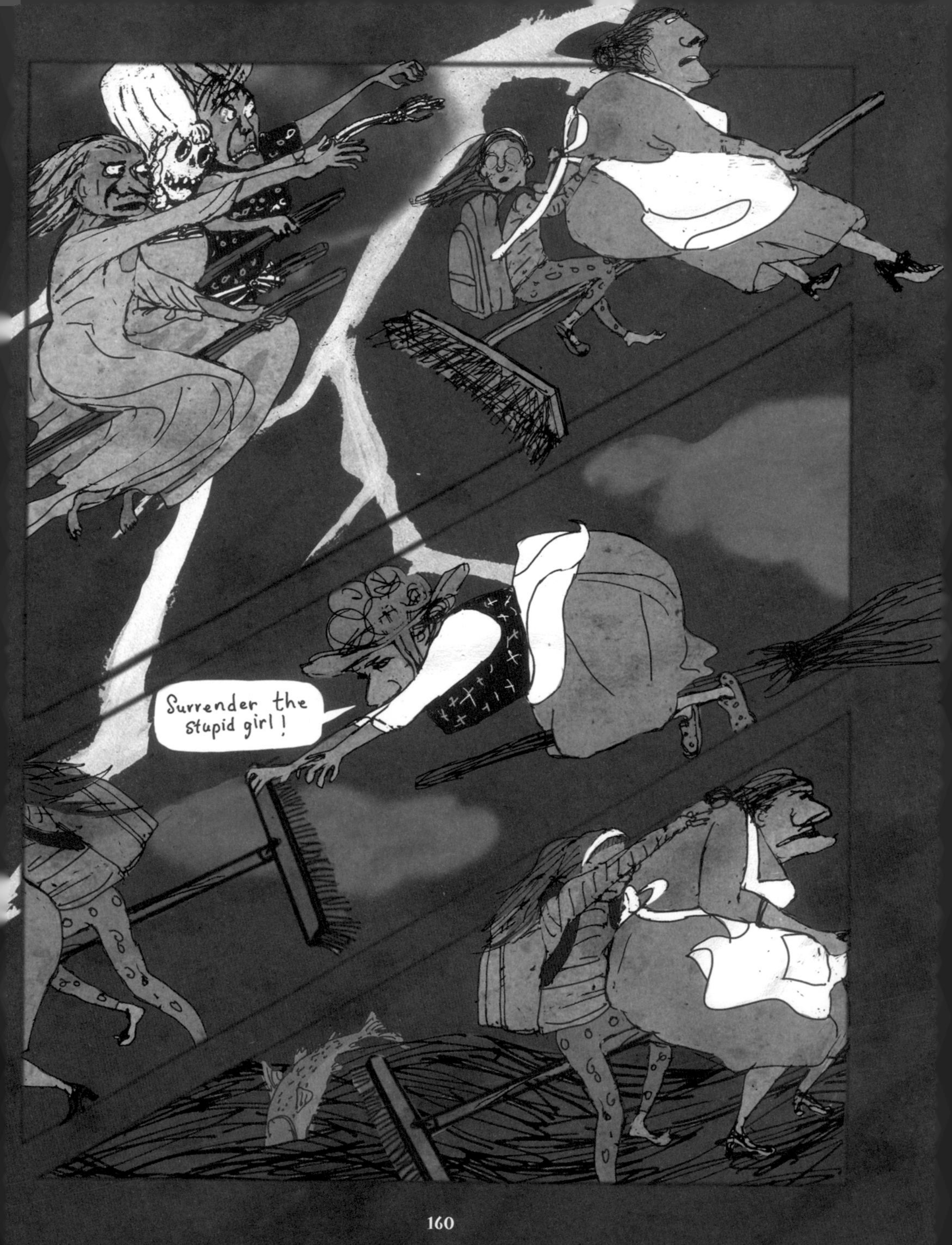
Surrender the stupid girl!

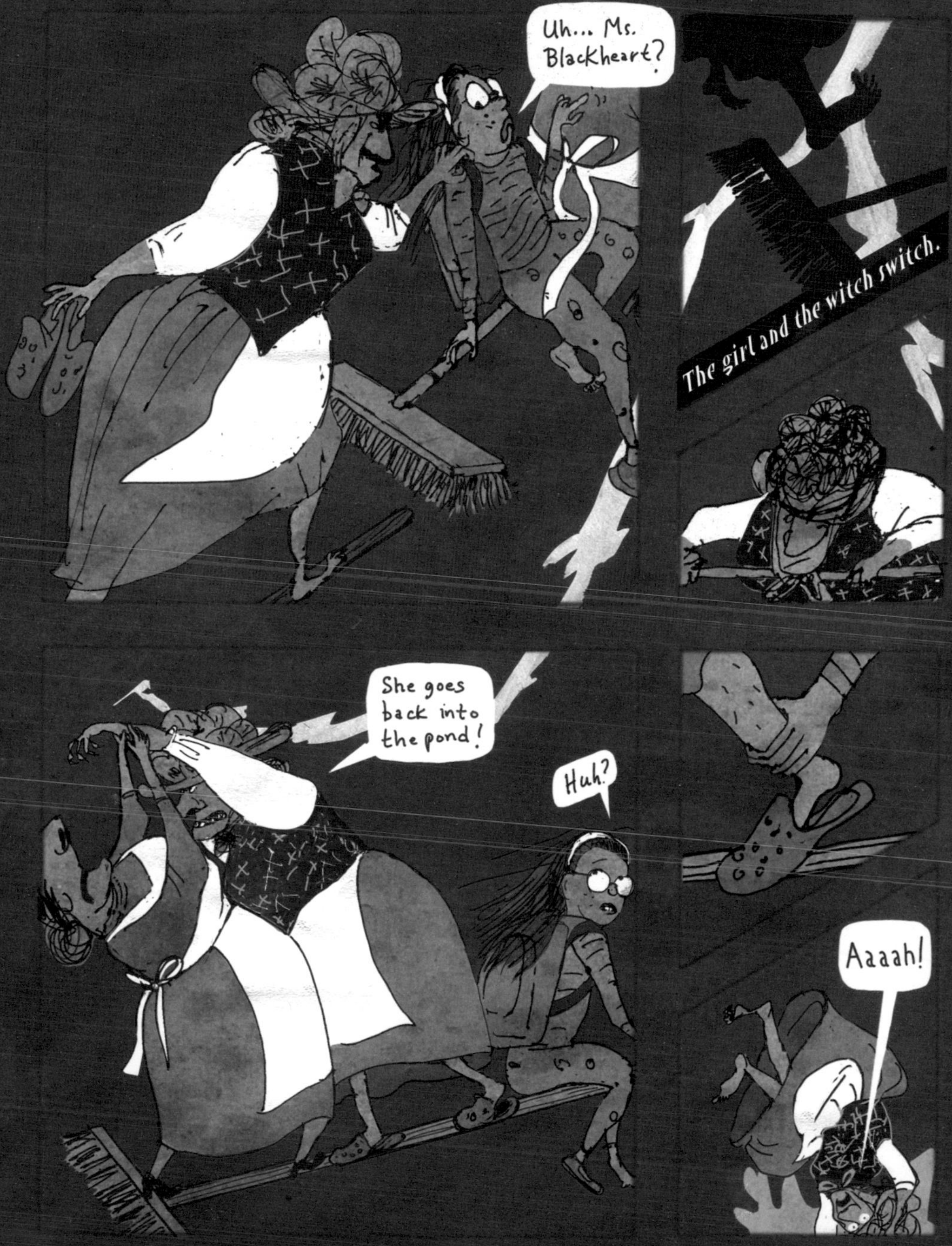
Uh... Ms. Blackheart?
The girl and the witch switch.
She goes back into the pond!
Huh?
Aaaah!

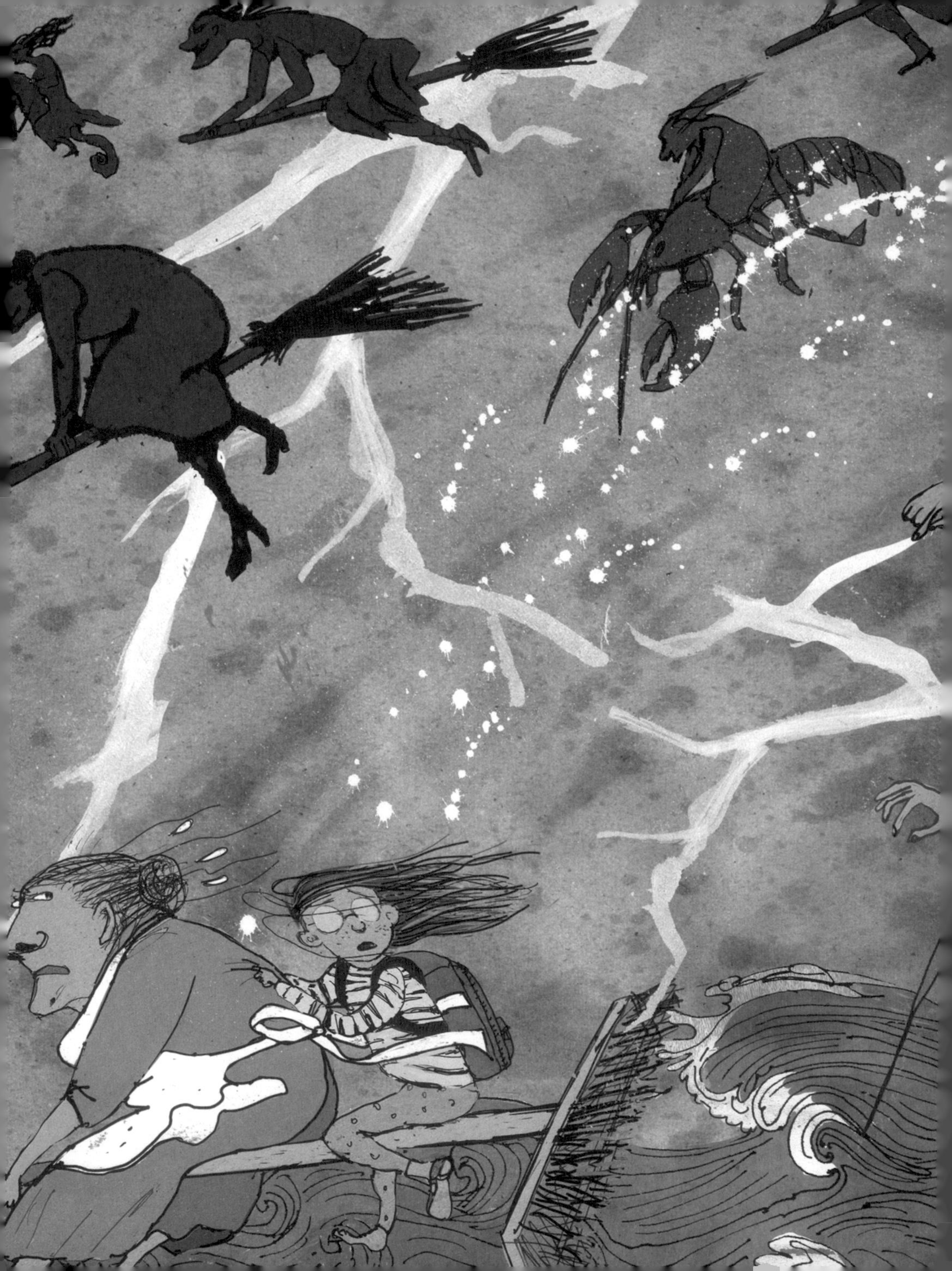

WATCH OUT FOR PAPERCUTZ

Welcome to the faintly-frightening first THE LUNCH WITCH graphic novel, by Deb Lucke, from Papercutz, those folks-who-usually-eat-lunch-at-their-desks and are dedicated to publishing great graphic novels for all ages. I'm Jim Salicrup, the Editor-in-Chief, and a big fan of witches—from Samantha Stephens to the Witches of Eastwick.

Believe it or not, this isn't the first time Papercutz has published a story about a witch. We've parodied the long-running hit Broadway play, with a story called, "Wickeder" in TALES FROM THE CRYPT. It really wasn't a parody, per se—it was more like the so-called "Wicked" Witch of the West's day in court. As much as I love L. Frank Baum's "The Wonderful Wizard of Oz" and the classic 1939 MGM musical based on the book, I always thought the Wicked Witch of the West was treated unfairly—after all, Dorothy's house did kill the Witch's sister, and Dorothy took her shoes (both silver and ruby incarnations). So, it only seems fair that Dorothy should stand trial for her alleged crimes.

© Guy Delcourt Productions.

We've also published a comics adaptation of "Hansel and Gretel" in CLASSICS ILLUSTRATED DELUXE # 2 "Tales from the Brothers Grimm," in which, so to speak, the owner of a gingerbread house is portrayed also as a "wicked witch." Again, those kids were clearly trespassing, and had no business eating her house. As for what they wind up doing to her in the end—that's too horrific to get into. Fortunately, the witch that appears in a few SMURFS graphic novels has managed to survive relatively unharmed.

© 2013 WWE, Inc. All rights reserved.

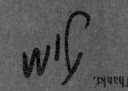

Also, believe it or not, we've even published stories featuring a lunch lady. Excuse me, a "lunch server," to be precise. In the pages of the WWE SLAM CITY graphic novels, all the WWE Superstars have been fired and have been forced to find real jobs. The monstrous, demonic superstar known as Kane, becomes a lunch la— er, server.

But this is the very first time we're publishing the story of a Lunch Witch, and we're hoping it won't be the last, as this is the first in a series of THE LUNCH WITCH graphic novels. This is also the very first time we're publishing a completely new character, appearing here for the very first time. Usually, Papercutz has brought you graphic novels based on popular books, movies, TV shows, toys, comic strips, comicbooks, video games, sports entertainers, even Pope John Paul II. We've also imported graphic novels from Europe and published English editions. But now we're ready to start publishing titles with all-new original characters. We certainly hope you enjoy THE LUNCH WITCH as much as we do—in fact, send us your comments! We'd love to hear what you think. After all, YOU'RE the one we're making these graphic novels for, so let us know how we're doing!

Thanks,

Jim

STAY IN TOUCH!

EMAIL: salicrup@papercutz.com
WEB: papercutz.com
TWITTER: @papercutzgn
FACEBOOK: PAPERCUTZGRAPHICNOVELS
REGULAR MAIL: Papercutz, 160 Broadway, Suite 700, East Wing, New York, NY 10038

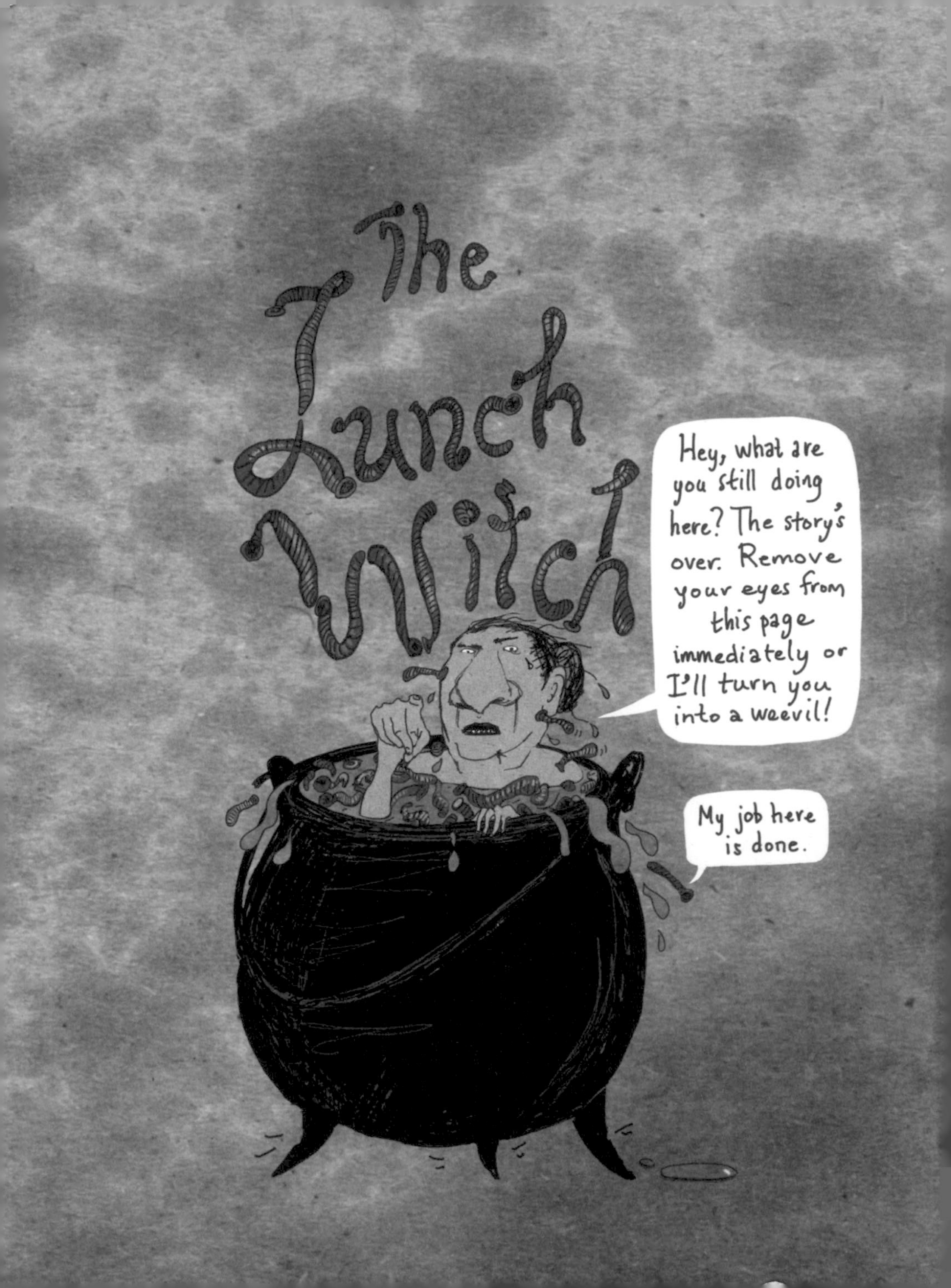
The Lunch Witch
Hey, what are you still doing here? The story's over. Remove your eyes from this page immediately or I'll turn you into a weevil!
My job here is done.

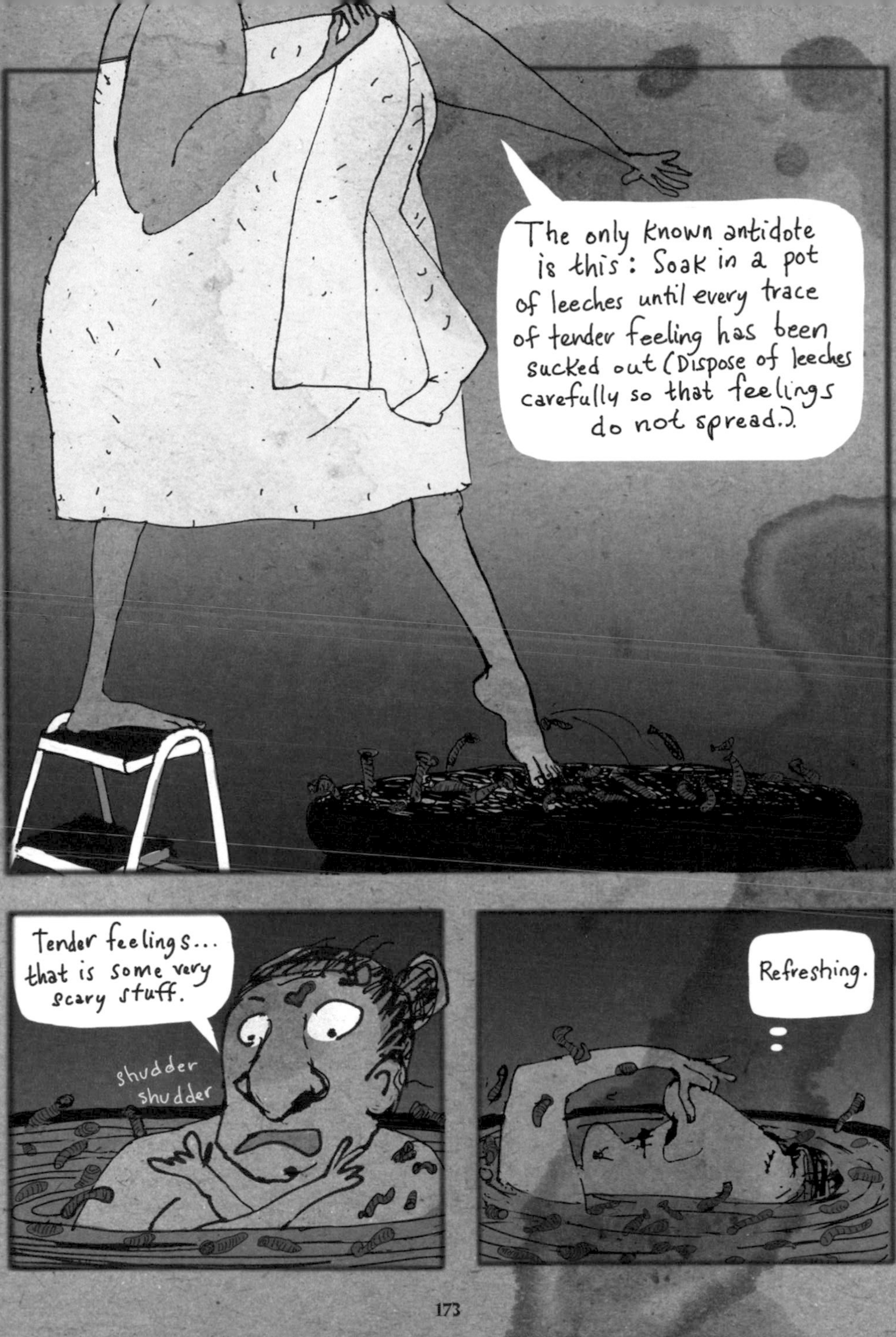
The only known antidote is this: Soak in a pot of leeches until every trace of tender feeling has been sucked out (Dispose of leeches carefully so that feelings do not spread.).
Tender feelings... that is some very scary stuff.
shudder shudder
Refreshing.

The End

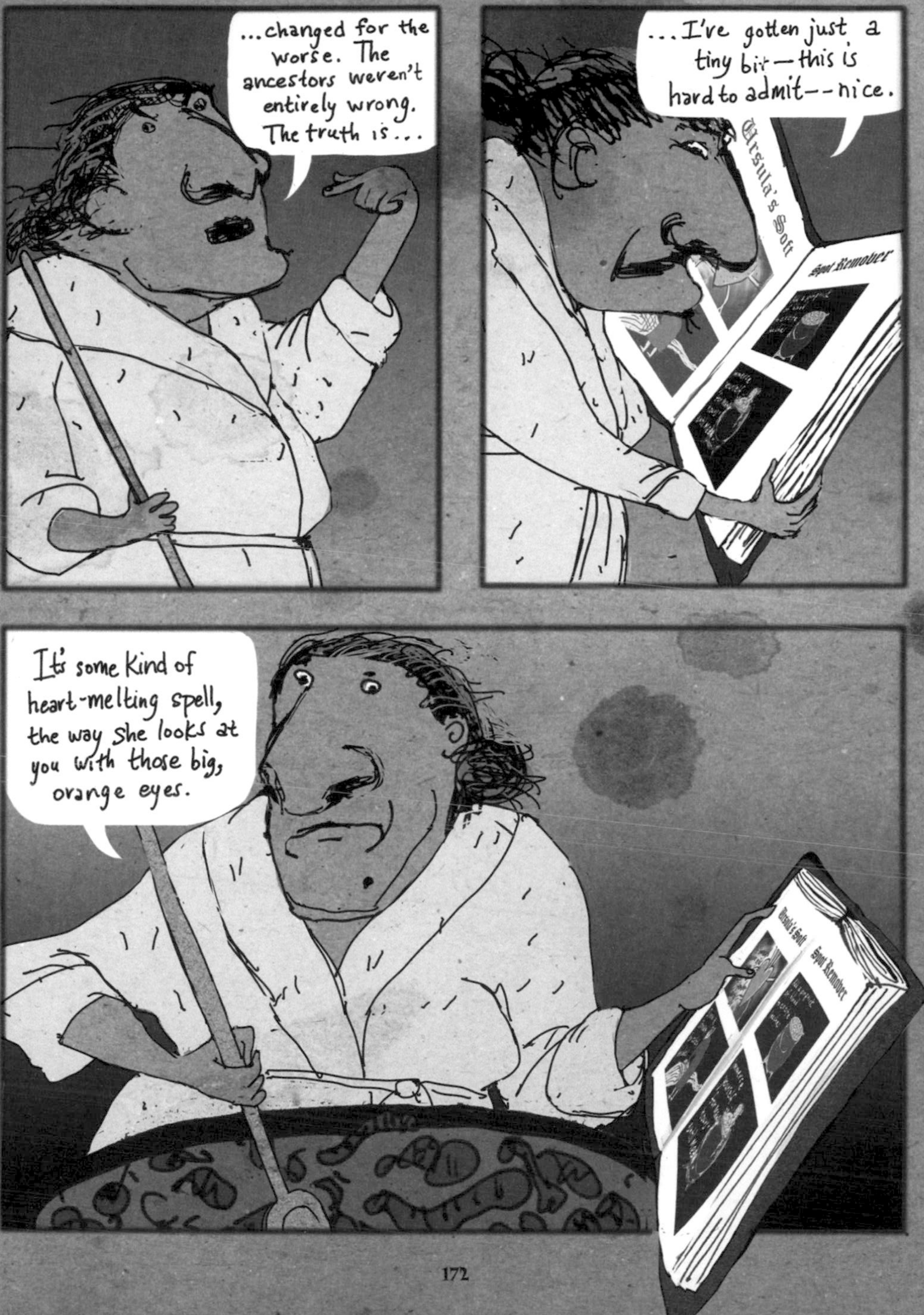
...changed for the worse. The ancestors weren't entirely wrong. The truth is...
...I've gotten just a tiny bit—this is hard to admit--nice.
Ursula's Soft Spot Remover
It's some kind of heart-melting spell, the way she looks at you with those big, orange eyes.
Ursula's Soft Spot Remover

The old Grunhilda would've hoped she had residual warts as well. The new Grunhilda was in the crowd cheering. We were both changed by the experience, but I was...

Last

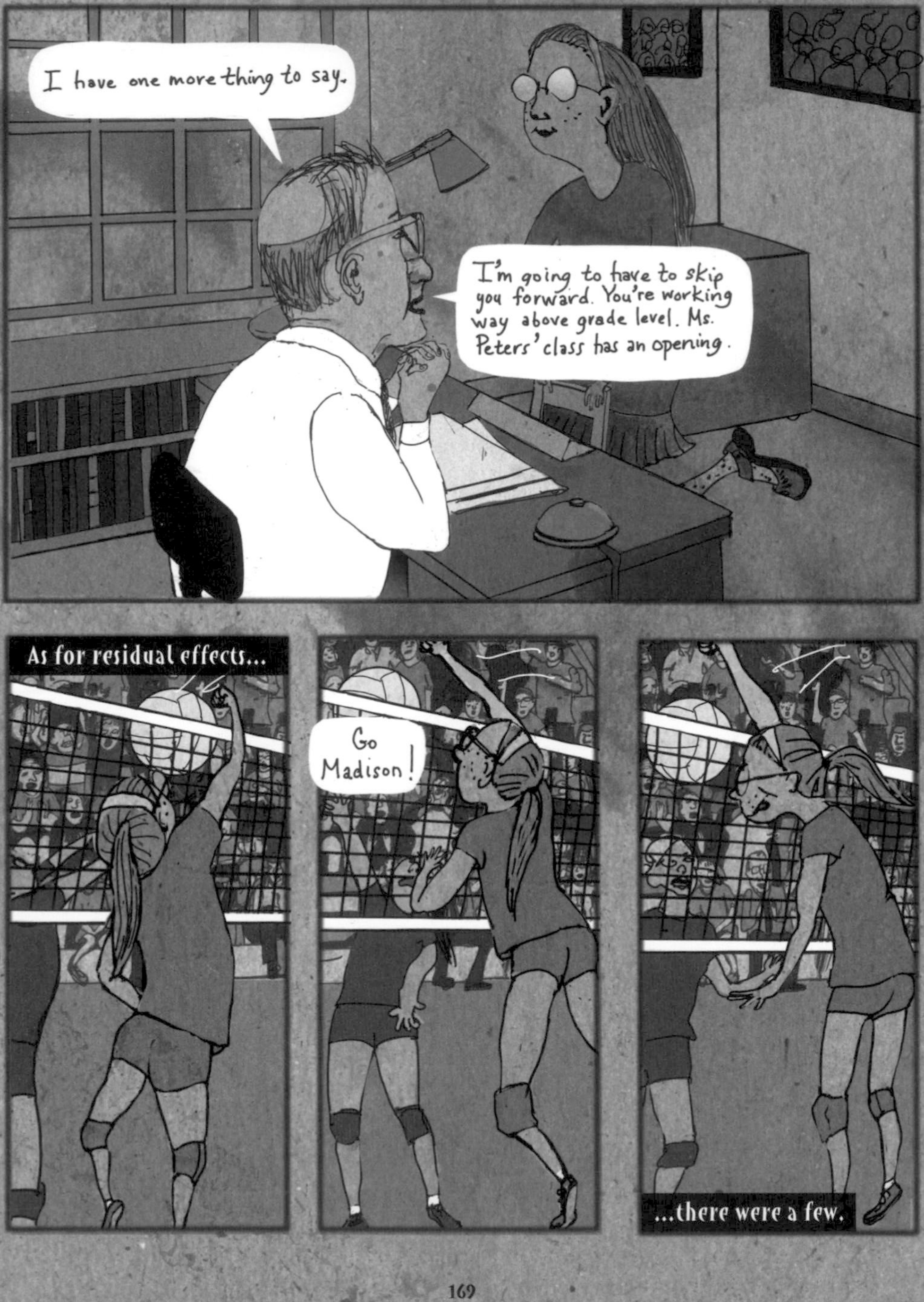
I have one more thing to say.
I'm going to have to skip you forward. You're working way above grade level. Ms. Peters' class has an opening.
As for residual effects...
Go Madison!
...there were a few.

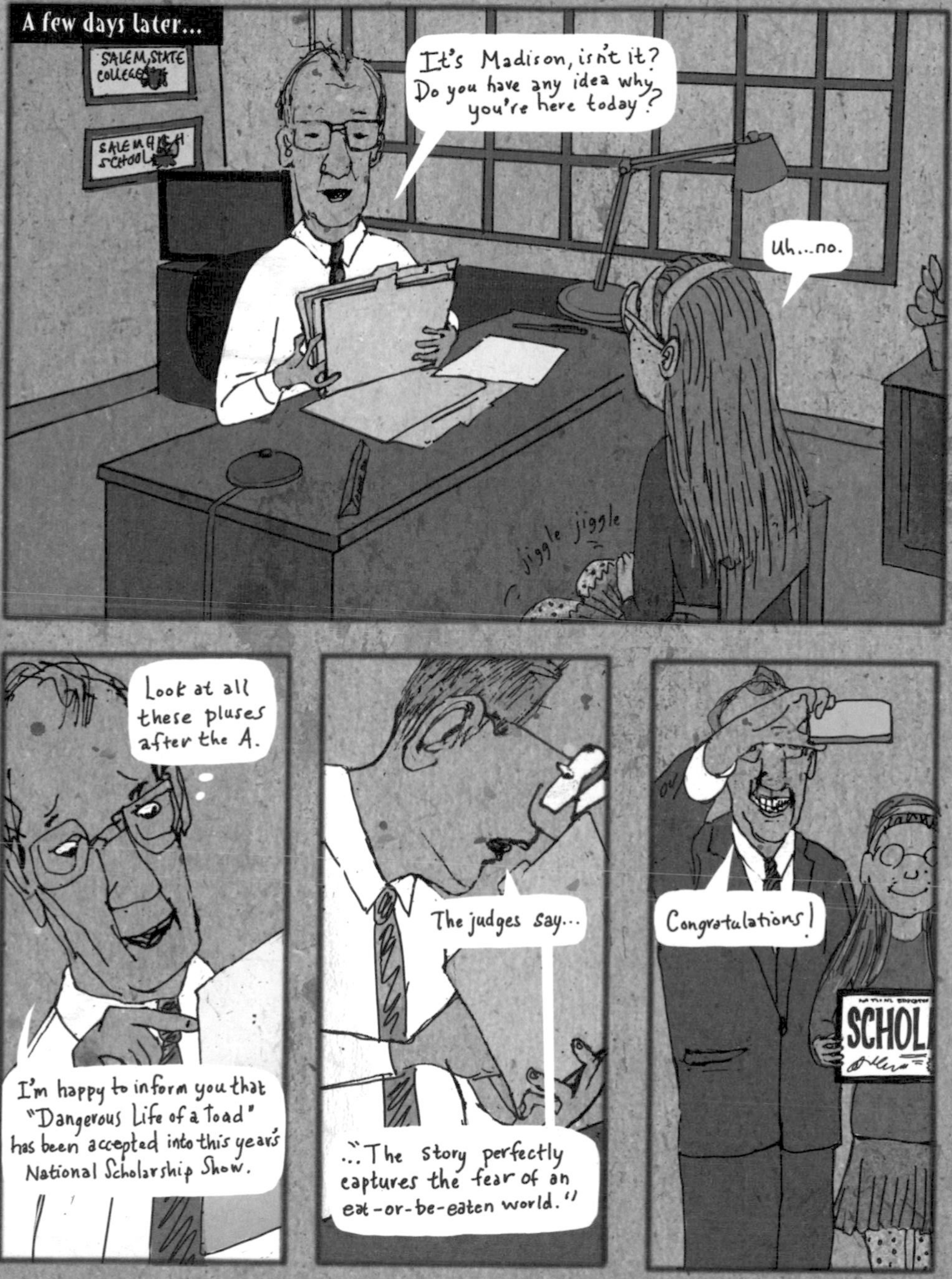

A few days later...
SALEM STATE COLLEGE
SALEM HIGH SCHOOL
It's Madison, isn't it? Do you have any idea why you're here today?
Uh...no.
jiggle jiggle
Look at all these pluses after the A.
I'm happy to inform you that "Dangerous Life of a Toad" has been accepted into this year's National Scholarship Show.
The judges say...
..."The story perfectly captures the fear of an eat-or-be-eaten world."
Congratulations!
SCHOL

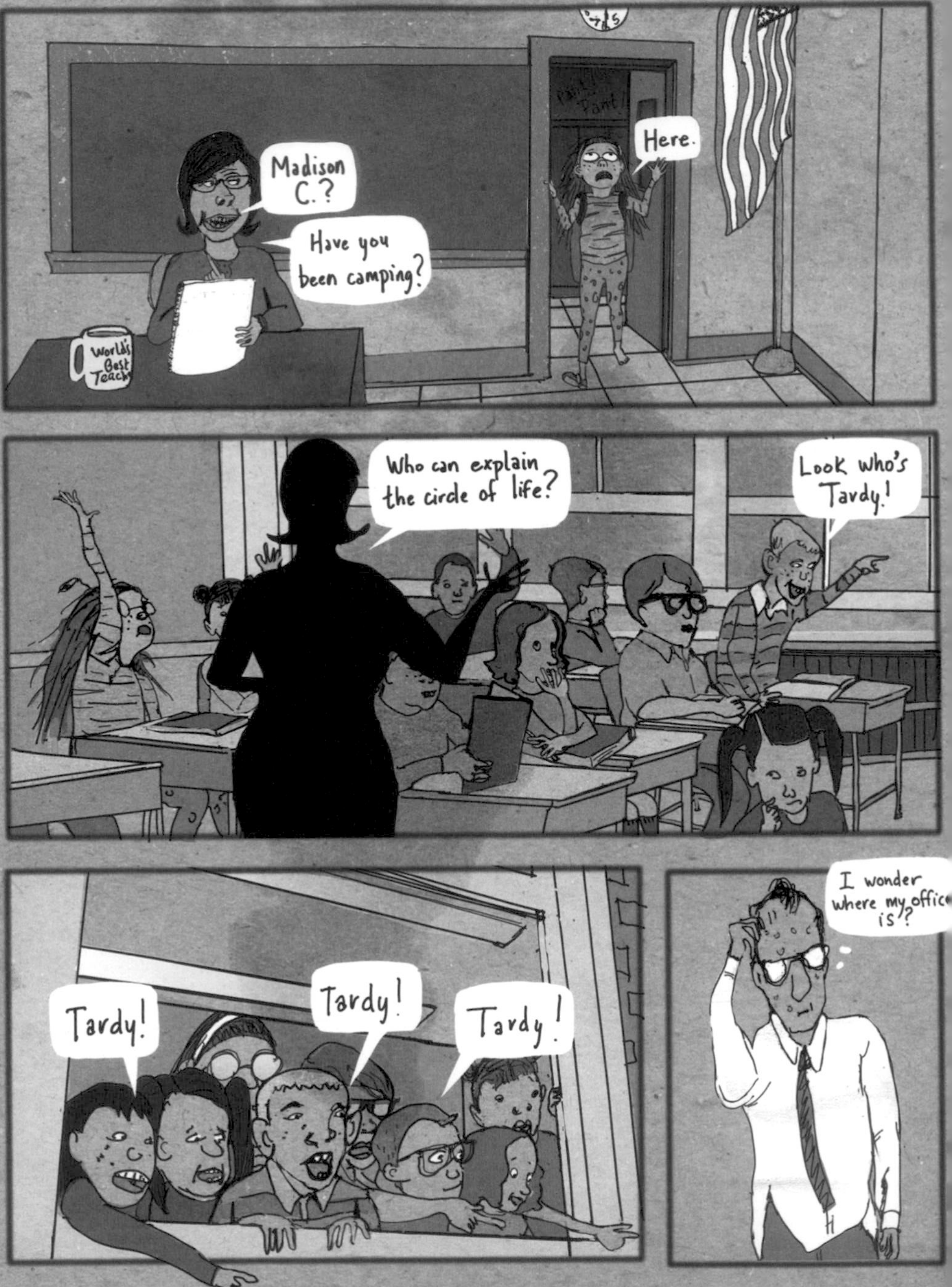
World's Best Teach
Madison C.?
Have you been camping?
Here.
Who can explain the circle of life?
Look who's Tardy!
Tardy!
Tardy!
Tardy!
I wonder where my office is?

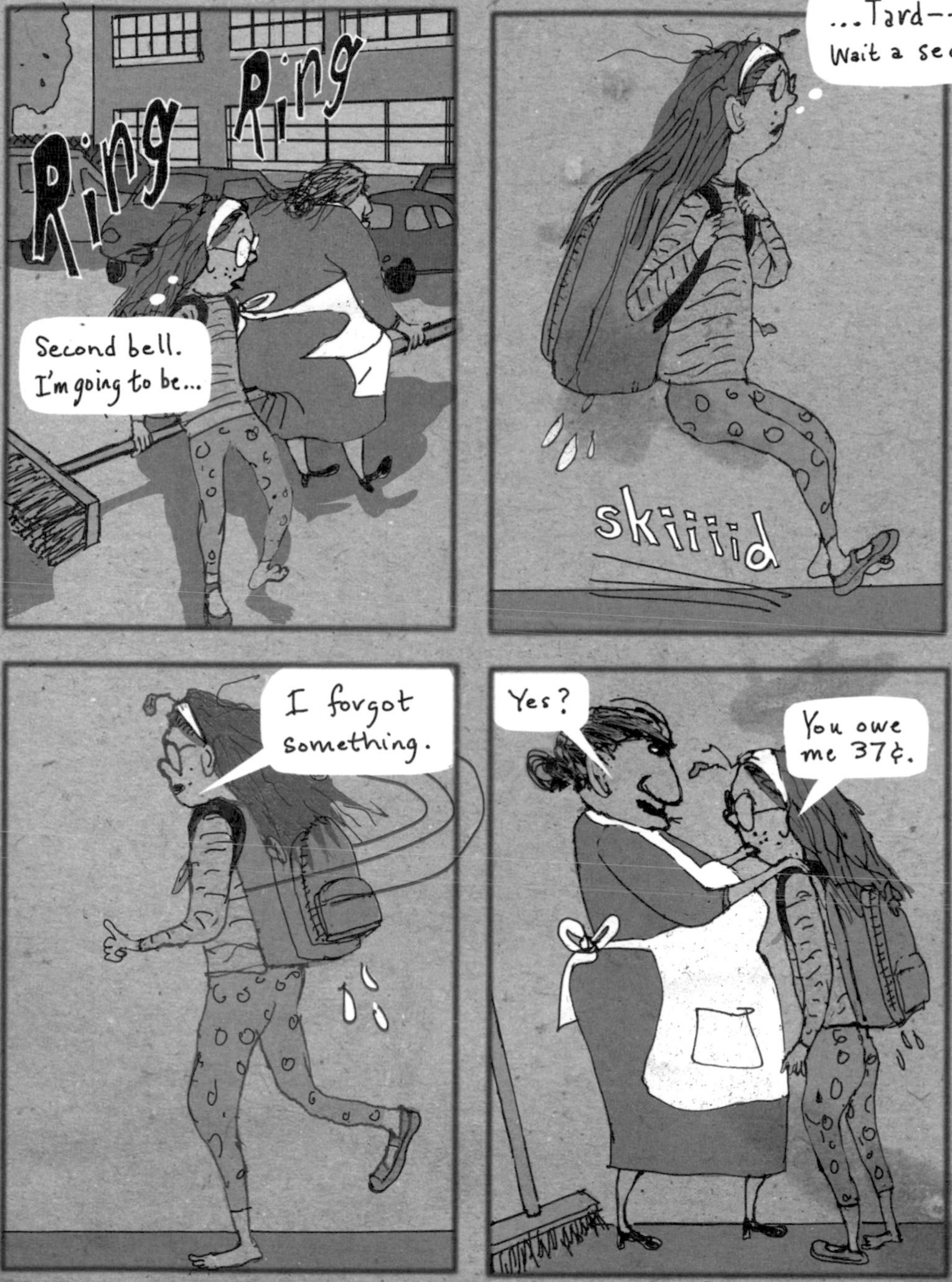
Ring Ring
Second bell. I'm going to be...
...Tard-- Wait a sec.
skiiiid
I forgot something.
Yes?
You owe me 37¢.

17th

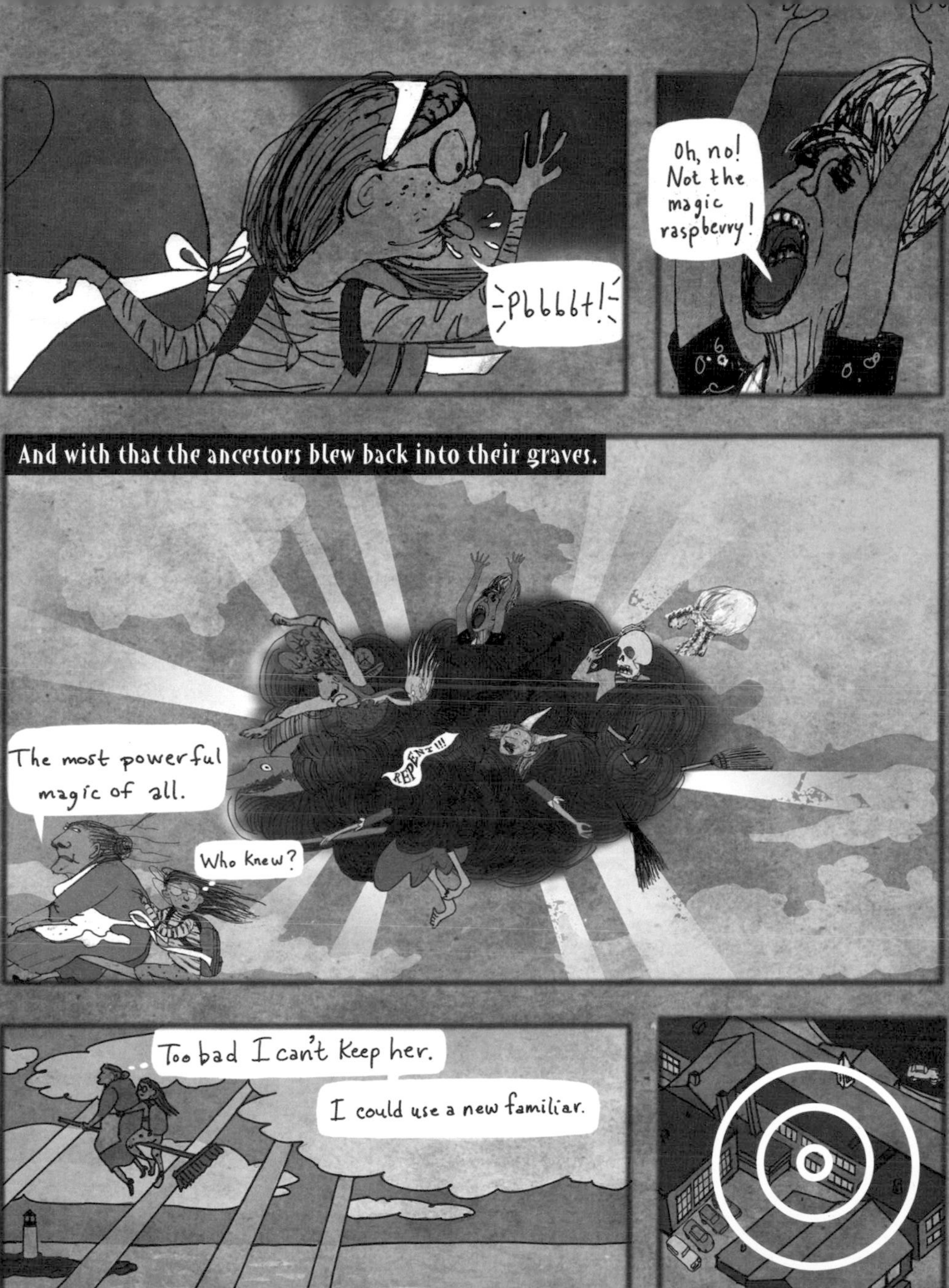
Pbbbbt!
Oh, no! Not the magic raspberry!
And with that the ancestors blew back into their graves.
REPENT!!!
The most powerful magic of all.
Who knew?
Too bad I can't keep her.
I could use a new familiar.

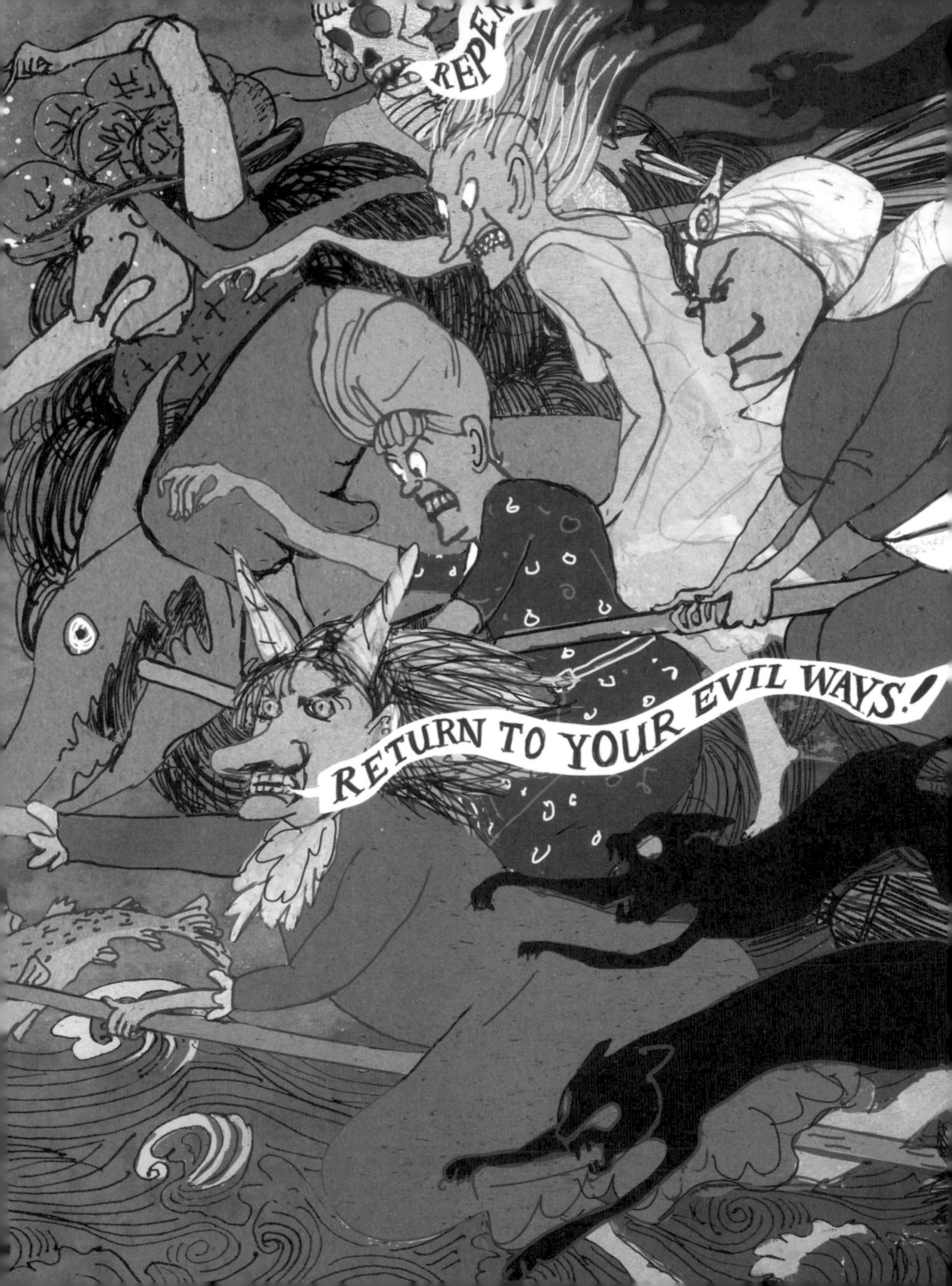
REPEN
RETURN TO YOUR EVIL WAYS!